Desert Rage

A Lena Jones Mystery

Betty Webb

Poisoned Pen Press

First Edition 2014

10 9 8 7 6 5 4 3 2 1

Library of Congress Catalog Card Number: 2014938543

ISBN: 9781464203107   Hardcover
         9781464203121   Trade Paperback

Poisoned Pen Press
6962 E. First Ave., Ste. 103
Scottsdale, AZ 85251
www.poisonedpenpress.com
info@poisonedpenpress.com

Printed in the United States of America

To the brood: Paul, Jason, and Colleen, Eric and Sandy, Ian, Alea, Ryan, Kyle, Sarah, and to cousins Jimmy and Kenny Webb, my childhood partners in crime.

Acknowledgments

Contrary to popular opinion, books are seldom written by just one person—there are a lot of helpers along the way. In the case of *Desert Rage*, many thanks to the Sheridan Street Irregulars, especially Scott Andrews, who filled me in on all things prison (but not because he's ever been in one!); to the legal expertise of Margaret Morse; to Deputy Fire Marshall Mike MacCrone, of the Scottsdale Fire Department; and to the memory of Armetta Zielsdorf, who allowed me to use her name. My gratitude also goes out to Robert C. Keezer, Louise Signorelli, Marge Purcell, and Debra McCarthy. If there are any mistakes in this book, the mistakes are mine, not theirs.

Prologue:

2:31 p.m. Monday, July 8

The first thing Ali saw when she came through the door was the blood. The next things she saw were the bodies.

"Why'd you kill my dog?" she asked Kyle.

Kyle waited, like, forever before he answered, almost like he didn't know what she was talking about, but then he shrugged. "Because she bit me?" He rubbed his leg like it still hurt.

Ali knelt down and placed her hand on Misty's side. The dog's body still felt warm. When she stroked the Yorkie's head, it whined. She looked up at Kyle. "She's not dead."

"That's all right, then. I didn't know you cared about the dog."

"She's the only thing I do care for." At the expression on Kyle's face, she added, "Besides you, of course. So what are we going to do now? We can't leave her like this."

He grabbed the baseball bat leaning against the sofa. "Want me to…?"

"No!"

"Hey, girl, don't get all jumped up about this. I only did what you wanted, didn't I?"

"Not the Misty part. We have to take her to the vet."

"How?

"My mom's car. The keys are in her purse. When we were talking about running off to California together, you said you knew how to drive."

When Ali stroked the dog again, it opened its eyes and licked her hand. Ali lowered her face to the blood-matted fur, held it there for a minute. "We'll drop her off at the vet on the way."

"Better get on the road, then."

"Wait a minute." Ali stood up, walked over to the thermostat, and turned it down as far as it would go. "I read in a mystery once where the killer did this so it would take longer for the bodies to, you know, decompose, give him time to get away."

"Good story?"

"Better than those stupid comics you read."

"They're graphic novels!"

"Like there's a difference." As cold air blasted out of the family room vents, Ali returned to Misty and picked her up. She cuddled the dog until she realized that Misty's blood was staining her new tee-shirt, the one with the picture of Rihanna on it. She made a sound of disgust.

"Hey, you okay?" Kyle asked.

"I'm always okay. Go up to my room and get me another top. I can't show up at the vet's with blood all over me."

"Well, duh, Ali. You'll be carrying in a bleeding dog, won't you? Nobody's going to think anything about your stupid shirt. Say you found her all messed up like that and brought her straight in, that, uh, your parents were out and you didn't want to wait."

Ali made a face. "Driving over there with blood on me. Ugh."

With that, the two fourteen-year-olds left the house, leaving behind the cooling bodies of Ali's mother, father, and ten-year-old brother.

Chapter One

Lena

I put the phone down and turned to my partner, who was, as usual, tapping away on his keyboard. "You won't believe who just called me."

"Santa Claus," he replied, not looking up. "The Tooth Fairy."

"The Honorable Juliana Thorsson, that's who."

Jimmy stopped typing. "The politician? The one in Washington?"

"Congress is in recess, so she's back in Scottsdale and wants me to come right over."

He grinned, his white teeth gleaming against his dark face. "Trying to win your vote, huh?"

"She wouldn't say."

"There's a politician for you."

Six years earlier, Thorsson had been elected to the U.S. Congress on a platform slightly to the right of Attila the Hun. At the age of thirty-four, she had already served two terms in the Arizona Senate, where her Olympic Bronze in skeet shooting earned her instant popularity with gun-loving Arizonans. When naked pictures of our then-U.S. Congressman surfaced in the *National Enquirer*, she ran for his seat. The possessor of an immaculate reputation, she won in a landslide. Now she was touted as a possible senatorial candidate. After that, maybe even the presidency.

And for some mysterious reason, this political paragon had summoned me into her presence.

I looked out the window of Desert Investigations and saw no pedestrians trolling the Main Street art galleries. No wonder. July has always been a rough month here in Scottsdale, and this year promised to be one of the worst yet. Only nine in the morning and it was a hundred and three.

"Something else is interesting," I told Jimmy. "The Honorable Juliana told me not to drive my Jeep, that it was too recognizable, which means she's already researched me. Did you get the air-conditioning in your pickup fixed yet?"

"If I say I did, are you going to ask if you can borrow it?"

"I'll have to borrow it regardless."

"Then lucky you. I took it in Saturday and now it's like Alaska in there. When are you supposed to see her?"

"As soon as I can get there."

"Bring my baby back in the same condition you borrowed it, that's all I ask."

Jimmy Sisiwan has been an equal partner at Desert Investigations since it opened. A full-blooded Pima Indian who lives on the nearby reservation, he performs three-quarters of our revenue-earning work—background checks for the human resources departments of local companies. Only rarely does he share field-work with me, but that's the way he likes it. Especially in July.

"Have fun," he said, tossing me the keys to his Toyota.

By the grace of our landlord, Desert Investigations had been granted three covered parking spots painted with the warning FOR DESERT INVESTIGATIONS ONLY. ALL OTHERS WILL BE TOWED. My pictograph-decorated 1946 Jeep took one of the spots, Jimmy's Toyota another, with an empty space left for a client. Or rather, it should have been empty, considering no clients had shown up. Yet there sat a nasty-looking black Hummer 2. For the third time in a week the space-hogging beast had parked so close to my Jeep that I checked my own baby for any dings on its custom-paint job. Lucky for the Hummer's driver, there were none.

I don't like Hummers on principle. They're oversized, heavy, and present a threat to the environment. They're also pretentious, a Scottsdale trait I am heartily sick of. Out of patience with the interloper, I hauled my pen and notebook out of my carryall, and in big block letters printed, PLEASE STOP PARKING HERE; IF YOU CONTINUE, YOUR CAR WILL BE TOWED AT YOUR EXPENSE.

After tucking the note behind Big Black Hummer's windshield wiper, I hopped into Jimmy's pickup and took off for the Honorable Juliana's residence.

Although called "the West's most Western town," Scottsdale hasn't lived up to that motto for decades. Long ago, strip malls had replaced cattle ranches when housing developments sprawled across once-pristine desert. Now, except for a few rare pockets, the city looked just like any other metropolis: overdesigned and overcrowded.

So much for truth in advertising.

A half-hour of bumper-to-bumper traffic later, I arrived at Arabian Run, a bland condo community situated on the site of a former horse farm. Nothing was left of the horses except the name and the black silhouette of a horse on the gate blocking off the development from the great unwashed. When I tooted my horn, a rotund guard emerged from the de rigueur security hut. I announced myself as Miss Brown, the name the Honorable Juliana told me to use. With that, he opened the iron gate and ushered Miss Brown and her borrowed Toyota pickup through.

The view that greeted me was of uninspired, uniform buildings lined up next to each other in ranks so unbroken that back East, they would have passed for government-assisted housing. This meant that unlike many politicians, Juliana Thorsson wasn't filthy rich. Not yet, anyway. The big money would roll in when, and if, she became a U.S. senator. For now she remained ensconced in an area more middle-class than upper, in a modest condo instead of one of Scottsdale's McMansions. But the landscaping was nice. I enjoyed a slow drive through curved asphalt streets made lush with planting of purple bougainvillea, pink oleanders, and here and there—as if to remind the residents they lived in Arizona—transplanted saguaros lifted their one hundred-year-old arms to the harsh July sky.

The Honorable Juliana's condo faced the narrow greenbelt that wove its way through the complex. At first I couldn't figure out why flags dotted the grass, then realized I was looking at a putting green. Par what? Two?

With the covered parking spaces reserved for tenants only, I parked on the street and put up Jimmy's sunscreen. On the exterior the sunscreen said PALEFACE GO HOME; on the other, a picture of Geronimo loomed over the sentence: FIGHTING DOMESTIC TERRORISM SINCE 1492.

That Jimmy, such a card.

The congresswoman met me at the door. "Come in quickly so the cold air doesn't escape," she said, waving me through. She looked somewhat older than in her campaign posters, but younger than the last time I saw her on CNN arguing about immigration with Anderson Cooper. A natural honey-blond, she downplayed her Nordic good looks by dressing like a banker. Gray suit, plain white blouse, sensible black pumps, But at age thirty-six, she was still a beauty and the dowdy outfit couldn't hide it.

As soon as I stepped into the frigid house, a small dog of indeterminate breed limped up to meet me. She wore a cast on her right front foreleg, and her back was shaved almost bald, revealing a map work of sutures. When I bent down to pet her, she backed away with a whine.

Thorsson scooped the poor creature up in her arms. "She wants to be friendly but she's not ready yet."

"Looks like she's been through a lot."

"You could say that. By the way, do you have a different sunscreen you could put on that truck? The whole point of my asking you to drive a vehicle other than your Jeep was to avoid notice."

"You don't think PALEFACE GO HOME sends a nice anti-immigration message?"

She gave me a sour smile. "I'll put the dog in the bedroom, then step into the garage and get you another sunscreen to replace that anti-American message."

Less than two minutes after saying hello I already doubted I'd take her on as a client, but business is business. Until I knew enough to issue a formal turndown, I'd listen to what she had to say.

Her brief absence gave me a chance to look around the large living room. Not fancy, but if she won the U.S. senatorial seat, that would change. Pale blue walls, pale blue carpet, pale blue sofa and chairs. If the air-conditioning hadn't been blasting away to beat the band, I would still have felt cold. I noted with amusement that she didn't own one gun cabinet, she owned three, each glass-fronted case filled with enough firepower to arm a small nation. In addition, a brass-fitted antique Winchester .22 hung over the sofa, flanked by two mounted elk heads. Apparently clay pigeons weren't her only targets. Other than the guns, I saw few personal touches. No art, no books, no knickknacks, just a couple of family photos and a pile of newspapers on the table next to the sofa. She must have loved reading about herself.

Several freshly inked campaign posters stood against one wall, giving away the congresswoman's future plans. THORSSON FOR SENATE! they announced. A WOMAN OF THE PEOPLE.

When Thorsson returned with a lizard-green sunshade extoling Geico Insurance, I went outside and made the switch. Despite my misgivings, I was curious about this Olympian-turned-politician.

"How about some iced tea?" she asked, when she let me inside again.

"Anything cold and wet would be much appreciated. It's over a hundred degrees already."

"Going to be a hot one."

"Maybe as bad as 2007." This is how Arizonans talk when they either have nothing interesting to say or are putting off what might turn out to be an unpleasant conversation.

"Nothing can be as bad as 2007, Miss Jones."

"Don't be so sure. Global warming, and all."

She frowned. "Global warming is a myth perpetrated by left-wing scientists. Sugar in your tea?"

"I like it bitter."

"Me, too."

At least we agreed on something.

She waved toward the sofa. "Have a seat. I'll be right back."

Apparently she had already made the tea, because almost by the time my rump landed on a blue sofa cushion, she returned and handed me a tall frosted glass filled to the brim. After a taste, I pronounced it excellent.

She sat down on the chair next to a magazine rack filled with more newspapers, sipped at her own glass. "There's nothing like cold tea on a hot day, is there?"

"No, there isn't. Look, I have an appointment at eleven thirty, so I would appreciate it if we got this show on the road. Why am I here? By the way, how should I address you? Congresswoman? Honorable Juliana?" I smiled to take the sting out of the questions. It was never a good idea to annoy a politician.

"Plain Juliana would be fine, Miss Jones. I don't stand on ceremony."

"Then call me Lena." I kept the smile plastered to my face.

"Do you read the papers, Lena? Watch the news?"

"Sure, but I try to stay away from the political stuff." The minute the words were out of my mouth, I knew they were a mistake because they immediately elicited the kind of political mumbo jumbo that numbed my eardrums.

"I encourage all citizens to educate themselves on the issues, especially those which concern the great state of Arizona."

"Can't argue with that." I finally stopped smiling. "Could we just get on with it?"

Regally, she inclined her head. "Of course. Before I called your office, I had you investigated. You were raised in foster homes. At the age of nine, one of your foster fathers raped you. After putting up with that for a while—there was something about a pet dog he threatened to kill if you told—you stabbed him. Almost killed him, too."

Since I'd been a minor at the time, the newspapers had refrained from printing my name or photograph, so the fact that Juliana had managed to unearth that old criminal case came as a shock. But I wasn't about to let her know it, so I shrugged.

"'Almost' being the operative word, Juliana. My foster father didn't die, just went to trial. And kudos for your own investigative skills, although I imagine that for someone with your contacts, everything is ultimately accessible, sealed records or no. Still, why does what happened to me almost three decades ago matter in the here and now?"

"I also know that the man who raped you will be released from prison sometime next month."

"Quite the detective you are. But as impressed as I am, I repeat my question: why am I here?"

She didn't answer right away, just kept staring at me with those cold eyes. Finally, she said, "You're very controlled."

"Part of my job description."

When her face relaxed, it was as if a different woman had entered the room. "Oh, yes. I know all about job descriptions and how necessary it is to live up to them." Her eyes flicked to the gun cabinets then back to me. "This entire conversation is off the record, correct?"

"Of course."

"Good. Have you been following the Cameron case?"

"I take it you're talking about the murders a couple of weeks ago."

"Nine days ago, to be exact."

The Cameron house, where an entire family had been slaughtered by a fourteen-year-old girl and her boyfriend, was separated from Quail Run by less than a mile, which meant that the Camerons would have been her constituents. The family was well-off, the kind of people who might want politicians for friends, so perhaps there was even a personal connection.

"I read about the case, yes. Dr. Arthur Cameron, his wife, and their ten-year-old son were supposedly beaten to death with a baseball bat by a fourteen-year-old boy. Tragic. And in my opinion, tragic for the girl in the case—the daughter—since from what I hear, she—supposedly, again—masterminded the whole thing. At least that's what they swore to in their confessions."

Juliana narrowed those cold eyes and studied me like I was a smear under a microscope. "Why tragic for the girl, if she was supposed to be the ringleader?"

"You're an educated woman, Juliana, so you must know that scientific studies prove that at the age of fourteen, the cerebral cortex isn't fully formed. It's doubtful the girl understood what she was doing, not that our court system will care. Considering the fact that Arizona loves to prosecute kids as adults, the girl's lucky the County Attorney filed in Juvenile Court, not in the adult system."

"Correct," she said. "You were nine when you stabbed your foster father. Did you understand what you were doing then?"

"I just wanted to keep him off me. If I'd been an adult in that situation, I would probably have contacted the authorities, not taken the law into my own hands." Uneasy, I shifted on the sofa. I didn't like talking about my past. Especially not that part.

To my surprise, she nodded, as if satisfied with my answer. Then she picked up one of the newspapers, and handed it to me.

RUNAWAY TEENS FOUND IN QUARTZSITE screamed the headline.

"Yellow journalism at its finest," I said. But at least the headline read RUNAWAY instead of KILLER.

"Now open the paper to the middle."

I did, and found a candid photograph of a teenage girl slipped between the pages. It was slightly out of focus, as if been taken from a distance by a shaky hand but you could still tell that the girl would grow into a beauty. Perfect oval face, blond hair, blue eyes, the lanky but perfectly proportioned build of a budding runway model. She'd been snapped carrying a load of books in her arms, walking down a palm-lined street.

"I took that picture," Juliana said.

"It's a bit out of focus."

"I'm not much of a photographer," she admitted.

"Who is it?"

"We'll get to that shortly. Now tell me what you think of this." She lifted the rest of the newspapers in the magazine rack, revealing a framed studio portrait hidden underneath.

When she handed the portrait to me, I still couldn't figure out why I was here. Comparing the blurred snapshot to the formal portrait, it was easy to see they were the same person, and I told her so.

She shook her head. "Wrong. The snapshot was taken two months ago, just before school let out. The studio portrait is more than twenty years old."

"But…"

"The girl in the formal portrait is me at the age of fourteen."

I inspected the two photographs more closely. The girls were so alike they could have been identical twins, but given the age gap, there could only be one explanation. On second thought, two explanations.

"Your niece?" I asked, recalling that Helga, Juliana's older sister, had a daughter named Ilsa. Both blue-eyed blondes often appeared in the congresswoman's campaign ads.

But Juliana shook her head. "Ilsa is two years older than this girl."

I had an idea where this was going, and I didn't like it. Cleaning up a politician's peccadilloes isn't my thing. "Then at some point you had an illegitimate daughter, who up until now, you've successfully kept hidden." I waved toward the campaign posters. "Obviously, you're about to make a run for the U.S. Senate, so you want me to make all this go away."

Those cold blue eyes never wavered. "You're right and you're wrong. The girl is my daughter, yes, but she's not illegitimate."

I realized I'd forgotten something. While still studying at Arizona State University, Juliana had briefly been married, but less than three months after the wedding, her husband was shot to death in a road rage incident. The tragedy had actually helped her first congressional run: brave widow carrying on despite personal heartbreak, still a staunch supporter of the Second Amendment.

"Fine. You had a child, but for some reason kept her a secret. What'd you do, adopt her out?"

"Once again, you're partially right and partially wrong. If you're familiar with my official biography, you know that my parents weren't wealthy, not even close, and they could barely afford my tuition at ASU. Getting a bronze at the Olympics didn't bring me much in the way of endorsement deals, either. My parents were prepared to take out a second mortgage on their home to see me through school, but there was no way I would accept such a sacrifice. They'd worked too hard to get where they were. I was about to quit school when I saw an ad in the back of the *New Times*, that leftist rag you can pick up for free on any street corner."

Here she paused to give me a frosty smile. "My politics weren't fully formed then, you understand. Anyway, the ad I'm talking about was paid for by a private party, and it offered fifty thousand dollars for the right young woman to perform a certain service. When I checked it out, I realized it was the perfect solution for my situation."

At the look on my face, her smile broadened, but somehow became even colder. "It's not what you're thinking. I didn't become an escort."

"But you…?" I let the sentence hang there.

"I became an egg donor."

It's not often, these days, that anything a politician says shocks me, but Juliana had managed. "You're telling me that to pay your tuition you sold your, ah, eggs?"

"Correct. Eggs from young women of my description—Nordic, tall, athletic, blue-eyed blondes with high IQs—we bring top dollar. Since I was all of those, I signed on. And was accepted right away."

Now I knew I didn't want her for a client. "Interesting, but irrelevant. Here's the deal. I really don't care what anyone does with their sperm or their eggs. Freedom of reproduction, and all that. What I do mind are your motives. You're afraid someone will leak news of your little clone to the media and you'll lose your extreme right-wing base. Well, Congresswoman, if you think you can hire me to hush this up and find some way to keep the girl hidden, maybe even funnel enough PAC money to pay for her removal somewhere else, you're asking the wrong private investigator."

I stood to leave, but her next words froze me in my tracks.

"Ask me the first girl's name."

Curious despite myself, I complied. "All right, Congresswoman. What's her name?"

"Alison Cameron. Yesterday, Ali—as she's known to her friends—was charged in Juvenile Court for masterminding her family's murder."

Chapter Two

I sat back down.

"No one knows about the egg donation, not even my sister," Juliana continued. "At first you thought Ali might be my niece, which is wrong. What you don't know is that Ilsa, my sister's daughter, is the result of in vitro fertilization, too. After more than ten years of marriage with no pregnancies, Helga learned she suffered from a condition that keeps her from producing viable eggs. It broke her heart. Her first thought was adoption, of course, but there's a long waiting list for infants, which she and her husband preferred. Also, adopting an infant from overseas can be both expensive and risky, so my first egg donation was to her."

The woman continued to surprise me.

"No money exchanged hands, just love and several weeks of intramuscular hormone shots. I've had better times, but it was worth it because now my sister and her husband have a wonderful daughter. Since she looks more like her father, whose features are different than mine, there has never been any question about her parentage."

"But she's still your daughter."

"No, she's my sister's daughter. Helga is the person who gave birth to Ilsa, raised Ilsa, loves and protects Ilsa. I'm merely the donor who facilitated that process."

"Donor? Nothing more than a campaign contributor?"

She gave me a look of distaste. "Sorry if I shock you, Lena, but yes, little more than that. I am not 'mother' to that child. I am her aunt, albeit an aunt who loves her very much." She paused and took a deep breath. "All Ali has is an uncle who's out of the country…" Another pause. "And her egg donor."

Sometimes the people you've made up your mind to dislike surprise you. "Look, Congresswoman, I can understand your feelings—I think—but at this point Ali is very, very fortunate that the case will be adjudicated in juvenile court. Considering the seriousness of the crime, it probably should have gone the other way, so I'm guessing you must have hired one hell of an attorney. Given that small miracle, what other miracle, exactly, do you think I can perform?"

"Find out who killed the Cameron family."

"Excuse me, but according to the newspaper accounts, Ali and her boyfriend confessed to the crime. She to planning the murders, he to carrying them out."

Juliana shook her head so fiercely a cloud of blond hair swirled around her head. "Impossible. I know my family's history and there's not a drop of violence in any of us." Seeing my eyes drift toward the elk heads on the wall, she frowned. "Game animals don't count."

"PETA might disagree."

"The electorate doesn't care what PETA thinks, and neither do I." She made a sound of disgust, then stabbed a finger at the newspaper. "Beating an entire family to death with a baseball bat? That is violence overload. Don't forget, one of the victims was Ali's brother, a child of ten. And before you ask, yes, I believe in the power of genetics. The science backs me up."

Ah, the old nature versus nurture argument. "Some science, not all. Upbringing counts for a lot."

The cold smile returned. "Upbringing? The kind you had? You were raised in a series of foster homes. If upbringing is all that counts, you should be a mess. But you're not."

Juliana didn't know me as well as she thought, did she? My nightmares…There was no reason to go into any of that. Still, I felt the need to further the argument.

"If genetics count for everything, with your own Viking heritage—which you so proudly pointed out to some of your more racist constituents during your first run for office—you'd be cleaving people's skulls with a battle axe instead of serving in the U.S. House of Representatives."

Another hair swirl. "The Vikings lived more than a thousand years ago. They've gentled since then. Now the Swedes, Norwegians, Danes, and Icelanders are some of the most peaceful people on Earth." As an afterthought she added, "If unfortunately Socialist."

"Aren't you forgetting Anders Breivik? 'Pure' Nordic blood, yet he killed seventy-seven people, most of them kids."

"A madman," said dismissively.

As a former police officer, I'd seen ghastly violence perpetrated by the most unlikely people—mothers, loving grandfathers, and yes, children. In rushing to the defense of her biological daughter, Juliana was forgetting something basic.

"Okay, let's pretend I buy your genetics theories, which, actually, I don't. How much do you know about her father? Dr. Cameron. After all, he's responsible for half of Ali's genetic makeup."

"Little more than the newspapers have reported," she admitted. "He was head of Emergency Medicine at Good Samaritan Hospital, in Phoenix. That's where you come in."

I raised my eyebrows. "You want me to check out his genetic heritage? Maybe find a wife-poisoner in his family tree? An axe murderer?"

She blushed, whether from anger or embarrassment at being called out for her borderline racist proclivities, I couldn't tell.

"I'm sure Dr. Cameron himself was an upright citizen, but there's always the chance he might have had unsavory connections. Many people do, not just Italians." The blush deepened. "Dr. Cameron's mother was Italian."

"Oh, you're hoping I'll find a Borgia, then. Or maybe a Mafia don here or there. Why? So Ali's attorney can raise the so-called 'warrior gene' defense in her case? That her genetics made her do it?"

"Don't be ridiculous!" Then, as if realizing she might have gone too far, she raised her hands in surrender. "If you dislike me, Lena, fine, but my politics are of no importance here. The only thing that matters is that little girl. Find out what really happened. If it means looking more deeply into my past, not just Dr. Cameron's, go right ahead. Now that you know my one secret, the rest of my life is an open book."

I doubted it. Everyone has something to hide, and the fact that Juliana had already admitted to one skeleton in her closet didn't mean there weren't more old bones rattling around in there. For instance, after her husband's death she had never remarried. What was up with that? Maybe she was gay. If so, her Religious Right supporters would run like rats in the opposite direction if they found out.

Despite my feelings about the woman herself, the case intrigued me. I didn't like the idea of two fourteen-year-old kids facing trial for multiple murders, but I was curious about their motives. Had Dr. Cameron and his wife really been the vessels of virtue the newspapers portrayed? Maybe they'd been secretly abusing Ali. Also, the news of the teens' supposed confessions bothered me. How, exactly, did a fourteen-year-old boy manage to kill a fully grown man, his wife, and a ten-year-old with a baseball bat? Oh, and batter the family dog half to death.

The dog.

"Juliana, that dog I saw when I came in. Is she yours?"

"Misty?" Juliana shook her head. "She's Ali's. When the murders made the ten o'clock news, the vet called the police. The information about the missing kids—and Misty—made the papers the next day. Upon reading that, I visited the vet and paid the bill, which turned out to be quite hefty, and he was more than happy to foster out Misty to me. Don't worry, it's on the up-and-up. I signed the requisite papers, agreeing to turn the dog over to its owner upon demand. Of course, I didn't mention my relationship with Ali, just told him I was happy to do something for the Camerons. And Misty."

"The vet wasn't suspicious about you?"

"Why should he be? He's a constituent."

I shrugged. "Even if he wasn't, the color of your money probably changed his mind. But what about the boy?"

"What about him?"

"Kyle Gibbs. Ali's boyfriend. Was he covered in blood when he showed up at the vet's?"

"No, the vet said he looked fine, but the boyfriend could have cleaned up, even changed his shirt after killing the family."

Yet Ali didn't? Something wasn't right.

"Before I decide whether I'll take the case or not, you need to tell me how you found out Alison Cameron was your biological daughter."

She sat back, remembering. "A couple of months ago I was at Fancy Feet, that shoe store in the Seville Shopping Center, looking for some comfortable flats. Ali was there with her mother. Both were so intent on shoes that they didn't notice me staring at them. When I walked in, I was struck by the girl's resemblance to that old picture of me, and when I looked down and saw the instep of her right foot, I knew."

She slipped off her left shoe. Just above the toes was a heart-shaped birthmark. "My sister and niece both have this, so did my mother. And my grandmother."

With such an obvious multi-generational reminder, no wonder Juliana was a dues-paying member of the nature-versus-nurture crowd. "Fine, so you saw her at Fancy Feet. What then? Did you follow them out of the store?"

"All the way to their house. It wasn't far. They live…lived… less than a mile away."

The snapshot. Ali had been carrying schoolbooks, not shopping. Which meant that the picture had been taken on a different day. "You've been stalking the kid!"

The flush came back. "Not really. Once I saw where she lived, I went back just that one day when I knew she'd be returning home from school. I fitted out my camera with a good zoom, and took the picture while she was walking up the street with some friends. She seemed happy. Normal. That was all I needed to know. I left her to live her life and never went back."

Happy. Normal.

So much for a book and its cover.

After thinking a moment, I made up my mind. "All right. I'll take the case, but only for seven days. After that we'll see where we are."

She closed her eyes briefly and moved her lips, probably in prayer to whatever fierce version of God she worshipped. When I explained my fee structure, she didn't blink, just wrote out a check on the spot.

"Paying for it with campaign contributions?" I asked, only half in jest, as I took it from her.

Frost again. "That would be unethical, as well you know. The minute I heard about Ali's situation, I cashed in some bonds. And if necessary, I'll take a second mortgage out on my condo. I am not going to let that girl rot in some horrible cell."

My dislike for my honorable congresswoman stepped back a bit.

But not completely.

Chapter Three

Ali

Married people don't know what love is.

I can tell by the way they're always fighting all the time about stuff like "Why do you keep hiding the broccoli in the crisper where I can't find it?" or "Don't you think that for just this once you could manage to clean the bathtub when you're done taking a bath?" Married people fight like that because if they didn't keep their minds busy picking each other apart, they'd have to face the fact that they married the wrong person to begin with because they never really loved each other, not one bit.

Kyle and I aren't like that.

We are truly and deeply in love for forever.

Kyle became my soul mate the day we were walking home from school together and he grabbed my arm to keep me from stepping off the curb when that Beemer blew through the red light and almost squashed me. He saved my life, and you don't forget something like that. When I was thanking him (trying hard not to cry or do anything else dorky), I looked into his eyes, those awesome dark blue eyes, and they pulled me in until my soul saw right into his soul. I understood then what life was all about.

He understood, too.

After that, it was Kyle+Ali=4ever.

To make sure I always remembered that moment, I stood in front of my bedroom mirror and scratched KYLE+ALI= 4EVER into my stomach with an X-ACTO blade, then rubbed black ink into the letters. It hurt, but it didn't bleed much, and it was worth the pain even if I forgot that mirror images are always reversed, so now I can only read it if I'm looking in a mirror. Which is kind of cool in a way, because it's like a secret code only Kyle and I can decipher. He did the same thing for me, scratched ALI+KYLE=4EVER into his stomach, only he remembered the part about mirrors.

Before gym the next day, we made a pact that we'd die for each other, just like Romeo and Juliet. If we had to, we swore we'd kill for each other, too, no matter who we had to kill. Our English teacher. My parents. Why, we'd even kill the President of the United States for each other! That's what real love is all about—finding and staying true to that one perfect person on Earth, because he is you and you are him and nobody else matters.

Kyle and me, we'll never complain about putting broccoli in the crisper or forgetting to clean out bathtubs. We're about deep, undying love.

So I don't let myself think about Dad or Mom or Alec because the whole killing thing was really, really necessary and what happened wasn't my fault, was it?

It was Mom's, that's whose fault it was! Sitting me down and telling me I had to cool it with Kyle for a while and that she'd already called Kyle's foster mom and told her the same thing. Oh, really? Kyle stay away? As if! And then the next day Dad came across like Godzilla because I only got a ninety-four on my algebra test. He didn't understand why I didn't ace it because he'd looked at the test afterward and said it was easy as pie. I told him it wasn't, but he just kept repeating the same phrase over and over again, easy as pie, easy as pie, until I thought I'd scream. He makes me crazy sometimes, he really does. As if that wasn't bad enough, an hour later Mom came up to my room and said she wasn't going to let me spend the night at Tiffany's house just because she found out the last time I was over there, her mom gave us a beer, helped me dye my hair black, and let me sneak out to see Kyle.

Tiffany's mom Suzy is mega super cool. She gets it about me and Kyle. My parents don't, especially my stupid dad.

Didn't, I mean. Past tense, considering what happened.

Whatever, no biggie.

Nothing I can do about any of it now, is there? Besides, it was their own stupid fault, wasn't it? Even Alec's. Talk about a snot-nosed little brat!

Well, screw him. Screw Mom, screw Dad, screw them all. I don't care what happened to them and never will.

All I care about is Kyle.

And Misty.

Chapter Four

Lena

Considering how tight access had become in juvie cases over the past few years, I was surprised at how easy it was to arrange a visit with Alison Cameron. Once I signed the contract as official investigator for the girl's attorney, all I had to do was place a call to the juvie complex at Mesa Detention Center, and the next thing I knew, I was sitting across from her in a pungent green and gray interview room. Someone had been sick in here recently.

The child I saw shocked me. Not because of what she had done—during my years on the Scottsdale Police Force I'd arrested several killer juveniles—but because of how she looked. The cheerful blonde beauty I'd seen in Juliana's candid snapshot was gone, replaced by a scowling dyed-brunette with line-shaped scabs up and down her left arm that her orange jumpsuit failed to cover.

"Good morning, Ali. My name is Lena Jones and I've been hired by your attorney to investigate the incident that led to your family's, ah, deaths. And by the way, have you been cutting yourself?"

No answer, just a combative jutting of chin.

"Okay, life sucks, I get it, and cutting releases the pressure, but here's what we have to do now. To begin my investigation, I need to ask you a few questions. You up to answering?"

Silence.

"I'll take that as a yes. Question number one. Did you take part in the incident? Or were you merely the, ah, planner of said incident?"

The silence was so deep that I could hear the guard outside the door scratch some portion of his body.

Time to call a spade a spade and a murder a murder. "Anyway, that's what you told the police, that you planned it. But I'm a little confused as to whether you physically took part in the murders themselves."

Silence.

"Then let me frame the question a different way. Did you kill or help kill, one, two, or all three of the victims?"

Silence.

"Where were you when the murders were committed?"

Still that eerie silence.

"Moving on. What about the dog? Why half-kill it, then turn around and take it to the vet?"

Finally a reaction. "Misty's a her, not an it."

The dog was the way through this, then. Killers, whatever their ages, frequently dissociated themselves from the more heinous elements of their crimes while obsessively focusing on some triviality. Not that the poor dog was a triviality.

"Cute dog. Friendly, too."

Ali's chin trembled. "You...you've seen Misty?"

"She came running up to me as soon as I walked in the door," I lied.

"At the vet's?"

I shook my head. "Now that she's recovering from her injuries, she's been fostered out to a good temporary home."

Ali leaned toward me, anxiety mapping her face. "Who?"

"A very nice lady." Another lie. "Nice" was the last word I'd use to describe Juliana Thorsson.

"She better not be one of those animal hoarders I've seen on TV!"

"No, no. Misty's the only animal there. She's getting plenty of pats and hugs, I promise you that." I crossed my fingers behind my back on that one, it being hard to imagine the frosty congresswoman cuddling anything.

"Can I see Misty?"

"Maybe if you answer my questions it can be arranged."

"Just maybe?" A fleeting expression of grief, but it immediately disappeared.

"I'm not going to make promises I can't keep, Ali. That said, judges do tend to be more lenient with cooperative inmates."

"Inmates?"

"That's what you and Kyle are now, yes. Inmates. And if you don't start cooperating, you and Kyle will continue to be inmates for a long time. In separate facilities, with no visits from Misty."

She looked down at the floor long enough that I took a quick glance at it, too. Maybe some of the vomit I smelled was still there? Then I saw a drop of moisture splash onto the dusty green tile. It sure as hell didn't come from me.

Softening my voice, I said, "Ali, I promise you I'll try very, very hard to get you a visit with Misty."

"Promise from the heart," she mumbled.

What did that mean? "Uh, yeah, I promise from the heart."

She lifted a teary face and gave me a ferocious stare. "Put your hand on your heart and say it!"

Remembering she was only fourteen, gifted with all the magical thinking that age entailed, I put my hand on my left breast. "I promise from the heart that I will try very, very, very hard to arrange a visit with Misty, so help me God."

"There is no God."

"Who told you that?" Another way in, perhaps?

"My dad. He's a doctor and sees a lot of dead people, so he should know. He says he never saw any god of any kind. Or angels. Or Satan."

Noticing her use of the present tense, I asked, "Is there anything else your dad tells you that might be important to your case?"

Her face shuttered.

"Ali, did your dad do anything bad to you? Touch you where you shouldn't be touched, maybe? Do something even worse?"

That damned silence again. Other than where the dog was concerned, the kid was an ice queen, just like her egg donor. Fleetingly, I wondered what the beautiful woman who raised her had been like. Not the same, I hoped.

There was no point in continuing down a blind alley, so I switched tactics. "Misty will be glad to see you. Although she's being well taken care of, she looks lonely."

Ali picked at one of the scabs on her arm, making it bleed. "Lonely enough to die?"

"Dogs don't die of lonely, Ali." At least I didn't think they did, but maybe I was wrong.

"People do." Her voice was flat, without affect.

"Do what?"

"Die of being lonely."

I thought about that for a moment, then asked, "Who are you lonely for?"

"Misty." She looked down again. "Kyle."

"Not your mother and father? Your brother?"

"I don't let myself think about them."

"Probably the wisest course of action under the circumstances." For some reason, I was finding it hard to talk. I cleared my throat. "Getting get back to my question, did you or did you not take part in the actual killing?"

She crossed her arms over her chest—never easy to do when you're wearing shackles—and jutted out her chin. But her voice was still flat. "Did I kill them all by myself? No."

"Do you know who did?"

No answer.

"Ali, Kyle told the police he did it, that you weren't involved in any way."

"I can't help what Kyle says."

"Maybe he was just confused. So answer me this. Did you *help* kill one, two, or all three of the victims?"

A shrug. "I wasn't counting."

Christ, what a little monster. "Do you know anyone who killed or helped kill any of the victims?"

Nothing.

"Did you plan the killing of one or more of the victims?"

She uncrossed her arms and rested her shackled hands on the table. "Like you said, that's what I told the police, isn't it?"

"Yes, but was it the truth?"

She looked down at her hands. The black-painted nails were bitten, the cuticles bloody.

"If you only planned it, and Kyle didn't kill anyone, who was your accomplice?"

"Some guy."

"Some guy you knew? Or some guy you just met?"

"Seen him around."

"School? The neighborhood?"

"Just around." She looked at the door, as if hoping for rescue. None arrived.

"What's the guy's name?"

"I can't remember."

"Describe him for me."

"He looked like, you know, just a guy."

"How old was he?"

A brief hesitation, then, "Old. Almost as old as you."

To a teenager, anyone past twenty was old, and since I was on the dark side of thirty, she categorized me as ancient.

"Short?"

"Yeah. Real short."

"Dark-haired?"

"Blond."

"Blue eyes?"

"Brown."

Of course that would be her answer. The newspapers had described fourteen-year-old Kyle as tall for his age, dark-haired, with blue eyes.

"Did you pay this short blond guy with the brown eyes to kill your parents?"

"Yeah."

"With what?"

"With money I saved up from my allowance."

I almost laughed. Instead, I asked. "Why did you take Misty to the vet?"

"Because she was hurt, you dumb-ass!"

Alison Cameron was a liar, and a bad one, too, but exactly where did the lies begin? As I drove back up the Pima Freeway toward Old Town Scottsdale, I replayed the interview in my head. When first arrested, the girl told the police that she had not only planned the murders, but took part in carrying them out. There'd been no mention of a hit man. Kyle Gibbs had done pretty much the same, swearing he and he alone was responsible, that Ali hadn't asked him to kill anyone. They were exonerating each other. Which story was closest to the truth?

By the time I exited the freeway and started the slow slog up Scottsdale Road, I'd just about decided both stories were complete fabrications. Then again…

The black Lincoln Town Car in front of me suddenly slammed on its brakes, jarring me back to the present. I braked in time to keep from hitting it, then sat back in frustration. Construction. It was eleven a.m. and the work on Scottsdale Road should have been halted due to the heat of the day, but several Hispanic laborers were still pouring chip seal onto hot asphalt. With brown faces flushed red and tempers to match, two of them were arguing with a third. The Town Car driver powered his window down. Due to the jackhammer roaring nearby I couldn't hear what he said, but there was no missing his upright middle finger.

I glanced in my rearview mirror, hoping I had enough room to back up and turn around, but saw that a silver Mercedes had just about crawled up on my Jeep's bumper. The Mercedes vented a sustained air-blast that nearly deafened me. But the white church bus idling next to me proved the most unsettling. Although filled with laughing children on the way to some harmless recreational activity, it bore an unpleasant resemblance to the bus that haunted my nightmares.

The bus where it happened, where I'd been thrown from at the age of four.

Question: What is a mother?

Answer: The woman who shoots her child in the face and leaves her to die.

I closed my eyes, wishing the bus and the memory away. When I opened my eyes again, the bus and the memory were still there.

A half hour later I arrived at my destination, a measly two blocks from the traffic tie-up and resulting fistfight. The law offices of Edwins, Zellar, and Hurley were housed in a marble and glass building that sat uneasily between a Western clothier and a store specializing in turquoise Navajo jewelry. From the parking lot, if you squinted your eyes, you could see the edge of the Salt River Pima/Maricopa Indian Reservation, and beyond that, the Superstition Mountains. This struggle between sleek modernity and rustic simplicity furthered Scottsdale's schizophrenic air, as if it couldn't make up its mind whether to belong to the nineteenth century or the twenty-first.

Stephen Zellar, Esquire, however, very much belonged to the twenty-first. His office, furnished in cream-colored leather and polished chrome, was not so much welcoming as efficient. Same with Zellar himself, a middle-aged man as pale and gaunt as his furniture. Dispensing with the usual pleasantries, he slid a box file over his desk to me as soon as I sank into a chair.

"Here are copies of the discovery we've received so far," he said. "Photos of the clothes the kids' were wearing the day of the murders—DPS found them in the mother's Lexus at a campsite in Quartzsite, by the way. We have the crime scene photos, autopsy reports, ballistics test, police interviews with the doctor's coworkers, interviews with the kids' teachers, friends, the live-in maid, who was, lucky for her, on vacation at the time of the murders, phone and computer readouts—you know, the usual. No DNA results yet. That'll take a while."

But I figured the disposition of this case wouldn't take long. Given Ali's and Kyle's confessions, however ridiculous those were, there would probably be a quickie plea deal and that would be that. The kids would serve time in the juvenile corrections system until they turned eighteen. After they were released, the taint of the murder conviction would follow them for the rest of their lives.

"How about surveillance cameras? Neighborhoods like that frequently have them."

He shook his head. "The Camerons had none, apparently believing that alarms were sufficient. Same for their two neighbors, unfortunately."

Or fortunately, if cameras had shown two bloodied teens leaving the house. Before I opened the box, I asked, "Is there any chance I'll be able to talk to Kyle Gibbs and get his version of events?"

"I doubt it," Zellar said. "As I explained during our telephone conversation yesterday, he and Miss Cameron have been charged separately, therefore he has a different attorney."

"Court-ordered attorney?"

A barely visible nod. His fingers began to drum on his glass-topped desk. "You may take the file back to your office. We're keeping the originals, of course."

"Of course," I murmured.

Zellar stood. "The girl's confession is nonsense, Ms. Jones, and I foresee no trouble in getting it thrown out. As to what happens with her case after that, well, I rely on you to come up with mitigating factors if we actually go to trial. Mental health issues, difficult home life, sexual abuse, you know the drill."

Yep, the standard drill when it came to killer kids. "You're not looking for a plea deal, then?"

"Depends on what we're offered. Anyway, if there's nothing else…"

A check of my Timex proved I'd been in Zellar's office less than five minutes. Remaining seated, I said, "I was hoping to ask a few more questions."

He glanced at his own watch, which appeared considerably more expensive than mine. "I have a luncheon appointment, so keep it brief."

"How well do you know Congresswoman Thorsson?"

Still standing, he answered, "She's an old family friend, but I'm not inclined to discuss the congresswoman further, other than to stress that this is the first time she has ever needed the services of a criminal defense attorney. Miss Thorsson has been an upstanding citizen all her life. Next question."

"You don't know why she's taken a personal interest in this case?"

"As I said, I'm not inclined to comment on that." A slight flicker in his eyes hinted that he might know about the biological relationship. It would be interesting to see how that played out if the case wound up in court.

But that was for later. "What are your impressions about your client?"

"Alison? Bearing in mind that impressions, as you call them, count for little except with juries—and there will be none here, just an unimpressionable judge—she appears to be a troubled young woman. Which, I remind you, will be part of our defense. If it's needed."

"Sounds to me like you're preparing to go to trial, then."

"Only a last resort. A good defense attorney always has a Plan B. As well as a Plan C and D. At this stage, anything can happen. Having a mental health evaluation in hand would be useful in either eventuality, so I'm arranging for a psych eval as we speak."

"A psychiatrist?"

"Most definitely a psychiatrist, and a child psychologist, and a social worker who specializes in juvenile issues. We must never forget that Miss Cameron is a minor."

"When you spoke with Ali, did she tell you she planned the killings?"

He looked with great interest at the far wall, which was painted a bald, glaring white. Nothing hung on it. A second glance revealed a large, white-on-white minimalist abstract bordered by a thin chrome frame. You could hardly tell it from the wall.

Zellar cleared his throat. "Given Miss Cameron's age, anything she might have told me about that afternoon would be suspect. Adolescents can be overly imaginative, you understand."

"Did she say anything about the short, blond, brown-eyed hit man she hired with her allowance money?"

Another glance at his watch. "You're kidding me, right? Now, I'm afraid I must bring this meeting to a close. If there's anything else you need to know, speak to my appointments secretary as you leave. I'll always make time for you."

Not much time, apparently.

"Before I leave, how about giving me the name of Kyle Gibb's attorney?"

Zellar's face grew even stiffer with disapproval. "He won't say anything to you."

"Just the same…"

A sigh. "Curtis Racine. Young, bit of a rebel, but savvy enough that he won't let his client talk to you, so you'd just be wasting your time." With that, Zellar walked over to the door and opened it. As I reluctantly rose from my chair, he said, "It's been a pleasure, Miss Jones."

After Zellar's frigid office, the July heat felt good, so I drove the eight blocks to Desert Investigations as slowly as possible. I wasn't eager to open the evidence file, having been warned in advance that it contained photographs of the murder scene. Seeing how two adults died is bad enough, but studying images of a dead ten-year-old was something even the most hardened detective dreads.

The trespassing Hummer had been nowhere around when I opened the office early this morning, but as I pulled into the parking lot, I found it parked diagonally across two of Desert Investigations' parking places. Ordinarily I would have done something about that, but right now I wasn't in the mood. In the face of tragedy, trespassing Hummers don't rate.

Jimmy wasn't in, so I had the office to myself, which turned out to be a good thing because the crime scene photos were among the worst I'd ever seen. The victims had been separated from each other by approximately eight feet, bound with duct tape. While they sat helpless, they were subjected to torture-by-battering with the Louisville Slugger found at the scene. A close-up of the bat showed it remained intact, which was surprising given the fury of the assaults. According to the medical examiner's report, the torture had gone on for some time. First their legs were broken, then their arms, then their ribs. The fatal blows to Alec and his mother came only after earlier blows shattered their faces. For some reason, after being tortured, Dr. Cameron had died via a 9mm gunshot to the head. Odd, that.

The medical examiner believed that ten-year-old Alec died first, while his parents watched. Alexandra came next, then Dr. Cameron, but only after a round of torture even more extreme than his wife's and son's.

The office door opened just as I was closing the folder. "Jesus, Lena, what's wrong?"

Jimmy. Carrying two Big Gulps from Circle K.

"Working on the Cameron case."

"Examining the crime scene photos?"

"Yep."

He thrust a Big Gulp at me. "Drink this, but slowly. Otherwise…"

I knew what "otherwise" meant so I didn't gulp my Big Gulp, just sipped at it while eyeing the hall that led to the bathroom. If the worst happened, the run would be a straight shot, nothing in the way, thus sparing our carpet.

"Deep breaths, Lena."

"Stop playing nursemaid, Almost Brother. I'm fine."

"You always fall to pieces over the kids."

"I'm not falling to pieces."

"And I'm the Lord Mayor of London."

"Then stop hovering, your lordship, and sit down."

Jimmy and I often carried on like squabbling siblings, which was one of the reasons I often called him my "almost brother." Despite our seemingly diverse backgrounds, we had much in common. After his parents died of diabetes, the Pima scourge, Jimmy had been adopted by a large Mormon family in Utah. When they relocated to a guest ranch in northern Arizona, he'd moved with them. Being in Arizona again awoke his indigenous spirit, and within his first year back in the state, he'd made telephone contact with his relatives on the Salt River Pima Indian Reservation. Then came the visits, followed by lessons in the Pima language, and finally, a rift from his adoptive family that took years to breach.

But he had been loved. Fiercely.

Me? Not so lucky. After being left to die on a Phoenix street, I began a grueling march through Arizona's foster care system, which seldom offered the solace of love. Madeline. Reverend Giblin. Only in their homes did I discover that such a thing could exist in this dangerous world.

"Stop looking at me like that," Jimmy grumped, as he sat down at the computer station across from my desk.

"I'm not looking at you any way. Stop being so paranoid."

"Pot calling the kettle black. Maybe you shouldn't have taken this case."

"Too late now. And you know something? I'm beginning to doubt the girl was involved."

"Girls can be as vicious as boys." He knew my history as well as I knew his.

"Given the right circumstances, anyone is capable of killing, but this?" I shook a crime scene photo at him. The sense that something was wrong was growing stronger by the minute.

"Don't let the fact that she showed mercy to the dog fool you."

"We all practice selective compassion, except for, maybe, the Dalai Lama. He pities everyone." I looked at the photos again. "Besides, the crime scene techs only found Kyle's fingerprints on the bat, not Ali's."

"So? From what I hear, she's a bright girl. If she'd carried out the killings herself, she'd have been smart enough to wear gloves."

I nodded. "No one believes she did the bat-swinging herself. According to the statement her boyfriend gave the police, he was the muscle."

Jimmy twirled around his office chair once, something he frequently did when playing devil's advocate. "Again, so? Under the law, if the girl planned the murders, she's just as guilty. More so, in some situations, especially if the partner-in-crime is the first to cop a plea. Good thing Arizona no longer executes fourteen-year-olds."

"Only because the Supreme Court won't let us. But look. What's puzzling me is the savagery of the attacks. This is Ali's family, not Kyle's, so if he murdered them, why so much rage? It wouldn't have been personal with him."

"The parents were probably trying to break them up." Another chair twirl. "That could have set him off."

"At her parents, but not at a ten-year-old child. Don't forget the little boy. And the dog."

"He's crazy?"

"Then if his court-ordered attorney has any sense, he'll plead insanity. I need to talk to Kyle's attorney." Although contact with an opposing attorney and/or his client could be a license-endangering offense, something about this case made me decide to risk it. "Even better, the kid himself."

"Good luck on that," Jimmy muttered. Finally halting the chair-twirling, he returned to work.

Curtis Racine, Kyle Gibbs' attorney, was in. Not that it did me any good. Once he was on the phone, he immediately denied my request for an interview with his client. He did it politely, I'll give him that.

"Ms. Jones, you've been in this business long enough to know that I could get in big trouble for even taking this phone call, let alone talking to another lawyer's investigator." But there was enough curiosity in his voice to make me forge ahead.

"Duly noted, Mr. Racine. But let me ask you this. If for some strange reason I eventually decide that Mr. Gibbs and Ms. Cameron are both innocent of the murders, where would be the best place for me to start looking for the evidence that might prop up my thesis?"

"I haven't the foggiest idea," he replied in a pleasant tenor. "And call me Curtis." Another good sign. Despite ethics considerations that should have hamstrung us both, this guy really wanted to help. He was the type of attorney who would either go far, or get himself disbarred.

"Think I should interview Kyle's family, Curtis?"

The attorney's answer was a dark silence long enough for me to suspect Kyle might have family problems of his own.

"Okay, then. How about his friends?"

The pleasant tenor returned. "I can't stop you from doing that, Miss Jones, but their families might. We're talking minors here. And we really, really, really shouldn't be having this conversation at all, should we? Come to think of it, we're not talking at all."

But he didn't hang up, and from his chipper tone, I deduced that Kyle Gibbs didn't run with a bad crowd, otherwise he wouldn't sound so relaxed.

"How about Kyle's teachers?"

A chuckle. "They'll tell you less than I have."

"Are there any leads you can give me that won't conflict with client confidentiality?"

"Let me think." I heard breathing, papers shuffling. A few moments later, he said, "Ah. There is one thing. Two, actually. As you must have heard by now, certainly not from me, that my client lived in a foster home."

"Huh!?"

Ignoring my outburst, he continued. "Remember, we haven't had this conversation at all. You never talked to me, I never talked to you. As to Mr. Gibbs' living situation, I can't give anyone the particulars on that, of course, especially not you, but word through the grapevine is that young Mr. Gibbs once owned a dog, a mixed breed of some sort. He had to give it up at some point, but it's being taken care of by his aunt. She's a nice woman, considering."

Considering? "Do you mean…?"

"A reminder. This conversation never happened. But, no, I don't mean anything, just that Mrs. Daggett's trailer out in Apache Junction seems awfully small for such a large dog. You know, Mrs. Edith Daggett, spelled with two g's and two t's, lives on Apache Trail in Whispering Pines Mobile Home Park, 2015 East Apache Trail…Oh, goodness, did I actually let all that slip? My, my, what a blabbermouth I am! Well, what you gonna do? When I don't keep my guard up, all sorts of things come tumbling out of my mouth. It's your fault, you being such a tough interviewer and all. Guess I'd better end this call before you manage to strong-arm even more information from me, such as the fact that I don't believe a word young Kyle says, because that sweet kid wouldn't hurt a fly. So *adios*, Miss Jones. *Hasta la vista*. Hope to see you around the courthouse sometime. And remember, we never had this conversation."

Dial tone.

Never underestimate the eely slipperiness of an attorney. Although making a big noise about client confidentiality, Racine had made certain I would talk to Kyle Gibbs' aunt, a Mrs. Edith Daggett, two g's, two t's, resident of an Apache Junction trailer park. Within seconds, Information supplied me with the woman's phone number and address. An hour later, I was angling my Jeep into a visitor's parking space at Whispering Pines Mobile Home Park.

Apache Junction is an oddball town in an oddball state. Hunkered down in the shadows of the Superstition Mountains, it's a salty mix of old Arizona natives, new Minnesota retirees, prospectors looking for the Lost Dutchman Gold Mine, wranglers from nearby guest ranches, and a few pin-striped commuters who aren't afraid to brave the snarled mess of I-60 all the way to downtown Phoenix. Because the bulk of its denizens live on fixed incomes, AJ is the state champ when it comes to mobile home parks. Most are country club-type RV resorts, but a goodly number play host to beat-up single-wides.

Mrs. Daggett's was one of the latter, a down-at-the-heels place where ailing trailers go to die. After threading my way through a sea of rusting hulks, I finally found her fifties peach-and-turquoise single-wide. Concrete blocks had been pushed together in front to act as stairs. A sign taped to the rusty screen door warned BEWARE OF PIT BULL. Despite the sign, the door stood ajar.

Not taking any chances, I stayed off the ersatz staircase and banged a fist on the side of the trailer.

"Knock-knock, Mrs. Daggett! It's Lena Jones. With Desert Investigations?"

"Well, don't just stand there lettin' everybody know our business. Get yourself in here!" creaked an elderly voice.

"Uh, the dog…?"

A cackle. "He ain't gonna kill you."

After slipping my hand into my carryall and grasping the handle of my .38, I started up the stairs. I like dogs, but I don't like being bitten by them. Especially not the pit bull kind; they're infamous for clamping those enormous teeth around you and not letting go.

The .38 turned out not to be necessary.

Greeting me at the door was a golden retriever mix so old he could have been one of the original canines on Noah's ark. All but toothless, he snuffled and drooled all over my new black jeans.

"Pit Bull, leave that woman alone!" the woman yelled from the darkness inside.

Fat, half-blind, and probably deaf, too, Pit Bull kept messing me up.

"I take it the name's a joke," I called back, pushing Pit Bull away before his inquisitive nose made it to my crotch.

"My nephew's little joke, not mine. Poor old thing was already on his last legs when Kyle drug him in here from the pound, and that's been four years ago easy. So you're a detective, huh? Peculiar job for a woman."

"I like it."

As I sidestepped Pit Bull and entered the oven-hot, dimly lit trailer, I could make out what appeared to be a rag-wrapped collection of sticks propped up on an afghan-covered sofa. Once my eyes grew accustomed to the gloom, the sticks revealed themselves to be the limbs of an elderly woman so emaciated it was a marvel she retained enough musculature to speak. Inserted into her nose was a cannula, which led to an oxygen tank sitting on the floor. A heavy stench of tobacco hung in the air.

"You ever shoot that gun I figure you got there in your purse?" the bag of bones asked.

"From time to time."

"Ever killed anybody with it?"

"I plead the Fifth on that, Ma'am."

Another cackle. The stream of sunlight trickling through the closed venetian blinds illuminated her almost lipless mouth, revealing a few lower teeth, none on top.

"Plead the Fifth, that's what I told Kyle to do when he got caught up in that Scottsdale mess, but he wouldn't listen. Teenagers. Don't know nothing, think they know everything." She gestured to a rickety-looking chair. "Take a load off. Just make sure you keep that gun on the other side of you so if it goes off, it'll shoot you, not me. And for God's sake, don't point it at Pit Bull. He'd have a heart attack."

I took a load off. With a loud groan, Pit Bull collapsed in the middle of the room.

"Ma'am, is that dog all right?"

"He's still breathing, ain't he?" She raised her voice to a shriek. "Pit Bull! You still alive?"

Pit Bull thumped his tail.

"Yep, still alive. For now, anyway. But you didn't come all the way out here to talk dogs, did you? You wanna talk about Kyle, but it ain't to help him, is it? You want to pin it all on the boy and let the rich girl off the hook. Satan Kyle, using his manly wiles to lead Saint Alison astray, right?"

She might have been old and sick, but she was far from stupid.

"What makes you think that, Mrs. Daggett?"

"'Cause I just got off the phone with his lawyer."

"Oh."

"Here's what I'm going to do, Miss Scaredy Pants When It Comes to Dogs, I'm going to tell you all about my nephew. And when we're finished, you tell me which one of them was the hell-child and which one of them got drug into something they didn't understand and got left out there twisting in the wind. Notice who got the hoity-toity Scottsdale attorney along with the fancy lady detective, and who got the cheap court-ordered attorney?"

"Don't sell your nephew's attorney short, Mrs. Daggett."

"I'm not, but I know the odds."

I leaned back against the chair. Although covered with dog hair, it was surprisingly comfortable. "So here's your chance to set me straight about Kyle, starting with why I'm talking to you instead of his parents."

She snorted. "Rats got better parents than that boy."

"Really?"

"You ready to hear a sad story, Miss Scaredy Pants?"

Oh, yes, I assured her. Lena Jones was always ready for a sad story. After all, hadn't I had plenty of practice?

Chapter Five

Still, the story of Kyle Gibbs' young life unsettled me. While listening to Mrs. Daggett's melancholy account, my emotions careened between sorrow and rage.

Kyle was the product of the rape of a fourteen-year-old girl by her uncle, who was subsequently convicted of sexual assault. At the age of three, Kyle was turned over to Child Protective Services after neighbors found the toddler alone and naked in a filthy apartment; his by-then crack-addicted mother had disappeared and was never seen again. With no relatives stepping forward to claim him, Kyle then began a merry-go-round of foster homes, some good, some bad. At the age of six, he was sexually abused by an older boy, and during his stay at his fourth foster home, he'd suffered cigarette burns on his arm, a broken wrist and a punctured eardrum before CPS stepped in and removed him.

The Scottsdale foster home Kyle had been living in when the Cameron murders occurred turned out to be his eighth, and most stable. He had been living with them for three years.

"Last time the boy was out here, he said they was going to adopt him," Mrs. Daggett said, although her voice carried little conviction.

"How'd you feel about that?"

She sneered. "I didn't feel nothing, 'cause that kinda thing's come up before and it ain't never happened. It was just Kyle, building castles in the air, the way he always does."

"Castles?"

"Always dreaming 'bout about better places, better days. I told him time and again he'd better stop doing that because things don't never get no better."

A bleak philosophy to instill into a child.

Unaware of my thoughts, she continued. "But blood is blood, and no matter where the state shipped that boy to, I always stayed in contact with him. Well, when I was able to."

Behind me, Pit Bull farted. I pretended I hadn't heard it. Trying hard not to cringe away from the stench creeping my way, I asked, "What do you mean, 'when I was able to' ? The boy needed a home and you were his aunt." A sudden thought struck me. "Were you married to the uncle who raped Kyle's mother?"

Before answering, she moved some magazines off the table beside the sofa, uncovering a can of air freshener. "Here. You do the honors," she said, handing over the can.

I sprayed, not that it helped much. Despite the tiny fan wheezing at us from the kitchen counter, the interior of the trailer was too small to allow for better circulation. And Pit Bull, at least in the power of his farts, was a mighty dog.

"Before the stink bomb, you was asking me about Kyle's mother and who raped her. I wasn't married to that piece of slime, my sister was. We haven't spoken since she let him move back in with her when he got out of prison. Jack's his name, in case you're interested."

"The only thing I'm interested in, Mrs. Daggett, is why you didn't provide a home for Kyle, letting Child Protective Services take him."

A flicker of something, perhaps guilt, crossed her face. "Because I was busy serving a five-year sentence for fraud. I ain't going to go into details, other than to say I didn't do what they said I did. Anyway, there was no way CPS would turn that child over to me, even if I'd won my appeal, which I didn't. Unlike my sister's precious Jack, I didn't get no time off for good behavior, either, did the full nickel. Once I got released my husband was dead, another no-count, but at least not a kiddie-diddler, and

Kyle had already been a ward of the court for four years. CPS had the decency to let me visit, though. Supervised visitation for a while, but they finally eased up on that, of course."

"Of course," I echoed, looking around for the evidence of ill-gotten gains. Cheap sofa, cheap chair, cheap rug, cheap lamp. The only thing of value was a shiny new Cuisinart Elite IV on the kitchen counter. Even at sale price it would still cost more than everything else in this place lumped together.

Seeing me stare at the Cuisinart, Mrs. Daggett explained with a note of pride, "Kyle gave me that. Said the blender would make it easier for me to eat. Paid for it out of his allowance, he did."

Like Ali paid her mysterious hit man.

"Hey, Miss Scaredy Pants, you wanna see a picture of Kyle?"

"Sure." Because of his age, the papers hadn't run the boy's picture.

She leaned forward and hauled up a vinyl handbag that looked as old as her trailer. Rifled through it. "Here you go."

She handed over her billfold, which had a thick, accordion-style insert for photographs. "Handsome boy, ain't he?"

Yes, he was. With his black hair, navy blue eyes, firm chin, and a clear complexion instead of the usual teenage acne, the boy resembled a darker yet more innocent Justin Bieber. I knew from my own history that foster care presents additional danger to pretty children, and many of them became violent in order to cope.

"You do realize, don't you, Mrs. Daggett, that Kyle shares a background with many murderers, not to mention serial killers? Broken families, sexual and other abuse, foster homes." I could be describing myself, too, but she didn't need to know that.

She gave me a hard look. "I may live in a trailer and I may not talk fancy, but I can read the newspaper. Murderers and serial killers start off practicing on animals. Kyle rescues animals, he doesn't torture them. Cats, dogs, even a couple of those white bunnies people buy for their kids around Easter then get tired of and throw out with the garbage. He'd find them, fix them up, get them good homes." She nodded toward Pit Bull.

"There was a dog present during the killings, and it was badly beaten."

"Not by Kyle."

I had met women like Mrs. Daggett before. Experts at denial, their minds rearranged ugly realities into a more acceptable fiction. I could almost sympathize. Her past had been difficult, and judging from her current health problems, her future looked worse. So I pretended to believe her fairy tale. "Let's talk about Ali, then. How did she and Kyle meet?"

"Went to the same Scottsdale school. Kyle told me she was being bullied by some of those mean girls, probably deserved it, too, but he stopped them. Same day, she damned near got herself run over in the street outside the school, but he jerked her back just in time. After that, he was her hero."

To me, such heroism sounded too good to be true, so I immediately became suspicious. "What's the name of the school?"

She shrugged. "Can't remember."

"Did Kyle tell you how he stopped the bullying?"

She looked away, an indication she was about to tell a lie. "He gave them a stern talking to. Since he's tall for his age, five-ten already, he scared them pretty bad."

"No physicality involved?"

"Kyle would never hit a girl."

"Does he hit boys?" I was thinking about Ali's ten-year-old brother. The picture of the child's battered body would haunt me forever.

Her lips formed a tight, narrow line. "Kyle never hit anybody."

No, he just beats them to death with a baseball bat. "When's the last time you saw your nephew?"

"Three weeks ago. His foster parents dropped him off here for a couple of hours to see me and Pit Bull. That dog's nuts over him, I tell you that? Anyways, this was before that Alison bitch killed her whole family and blamed it on Kyle."

"That's not the way I heard it went down."

The sneer she gave me collapsed half her face into downward folds; the other half looked like it was held up by invisible strings.

"Yeah, now that the little snot sees how much trouble she's in, she's switching her story. Them rich girls are like that, spoiled rotten. Never take responsibility for nothing, always blaming other people when things go wrong."

Alison Cameron hadn't come across as spoiled when I talked to her. Terrified and stubborn, maybe, but not spoiled. And the only person she blamed was a non-existent short, brown-eyed blond hit man.

"Kyle confessed that he killed the Camerons, Mrs. Daggett."

"According to the papers and the cops, and you know how they all lie."

An idea occurred to me. I might not be able to interview Kyle, but Mrs. Daggett, as next-of-kin, had access. Although any report she gave me would be filtered through love and denial, a few dregs of truth might remain.

"I take it you'll be visiting him at the detention center."

Her head drooped and she said something I couldn't hear.

"Could you speak up, Mrs. Daggett? I didn't catch that."

She raised her head and stared at me defiantly. "I'm not on the visitor's list."

"That can be easily rectified. I'll call his attorney and get him to petition the Probation Department to add you. If necessary, he can get a court order."

Her voice lowered again, but this time I could still hear her.

"You don't understand, Miss Jones. Kyle don't want to see me. Said he doesn't want to spread his trouble around any more than he already has."

Later, while driving away from Whispering Pines Mobile Home Park, I pondered the Saint Kyle problem. Unless the kid changed his mind and allowed Mrs. Daggett to visit him in the Durango facility, she wouldn't be able to relay back to me the boy's version of events. If nothing else, the woman and I shared the same distrust of the media, but the fact remained that the newspapers' coverage of the murders pretty much tallied with the police report, which suggested an unnamed source inside the department. Regardless of what Mrs. Daggett professed to believe, Kyle was probably the Camerons' killer. After all, his fingerprints were on the bat. My job was to figure out Ali's involvement. That, and nothing else.

Mrs. Daggett was wrong about another thing, too. Curtis Racine was an excellent attorney, if a bit on the loosey-goosey side where codes of conduct were concerned. By sending me to see Kyle's aunt, he'd aroused a smidgen of pity in my hard-panned soul.

Not that pity would do either kid any good.

A call to Stephen Zellar, Ali's attorney, elicited the information that the girl attended Four Palms Middle School. Term was over, but summer school and extra-credit classes might still be in session. I crossed my fingers and headed for the school. Although Scottsdale is only a short drive from Apache Junction, the two towns could be on separate planets. As my Jeep cruised along I-60, raw desert gave way to irrigated greenery. Saguaro cacti diminished, replaced by towering palms and silvery leafed eucalyptus. The mobile homes disappeared, and in their place, Mediterranean mini-mansions strutted their stuff.

Four Palms Middle School was tucked into a plush oasis near the intersection of Lincoln and Mockingbird Lane, an Episcopal church on one side, an art academy on the other. The school's grounds were immaculate, and its football field would turn Notre Dame green with envy. Summer or no summer, a group of tweens carrying heavy-looking backpacks hovered near the school's main entrance. Maybe their parents couldn't get away for the summer, and the brainier kids were utilizing the hot downtime by working on extra credit projects. If you lived in Scottsdale, you were expected to go to college—a good one—and sometimes those extra credits even trumped the size of Daddy's bank account.

As I drove up, several post-tweens trying hard to look like jaded thirty-year-olds were exiting the main building. Remembering Ali's dyed black hair, I zeroed in on a similarly dyed girl around her age. In her all-black outfit, she could have been headed to a funeral.

Since I was wearing all black, too, I hoped she might mistake me for a sister Goth. Here is where a female detective has a jump on the opposite gender. Girls, especially savvy Scottsdale teens, would be wary of talking to a strange man, but a woman flashing a private investigator's ID might arouse more curiosity than distrust.

"Excuse me, Miss," I called to the mini-Goth as I exited my Jeep. "I'm a detective…" Here I pulled out my ID…"and I'd like to ask you a few questions."

She looked at me, then at my ride. Studied the Pima symbols. Frowned.

"That's no cop car."

"Because I'm a private detective, accent on private. Alison Cameron's attorney has hired me to look into her case. Do you know Miss Cameron?"

Ignoring my question, she moved toward the Jeep. "That thing on the hood, it's the labyrinth where Earth Doctor went to hide when Elder Brother overthrew him, isn't it?"

My lucky day; the kid knew her petroglyphs. Could she be part Pima? A closer look revealed skin as pale as mine, although her eyes were blue, not green.

"Sure is. And as you can see, that's Coyote on the passenger-side door. He's escaping in his reed boat while First World is being destroyed by flood. Flying above him are Night Singing Bird and Sky Hawk."

"Spider Woman's on the front fender, weaving her magic."

"And Kokopelli's on the other fender, playing his flute."

She stepped off the curb and walked around to the other side. Nodded. "I'm writing an essay on the Pimas for my Arizona History class, and I'm really getting into them, so if you give me a ride home in that Jeep, you can ask me questions. But it doesn't mean I have to answer."

"Of course not. I'm just a petroglyph-loving woman doing a favor for another petroglyph-loving woman."

A touch of genius, the "woman" part. As she climbed in the Jeep, the kid's smile half-blinded me despite its expensive orthodontia. By the time I dropped her off at her house, a rambling Mediterranean backed up against a golf course, she had given me some interesting information about Ali, as well as the name and address of Kyle's foster parents. In case I needed more information, the little Gothette shared her name—Tiffany Browning-Meyers—and her private cell number. She also confessed to being the daughter of the forever-banned Suzy, she of the free and easy black dye jobs and the open bar for minors. In turn for all this information, Tiffany made me promise to give her another ride in my Jeep sometime in the near future, and to friend her on Desert Investigations' Facebook page.

My cell rang just before I pulled away from Tiffany's house. Ali's defense attorney.

"Looks like we have a complication, Miss Jones. I've just been alerted that a Dr. Bradley Teague, of Pasadena, California, is the dead man's half-brother. Same mother, different fathers. Dr. Teague also happens to be the executor of Dr. Cameron's will, which, now that the wife and son are deceased, makes Alison the sole recipient of her father's estate."

Good thing I was still at the curb. In the private investigation business, *cherchez la femme* was outscored by *cherchez le money*. This meant that even if the judge threw out Ali's confession, the prosecutor would argue that avarice was the main reason Alison wanted her family dead. It would be a crushing blow to the defense, suggesting the murders might have been planned for material gain, and despite their sadistic trappings, carried out in cold blood.

"Mr. Zellar, the murders happened nine days ago. Why is this information coming to light only now? Shouldn't Dr. Teague have already announced himself as executor and arranged for his niece to have counsel?"

A sigh. "Because he was somewhere off the map in Kenya, doing volunteer work for Doctors Without Borders."

"They have satellite phones in Kenya. I hear they even have computers, television, and radios."

Another sigh. "Not where he was. When news reached DWB's main camp, he'd already left to work in a small village out in the bush. From there, he moved on to another village, and somewhere along the line, his phone was stolen. He wasn't tracked down until the day before yesterday, and he's been on the road since then. Be that as it may, he arrived back in the States late last night, and first thing this morning, called his brother's attorney, one Sebastian Showalter, who in turn, called me. Mr. Showalter informed me that the deceased and his wife also named Dr. Teague as guardian of both minor children in case the parents predeceased them."

"Then Mr. Showalter will become Ali's attorney of record, which effectively pulls me off the case. Right?

"Wrong. Mr. Showalter specializes in civil litigation, not criminal defense. After a brief conference call with Dr. Teague early this afternoon, it was decided that I remain as Ali's attorney."

I thought a moment. "Did you inform him that Congresswoman Juliana Thorsson was the actual person who hired you?"

"Not at this point." The frost was back in his voice. "I merely said it was a friend of the family who wished to remain anonymous."

"One more question. How will this affect my investigation?"

"Positively, as it turns out. Dr. Teague doesn't believe Alison is capable of murder, and is eager to have his niece exonerated. In fact, he is so adamant that you continue your work, he's authorized you to enter his brother's house." He cleared his throat. "The scene of the crime, so to speak."

"I need to talk to Dr. Teague."

"He'll arrive in Phoenix this evening, so I'll work with Mr. Showalter to arrange something early. In the meantime, you'll be given free access to the property, always providing the police are amenable. They've had to station a patrolman at the house to scare away vandals and looters, but the crime techs have already gone over the place from top to bottom and cleared it. Shall I call Mr. Showalter and have him messenger the keys over to your office?"

"Absolutely." I couldn't have asked for better news, because there was always the chance the crime techs had missed something.

"Nice talking to you, then, Miss Jones."

"Nice talking to you, too, Mr. Zellar," I replied, and for once, it was true.

I'd been back at Desert Investigations less than an hour when an InstaMessenger dropped off the keys.

Ten minutes later I drove through the entrance to Palomino Estates, a small enclave off Indian Bend Road, where house prices ran from eight hundred thou to a million and change. Designed for privacy, the main drag of Palomino Circle linked ten cul-de-sacs, where most of the custom-built homes, only three per cul-de-sac, backed up to the Greenway Golf Course. After a few wrong turns in this circle-within-a-circle development, I finally found 16733 East Yellow Horse Drive, where a uniformed police officer waited to escort me through the house. His name tag identified him as L. Bocelli. When I asked him if he was related to Detective Louis Bocelli, my former partner at Scottsdale PD, he smiled.

"My uncle. I was named for him."

"Then tell Louie I said hi."

A makeshift memorial had been set up in front of the Camerons' house. Smiling photographs of the victims, flowers—both real and fake—candles, stuffed animals, a toy rocket, and sympathy cards and notes sprawled against a hand-painted sign that said, in shaky blue letters, REMEMBER THE CAMERONS. I spent a moment reading the notes—one of them, unsigned, written in a delicate woman's handwriting—said *I will always love you.* That singular "you" made me wonder which of the Camerons the note's writer grieved for. Maybe Dr. Cameron had a lover. If so, we should find her. Rejected lovers sometimes revenged themselves in brutal ways.

"Ready to go in?" Officer Bocelli asked.

"Ready as I'll ever be."

The architecture of the Cameron house wasn't remarkable, just your basic Mediterranean sprawl. But its location explained why the bodies hadn't been discovered until six p.m., when Mrs. Cameron's book club had shown up to discuss Jonathan Franzen's *Freedom*. Like its neighbors, the house was located at the end of a cul-de-sac, and backed up on the opposite side of the same golf course as Tiffany Browning-Meyers' home. At midday on a sweltering mid-July Monday, that golf course would have been pretty much deserted. Not that the house's isolated situation mattered, since photographs of the Camerons' bodies showed duct tape over their ankles, legs, and mouths.

"You might want to look in the garage first," Louie's nephew said, pulling me away from that image.

"The garage? Why?"

"To start off slow. The house, well, I was in there once, and it's intense. Besides, what happened in the garage is interesting, too."

There's not much I haven't seen, but the fact that Bocelli wanted me to begin the tour in a four-car garage intrigued me. As soon as we rolled up the door, I understood why.

The killer, whoever he/she was, hadn't even spared the family's cars.

The windows of a 1957 Corvette convertible were smashed, its Polo White and Inca Silver body defaced with red spray enamel. Even the red Venetian leather upholstery was slashed. But it was the damage done to the 1955 Ford Thunderbird convertible that made me want to weep. The gorgeous turquoise thing was keyed in a crosshatch pattern, then spray-painted with red stripes. What looked like acid had eaten away at the whitewall tires and turquoise-and-white upholstery. Shredded bits of the soft top lay scattered on the garage floor. Similar damage had been inflicted on a silver Escalade.

"Impound yard has the mother's Lexus LS, the one the kids escaped in. Turned out not to be hard to spot, a brand new silver

Lexus LS sedan partially sprayed red, paint all bubbled up in the acid attack. Still had the dealer's tags."

"Acid's rough on cars," I said, still mourning over the Thunder-bird.

He looked down at the garage's cement floor. "Yeah, but that's nothing compared to what happened to the family."

I studied the young cop's face. He was in his early twenties. "You saw?"

"I caught the welfare check. One of the book ladies called it in when Mrs. Cameron didn't come to the door. They noticed that it was ajar, so after repeatedly ringing the doorbell and rousing no one, they walked in. And saw what they saw. They're probably still screaming."

"Finding the Camerons like that must have been rough on you, too."

"My first homicides, and wouldn't you know one of them had to be a kid." A quick, stricken look. "Whoever did this disabled the alarm first." He jutted out his chin, making a big show of being tough.

"You say 'whoever,' Officer Bocelli. Does that mean you don't believe the story that Alison Cameron and her boyfriend committed the murders?"

"What I think doesn't matter. I'm just a patrolman. Ready to see the house?"

"Let's do it."

When I opened the door leading into the kitchen, the com-bined stench of blood, rotting Chinese food, and another odor I couldn't quite identify rocked me back. Certain companies specialize in cleaning crime scenes, but probably because of the difficulty reaching the victim's brother, they hadn't yet begun their job. The kitchen looked and smelled like a battleground, which I guess it was. Glasses lay smashed on the floor, food cans and milk had been opened and dumped on the black granite counters. The same red paint that defaced the cars had been sprayed on the Sub-Zero refrigerator door, and it had dribbled down to collect in a pool on the black-and-white marble tile floor.

After taking a few pictures with my iPhone, I moved into the formal dining room, Bocelli following close behind.

When the murderer broke in, the Camerons had been eating lunch at a long mahogany table. The few dishes not broken or carried away by the crime techs still held rotting portions of Chinese takeout. The crime scene photos showed three takeout cartons from Zhou's Mandarin Wok, but remnants of their contents—possibly almond chicken—were still puddled on the table. Because the house was almost hermetically sealed, as most Arizona homes are during the hot summer, insect infestation wasn't too far along. Still, the food appeared to be moving.

All it takes is one fly.

A plate lay smashed on the floor, its contents spilled onto pegged-oak flooring. Other plates, riffled from the big mahogany china hutch, had been hurled against the wall, splattering the damask coverings with sweet and sour sauce. Or blood. Each chair was overturned, splintered into kindling. So, too, the hutch, either a Duncan Phyfe, or a good copy. Tiny bits of gilt and glass littered the floor and the dining table, a mystery until I looked up and saw the dangling remnant of a crystal chandelier.

Black fingerprint powder was sprinkled everywhere.

I took more pictures.

The living room had once been beautiful, a symphony of oak, marble, and silk underneath a three-story vaulted ceiling. The oak floor was broken up by three Oriental silk rugs, their pastel hues mirroring beautiful peach- and blue-tinted sofas and chairs, but all the upholstery had been slashed to ribbons. Above the marble-fronted fireplace hung a life-sized oil portrait of Alexandra Cameron, who had also once been beautiful. Dark hair, dark eyes, perfect features accented by a lush mouth—her face and figure bore a strong resemblance to the actress Angelina Jolie. The painting was the only thing in the room that remained undamaged, almost as if the killer had relished the thought of it looking down on the carnage below.

The walls and floor where the bodies had been found were dappled in blood spatter, so much so that it dizzied my eyes, forcing me to concentrate on the three darker areas where the Camerons had finally, and mercifully, died. The boy, next to an ottoman; the mother, near the fireplace; Dr. Cameron, duct-taped to a chair facing them. If the medical examiner was right, he had been forced to watch his wife and son tortured before dying himself.

"Christ," Bocelli muttered under his breath.

"Don't see him around." After I'd photographed every drop of blood, spilled food, and gutted piece of furniture, I said, "There had to be a lot of noise while all this was going on, even with their mouths taped shut." When bones break, they don't break silently. A baseball bat hitting a skull makes some noise, too. As does a gunshot.

Bocelli cleared his throat. "I hear these high-end houses are pretty much soundproofed. Even if they weren't, the neighbor on the left was in Venice, the one in Italy, not California, and the neighbors on the right were at their ranch in Wyoming."

In Scottsdale, everyone who could manage it left town during the summer months. Those who had to work remained, such as maids, cops, and Emergency Room physicians.

"Yeah, and since the golf course in back was pretty much deserted on a hot Monday afternoon—my research says the temp made it to one-seventeen that day—few golfers would have been around to hear anything, either," I responded.

"If two kids really did do this, it would make you think twice about having a family, wouldn't it?" Bocelli said.

There was nothing to say to that, so I just kept snapping pictures until it was time to check the other rooms. With Bocelli trailing behind, I walked down the hall to Dr. Cameron's den, where a new stench met me. Most dens are small hidey-holes, usually repurposed bedrooms. Not the good doctor's. Two brass-plated oak doors opened into a suite-sized space furnished with a wall of built-in mahogany cabinets and an antique desk the size of the ruined Escalade in the garage. But like the dining and living rooms, the desk's beauty had been destroyed, this time by a brown smear of what looked and smelled like feces across its surface.

Seeing my expression, Bocelli volunteered, "Dog shit. That's what I hear, anyway."

"Why dog shit?" I'd seen plenty of feces-smeared rooms in my career, but in every case, the feces had been human. This departure from the norm unsettled me.

Bocelli shrugged. "Who knows what went through those sickos' minds."

I moved away from the reeking desk and studied the walls. The glass-covered prints of classic cars had been knocked off their hangers, and lay shattered and ripped on the oak floor. More red spray enamel took the artworks' place. Near the sliding glass doors to a private patio, the remnants of a Samsung E2420L monitor lay on its side, but the hard drives of every computer in the house, along with every iPhone, were at the police lab. Their read-outs were in the case file back at Desert Investigations.

Wreckage this complete and planned—the killer or killers, plural, had to transport a giant helping of dog feces to the household—signaled an intense and personal animus, not random violence. The fact that Dr. Cameron's body was positioned so that he was forced to watch the torture-deaths of his wife and child identified him as the target victim. The agonies of Alexandra and Alec were merely a means to that end.

Further searching revealed nothing useful left in Dr. Cameron's den. Every drawer in the desk and file cabinets had been opened, their contents confiscated by the police.

"Lots of rage here," I said, to Bocelli.

"Seems to be everywhere these days, doesn't it?"

Another unanswerable question. Leaving the young cop to reflect on the state of the world, I got busy taking pictures. Since so little was left, I wound up spending much less time in the den than in the previous rooms, so a few minutes later I was climbing the stairs to the second floor, Bocelli trailing behind me like a loyal puppy.

The master bedroom was a disaster, with the mattress slashed to a fare-thee-well, but at least the Camerons' attacker hadn't massaged dog feces into the Tempur-Pedic. The master bath was worse. Every mirror had been shattered, the long granite countertop split in two, the porcelain top on the toilet bowl smashed against the tile floor. More feces had been smeared in the sauna-sized bathtub. I held my breath as long as I could, but finally had to inhale. Due to the hard surfaces and closed nature of the bathroom, the stench was worse than the den's.

"You about done?" Bocelli called from the window, where he stood looking out. By this point, he had seen all he wanted to see.

"There's still the kids' rooms," I called back. "And the maid's."

"No damage in the maid's."

I still wanted to see for myself, but a quick check found Eldora Morales' room immaculate. The Camerons hadn't skimped on her comfort. As maids' rooms go, hers was large and well-furnished, with a roomy double bed, a dresser, a chest of drawers, a small desk-and-chair setup, a comfy-looking recliner, a radio, and a flat-screen TV. It could have served as a room in any mid-priced motel, except for the photographs. Like most live-ins, Morales surrounded herself with pictures of her family. From the landscape in the backgrounds I could see they lived in Mexico. I recognized the beach at Rocky Point.

Obviously, the killer held no grudge against her.

But the fact that the murders happened during the maid's trip to Mexico made me wonder about the timing. A coincidence? Or did the killer know the maid's schedule? If it was the latter, then the killer was either someone who knew them well, or someone who had been casing the house over a period of time. That, as well as other things I'd seen since entering the house, nagged at me.

"Ready for the kids' rooms?" Bocelli asked.

"Not really."

"Me neither. In a way, those are the worst."

When I looked into Ali's room, that nagging feeling grew even stronger. Girls were hyper-protective of their belongings, and I couldn't see her allowing anyone to slash her collection of stuffed animals, or smear dog feces all over her pink walls. But everything in here was as savaged as most of the other rooms I'd seen.

"Used to be very girlie," Bocelli remarked, behind me. He didn't step into the room.

"Not so much now."

Alison Cameron's white-carpeted room had once been a young teen's dream. A canopied bed stood in the middle of a room painted a muted pink, trimmed in darker, but still muted, lavender. It had been spray-painted, then finished off with dog feces. The bed's white coverlet and hangings hung in ribbon-like tatters. Degas prints of horses and ballerinas still decorated the walls, both species flaunting long, muscular legs. Their protective glass frames were shattered. No laptop or cell phone, of course; the police had confiscated them, whatever condition they'd been in.

Just about the only intact items in the room lay on Ali's dresser—a silver-backed brush and comb set and an emptied jewelry box. The box had been dusted with the same fingerprint powder I'd seen on other bits of carnage, but a few smashed pieces of jewelry remained on the floor. Of most interest to me was the antique silver locket that might have been a family heirloom. It was now bent, the chain snapped. When I opened the locket, I saw a tiny photograph of Ali's mother. The mother who wasn't a biological mother. As I held the locket, Alexandra's picture fell out, revealing another photograph, this one of the handsome young man whose picture I'd seen at Mrs. Daggett's. In this one, too, Kyle looked harmless enough, but despite what most people believe, most killers do.

I took a picture of the picture.

For all her pink-and-white frou-frou, Ali was a reader. Scattered in front of the bookcase across from her bed was a full set of C.S. Lewis' *Narnia* books, Tolkien's *Ring* series, and a veritable shrine to the young adult novels of Judy Blume. All ripped in half. Safe enough reading for a young teen, but lying on the bottom shelf, oddly untouched, I saw the complete set of the *Hunger Games* books, as well as a scattering of other harder-edged sci-fi, such as Cory Doctorow's *Little Brother*, and Ursula Le Guin's *The Lathe of Heaven*. Fantasy and violence. At least that's the way the county attorney would play it if this case ever went to trial.

After finding nothing more of interest, I moved down the hall to Alec Cameron's room. No casual reader, Alec. If he'd set up any shrine, it was to the Arizona Diamondbacks, Cardinals, and Coyotes. Remnants of sports pennants and posters covered the walls, the one exception being a large photograph of Albert Einstein. The only books around were textbooks, but they looked advanced for a boy of ten. *Supersymmetry and String Theory. Introduction to Astrophysics.* No cell phone, no laptop. Like Ali's room, everything was either ripped, smashed, or covered in dog feces.

There were two upstairs rooms left to check out, a hobby room Alexandra Cameron had used for weaving—shreds from a brightly colored blanket hung from a small loom—and a nicely appointed guest room. Neither of those rooms had been defiled—not personal enough, I imagined—but I photographed them anyway while Bocelli, now confident that I wasn't about to pocket anything, waited in the hall.

I was about to leave the guest room when I noticed something out of place. Like the other rooms, it had been tastefully decorated in a soothing, if bland, color scheme: beiges, browns, and rusts, accented by discreet touches of turquoise. Yet resting behind the Indian-print pillows tossed on the bed was a small, navy blue bolster, looking out of sync with the room's overall color scheme. Curious, I walked closer. Was it my imagination, or was the bolster slightly misshapen?

After checking to see if Bocelli remained in the hall, I picked up the bolster and found it much heavier than any self-respecting mini-pillow should be. When I gave it a squeeze, something crumpled. Like many bolsters, this one had a zipper so that the cover could be washed. When I zipped it open, money fell out.

Lots of money. Eighteen bundles of ten one-hundred dollar bills. Wrapped around one of the bundles was a deposit slip for eighteen thousand dollars cash, dated the day before the murders. That was a lot of money to leave lying around the house, even for a doctor. I spread out the bundles and snapped pictures as quickly as possible, getting several close-ups of the deposit slip.

Then I called out, "Officer Bocelli, you'd better radio the station. Looks like we've found something interesting."

Chapter Six

While we waited for detectives to arrive, I emailed the photos I'd taken to Jimmy's computer, beginning with the close-ups of the deposit slip. Emergency Room patients don't pay their doctors in cash.

WHAT CN U FND OUT BOUT THIS? I texted.

By the time the unmarked police car arrived, I had finished sending the last picture.

We'd pulled Bob Grossman and Sylvie Perrins, excellent cops and old friends of mine, but right now both looked worried. With good reason, since they were the detectives who originally processed the murder scene.

"Captain Ulrich is fit to be tied," Bob mourned. He was a big, comfy looking man whose laid-back demeanor had fooled many a perp into dropping his guard. "Claims we did a lousy search."

Sylvie, a thin nervy woman, twitched all over, par for the course for her. "Heads are gonna roll, probably ours. You know what she's like."

I did my best to soothe them, explaining that the money had been hidden in an undamaged room, which wouldn't have been subjected to as rigorous a search. "The reason I noticed was because the bolster didn't fit the decor."

They gave me blank stares.

"Navy blue in a room done up in earth tones."

Bob still looked confused, but Sylvie, who had visited my redecorated apartment upstairs from Desert Investigations, nodded. "Yeah, you'd notice that, Miss Interior Decorator. Oh, well, water under the bridge. C'mon, Bob, let's visit the scene of our sure-as-shit demise."

Officer Bocelli remained downstairs while I led the two detectives to the guest bedroom and pointed out the bolster, which I'd re-stuffed with the money, and tucked back into its original position. It was almost hidden again underneath more appropriately colored pillows.

"Oh, shit," Sylvie sighed.

Bob recovered enough to quip, "No, that's in the other bedrooms."

They began tearing the place apart.

When I arrived back at the office, Jimmy was locking up for the day.

"How about an early dinner over at Malee's, Almost Brother?" I suggested, gesturing toward the Thai restaurant across the street. The echoes of carnage at the Camerons' house had disturbed me and I didn't want to be alone. Not that I would ever admit it.

"Sorry. Promised my cousin Rita I'd have dinner with her. Tomorrow, maybe?"

"Whatever."

He narrowed his eyes. "You okay? You don't look so good."

"Just the heat. I'll feel better when I get upstairs. Well, see you tomorrow."

"Lena, if you need…"

"I said I'm okay!"

He raised his hands and backed away. "Fine. You're all right. Never better. But you know where I live and you've got my phone number. I should get back from Rita's around eight, and the only thing planned for the rest of the evening is sitting in front of the tube watching *Iron Chef* reruns."

"What an exciting life you lead," I muttered, as I picked up the case file box and started up the stairs to my apartment. "See you tomorrow."

He said something else, but I was moving too fast to hear.

Years ago I had leased the space for Desert Investigations mainly because of the apartment above, a furnished one-bedroom efficiency that made up for its lack of character by its ten-second commute. At the time, the impersonal beige-on-beige color scheme didn't bother me. Due to a childhood spent in one foster home after another, no place felt like "home," and I saw no reason trying to convince myself otherwise just because I was no longer forced to live where Child Protective Services deposited me.

Eventually, though, I began to see that turning an apartment into a home could be a sign of hope, not futility, so I went shopping.

Sylvie called my apartment Cowgirl Modern. The sofa and chair were crafted from bleached saguaro cactus skeletons, made sittable with thick cushions covered with Navajo designs. Kachinas danced along the living room's long window ledge, and a bright painting by the Apache artist George Hazous thumbed its nose at the still-beige wall. In my bedroom, a spread depicting the Lone Ranger and Tonto covered my double bed, and a table lamp in the shape of a horse's head threw off a soft, welcoming light. Only after the frenzy of redecorating was finished did I realize I'd created a bedroom identical to the one I'd had at Madeline's, the foster mother who showed a lonely child that love could exist in this cold world.

Usually, whatever rough day I'd endured, stepping into my apartment calmed me. Not this evening. In my mind's eye, I saw blood splatters on the wall, pooled blood on the carpet.

I saw death.

After a moment's reflection, I put the case file on the floor, grabbed my landline, and called Madeline. When she answered, I said, "Hey, how about I drop by with some vegetarian takeout from that new Indian restaurant in Apache Junction? Haven't seen you in almost a month!"

"Drop by?" she laughed, the cascade of warmth easing my tension. "Have you forgotten I live sixty miles away? Normally I'd love to see you, honey, but that oil painting class I was thinking about giving, well, I decided to do it, and it starts tonight. Twelve people will be arriving in less than an hour. You're welcome to join them, though."

"That many people signed up, all the way over in Florence?"

"Don't dis Florence, kid. Lots of talent hidden out here in the desert. So how about it? You ready to try your hand at Painting 101?"

"I'll pass on that."

"There's another class scheduled for tomorrow, so how about I drive up there Friday and treat you to an eggplant Parmesan dinner at Green's? You're right, it's been almost a month, way too long for me not to see my favorite daughter."

Favorite daughter. The expression brought a smile to my face. Before she'd been sidelined with breast cancer and eventually whipped its ass, Madeline had fostered several children. For all I knew, she still called each one of them her "favorite daughter" or "favorite son," but hearing her say those words took the edge off my misery.

"Friday's good, as long as nothing new blows up with this case I'm working on."

Even through the phone I could hear her smile. "There's always a case with you, isn't there?"

I hoped she could hear my smile, too. "An astute observation."

After promising I'd call if something came up, we rang off.

But as soon as her "Good-bye, honey" faded, my misery returned.

Walls smeared with dog feces and blood.

Shaking the image out of my head, I turned on the TV, but most of the channels featured brawling basketball wives, men pretending to be lost in the wild, widows hoarding used Kleen-exes and rotted food, drug addicts ruining their loved ones' lives, collapsing apartment buildings in New York, or suicide bombings in the Middle East. As I scrolled through the evening's offerings, it got to the point where I could no longer tell which was which, real reality or made-up reality.

But nothing was as bad as MSNBC, which featured Congresswoman Juliana Thorsson denying that she had made up her mind to run for the U.S. Senate. She was being interviewed as she left some government building, minions in tow.

"I act on the will of the people," she said, fending away a dozen microphones stuck into her face. "Nothing more, nothing less."

The campaign posters I'd seen in her house told a different story. Like all politicians, the woman was a practiced liar.

Walls smeared with dog feces and blood.

I switched the set off. I couldn't stay here, not feeling the way I was feeling, so I grabbed my keys and left in search of comfort food. Ten minutes later I was sitting at a deuce in the Olive Garden, surrounded by happy families or families faking happiness. Even worse, a party nearby was celebrating a young woman's birthday, their merriment reminding me that I didn't know my own birth date. How could I?

I had been found at the age of four—at least that's the age the admitting physician estimated—lying beside a Phoenix street, the bullet in my head wiping out all memories of birthdays. When I emerged from my coma, I couldn't remember who my parents were or who had shot me. The only thing left of my former four-year-old self was a burning rage that five years later found its target in the belly of the man who raped me.

Why had my parents left me to die?

Walls smeared with dog feces and blood.

My life didn't feel right.

The murder scene didn't feel right.

By the time the waiter arrived and began reeling off a list of specials, my appetite had disappeared, so after slapping down a ten dollar bill on the table for his trouble, I left.

Once back in my apartment and as relaxed as I ever get, I opened the case file and started reading the material the crime techs pulled off Dr. Cameron's personal computer. I don't know what I hoped to find, but nothing there looked even halfway suspicious. His emails contained nothing more than messages back and forth to various medical colleagues, and his search history was downright boring. No visits to porno sites, no sexplicit love letters from other women, just dozens and dozens of sites focused on collectible cars. Most of the older hits were for American classics, like the ruined Corvette and T-Bird in his garage, but the more recent searches were for new and exotic foreign cars. I found no history of sexting on his iPhone, either, just interminable calls back and forth to Good Sam.

The man had no life.

Alexandra's laptop was a little livelier, although not by much. Emails to and from her Sigma Gamma sorority sisters tended toward the salty, but never crossed the line into vulgarity. Same with the emails to her book club. Myriad emails between her and various functionaries of a Chicago organization named Big Kids Dream Big, for which she apparently did volunteer work, as well as emails to and from dozens of friends. None sounded the least bit suspicious. Her search history wasn't overly exciting, either, consisting mainly of searches for universities, scholarship information, child-guidance sites, and anything having to do with hand-looms and weaving. No porno. Her phone revealed no sexting, no nude selfies, absolutely nothing of a racy nature.

Same for ten-year-old Alec, who, judging from his laptop and his phone, felt no interest in anything that didn't fall under the heading of science or sports. Like his father, he didn't appear to have many close friends, as shown by the sparse list of names and numbers on his contact list.

Saving what promised to be the most complicated for last, I finally opened Ali's material. While I was certain her parents normally policed her laptop, they didn't appear to have done so recently, because some of the sites on her search history were eyebrow-raising. After having what appeared to be a long-distance, and unrequited, love affair with the trembly lead singer of Antony and the Johnsons, she had dived headlong into the Goth lifestyle. She subscribed to Goth eZines *Gothic Beauty* and *Lady Amaranth*, to which she'd posted several comments, mainly about the hopelessness of life. She'd also downloaded music from bands such as Fields of the Nephilim, Nox Arcana, Bluetengel, and Christian Death, which was dark enough to make Marilyn Manson look giggly by comparison.

And as for sexting, well, she must have kept Kyle Gibbs one happy boy.

Unfortunately, the sexting wasn't the most disturbing material the techs found on her phone. A month before the murders, she and Kyle had exchanged texts about running away together. The plan was to take one of Ali's parents' cars and drive to Hollywood, where they would get jobs in the movie industry, he as a leading man, she as his leading lady. Although these weren't uncommon teenage fantasies, given the timing, they were worrying. Then, on the week before the murders, Ali's texts had become more and more vitriolic about her parents. The phrase WSH THEY WER DED was repeated several times.

Those messages wouldn't play well in any courtroom.

After reading what had to be Ali's fortieth wish for her family's early demise, I put the information back in the file and turned on the TV. I channel-surfed for a while and paused briefly on yet another interview with Congresswoman Thorsson, heard her tell a few more lies, before I settled on Me-TV and watched reruns of old sitcoms. Perhaps they would drive away my memory of the Cameron house. Around midnight, I trudged off to the bedroom, but lay there wide awake until almost three. When sleep finally greeted me, I dreamed of a mine shaft filled with dead children.

Or maybe it was a memory.

Knowing what I know about the way most foster homes are run, the next morning I waited until nine o'clock to arrive at the house of Glen and Fiona Etheridge, Kyle's foster parents.

Although the house was within walking distance of the same golf course the Camerons' place fronted, it was in an older development that in a few years would probably be torn down to build new mini-mansions. The lot was small, and desiccated desert landscaping decorated the tiny front yard. As for the house itself, the eaves needed repair, and the stucco facing could have used a fresh coat of paint. A banged-up green Volvo emblazoned with fading political bumper stickers sat in the open garage. One tire was flat. The doorbell was ailing, too, and it was only after I pounded on the door with my fist that a woman's voice shrieked over the noise of a vacuum that she'd be with me in a minute.

A few seconds later the vacuum shut off and the door opened.

"Jesus, lady, where's the fire?" A frowsy brunette in her mid-forties. She looked like she'd fallen off a dump truck, but her assertive manner signaled she wasn't the maid. Besides, no self-respecting maid would be caught dead in that filthy apron. From somewhere behind her, I heard a baby muttering.

"Mrs. Etheridge?"

Scowling, she brushed a lank lock of hair off her face with a broken-nailed hand. "If you're selling anything, I'm not buying, and if you're doing a marketing survey, go annoy someone else."

I stuck my foot between the door and the jamb. "My name is Lena Jones. I'm a licensed private investigator, and I'm here to talk about Kyle."

The scowl deepened. She looked down. Saw the foot. "You've got three choices. I slam the door in your face, call the cops, or get out my Glock and shoot you where you stand. Pick your poison."

Before I could answer, the scowl relaxed into a mere frown. Then she stared hard at me, as if bringing my face into focus. "Wait a minute. Did you say your name is Lena Jones?"

"Yes, Ma'am."

She motioned to my pictograph-covered Jeep. "Anyone see you drive up in that thing?"

"Not that I'm aware of."

"Good." She grabbed me by the arm and jerked me into the entrance hall so quickly I almost fell.

"You're probably on a few new security cameras, though," she muttered, walking away from me toward the babbling sounds. "Ever since the murders, this neighborhood's been paranoid as a chicken on a fox farm. They're afraid Kyle's going to be released for a home visit and kill them all in their beds. As if.

We can't even visit him. Not yet, anyway. We're appealing the judge's decision but as for now, Glen and I have no legal standing. Crazy, huh? When I think about that boy sitting all alone in that juvie hellhole…Well, nothing I can do about that. Not until the judge changes his stupid mind." She took a breath. "So, Ms. Jones, what do you want to know? Push comes to shove, I'll deny I told you anything. You'll back me up on that, right?"

Confused by her quick turnaround, all I could do was answer, "Uh, right."

"Good, 'cause I'm not about to give up the others, too."

She didn't explain, just kept moving. We passed through a two-story great room filled with toys in various states of shabbiness and elderly furniture in need of repair. Some money once, not so much now. But still enough to buy out the stock of Toys "R" Us.

I kicked a Tickle Me Elmo out of my way before I tripped over it. "Mrs. Etheridge, do you know me from somewhere?"

Without turning her head, she continued in those short, choppy sentences of someone perpetually in a hurry. "Call me Fiona. You helped my sister once. Stacey Larchmont? Married to that sleazy dope dealer? You were a cop at the time. Damn near got yourself killed saving her stupid ass. Took a bullet for her. How's the hip? Kept up with you ever since. So does she. Not that hard to do these days, damned Internet. No privacy anymore. We're all doomed." At the entrance to a large, well-lit kitchen, she stopped and turned around. "That's what you want, isn't it? Me to give up Kyle's right to privacy?"

The baby's muttering rose to a wail. No. Make that two wails.

"Twins," she said, noting my surprise. "You never saw them. And don't bother asking their names because I won't tell you."

Fostered-out twins. She didn't have to tell me their names. I knew who the children were and why they'd been removed from their parents' care. With luck, the parents—who didn't deserve the title—would stay in prison until they rotted.

"We'll talk while I feed them, okay, Ms. Jones? Not quite their mealtime, but babies aren't clocks."

"Sounds good to me. And call me Lena."

At first glance, the kitchen was every woman's dream. Big skylight shining on a cream marble floor and countertop, mahogany cabinets, a prep island as long as a '76 Cadillac, a shiny Sub-Zero refrigerator, and a massive Viking range that could have prepared a meal for the entire crew of a marauding longboat. On closer inspection, I saw that one of the cabinet doors hung crookedly, and a large crack ran the entire length of the marble countertop.

But the toddlers she settled into matching high chairs weren't in perfect shape, either.

Despite their obvious injuries—scars from old cigarette burns running up and down their arms—they looked happy and well cared-for. I thought back to the media coverage of their parents' arrest and trial and guestimated that Fiona had been fostering the twins for around eight months.

Crooning something sappy from *The Sound of Music,* she began spooning yellow gook into the toddlers' mouths. "So what do you want to know about Kyle?" she asked, after the boy spit the gook into her face.

Me, I would have gagged, but she just laughed, wiped it away, and thrust another spoonful into the spitter's gaping maw. This time it stayed in.

"Fiona, do you think Kyle murdered that family?"

"Does a bear shit in a Manhattan subway?"

"Uh, no."

"There's your answer."

In denial, just like Kyle's aunt. I tried a fresh approach. "Let me see his room. If he's as innocent as you claim, it'll give me an idea of what he's really like, not what the arresting officers say he's like."

She was silent for so long I thought she was going to deny my request, but eventually she nodded. "Upstairs, first room on the left, right next to the twins' nursery. Won't do you any good. Cops took everything."

Before she could change her mind, I left her shoveling more food into the toddlers' mouths.

Two of the stairs creaked loudly, and one of the balusters had crumpled under the weight of the heavy oak handrail. More evidence that the Etheridge household was tight for cash, probably the reason they had started fostering in the first place. Fostering pays, which is one of the reasons it sometimes attracts the less-than-kid-friendly.

Once I walked into Kyle's room, I understood why Fiona had allowed me access. The room was almost as large as the master bedroom across the hall, and twice as crowded. No electronics, though. The police would have taken them away. Still, it was nice, for a change, to see a kid's room that hadn't been trashed.

Nothing but the usual boy-clutter. Shoulder pads, a catcher's mask and mitt, an aluminum bat, hockey knee guards, and a few items I couldn't identify. But sports played second fiddle to the supposed killer's obsession with animals. Only one sports poster decorated the walls: a photograph of Hank Aaron hitting his seven hundredth and fifty-fifth homer. The other posters showed various young animals at play: colts, puppies, kittens, kangaroo joeys, tiger cubs, fawns…There were so many, you could hardly see the pale blue walls that perfectly matched the bedspread.

Kyle's obsession with animals didn't stop at posters. In a large Plexiglas cage on the top of the chest of drawers, two gerbils snuffled happily through wood shavings while a third exercised its stumpy legs on a wheel. In the corner, a forty-gallon aquarium played home to an assortment of colorful fish swimming around a tiny plastic castle. On a sunlit window seat, two fat gray kittens snuggled alongside an equally fat mixed-breed puppy.

Other than Hank Aaron, the only human presence in the room was two photographs on the nightstand. One showed Fiona with a man I took to be her husband. The other was of a still-blond Ali, her face glowing. When I opened the nightstand's drawer, I found it bare.

The desk drawers looked the same. The police hadn't left so much as a paper clip. There was nothing under the bed, either, nor in the chest of drawers.

As I crossed the room to check out the closet, a movement out of the corner of my eye startled me. I turned to see a minor scuffle between two of the aquarium fish—an orange and yellow something-or-other nipping at the fins of a blue something-or-other. Amused, I watched as Bluefish—who had to be twice the size of its attacker—head-butted Yellowfish, knocking him into the side of the tiny castle. Chagrined, Yellowfish swam away with Bluefish chasing him through a small forest of seaweed. I'd started to turn away when I noticed something out of place.

The fish fight had moved the castle about a quarter of an inch, revealing what looked like a white strip of plastic underneath. It was probably nothing, but I dipped my hand into the cool water, lifted the castle off its base…

And pulled out a fat plastic envelope waterproofed by generous application of duct-tape.

At the sound of footsteps on the stairs, I stuffed the envelope into my carryall. I was just drying my hand on my jeans when Fiona stepped into the room. Fortunately, she didn't notice.

"So, you think this looks like the bedroom of a homicidal maniac?" She sounded more relaxed now that the twins had been fed.

"Not at first glance."

"Hmph." She stared at the two fish. They were fighting again.

Eager to turn her attention away from the aquarium, I pointed to the kittens and pup on the window seat. "Who's taking care of Kyle's pets now?" I asked, although I could guess the answer.

"Me, since I have so much time on my hands." She walked over to the seat and scratched a variety of heads. Only one, the puppy, opened its eyes briefly in grateful acknowledgement. "Kyle's rescues. Along with dozens of others. Squirrels. Snakes. A desert tortoise with a broken shell. Carried home a three-legged coyote pup, once. Turned it over to Adobe Mountain Wildlife

Rescue. Always nagging me to drive him up there to visit it. Know how far that is?"

I nodded. The rescue center was on the opposite side of the county.

"Damn near thirty miles. He named it Bruce. Cute little thing. Semi-tame now. Never be returned to the wild. Too crippled up."

For obvious reasons, it was rare for foster parents to allow their wards to adopt animals. When a child is on the move through the foster system, he or she must remain unencumbered. Only once had I been allowed to keep a pet, a yellow dog named Sandy. It hadn't ended well.

Not for me, anyway.

"Why'd you let Kyle keep all of them?" I asked Fiona. "If he was moved to a different foster home he'd be forced to leave them behind."

"We were having adoption papers drawn up when, well, when Ali's family was killed."

"You were going to adopt him?" I couldn't keep the surprise out of my voice.

"Still will when this mess is over."

That day sounded like a cold day in Hell to me, but I let it slide. "What does his aunt think about that?"

A variety of emotions swept across her face: anger, contempt, pity. "She knows it's for the best. Given her criminal record, they'd never allow her to take custody. She loves him, though, so we've promised to let her see him. We drive him over to her trailer every week, drink crappy coffee in that greasy spoon down the street while he visits."

I noted her use of the present tense, as if nothing had changed. "That must be a comfort to them both."

"Hmph. I happen to believe, although I've never said this to Kyle, that the less he sees of what remains of his so-called family, the better. Still, love is love, no matter where you find it."

There was nothing to say to that, so I opened the door to the closet, peered inside. Nothing. The closet was as empty as the drawers.

"They really cleaned everything out, didn't they?"

"He had a laptop and iPod we bought for him, but the cops impounded them. Along with his cell. They hauled out cartons and cartons of stuff, all the new clothes we bought for him. Probably looking for blood stains." She sniffed.

"Did Kyle keep a journal?"

"What teen doesn't? The cops took it before I could do anything. I would've burned or buried it in the backyard before I let them get their hands on it. And I can guess your next question, so no, I never read his journal. Kids have a right to their private thoughts. Especially foster kids."

"Then you don't know what he wrote about."

"Nope, although I guess Ali figured heavily, young love and all that. If you're finished here, let's go back downstairs before the twins make a break for it." The rushed tone came back into her voice.

We went downstairs, where I discovered that before Fiona had come upstairs to check on me, she'd cleaned the twins up and transferred them to a large playpen filled with stuffed animals. The boy was trying to eat a teddy bear while the girl poked a turtle into his ear. Fiona picked up each in turn, giving prolonged hugs. I couldn't tell if they appreciated it or not, because both tried to ram their toys into her eye. Maybe they were aiming for her mouth.

"What's going to happen to them?" I asked.

"There's a long line of people wanting…" Suddenly hoarse, she cleared her throat. "…wanting to adopt them, so they'll be fine. Caucasian newborns and toddlers, they're the adoption superstars. It's the mixed-race children and older kids, teens like Kyle, who have trouble finding permanent homes. Given your own background, you ought to know that."

Yes, I did. After entering the CPS system at the age of four, I'd dragged my garbage-bag suitcase through a dozen foster homes before I aged out of the system at eighteen. In a way, it was understandable. Not everyone felt comfortable caring for a parentless child who'd stabbed someone. Oh, well. Water and blood under the bridge.

"How 'bout some coffee?" Fiona asked, gesturing toward the kitchen. "I was up with the twins half the night, and if I don't get a jolt of caffeine, I'm going to fall flat on my face." Without waiting for my answer, she headed for the kitchen again.

The coffee tasted like mud, but I drank it anyway. Anything to keep her talking. Back in the living room, the twins gibberished happily to each other.

"What does Mr. Etheridge do?" I asked.

"Glen owns a print shop. Used to employ fourteen people. Down to eight. Economy, you know." She looked around, at the damaged countertop and broken cabinet door. "We're barely hanging on, so the money from fostering helps. Some, anyway. We wind up blowing it on the kids. Kyle and the twins aren't the first we've fostered, they're more like the…" She closed her eyes, counted silently, opened them again. "Right, right. They're the sixteenth kids we've taken in. Need everything from underwear to shoes. Glasses. Hearing aids. Prosthetics. The state's supposed to cover those expenses, but we add to it out of our own pocket. Our sofa's so old Napoleon probably warmed his ass on it."

I surveyed the kitchen again. Chips on the mahogany cabinets, a couple of drawers with broken pulls. Such bedlam wouldn't be everyone's cup of tea, especially in Scottsdale. Curious, I asked, "How does your husband feel about this?"

She laughed. "Glen wouldn't notice if the refrigerator fell on his head unless it clipped one of the kids on the way down."

"He likes kids, then?"

"Came from a big family. Eight brothers and sisters, he was the youngest. Me, I was one of those lonely-onlys, spent my childhood wanting a big family, so when Glen and I married, I got pregnant right off the bat. We had Drake and a year and a half later, Emilie came along. Happiest years of my life." Her smile faded. "Both away at school now. Empty nester, that's me."

"Thus the foster thing."

"Seemed like the perfect answer. Extra money, and kids running around again. You don't know how quiet an empty house can be."

I thought back to my apartment over Desert Investigations, the lonely nights there. But I said, "You're right, I don't."

"You get used to a certain level of noise," she continued, her hurried speech slowing, warming. "And you get used to doing things for other people, not for yourself. Hey, I know I look like hell, but I'm okay with it. The babies keep me off the streets, right? If I had my way, Drake and Emilie would still be living here and attending ASU, letting me fuss over them, but no, Drake was determined to be an aerospace engineer and just had to go to Cal Tech. Emilie's at Julliard."

"She's a musician?"

"Cello." Fiona's wry expression didn't hide the pride in her eyes. "You have any idea how much a decent cello costs?" Without waiting for an answer, she continued, "You're looking at ten thousand for starters, and they go up from there. God help us if she gets a job with a symphony orchestra. We'd have to take out a second mortgage on the house. A third, I mean. Already have a second." She brightened. "Maybe she'll get a job with the Phoenix Symphony. Then she could move back home, save us some money."

She looked into the living room, where the twins' babbling had stopped. "Uh oh. When it gets quiet, that's when you have to worry. Excuse me while I go check."

Fiona was gone long enough for me to reflect on some of my own foster mothers. Madeline topped the list of the good ones, with Mrs. Giblin close behind. Some women seemed to be born maternal, whether they could give birth or not. Whereas others…The act of giving birth was no guarantee of decency. If it had been, the twins wouldn't be covered with scars.

Fiona finally returned, smelling like shit. Literally. "They've found a new game," she grumbled, as she wetted down a towel in the sink. "Look, can we wrap this up for now? I need to spot-clean the carpet."

"One more question." The one I'd purposely put off until last. "Did Kyle shoplift?"

She didn't turn around. "What makes you ask that?"

"The Cuisinart Elite IV sitting in his aunt's kitchen."

Her answer was so soft I had to ask her to repeat it. "We give him an allowance," she finally said.

"That model can run to six hundred dollars."

She dropped the towel into the sink and turned to face me. "Oh, all right. Yes, Kyle used to shoplift, but he hasn't done that in a long time."

"The Cuisinart looked brand new to me."

"Appearances can be deceiving." She bent down and began hauling out bottles and cans of various cleaning solutions. "Not that I haven't enjoyed our little chat, but I've really got to spot-clean that carpet before the stains set." She straightened back up and blew a stray hair out of her face. "Now, if you don't mind…"

We were at an impasse, but fortunately I was able to talk her into seeing me again tomorrow at three, the twins' nap time. By then she would have either come up with a better cover story for Kyle's supposedly former bad habits, or tell the truth. I hoped it would be the latter.

"You've given me a clear sense of Kyle," I said, as she hustled me through the reeking living room. "Maybe tomorrow we can talk more about his relationship with Ali."

Opening the front door, she said, "Sure, but long story short, they were a real-life Romeo and Juliet couple." For a moment, fear flickered across her face. "And you know how that turned out."

As the door closed behind me, I recalled how the play ended. With a double suicide.

Not wanting to wait until I got back to Desert Investigations, I drove down to the end of the block and parked under a shady eucalyptus. After making certain she wasn't peeking out her window, I pulled the envelope out of my pocket and slashed through the duct tape with the penknife I kept in my carryall.

Unwrapped the notes inside. Most were the usual moony teenage professions of love. Except for the last one.

It read…

I HATE MY PARENTS. I WISH SOMEBODY
WOULD JUST KILL THEM. MAYBE YOU????

XOXOXO

LUV LUV LUV YOU MADLY

ALI

Chapter Seven

The next morning I learned that the Camerons' former maid, Eldora Morales, already had a new job. Once she returned from her vacation with her family in Mexico, Margie Newberry, the Camerons' next door neighbor, called around on her behalf, finally securing her a position with a family in Paradise Valley, an even more upscale community west of Scottsdale. Armetta Zielsdorf, her new employer, had graciously given her permission to speak to me, even though it meant Mrs. Zielsdorf would have to prepare lunch for herself, her four children, and three visiting friends. Judging from the burnt smells emanating from the kitchen, Mrs. Zielsdorf wasn't much of a cook.

Driven out of the house by the stench, Eldora and I sat on the back patio, overlooking Camelback Mountain and the one hundred foot-high rock formation called the Praying Monk. The day's heat hadn't climbed to its peak yet, and an updraft from the canyon below kept the temperature bearable. Over glasses of iced tea, Eldora told me her story.

After being widowed, she came north—legally, she stressed—to find a job so she could send money home to her children and her mother and father, who were caring for them. Several stints as a hotel maid later, she wound up with the Camerons, where she stayed for twelve years, until their deaths. According to her, the Camerons had been the perfect employers and both children were utterly delightful.

"Even Ali?"

Eldora avoided looking at me by turning slightly so that she faced the Praying Monk. He perched so tenuously on the face of the mountain that it looked like he was about to tumble down to the street below. "Miss Ali a nice girl. Not kill her parents."

"Look at me, Eldora."

She turned back, but her eyes still wouldn't meet mine. Somewhere in her fifties, Eldora's hair was long, streaked with gray, and braided into one long plait down her back. Her short-nailed fingers fluttered nervously on the table's surface.

"Nice girl. Very nice."

Eldora wasn't in denial about Ali and any misbehavior problems the girl might have had; her hesitancy came from the fact that maids who tell tales soon found themselves out of a job. The trick here would be to ease her past that concern.

"The Zielsdorfs seem like nice people, too," I said. "It was understanding of them to give you this time off. Especially at lunchtime, when they have company."

"Nice people. Very understanding. Miss Armetta driving me to funeral, too." Her dark brown eyes flickered back to the Praying Monk.

"That is nice. Is your room here nice?"

"Very nice. Very pretty."

"Do you have a television set, like at the Camerons'?"

"Big TV. Very nice."

Time to shift back to the subject. "Was little Alec Cameron nice?"

Her lower lip trembled. "Sweet boy. Very nice."

"So Ali and Alec were both nice children."

She nodded furiously. 'Oh, yes, yes."

"Neither of them ever gave you any trouble?"

"Mister Alec was a good boy. Smart, too. Wanted to be astronaut." The tremble increased. She had loved Alec.

"How about Ali?"

The tremble stopped. "Nice girl. No trouble."

Judging from her reaction, Alec had been the easier child. No big surprise there since Ali was fourteen, and subject to all the hormonal craziness that arrived with puberty.

"Did you ever see Ali hit her mother or father? Or Alec?"

Alarmed, she looked straight at me. "Miss Ali never hit anyone!"

"But there was some trouble, right?"

A pause, then a hesitant nod. "Over boy. Miss Alexandra wanted her not see boy so much. Said she was too young to be serious like that."

I wondered if Alexandra had suspected the duo's runaway plans. "Was there a fight? I mean, an argument?"

A hawk called out somewhere down in the canyon. Another answered back. Looking out from this vantage point, we could have been in the wilderness, but the steady sound of traffic on the street on the other side of the house gave the lie to that. We were in the middle of the city.

"Eldora? Was there an argument over that boy? Kyle?"

She looked back at the Praying Monk, as if pleading for him to save her, but he remained silent.

"Tell me, Eldora. I'm going to stay here until you do." I hated bullying her, but Ali was my client, not Eldora.

The edge in my voice must have reached her because her thin shoulders slumped. She was getting tired of lying. Returning her gaze to me, she said, "Maybe Miss Ali yelled some. Girls do. That all. No fighting. No hitting. Just yelling."

"How about Dr. Cameron? Did he yell at Ali when they talked about Kyle?"

A faint smile. "No. Dr. Cameron not care what she do. So no yelling."

"Really?"

"Dr. Cameron not care what anybody do. Just so long they don't scratch his pretty cars."

My next question was a shot in the dark, but sometimes shots found their target. "Eldora, do you know who killed the Camerons?"

Her mouth began trembling again, then her hands, her shoulders. Then her attempt to control her emotions failed utterly. With tears streaking her cheeks, she lifted her face to the sky and wailed, "If I know who, I not wait for cops, I kill them myself!"

I spent the rest of the day at Desert Investigations digging through the case file again, studying the crime scene photos, rereading the detectives' interviews, double-checking the autopsy report on the victims. Alexandra and Alec had died of massive blunt trauma, Dr. Cameron by gunshot. No semen had been found in or on Alexandra, and there was no sign of vaginal bruising; she hadn't been raped. The stippling around Dr. Cameron's wound showed that the gun had been fired approximately three inches from his head, a *coup de grace*, much like a hunter puts a wounded animal out of its misery.

During the autopsies, the M.E. found all three victims had small portions of partially digested almond chicken, moo goo gai pan, rice, and egg rolls in their stomachs. Based on those findings, and the fact that when the police arrived at 6:12 p.m., rigor mortis had already begun in the Camerons' eyelids, necks, and jaws, the M.E. estimated their times of death as between 11 a.m. and 3 p.m. The time was further narrowed by the statement of the delivery boy from the Chinese restaurant, who said he dropped off a takeout order to a still-living Alexandra Cameron a few minutes before noon. The Camerons managed to get small portions of the takeout into their stomachs before they were bound with duct tape and slowly tortured to death, which gave a more realistic timeline of death to somewhere between noon and three p.m. After flipping through more pages, I found a note saying that Ali and Kyle had arrived at the vet's with the badly injured Misty at 3:02 p.m., as shown by the camera in his reception room. Given that the vet's office was an approximate thirty-minute drive from the Cameron house, I condensed the timeline of the murders to between noon and 2:30.

I did find one other thing interesting. Tests found fibers from both Alexandra's and Alec's clothing on the back of Dr.

Cameron's sports shirt and slacks, leading me to believe that despite his seeming lack of warmth, he tried to protect his family from the killer. Or killers. Gun or no gun, I wasn't convinced the damage I saw had been carried out by one person.

"How you doing over there?" Jimmy asked, turning away from his computer, where he had been busily working all day. "You've been pretty quiet."

"Just a little light reading."

Before I could cover them up, he glanced at the photographs laid out on my desk. "I don't know how you can look at that stuff."

"Just part of the job. It doesn't bother me."

"Right."

"Tell you what, though. After all this sitting around and reading, I need to loosen up, so I think I'll go to the gym."

"Which one?"

For the past few years I've been a member of L.A. Fitness, but a couple of months ago I'd also been going to Scottsdale Fight Pro. The gym was only two blocks from Desert Investigations and offered, besides the usual workout machines and free weights, a wide choice of martial arts classes that included various styles of cage fighting, as well as other hand-to-hand combat techniques. Since my days with Scottsdale PD I'd been a practitioner of karate and jiu jitsu, but due to an ass-whopping I had been given during a recent case, I'd begun classes in Krav Maga, an Israeli armed forces discipline. Well, maybe "discipline" is the wrong word to use, considering that head-butting and eye-gouging are a big part of Krav. The point of Krav is, when you are shorter and lighter than your opponent, you need some sort of edge to deal with an attack, prevent the perp from hitting you again, then quickly neutralize him. Firearms work well, too, but lethal force isn't always called for. And then there are those cases when, for one reason or another, you're not armed.

"Fight Pro," I told Jimmy, in answer to his question.

Being an L.A. Fitness fan himself, he frowned. "No accounting for taste."

"No, there isn't." I repacked the case file box, ran it upstairs to my apartment, and grabbed my gym bag. I'd probably go through the file again tonight, but for now, I needed to get physical.

A wall of heat hit me when I ran down the stairs and stepped outside. The thermostat on the outside of Cactus Kitty's, a new pseudo-cowboy bar across the street from Desert Investigations, informed me that the late afternoon temperature was one hundred and eighteen. Oh, joy. It was too hot for even the ever-present tourists, and Main Street was pretty much deserted. Maybe they were all huddled in the bar, since its sign proudly advertised ICE COLD BEER AND AIR-CONDITIONING. Despite the heat, I began to walk to the gym. The two-block distance wasn't going to kill me. Besides, since Fight Pro had started resurfacing its parking lot, parking had become a problem, and chances were good that I wouldn't be able to find a spot anyway.

It soon became apparent I'd made the right decision. Fight Pro's lot was a mess. Several cars were circling the lot again and again, hoping that since their last pass, a space might have opened up. Wishing them luck, I hurried inside where the frigid air-conditioning immediately dried off my sweat.

Because of the mess outside, few of the other usual gym rats were there, just several people trying to outdo each other with free weights, so I had my pick of the equipment. After a brief warm-up on the treadmill, I cranked up the speed, pounding out one mile in ten minutes, forty-three seconds. Satisfied, I slacked off to a leisurely jog for another two miles, then stepped off the treadmill. Since there were no Krav Maga classes scheduled today, I walked over to the free weights area. I'm no competition bodybuilder like some of the women who frequent Fight Pro, but I am strong for my size, and can squat a hundred and forty-five on a regular basis. I was a bit off today—probably due to the heat—but I still managed a hundred and thirty. Then it was off to the bench press, where I redeemed myself by lifting one-sixty. Arms sore, I headed back to the treadmills, and finished my workout by running another three miles.

Before heading to the showers, I noted that one more regular had come in, a weirdly overdeveloped woman who seldom talked to anyone. Around thirty, at least six foot two, and a bad peroxide blonde, she was more or less normal from the waist up—normal for serious weight trainers, that is. But most of her workouts were dedicated to increasing the size of her massive thighs, each of which already appeared larger than her shoulder width. She was now so grotesquely disproportioned that the other gym rats had taken to calling her Monster Woman.

Right now, Monster Woman was in the grunt corner, doing squats with weights that drew admiring looks from everyone. From where I stood, I couldn't see the markings on her weights, but from the size and number of them, it looked like she was hefting upwards of three hundred pounds. Surely that couldn't be right?

Then again, maybe it was. A couple of months earlier, I had discussed her with Elena Muinsiere, another ex-cop involved in Krav Maga. A bodybuilder herself, although a sane one, she told me that during a rare conversation, Monster Woman bragged that her biceps measured eighteen inches, her quads forty-two. Each.

"A clear case of testosterone abuse," Muinsiere had said. "It's messed her head all up. Talk about 'roid rage! I'm no wimp, Lena, but I keep as far away from her as possible, and I suggest you do the same."

I'd taken Muinsiere's advice, so today I made a large detour around Monster Woman while heading to the showers. Whatever drama was being played out in the woman's head, I didn't want to become a part of it.

Chapter Eight

Friday morning I had a meeting with Dr. Bradley Teague, the dead man's half-brother, who had checked into a Scottsdale resort hotel after his long flight from Kenya. He wasn't what I expected.

Somewhat north of sixty, he sported a swollen jaw, a split lip, and a missing front tooth, injuries he'd received when trying to inoculate a Kenyan girl against polio. He also exhibited the behavior of a man who feared he would never sleep again, no matter how firmly he clutched at the crucifix dangling from his neck.

"The mother was willing but the local warlord wasn't having any of it, and in that part of Kenya, the warlord is king," he lisped. "Fortunately, I was able to inoculate most of the kids in the village, including the girl, before he hit me with the butt of his rifle. Where are their bodies?"

I was stymied for a moment, but Stephen Zellar, Ali's attorney, answered without a blink. "Now that you're here, the medical examiner is releasing them, and your brother, sister-in-law, and nephew will be transferred to your funeral home of choice today," he said. "In the papers on file with his estate attorney, your brother was very specific about what he wanted, so everything should run relatively smoothly. The only thing you need to do now is choose a suitable reception hall for the after-funeral get-together."

"Reception hall?"

"The Camerons, especially your sister-in-law, had many friends. He left instructions for them to gather at his house after the funeral, but after what happened there…" Zellar cleared his throat. "Any reception hall would do. What church did they attend?"

"None. That I know of, anyway. We weren't close, so I, ah, I think we should skip the reception. Considering everything, the publicity and all, it doesn't seem appropriate."

Zellar raised his eyebrows.

Dr. Teague took the subtle hint to explain himself. "As I said, Arthur and I weren't close. I was already in high school when my father married his mother, and shortly afterwards left for college. Then there was medical school, then the Army, then marriage, and well, you know how it goes. Life, and all that. When I set up my practice in Pasadena, that took an enormous amount of time and energy, and I was, well, to come right down to it, I had my own life. Sure, I visited Arthur and his family from time to time, sent Christmas and birthday presents to the kids, but…" He trailed off, and touched his crucifix, as if to make certain it was still there.

"I see," Zellar said. "About the house, then. It remains rather, ah, disorganized, so do you want me to place a call to one of the companies that specialize in that sort of, er, cleanup?"

"Oh, God." Dr. Teague let go of his crucifix for a moment and buried his ruined face in his hands. Then, as if he couldn't bear his own touch, he jumped up and crossed the room to the sliding glass door that led to the suite's balcony. He opened the door, took a deep breath, and immediately closed it again. But he remained there, his face pressed against the glass. "Yes. Get it cleaned up. Then sell it. At a loss, if necessary. The furniture, too, if there's any left after…" He paused, then added, "But the portrait of Alexandra, I'll take possession of that in the meantime, even if it needs repair. The painting was done by Max Trattner, and is quite valuable." He paused again. "I'm the one who commissioned it, as a wedding present for Arthur."

Every time he said "Alexandra," the tone of his voice changed. I looked at Zellar to see if he'd noticed, too, but the attorney's face remained expressionless.

It was the morning after my interview with Kyle's foster mother, and we were sitting in Dr. Teague's suite at the Scottsdale Valley Ho, a fashionable retro hotel located a few miles south of the Cameron house. Considering the subject matter of the past hour, the suite's hipster fifties decor at first seemed wildly at odds with the conversation we were having. Then again, its very hipness might help ease Teague back into the twenty-first century and a country where children didn't have to duck ignorant warlords in order to receive medical care.

For the last hour, Zellar had been explaining the intricacies of juvenile law. If Zellar couldn't get Ali's confession thrown out and the charges against her dropped, there was yet another fallback: a plea agreement.

"Failing that, we present our case to the Juvenile Court judge. If, at the end, he finds her guilty, her age will be taken into account during the sentencing phase, and the law is much more lenient when it comes to juveniles. She and Kyle Gibbs will be tried separately, and it should be relatively easy to shift the onus of guilt onto him, since he's the actual killer."

"Make that 'alleged' killer," I corrected, ignoring the damning note I'd found in Kyle's room. Maybe I would tell Zellar about it later, maybe not. "Innocent until proven guilty, and all that."

Dr. Teague threw me a questioning look, but Zellar, merely pursed his lips. "Mr. Gibbs isn't our concern."

True enough, legally speaking. The sooner we finished here, the sooner I'd be able to talk to Dr. Teague alone. That moment arrived twenty minutes later, when Zellar called Dr. Teague away from his view of the hotel's parking lot to sign some papers. After offering his condolences once again, he stuffed everything back into his massive briefcase and left.

Dr. Teague appeared surprised when I remained behind. "Is there something else, Ms. Jones? If so, make it quick. I have to get out of this room, take a walk, do anything but sit around here thinking."

I smiled. "Come to think of it, I could do with a walk myself, and I'd be more than happy to keep you company." Playing on his apparent familiarity with art, added, "The Main Street galleries are open, and it's not all that hot yet. At least, not as much as yesterday."

At first I thought he would turn down my offer, but he didn't. "Anything's better than staying cooped up in here." He started toward the door. "Not that you're just 'anything,' Ms. Jones. Sorry if it sounded that way."

"No offense taken."

"Not all that hot" is a relative term in Arizona. The temperature had already nudged past ninety, but in a climate this dry it was bearable, and Teague, used to the heat of Africa, had no problem with it. At first he strode briskly along as if disinclined to talk, but by the time we reached the Arts District he loosened up enough to discuss what was left of his family. Namely, Ali.

"I will help my niece, regardless of what she may have done," he said.

"Regardless?" I didn't like the sound of that.

He slowed, examined a fingernail. It looked fine to me. "Zellar says he can get her confession thrown out. What do you think, Ms. Jones?"

What I thought didn't matter; it was what the judge thought that counted. "Zellar will make a strong argument that the arresting officers in Quartzsite strong-armed Ali, and since she's only fourteen, it might work. But better cross your fingers. As Zellar told you, she repeated the same story, on videotape, when she was returned to Maricopa County."

"Zellar says there was no attorney in the room at the time."

"Which will work in her favor."

It was early enough that Main Street was still fairly deserted, so we were able to talk freely. Not that anyone would have paid attention even if we'd been discussing an imminent alien invasion. The few tourists who were already out and about were more interested in window shopping than they were in us.

This section of Scottsdale was perfect for a leisurely walk.

More than fifty art galleries were located within a twenty-block radius, and their windows showcased everything from impressionism to photo realism, to post modernism, to downright kitsch. Interspersed among the galleries were jewelry stores, most of them offering Native American work, Navajo turquoise and silver being the big thing at the moment. For a while, Dr. Teague seemed content to amble along like the other tourists, the flashy window displays working to take the edge off his earlier edginess. Eventually he stopped in front of one of Scottsdale's less prestigious galleries. The painting in the window featured a large oil of three dolphins frisking with a mermaid. They glowed in the roseate light angling through a pyramid hovering above the waves.

"Thomas Kinkaid goes to sea," he said.

"All it needs is a unicorn."

Still staring at the painting, he asked, "Do you think she was telling the truth?"

I knew he wasn't talking about the fakey mermaid. "Teenage girls have done crazier things. But the part about hiring a hit man with her allowance money, I'm doubtful about that. Kyle seems the more likely suspect." Not that the thought made me any happier. The grudging pity I felt for the boy kept nagging at me.

Ali's legal situation having been fully covered over the last hour, it was time to ask the question we'd been dancing around since leaving the hotel. "Dr. Teague, you said a couple of times you and your half-brother weren't close, but did you know the, ah, details about Ali's birth?"

He grabbed at his crucifix, then let go as his shoulders tensed and his hands began to twitch. It took him a few moments to answer. "Of course. We, ah…that IVF business, then the… Well, siblings don't always see eye to eye, do they? Do you have a sister?"

"Not that I know of."

The dolphins lost his interest. When he turned around to face me, I could see a vein throbbing on his temple. "What an odd answer."

I gave him the thirty-second version of my childhood.

Fresh from the horrors of Kenya, he wasn't all that shocked. "I'm sorry about the foster homes, but adopting a child with your background would have been risky."

"Agreed."

"Even adopting a newborn, if you don't know the parents' background and genetic makeup, that can be risky, too. All sorts of problems are inheritable, say, from paranoid schizophrenia to amyotrophic lateral sclerosis. That's…"

"Lou Gehrig's disease, yes, I know. Is that why your brother opted for IVF rather than adoption?"

He wiped his brow, where a line of sweat had formed and threatened to run into his eyes. "Arthur discussed it with me before he and Alexandra had the procedure done, not that anything I said swayed his decision."

"Did you try?"

"Once Arthur makes, made, I mean, *made* up his mind to do something, he became obsessed with it. It's what made him an excellent physician, but a difficult person to talk to. Asperger's people are like that."

I looked at him in surprise. "Asperger's?"

"Sorry. You're probably not familiar with it."

Actually, I knew a little about the syndrome. It was at the high end of the autism spectrum, frequently characterized by obsessive behavior. People suffering from it—although *suffering* probably wasn't the right word to use—can function quite well, frequently at the genius level. But because their brains do work differently than the average person's, they can have trouble with social interactions, coming across as aloof or remote. And they don't like to be touched.

"I've heard of Asperger's," was all I said.

"Good, then I don't have to explain it. Well, Arthur had it in spades. For instance, I learned never to bring up the subject of cars, because if I did, he'd talk for hours obsessing about the things. He was always emailing me pictures of some classic car or other, as if I cared, out there in the bush where so many kids were dying. He should have stopped..." Another grab at his crucifix. "Anyway, you couldn't turn him off once he got started, and it drove Alexandra crazy. She finally had to tell him if he mentioned any car of any kind in her presence, she'd leave him, although I don't think she really meant it.

"Alexandra wasn't only beautiful, she was a good and decent woman. She had a job when they met, but she quit it when they got married to make a home for him. Not that Arthur ever appreciated it. That thing about children, for instance. When Arthur realized she couldn't get pregnant, he started obsessing about IVF like he obsessed about cars. Being a good Christian, Alexandra didn't want to undergo the treatments at first, but the son of a bitch kept on and on at her until the poor woman finally gave in." He heaved a big sigh. "Oh, well, what difference does it make now? What's done is done, and now Alexandra is with the angels."

When he said the name *Alexandra*, his voice sounded tender. It made me suspect that he harbored something other than Christian love for his brother's wife. "But now there's Ali," I said. *And there used to be Alec.* I touched him on the arm, only to have him flinch away. Also interesting, since Asperger's was believed to have a genetic component.

Dr. Teague shook himself, as if to rid himself of my touch. "Oh. Ali. Right. If you must know, as a practicing Catholic I refuse to have anything to do with artificial means to end pregnancy, prevent pregnancy, or even encourage pregnancy through drugs or any other procedure which attempts to circumvent natural law, so when Arthur brought it up, of course I argued against it."

"Really? I know plenty of Catholics who don't agree with you on the IVF business, priests among them."

"Apostates!" When he turned to me, his eyes glittered with religious fervor, and for a moment I feared I would be on the receiving end of a sermon about the evils of free thought. It didn't happen, though. He grunted, stroked his crucifix, and turned back to the dolphins.

Only by reminding myself that this man had risked his life to inoculate Kenyan children was I able to temper my next remark. "Apostates? That's rather a harsh judgment, don't you think?'

He looked at me again. "God is sometimes harsh, but we must submit to his will."

I studied his crucifix. It was larger than the usual cross, almost aggressively so. Had a touch of Asperger's caused him to obsess about God instead of collectible cars? "Using your own logic, then, wouldn't it follow that the Kenyan children you inoculated against polio should be left to contract the disease?"

"Don't play word games with me, Ms. Jones. The situations are nothing alike. Anyway, you have your beliefs—perhaps—and I have mine. Suffice it to say my brother and I clashed over the IVF issue, much as we clashed on others. Arthur was always a hardhead, so he paid no attention to me, just maintained that the Camerons had never displayed any genetic problems, none that we knew about, anyway. And since extensive DNA and psychological testing is required of any prospective egg donor, he believed the procedure was the next best thing to having children with Alexandra."

He paused, sighed. "Talk about a beautiful woman. And such a good one, too."

Yes, she'd been beautiful, but I'd seen Alexandra Cameron's before and after pictures and it was the *after* that haunted me.

Before he became mired in his memories, I said, "By the way, Dr. Teague, a large sum of money, eighteen thousand dollars, to be exact, was found hidden in your brother's house. Do you know anything about that?"

A vein throbbed in his forehead. A tell? "There's nothing I can tell you about that."

I tried again. "Is there anything you can tell me, *anything*, that could have led to Ali's problems with your brother? Or his murder? "

"How would I know? Other than a phone call now and again and the obligatory holiday cards and presents, like I've explained, we didn't keep in close contact. Looking back, I wish it could have been different, but we were on separate life paths."

"Not so much. Both doctors, both…" I paused, belatedly realizing how little I knew about Bradley Teague's personal life. "Do you have children?"

He gave me a wintry smile. "Not that I know of."

"Touché, Dr. Teague, but considering the situation, my question is relevant. Despite your different philosophies, your brother named you as his children's guardian if something happened to him or Alexandra. Zellar mentioned in passing that you're a widower. Any future marital prospects? Someone who might serve as a mother figure for Ali?"

The vein in his temple throbbed even harder. "No. My marriage wasn't happy. When Jeanette contracted a particularly aggressive form of pancreatic cancer, we'd been contemplating a legal separation, but of course after her diagnosis…" He let the sentence trail off, cleared his throat and began again. "After my wife died, I confronted the fact that our problems were due mainly to my inability to, as Jeanette put it, maintain close human contact." He sighed. "That appears to be a family trait."

Like Asperger's.

Unaware of the way my mind was working, he continued, "Catholicism aside, I didn't go to Kenya and similar hellholes because I'm some walk-on-water saint. The unvarnished truth is that, other than a brief infatuation with my brother's wife, I've never really cared much for people. Just their symptoms."

Despite the day's heat, I felt a chill. How would the troubled Ali fare under the guardianship of this man? And, come to think of it, how had she really fared under the guardianship of her own father? Had Alexandra been warm enough, empathic enough, to make up for her husband's remoteness?

As if he'd read my mind, he said, "My niece will receive good care, Ms. Jones, I assure you of that. As for the rest of it, what you'd probably call the 'emotional' part…" He shrugged. "Well,

I'll try. You see, working with Doctors Without Borders has more to do with the expiation of guilt than anything else, and I certainly do not want to accumulate more. So Ali will want for nothing. Now please excuse me, but I need time to myself."

Dismissal delivered, he clutched at his crucifix again, then left me with the capering dolphins and moved on down the street.

Alone.

Chapter Nine

Kyle

I need to see Ali.

Need to see her.

But they're keeping Ali from me, telling me I'll never see her again except maybe in court but probably not even then because we're going to have different trials.

Why can't I see her?

I need to see her, need to talk to her, need to tell her to stop saying the things everybody tells me she's saying, crazy stuff like she planned it and stuff.

She's got to stop saying that, needs to tell them it was all me, that I did it all, did it, did it, did it.

She's got to shut up.

When I told the guard the other day that I wanted to tell Ali something, he just laughed and laughed, said he knew what I wanted to do, tell her what to say and what not to say. He said Ali and me should've got our stories straight right off the bat instead of making it up as we went along. He also said we were mean-stupid to kill her mom and dad and brother, mean to kill them in the first place, stupid to believe we could run away to Hollywood and get jobs in the movies, buy a big house with a big pool, and throw big expensive parties and stuff. He kept calling us mean-stupid, mean-stupid like all the other kids in this place.

Ali's not mean, except to people she thinks might hurt me. And she is so not stupid. She's smart, real smart. She knows all about things I never even heard of. She reads books on medicine and stuff, knows the names of all the bones in the human body, can recite them all by heart.

That's smart!

Me, though? Compared to Ali, no way, and compared to maybe the guard and everyone else I've ever known, maybe I am stupid.

A real no-hoper.

But Ali keeps on reminding me that I get B's and C's on my report cards. Okay, so maybe there was that D in algebra, but I didn't fail, did I? Ali said that what with all that moving around from place to place I had to do, I never failed any class, which she thinks is pretty good. Most of the kids in here got moved around all the time like me, but they don't get B's and C's, just mainly D's and E's.

She told me to remember I even got an A in English once! We was supposed to write one of those dumb "What I Did On My Summer Vacation" essays, so I did and the teacher said it made her cry, that she'd been going to give me a B in the class but that after reading my essay she changed her mind and gave me an A.

When I took it home and showed it to Mom Fi, she cried, too.

So did Ali. After she read it she put her arms around me and hugged and hugged, crying like a baby.

Not that Ali's a crier. I only saw her cry that once, and it was for somebody else, me, not for herself.

Maybe Ali's right, maybe I'm not as stupid as everyone says I am. Well, everyone except her and Mom Fi and Dad Glen. They don't think I'm stupid at all. They think I'm smart, they say it all the time, they tell me I just missed a lot of school and most of the time there was nobody around who made me do my homework.

I miss them, even though they made me do my homework.

I especially miss Mom Fi. Almost as much as I miss Ali.

I hear Mom Fi was awful mad when she found out I took off to Hollywood with Ali, but I left a note, didn't I? I asked her to please feed Chester, Wendy, Alice, Veronica, and Archie, that I'd call her collect as soon as me and Ali got to California, so not to worry, we were fine, and when we got our jobs in the movies I'd send money home so she and Dad Glen could fix up the house and buy toys for the twins.

I miss the twins, too.

Crazy screaming little monsters but so cute you can't get mad at them. Besides, they're really only babies, aren't they? Babies don't know nothing yet, don't know about...

No, not going to think about all that stuff.

Have to see Ali.

Have to tell her to tell them I did it.

Did everything.

Thought about it. Planned it.

Did it!

Chapter Ten

Lena

After watching Dr. Teague disappear into a gallery that specialized in Navajo silverwork, I continued my way to Desert Investigations. The Valley Ho being so close to my office, I'd left my Jeep in its designated covered parking spot, but as I passed by the private parking lot next to our building, I saw Big Black Hummer hunkered down in Jimmy's spot again. A glance along the street revealed Jimmy's Toyota pickup, sitting in the soon-to-be-broiling sun.

Patience at end, I called the tow company.

Stepping out of the blazing Arizona sunshine, the office looked dark in comparison. I could smell coffee, but something seemed off about it.

"Top o' the morning to you, kemo sabe," Jimmy quipped, staring at his computer screen. He had to have been in the office for at least an hour, because his desk swam in a sea of paper.

"How could you tell it was me? You didn't even turn around. It could have been a client."

"Yardley's lemon verbena soap. You're the only person I know who uses it."

I segued away from the intimate subject of my bath soap. "I called the tow truck on the Hummer."

He made a face. "You sure that was necessary?"

"Positive. I'm surprised you didn't."

He shrugged. "I've learned to pick my battles."

Irritated by his lack of irritation, I changed the subject. "Whatever happened to the theory of the paperless office?"

"Like most theories, it didn't pan out." When Jimmy spun around in his chair, his long black hair swept several papers off his desk. He ignored them. "So how'd things go with Ali's uncle this morning?"

While pouring myself a cup of coffee, I summed up the conversation. "Dr. Teague is handling the situation as well as anyone could, I guess, and appeared open enough during our interview. He even displayed a not-too-secret love for his brother's wife. Oh. And he's religious."

"But?"

I took a sip of the coffee. Some sort of frou-frou vanilla/hazelnut blend, not my type of thing, but what the heck. It was caffeinated. "What makes you think there's a 'but'?"

"Because I know you."

"I wish you'd go back to Blue Mountain. This crap tastes like candy."

"There's an unopened bag of Blue Mountain beans in the cupboard, and the grinder's clean. Have at it."

"I hate the noise the grinder makes."

"Poor you. Tell me why you're not comfortable about the interview. It's all over your face."

"That's disgust at the coffee."

"If you don't tell me, then I won't tell you what I've found out about Dr. Cameron's bank account."

"All right, all right. Here's what I think. For all Teague's supposed openness, I could tell he was holding something back. He admitted he and his brother weren't close, but put it down to Asperger's behavior on his brother's part. After sounding a bit disapproving over the egg donor situation, he started to add something, then changed his mind and just said that siblings don't always see eye to eye. There's more there, I can feel it. From the way he talked about his brother's wife—he even commissioned a painting of her, pretending it was a wedding present—maybe there was tension between them over Alexandra. Still, he seemed forthright enough, accent on the word *seemed*, so maybe it was something other than unrequited love. I'll have another go at him before he leaves town, which will probably be right after the funeral."

"Back to Kenya? But Lena, now that he's Ali's designated guardian, I don't see how that's possible."

"Not much guardianship involved if the girl remains in juvenile detention until she's eighteen."

I thought back to Dr. Teague's confessed lack of close human relationships. Even if Ali was eventually found guilty of all charges, she was still only fourteen, and Arizona judges tended to be lenient toward minors. White, non-gang-affiliated female minors, anyway. If, despite all Zellar's legal and medical arguments about a teenager's "unformed cerebral cortex," Ali wound up serving time, she would need a stable and loving person to come home to when her sentence was up. It was hard to see her uncle fulfilling that role.

Harder still, Ali's biological mother—the Honorable Juliana May Thorsson, if the polls were correct, would be busy in the U.S. Senate.

Poor, messed-up kid.

"Even if the kid does time, guardianship is more of a job than you'd think," I pointed out, after taking another sip of the god-awful brew. "But then it would be mainly legal stuff, not actual day-to-day supervision. I don't want to think of what might happen when she's finally released, so let's not go there. Tell me about Dr. Cameron's secret bank account. You finally hacked your way in?"

He waved some papers. "Child's play, since we had the account number on the deposit slip. Turns out this was the doctor's private account. His wife's name isn't on it."

"Sounds to me like he was keeping a mistress." I remembered the portrait of Mrs. Cameron over the mantel of the murder house. How could a man married to a woman that beautiful stray?

Unaware of my thinking, Jimmy said, "For all we know, the doc was keeping a half dozen mistresses, but not with this account. Turns out it's a savings account he set up three years ago. No withdrawals. Ever. Now here's what's interesting. He made a total of four eighteen-thousand-dollar deposits this year, not counting, of course, the money you found in his house. Before that, he made only one deposit early last year, and four the year before that."

"Sounds like business, whatever it was, was getting better."

"Maybe."

"Just maybe? Don't keep me in suspense."

A slight smile. "Those deposits were made at irregular intervals. This year, he made two in January, one each in March, May, and July. Last year, only one, in January. The year before that, one each in April, May, June, and July. All made in cash, like the bundle you found in that pillow."

"It was a bolster."

"Whatever." Jimmy leaned even closer, and for a moment I thought he would touch my face, but at the last second his body bent down and to the right, as he picked up the fallen papers from the floor. Straightening, he added, "As you know, cash deposits are untraceable."

"Unless you can find the original account the money was withdrawn from. Good luck with that."

He put the papers back on his desk. "Or we could get a copy of the victim's tax returns. The IRS demands specifics, even if the money comes from gambling or hooking. Drug dealers, the small-time ones, anyway, sometimes declare their income as gambling winnings."

It was hard to envision Dr. Cameron a drug dealer, but these days, anything was possible. What argued against a drug connection, though, was that each deposit was for the same amount: eighteen thousand dollars even. Drug-running tends to be an up and down business, not to mention more profitable. And there are seldom year-long breaks, the cartels not being in the business of giving their employees sabbaticals.

"However Cameron got the money, it looks like he was saving up for something big," I pointed out. "Otherwise, why not just blow it on a vacation with the wife and kids? Answer: he didn't want his wife to know about this extra income. Or its origins, or its purpose."

"That's my thinking, too."

Then I remembered the ruined Corvette and Thunderbird in the family's garage. "Another car, maybe?" I asked. "His computer searches showed he was looking at some pretty ritzy newer models. Maybe he figured once he brought it home, the deed was done and his wife would have to lump it."

Jimmy raised his eyebrows, which made the curved tribal tattoo on his temple almost disappear into his ebony hair. "Have to be one heck of a car, Lena. There was already a hundred and eighty thousand dollars in that account, and your dead man was about to add another eighteen thousand to it."

"So what kind of car costs more than two hundred thousand dollars?"

When Jimmy grinned, his teeth were a startling white against his bronze skin. "Let's start with an Aston Martin V12 Vanquish, or a Lamborghini Gallardo, or…"

I lifted my hands in surrender. "Stop. Please. Since when do you know so much about high-end cars?"

The smile grew broader. "Every man has his dreams."

The idea of Jimmy, a dedicated Toyota truck man, lusting after a Lamborghini made me smile, too. "Be sure to give me a ride in your new Lamborghini as soon as you buy it. Seriously though, is there any way you can backtrack that cash? I took close-ups of some of the bills in case you were able to trace the serial numbers."

"I'm working on it. The timing of the deposits, too. If I can connect the deposit dates to a recurring series of events, we might—just might, mind you—zero in on who he was doing that under-the-table business with. And whatever services the good doctor was providing for them."

"Has to be something illegal, Jimmy. Another thing. I want you to see if anyone has posted something negative about any of the victims, especially Dr. Cameron. And check to see if there were any malpractice lawsuits against him. I didn't see anything like that in the case file."

"He wasn't in private practice, and it's those physicians who usually get hit with big malpractice suits. Like, 'You misdiagnosed my mother with an ulcer and it turned out to be stomach cancer, but by the time they found out what was really wrong, it had metastasized.'"

"Granted, but some sketchy people wind up in ERs, people getting shot because they were doing something they shouldn't be doing, gangbangers, et cetera."

He looked dubious. "Not a lot of that going down in Scottsdale."

"Except Cameron worked at Good Sam in downtown Phoenix. Lots of gunshot victims there. On weekends, it's a regular assembly line. Maybe somewhere along the way he let the wrong person die and now the dead banger's buddies…"

Jimmy interrupted. "Aren't you forgetting the confessions? Ali's and Kyle's? Plus there's that note you showed me, the one where Ali not only wished her family dead but suggested that Kyle kill them. And by the way, have you given the note to her attorney yet?"

"I will." Maybe. Possession of the note would place Zellar in a dicey legal position, something I wanted to avoid. "For now, forget the note and think about the confessions. *Conflicting* confessions, I'd like to point out. Here's the thing. On my way back from the meeting with the brother, it occurred to me we're taking too much for granted when it comes to Ali. Her story about paying a hit man with her allowance money is bullshit, so what other lies could she be telling? And what about Kyle's version of events? We need to compare Ali's story with his, but I haven't yet figured out a way to get to him. Sending him questions via his aunt might have worked, but he doesn't want to see her. Kyle's foster parents can't help, either, because so far, the judge is denying them permission to visit."

Jimmy frowned. "You're kidding me? They're his guardians."

"Foster parents. Which means that technically, the kid's still a ward of the court, not them, so what the judge rules goes. I called Kyle's attorney first thing this morning and he told me he's appealing, but right now, the kid remains in a state of legal limbo. Still, there is one bit of good news. Kyle's guardian ad litem says she'll go with the attorney to talk to the judge, but it might take a couple of days. The judge has a full docket."

Jimmy frowned. "Kyle's attorney actually talked to you? Gave you information? Geez, Lena, he could get disbarred for that. And you could lose your license."

"I'm not going to lose my license." I recapped the conversation, ending with, "And at this point in Racine's career, he's more interested in the truth than in ethics."

"And here I thought truth and ethics were one and the same. Silly me. But back to the kids. Kyle…" Something outside drew his attention. "Well, will you look at that!"

A truck from City Towing was passing by, with Big Black Hummer loaded onto its flatbed.

"You can move your pickup out of the sun now," I gloated.

He gave me a disapproving look. "Please don't tell me you called the city." Left to his own devices, Jimmy would rather park in the hot sun than turn in a parking space thief. He had always been too tenderhearted for his own good.

"Whoever keeps parking in our spots didn't pay any attention to my notes, so yeah, I called. Someone had to. But what were you about to say when we were so pleasantly interrupted?"

He turned away from the window. "I was going to remind you that Kyle wouldn't be the first teenager to kill for his girlfriend."

"You think I don't know that? But something…" I shook my head. "Something's off about this case. Way off. I just can't figure out what."

"Well, let me know when you do." He grabbed his keys and went outside to move his truck.

The hours passed slowly while I informed various clients on the status of their cases. Gerald Jenks, the human resources director at Charge-O-Matic, who'd been suspicious about the behavior of a stockroom employee, was shocked to learn that the man had done time for grand theft in Kansas, been arrested for shoplifting from a Phoenix Costco, and missed his last appointment with his parole officer.

"Didn't you run a background check?" I asked him.

Jenks' long silence was my answer.

I sighed. "Here's the good news, Mr. Jenks. Since he handles money, even if it's only the petty cash, you can let him go for cause and not worry about getting sued. But in the future, you might want to run these sorts of checks before you hire someone, not after. Or at least check their references."

"But he looked so honest," Jenks mourned.

"Good crooks usually do."

Human nature never ceases to amaze me. Despite a recent deluge of newspaper articles about upright church deacons caught watching kiddie porn and sweet-faced grandmothers on trial for running meth labs in their basements, most people still judged the human playbook by its cover. The fact that a simple Internet search could reveal the guilty truth behind innocent masks never occurred to them. Whatever the reason, their naïveté kept business booming at Desert Investigations.

I heard the same sort of story again, one client after another ruefully admitting to trusting the wrong person, lonely men trusting the wrong women, lonely women trusting the wrong men. After a couple of hours of this, I was ready to tear my hair out in frustration.

Finally, in late afternoon, after myriad attempts, I reached the Honorable Juliana Thorsson, who had either been ducking my calls or doing what politicians love to do—making life more complicated for the rest of us.

"Keep it brief," she said in a hurried whisper. In the background, I heard the buzzing echo of voices in a large room. Another fund-raiser, probably. What did that make—four this week? Every time I turned on MSNBC, there she was, surrounded by her minions, pretending she hadn't already made up her mind to run for the Senate.

"There's not much to tell you yet." I gave her a quick rundown on what I'd discovered so far, finishing with Ali's damning note to Kyle.

"I don't believe it," Thorsson snapped.

"Don't believe Ali wrote it, or don't believe she meant it?"

"Just a minute."

I heard the clippety-clop of high-heeled shoes, what sounded like doors opening and closing, then her voice returned at a more or less normal level. "I'm in a restroom stall now so I can talk freely."

"Did you check the other stalls?"

"I'm famous for my attention to detail. But back to Ali. I don't know how familiar you are with teenagers, girls especially, but there's a lot of frustration that goes on at that age, a lot of unfocused anger, especially toward authority figures. I'm sure she was just blowing off steam. She didn't mention her younger brother, did she? But whoever broke into the house killed him, too."

"Then why did Kyle hide the note?"

"Didn't you say you found several other love notes with it? Regardless of all that emailing and texting, kids still love to pass notes to each other. Maybe a lot of that intensity came about because Kyle's foster parents didn't approve of their relationship, and Ali knew it. She was having the same kind of trouble on her own home front, so that would just double her angst."

I suddenly became aware that I hadn't discussed Ali with Fiona, the boy's foster mother. I needed to remedy that. "Good point, but…"

Over the phone I heard a door opening again, laughter, two women discussing a third. They weren't being complimentary.

"Talk to you tomorrow," the Honorable Thorsson whispered before she killed the call.

Six o'clock found me parking my Jeep outside Jimmy's trailer to carpool over to his cousin's new restaurant.

Louise's Fry Bread Shack was located just off the eastern boundary of the rez in a commercial area hard-hit by the recession. It sat next to a second-hand furniture store, across the street from a failed shopping center where the only signs of life were two coyotes snuffling through an overturned dumpster. The out-of-the-way location hadn't hurt the restaurant's business, because when we arrived, a long line of Pimas and Anglos were waiting for service at the takeout window. We bypassed them and went inside.

Like many fry bread restaurants, Louise's place was bare bones. Other than the large framed print of Geronimo that hung on one wall, there was no décor to speak of, which only highlighted the large, hand-printed sign above the order counter: IF YOU ARE TALKING ON YOUR CELL PHONE WHEN YOU TRY TO PLACE YOUR ORDER, WE WILL TAKE THE ORDER OF THE PERSON BEHIND YOU.

Pimas take good manners seriously.

The menu wasn't complicated. Fry bread is a popular Southwest Indian staple and the Pimas cook up some of the best. Plate-sized slabs of dough deep-fried until golden, then slathered with mixtures of your choice. In my case, I opted for the chorizo, beans, lettuce, and cheese combination. Louise, a cheerful Pima beauty with mahogany eyes that perfectly matched Jimmy's, suggested I might be happier with the milder green chili chicken entree, but I didn't want to seem like a wuss, so I stayed with the chorizo. Jimmy, even less cautious than I, ordered the house special, which included just about everything—chorizo, mutton, chicken, and God only knows what else.

When I looked appalled, he just smiled: "I'll still have room for dessert fry bread—honey, butter, and cinnamon."

"That's two days' worth of calories," Louise warned, before she headed to the kitchen. "You'll get fat."

"Fourteen hours a week at L.A. Fitness says I won't," he countered.

"How come I never see you there?"

"Different schedules, Lena. You're a night owl, I'm a morning person. Anyway, haven't you been spending more time at Fight Pro lately? Working on that, what's it called, Cro Magnon stuff?"

"Krav Maga. It's an Israeli form of martial arts."

"You and your…"

I interrupted. "Hey, Almost Brother, I just had a thought."

"I wish you wouldn't do that."

"What? Interrupt you?"

"Have one of your 'thoughts.' They always wind up causing trouble."

I made a face. "Seriously, how long has Big Black Hummer been trespassing in our space?"

"About a week. Why?"

"That's when Fight Pro started resurfacing its parking lot, and finding a parking space got tough. I'll bet the Hummer belongs to one of the members."

"Could be. But wouldn't that…?"

At that moment, our food arrived and all conversation ceased. As Jimmy had promised, the fry bread was delicious, if spicy, so I downed three glasses of iced tea to offset the heat. It didn't help.

Louise joined us for a few minutes while she and Jimmy discussed all things Pima. The tribe's new casino and resort on the northern edge of the rez was raking in big bucks. Their child-friendly Butterfly Pavilion, located near the new Diamondbacks spring training facility, was doing well, too.

When I facetiously asked if the tribe would eventually build a Disneyland Pima, they both laughed.

"The Mouse got rich without our help," Louise replied, brown eyes sparkling. "But don't discount a Pima Magic Mountain. I've always been partial to roller coasters, and wouldn't mind living within walking distance to one."

Hanging out with the mellow Pimas always calmed my restless soul, so by the time we'd finished our meal, I felt relaxed and happy. It wasn't to last.

On the way back to Jimmy's trailer to pick up my Jeep, the chorizo-laced fry bread took its revenge.

"Uh, I need to use your bathroom," I said, as he pulled his pickup up next to my Jeep.

Jimmy gave me a pitying look. "Didn't I warn you about the chorizo?"

"Always one to say, 'I told you so,' aren't you? Now are you going to let me in there or do I have to find a friendly ditch?"

Ordinarily I like to see the sights at Jimmy's trailer, which is decorated with Pima designs, but this time, I rushed straight to the bathroom, where I spent the next few minutes contemplating my gastronomic sins. Finally, I emerged and joined Jimmy outside. He'd pulled two lawn chairs together and sat looking up at the stars. They were bright tonight, especially the Milky Way, a broad spackling of white against the indigo sky.

"Feeling better?"

I eased myself into the chair beside him. "I might live."

He chuckled. "Next time temper that adventuresome spirit with some common sense."

"Nag, nag, nag."

I checked my watch. Almost eight thirty. "Mind if I stay here a little while longer? It's Art Walk night on Main Street, and I'm not in the mood for teeming crowds right now."

"Told you we should have leased that office on Indian Bend."

"Too far from the action."

"It had a great bathroom, though. Shower, the whole deal."

"Uh, which reminds me, I better use yours again."

As I staggered toward the trailer, he called, "There's a new issue of *Arizona Highways* in the magazine rack next to the sink. A few *National Geographic*s, too. Not that you're in a reading mood."

After my shaky return, we sat in companionable silence for a while, each lost in our own thoughts. A warm breeze delivered scents of sage, mesquite, and fresh earth, while nearby, two coyotes yipped at one another. I-love-you calls? Or a let's-team-up-and-kill-something conversation?

"Did you know we're part of the Milky Way?" Jimmy asked, when the coyotes' dialogue ended in a rabbit's shriek.

"Learned it in Astronomy 101. From here it looks like it's way out there in the distance, not that we're looking at it from the inside. Just think—billions of stars, and probably a thousand planets like our own. Makes me feel small." I sighed, oddly comforted by the thought. Compared to the enormity above us, my bad memories weren't that big a deal.

"We Pimas have our own version of Astronomy 101, you know," he continued. "Our ancestors believed the Milky Way was created when a mule bucked off a load of flour. Coyote ate some, but Earth Doctor picked up the rest, and with his walking stick, swirled it across the sky." In a soft tenor, he sang Earth Doctor's ancient psalm,

> *I have made the stars!*
> *I have made the stars!*
> *Above the earth I threw them.*
> *All things above I have made*
> *and placed them to glow*
> *above Coyote's home.*

When Jimmy's song ended, Earth Doctor's creation swung its way through the now-silent night.

A rare feeling of contentment remained with me during the drive home. Past the widely spaced Pima homes, through the creosote thickets, around the newly harvested cotton fields, and onto the glittering streets of Scottsdale.

My contentment died only when I turned onto Main Street and saw Desert Investigations ablaze.

Chapter Eleven

A fiery starburst of light shape-shifted beyond the remnants of the gold script sign DESERT INVESTIGATIONS, which now read only ERT INVES. Tendrils of black smoke curled through what was left of the plate glass window. As I braked my Jeep on the other side of Main Street, the rest of the glass shattered, and a storm of wickedly sharp shards blew outward. The crowd gathered in the street made scared sounds and moved back en masse.

Being an ex-cop, my instinct was to run toward the inferno to rescue, well, something, but as I leapt out of my Jeep and started toward ERT INVES, a hand reached out and dragged me back.

"Fire department's on the way," a familiar voice said. "We all called about the same time."

I turned and saw Cliff Barbianzi, owner of the Damon and Pythias Gallery across the street from Desert Investigations. "Lena, if you think I'm letting you run in there, you're crazier than I already think you are."

"But it's burning!"

"Better your office than you."

Orange and red tongues of flame. Tinges of blue. An acrid smell jabbing tiny pitchforks in my nostrils. Waves of hellish heat in the already hot night.

"Cliffie, I need to…" I strained away from him.

His hand, which up to that point had been lightly holding my arm, tightened. "Wait until Rural Metro gets here, which should be any minute. They're only six blocks away. No point in getting killed over something you can't do anything about."

Cliffie wasn't a large man, nor an especially strong one, and I could easily have broken away, but I didn't because he was right. There was nothing I could do about the situation, other than wait for the fire trucks and hope my upstairs apartment wasn't burning, along with my office.

Our helpless vigil was joined by several other gallery owners who had stayed late after the Thursday Night Art Walk to clean up the mess the art-loving crowds had left. Anastasia, the owner of the Orthodox Art Gallery, offered me a glass of champagne left over from a Russian icon painter's opening, while Jeff, who ran the Native Trails Gallery, offered me a toast triangle spread with caviar. Another gallery manager, a woman new to the neighborhood and who didn't know me all that well, offered me a dainty handkerchief to sob into. I 'thanks-but-no-thanks'ed everyone, but did wind up accepting the bottle of Evian someone shoved into my hand. As I took my first sip, sirens filled the night.

"What happened?" I asked Cliffie, while the sirens grew louder.

"You were firebombed, Lena. I was putting away the punchbowl when I heard some god-awful noisy truck or motorcycle or something equally as obnoxious roaring up the street. It was annoying, yeah, sure, but getting that big punchbowl into that tiny cupboard isn't the easiest trick in the world, so that was what I was focused on. At first, anyway. Then I heard glass breaking and out of the corner of my eye saw a flash, then the sound of the truck or cycle or whatever the hell it was roaring off, and next thing I knew, I was looking at flames. Well! It didn't take a genius to figure out what was going on, so I grabbed my cell and speed dialed 9-1-1 while running across the street and upstairs to your apartment."

He paused for breath, then continued. "I banged and screamed and kicked at your door, and redialed and redialed and re-redialed your home number, but you didn't answer, so I started to run around to the back where the fire escape is, 'cause

I was going to break your window and drag you out by your glorious blond hair, but when I turned into the parking lot, I saw your Jeep was gone, thank God." Another deep breath. "So I sensibly removed myself from harm's way and came down here to wait for the beautiful boys of Rural Metro."

Just then several fire trucks rolled up and the beautiful boys of Rural Metro got busy with hoses and axes. Immediately afterward, two cars from Scottsdale PD pulled in and blocked off the street. Assured that I was no longer tempted to run into the inferno, Cliffie loosened his clutches and continued. "It could be worse. There's a good chance they'll be able to save that cunning little apartment of yours, maybe even most of your office, and anyway, I'm sure that gorgeous Indian partner of yours backs up everything, right?"

"Right." Jimmy was compulsive that way, backing up Desert Investigations' files on his home computer as well as every cloud site known to man. He'd even made me buy fireproof file cabinets and a safe, purchases I'd pooh-poohed at the time. I would pooh-pooh no more.

But at the moment, all those safety measures brought me little comfort.

At a time of borderline sanity, Desert Investigations had saved me. I'd begun the business years earlier after leaving the Scottsdale Police Department with a bullet in my hip, souvenir of protecting an innocent bystander during a drug raid gone bad. It's true what they say about the mental anguish of a gunshot often being more difficult to recover from than the physical injury itself. The days became a litany of "What if I'd done this, instead of that?" "What if I'd moved to the right instead of the left?" Or even the more wounding, "What if I'd refused to follow orders?"

Mistakes had been made. Three officers were shot. One died. Two lived on in the company of nightmares.

Desert Investigations—my savior.

Now it was dying.

And all I could do was stand there and watch.

The roar of the fire trucks' big engines only partially eclipsed the moans of buckling furniture. The firemen's shouted orders hardly muffled the sounds of breaking glass. Blue, red, and yellow flashing lights paled next to the crimson tongues licking across my desk. Splash-back from thick streams of water couldn't cool the heat that scorched my face.

"So much for my carpet," I said lightly, wanting no one to sense the despair I felt.

Cliffie, my would-be lifesaver, wasn't fooled. He gave me a hug that almost cracked my ribs. "But you're safe and well, dearest heart. And so is Jimmy. So it's all good."

Jimmy.

The name jolted me out of my self-involved misery. Desert Investigations was as much his baby as mine, so I pulled out my cell and hit his number. When he answered, I could hear coyotes yipping in the background. He was outside, probably still singing ancient Pima songs about the beginning of the Universe. Jimmy was purpose. Jimmy was peace.

I was about to change that.

He listened to my hurried words in silence until I was finished.

"I'm on my way." His voice was calm.

"Not necessary. I can take care of this."

"It's my office, too, Lena, so just this once, don't try to handle everything all by yourself. Let the police and the firemen do their jobs."

Giving up control has always been difficult for me, but I grunted something that might have been taken for agreement. Before I could clarify, he hung up. Deciding not to call him back, I stuffed the cell into my carryall and stood there, watching my life incinerate.

Jimmy must have broken all kinds of traffic laws driving in from the rez, because before I finished the bottle of Evian, he came running up.

"Had to park a couple of blocks away," he panted. "Main Street's blocked off."

"I told you I could have taken care of all this trouble by myself." There went that control thing again.

He said nothing, yet I could tell he was almost as upset as I was. He wasn't losing his home, but the man was so empathetic he'd always felt my pain, and tonight was no exception.

"Who do you think did it?" I asked.

"Considering the timing, I'd say the owner of Big Black Hummer is the obvious suspect. A person who drives a vehicle like that is all about show, and when you had his baby towed, you hit him in the ego."

"Thanks for not saying 'I told you so' this time. But you did warn me, didn't you?"

The glow from the dying fire flickered across his face. He didn't appear to be nearly as upset as I was. If anything, he looked cross. "I warn you about a lot of things, Lena, but you're in the habit of not paying attention."

"That amounts to an 'I told you so,' I think."

"Yeah, well. If the shoe fits."

Being firebombed involves a lot of paperwork. After the last of the flames disappeared, the deputy fire marshal pronounced the fire "suspicious," needing a full investigation. When Jimmy and I told him about Big Black Hummer, and Cliffie related what he'd seen, the fire marshal stepped away for a few moments to make a quick phone call. Once the conversation finished, he handed over a batch of forms to sign and said he'd see us tomorrow. Then, while the beautiful boys of Rural Metro were loading their trucks back up, a Scottsdale PD detective—a woman I only vaguely knew—arrived, wrote a report, and we signed more forms. Hard on her heels came Gavin Biddle, our insurance agent, followed by a cleanup crew from Scottsdale Restore. All bore forms of their own. It was almost eleven before we were through signing everything.

"Am I clear to check out my apartment now?" I asked Gavin.

He looked at me as if I'd lost my mind. "Not until the authorities declare it safe for access."

"The deputy fire marshal's already gone," Jimmy put in.

"He'll be back tomorrow," Gavin assured us. "Meanwhile, you don't want to even think about going in there tonight. Thanks to your neighbors, the fire department got right on this, but there's always a danger of hot spots, flare-ups, and the like. In such an eventuality, the last thing you want is to be caught on the second story with a blocked stairway for an exit. Not to mention the fact that it appears the fire reached the ceiling in one spot, so the upstairs flooring needs to be checked before you take one step on it. Don't want to be falling through, now, do we?" Although Gavin was barely thirty, and baby-faced to boot, his tone was that of an elderly grandpa delivering a warning to a misbehaving grandchild.

"No, we don't, do we? So where am I supposed to sleep tonight, in my Jeep?"

A gentle smile. "Perhaps now is the time to remind you that in the event of a fire, your policy covers not only cleanup and restoration, but ten nights in a motel. It being July, I'm sure there are plenty of vacancies within your policy's price point parameters. Why don't you let me call around and…"

"Um, Lena." Cliffie, that faithful friend, had remained behind after all the other gallery owners slowly drifted away. "I have a pied-à-terre in the Arcadia District, and I'd be honored to have you as my houseguest for the duration. Or if you want to be closer to what's left of your office, there's a daybed-and-desk setup in the back room of my gallery. You're more than welcome to use that. For as long as you like, no ten-day limit."

Before I could accept his offer, and I was about to, Jimmy spoke up. "That's generous of you, Cliff, but here's another option. When I built that office extension onto my trailer last year it freed up the second bedroom. It's small, but livable. My home computers are linked to our case files, which means Lena can continue working without interruption." As Gavin and Cliffie looked at me expectantly, Jimmy continued, "But whatever you decide, we'll work it out."

Pied-a-terre. Art gallery. Reservation trailer. A good range of choices, but for reasons too worrying to disclose, I followed Gavin's advice and opted for a motel.

Two hours later, after stopping at an all-night Walmart for emergency clothes and toiletries, I checked into the Best Western on Indian School Road. My upstairs room wasn't luxurious, but the business center on the ground floor provided a computer, printer, and copier. Since an IHOP was within walking distance, I figured that after a few hours' sleep and a decent breakfast, I could resume work on the Cameron case.

That is not what happened.

By four a.m. I hadn't yet fallen asleep. Instead, I lay awake in the king-sized Sleep Zone bed, staring at the ceiling. Gavin Biddle had warned me to be prepared for, at the very least, smoke damage to my apartment. Clothes could be easily replaced, as could office equipment, but I couldn't seem to stop cataloging the items I felt most concerned about. My collection of blues vinyls, some of them original pressings. My Lone Ranger bedspread. The Two Gray Hills Navajo rug hanging over my saguaro-rib sofa. The Hopi kachina doll I'd bought at the Hubbell Trading Post. The George Haozous oil painting. The black satin toss pillow emblazoned with the words WELCOME TO THE PHILIP-PINES I'd stolen from my fourth foster home.

Keepsakes of good times, reminders of…Well, other times. When you lose a memory, you lose part of yourself.

And I'd already lost so many.

Memories of my childhood, memories of my parents—who-ever and wherever they were. They had vanished with the bullet that left the scar on my forehead.

It's always a mistake to shop when you're upset. None of the clothes I purchased the night before fit, so first thing the next morning I drove back to Walmart. The rest of the day continued down the same path, playing catch-up, fixing screw-ups—I'd forgotten to buy workout clothes, too—and placing calls to a bevy of insurance companies. Before I realized it, the day was over, and although exhausted, I'd accomplished little. At least the Sue Grafton novel I'd bought on my third trip to Walmart was good, but I fell asleep reading it, only to wake at three a.m. to stare at the ceiling for the rest of the night.

The sun rises early in July. At six thirty, giving up any hope of sleep, I slipped into my Walmart workout clothes and headed to Fight Pro, hoping an hour on the treadmill and a few rounds with the Nautilus equipment would calm me down. Given the early hour, there were plenty of parking spaces to be had and the gym was all but deserted, except for the usual gym rats: Cage Fighter Man, slamming a punching bag. Steroid-enriched Monster Woman, grunting in the free-weights section. We ignored each other, caught up in our own private worlds of sweat and pain.

Showered and changed into my new tee-shirt and jeans, I stopped by Desert Investigations to see if anyone from Scottsdale Restore was there yet. No sign of them, other than the chain-link fence which now surrounded the building so that I couldn't sneak into my own apartment. The woman working the phones at the company's emergency number told me the clear-out and reconstruction couldn't start without signed permission from the fire marshal. Did I want her to call over there and find out exactly when he'd be by?

I did, and was told she would call me right back.

I settled back in my Jeep, prepared for a long wait. In the meantime, I enjoyed the rare quiet. The art galleries weren't open yet, and the tourists were still asleep. Now and then, a solitary car rolled by on Scottsdale Road, but other than that, the only movement on the street was a nasty-looking crow strutting behind the chain-link fence, picking through debris. As I watched, two slumming cactus wrens joined him.

My cell phone rang, startling me, but not the birds. The fire marshal himself was on the line, sounding like he was calling from his car. After the usual pleasantries, he told me the inspection was scheduled for two thirty.

"But I'd hoped we could get this show on the road much earlier," I protested. "I'm anxious to get back into my apartment and the cleanup crew won't start without your sign-off."

"Sorry, Ms. Jones," the fire marshal said, not sounding sorry at all. "Two thirty or thereabouts is the best I can do. Yours isn't the only property I need to look at today. To show you how busy things are here, you're number four on the list. You know how it is in summer, all those overworked air-conditioners setting roofs on fire, all those backyard barbeques setting everything ablaze…. Well, summer's a bad time for us. Come to think about it, we'd better make that three or thereabouts, since the property before yours is all the way up in Grayhawk, and that was a nasty one, although I'm relieved to say even the pets were saved. One of the firefighters made it onto the morning news, giving CPR to an unconscious kitten. Feisty little thing. Scratched his face all to hell when it regained consciousness."

Grumbling, I agreed to meet him at "two thirty or there-abouts," and hung up. When I checked my watch, I saw it was almost seven. I could call Jimmy without getting him out of bed, so I hit speed dial. He picked up right away.

"I'm shocked," he said. "I expected your call long before this."

"Every now and then I do try to be considerate."

I interrupted his laughter with another bad thought from my sleepless night. "The Cameron case file was in the office."

A long silence, then, "It's toast, then. But it was just a copy of the original, wasn't it?"

"A copy of a copy. I'll have to ask Ali's attorney for another one, or have his office email me what they can. That's probably what I should've done in the first place. You know how…"

"It's Saturday, Lena."

"So?"

"Zellar's office won't be open."

"Since attorneys bill by the hour, I'm betting you're wrong. By the way, have you had time to check out the owner of Big Black Hummer?"

"Where are you calling from? Not your motel. I hear birds."

"I'm in front of what's left of Desert Investigations. Well, did you?"

A grumbling noise. "Take me more for granted, why don't you? Okay, if you must know, I ran a quick check of the plate and found the vehicle registered to a Terry Jardine, who lives at a south Scottsdale resident address, which comes as a surprise, since a Hummer's a pretty pricey vehicle. I would have done more checking, grabbed his driver's license and other info, but I'm still busy working on the Cameron case. Just please don't tell me you want to go talk to Hummer Guy."

"So what if I do?"

"Bad idea. Regardless of the suspicious timing, Hummer Guy might not be the guilty party. We've irritated enough people over the years, and given all this heat lately, one of them might have snapped. Ray Bradbury wrote a story about something like that once, the effect of hot weather on crime. 'Touched with Fire,' I think it was called. Anyway, there's no point in going off half-cocked with Mr. Jardine, whose vehicle might simply have been in the wrong place at the wrong time."

"In other words, you think I should just sit around and wait for the cops to do something? Given their backlogged caseload?"

"Arson is a felony. They'll get to it."

"Yeah, sometime next month, maybe. I just got off the phone with the fire marshal. He can't check out the building until around three. Or thereabouts."

"Lena…"

One of the cactus wrens found a Reese's Peanut Butter Cup wrapper. After much cheeping and cawing, the crow wrestled the wrapper away and flew off with it to one of the tall palm trees lining Main Street. For a moment the wrens looked like they were considering a pursuit, but then changed their minds and resumed pecking through the rubble.

"Lena, don't…"

"Don't worry, I won't do anything rash. Now give me Mr. Jardine's address, then you can get back to finding out where Dr. Cameron was getting all that cash."

Amid much grumbling, Jimmy gave me the information.

Despite Jimmy's belief, I seldom go off half-cocked, but as an ex-cop I disliked coincidence. Desert Investigations had been firebombed the same day I'd had Big Black Hummer towed. Cliffie had described the vehicle that delivered the firebomb as loud, something Hummers tend to be. Ergo, its owner was Suspect No. 1.

And I had every intention of checking him out.

Terry Jardine lived in a tidy south Scottsdale neighborhood near the intersection of Miller Road and McKellips. Basically blue-collar, most of the small ranch homes that lined Buena Vista Drive were immaculate, with groomed desert landscaping, well-trimmed palm trees, and here and there, a decorative fence painted the same color as the trim on the house.

The Jardine house wasn't so well-kept. Its weedy lawn, crumbling stucco, and disintegrating sun screens screamed *cheap rental,* and as I drove my Jeep by to hide it on a different side street, I wondered how Mr. Jardine afforded his expensive Hummer. Drug sales? Possibly. Many street-corner hustlers had flashy cars but lived in non-flashy housing. Unless they were higher end dealers, that was, which didn't appear to be the case here.

Once I found a parking spot between a perfectly restored '76 Camaro and a nearly new Toyota 4Runner, I strolled casually toward the house. Jardine might recognize my Jeep, but probably not me, so I felt safe. As I drew near the house, I saw a big BEWARE OF DOG sign on the tall wooden gate to the backyard. The sign was punctuated by the sound of frantic barking. From the bass timbre of the woofs, I envisioned a large dog. Shepherd? Pit bull? Rottweiler? That meant no in-place reconnoitering.

I'd just reached the far end of the yard when Big Black Hummer, bailed out of the impound lot, growled its way up the street and into the drive. A night-shift worker? A playa back from a night on the town?

I bent down and fumbled with my shoelaces as the Hummer came to rest. Jardine didn't get out right away. I could barely see him through the dark-tinted windows, but I could tell he was fussing around with something next to him.

Then the Hummer's door opened and out stepped Monster Woman.

Shouldering her gym bag.

The air surrounding her thrummed with adrenaline, steroids, and rage. Huffing like an out-of-breath Clydesdale, she stomped up to the front door, her hands clenching and unclenching, readying themselves for whatever adversary might present itself. Because of her dark sunglasses—even darker than the Hummer's tinted windows—I couldn't see her eyes but could imagine them. Ice blue, black pinpricks for pupils, focused on individual pieces of her body, never once seeing the whole.

Fascinated, I continued to study her through the corner of my eye as she stuck her key into the front door, her glutes bunching as she did so. When she disappeared into the house, I hurried back to my Jeep and drove away.

Later, in a very different neighborhood, I caught up with Tiffany Browning-Meyers, my mini-Goth Facebook friend, a block away from her house. She was headed in the direction of Four Palms Middle School.

"School on a weekend?" I asked, pulling over to the curb.

The little tween recognized me at once. "Yeah, if your parents pay extra. The class is going to visit some old Hohokam ruins."

"Have time for a short ride first?"

She checked her watch, which I could have sworn was a four thousand dollar Clerc. I consoled myself by pretending it was a knockoff.

Oblivious to my watch envy, the little tween's face broke into a big smile. "Majorly. But I have to be on the bus in a half hour."

"No prob. Hop in."

The girl was as smart as she was Goth, so once she had settled herself, she said, "So what do you want to grill me about this time? Ali or Kyle?"

"You like Kyle, right?" I pulled away from the curb and headed toward the school.

"Yeah, but not in *that* way." She shot me a look from kohl-rimmed eyes.

"Something about him worry you?"

She tossed her head, creating a waterfall of long black hair. "As if. Nah, Kyle's great-looking and all, even with all those scars on his arms he got from his bio-parents, but he's too much wanksta for me."

"Wanksta?"

"You know, somebody who tries to act tough but is just the opposite. Anyway, Jacob Finn and me, he's my only, and still will be when he gets back from Denmark. Unlike certain people I could mention, we don't step out on each other." She then proceeded to give me a comprehensive synopsis of the mating habits of fourteen-year-olds in the twenty-first century. It was terrifying.

I cleared my throat. "Well, that's, ah, nice to know, but unlike the others, Kyle and Ali were, um, true to each other?"

She held up two fingers close together. "Siamese freaking twins."

"How did their parents feel about that? I've been told they were worried."

"Depends on who told you. At first Ali's parents knew zip 'cause she didn't tell them about him right away. When she finally did, they were okay at first, but after a while Ali's mom started thinking they were too intense and should maybe cool it. But, like, who cares, 'cause her parents could be weird, okay, well, maybe just her father. Mrs. Cameron was okay. More or less, but, kinda like…" She frowned, creating a thin little line of black lipstick. "Oh, I dunno. As for Kyle's folks—they're just foster parents, you know—from what I hear, they were flat out trying to break them up."

"Are you sure of that?"

She nodded that yes, she was.

"But if Kyle's foster parents were trying to break them up, what was their reasoning?"

"Dunno. Better ask them."

"I will. In the meantime, what was so 'weird' about Ali's parents?"

She thought about that for a moment, then said, "Okay. Here's the deal. Her mom was sweet, everyone liked her, mainly because she was so beautiful and always making things for us, like homemade trail mix, fancy little cut-out veggies, sometimes that Greek thing called hummus, dips, you know. With olives and some spicy stuff. Ground it up herself. At times she seemed so smart, but other times, she was kinda clueless, you know, like, walking around in a fog, knowing nothing about nothing, like, about Ali always sneaking out the window at night to see Kyle, stuff like that. But you just had to love her. My boyfriend was over there once, and he said she was like this beautiful lost princess, just waiting for someone to rescue her. But that's guys for you, hopeless romantics, right?"

"Uh, right." Good grief, did this little girl already know things about men I still didn't?

Her next comment jerked me back from my self-questioning. "Ali's dad, now there's the weird one."

"Weird in what way?"

An exaggerated shrug. "Creepy."

"'Creepy,' as in flirting with young girls, trying to touch them?"

A laugh. "That's so random! You're a bit weird yourself, you know that? Nah, Dr. Cameron wasn't into little girls, he was just, I don't know, like I said, creepy. Like when he walked into a room he sometimes tried to act all jolly and stuff, but everybody else got real quiet, see what I mean?"

Oddly enough, I did. She had just described someone with Asperger's trying hard to fit in and not doing a very good job.

"Because of him, none of us really liked going over there," she continued. "That's why when we all got together, it was always at somebody else's house. Usually mine, because my mom…" She blinked, probably belatedly remembering the trouble her mother's hair-dying, beer-supplying habits had caused.

I rescued her from her embarrassment. "Did Ali ever show up at school with bruises?"

"You mean, did her old man beat her, rape her, knock her up so she had to have an abortion? Hey, the dude was creepy, but not that kind of creepy. Ali never had a mark on her 'cept what she got playing soccer. You ought to see that girl on the field, competitive as hell, she'd plow through a line, like, like a tank or something. Talk about an animal!"

I pulled up in front of the school, which, given what I'd just learned about tween romance, I now viewed with considerably more cynicism. "Have fun in summer school," I said.

Another head shake, another waterfall of black hair. "It's not summer school, it's a Special Projects semester, and I'm hoping mine gets me into Vassar. Know what it's about?"

"Lay it on me."

"Native American slavery in the Southwest. Did you know Spanish friars used Indian slaves to build their missions?"

When I nodded, she looked disappointed. "Anyway, Special Projects ends next Friday. Then you can give me that Jeep ride you promised."

"You just had it."

"Five blocks? I don't think so! You're taking me off-road, somewhere in the Tonto National Forest, that's what you're doing. Just email me the day and time and I'll make room for it in my calendar."

With a final toss of her black-dyed hair, she walked away, leaving me feeling very, very old.

Still parked outside the school, I phoned Zellar's office. I was right. He was in. When I informed him what had happened to Desert Investigations, he switched me over to Babette, his secretary.

"Your boss makes you work on weekends?" I asked.

"For double time-and-a-half I'd work on Christmas, too. He says you need another copy of the case file?"

"Afraid so."

"It'll take a while," she said, sounding apologetic.

"How long's 'a while'?"

"Two or three hours, maybe."

Having expecting a couple of days' wait at the very least, I could have kissed her. "Just give me a call the second you're done, okay? One other thing, could you also copy everything on an attachment and email it to me at desertinvestigations.com?" *In case the second file got firebombed, too.*

"Give me four hours, then. I'll make so much money working today I won't even know how to spend it."

Thank God for greed. After singing Babette's praises to the skies, I hung up and pulled away from the curb.

Fiona Etheridge, Kyle's foster mother, was home but the twins weren't.

"CPS turned them over to their grandmother," Fiona explained. Her eyes were red from weeping, but her voice was steady as she led me through a clean, toy-free living room into a spotless kitchen. I missed the mess.

"Which grandmother? Paternal or maternal?" From my reading about the case, I remembered that both grandmothers had troubled backgrounds.

"Paternal, although I'm not supposed to tell you. Apparently she's been clean since her last stint in rehab."

"How long ago was that?"

"Six months."

Not a decision I would have made, but Child Protective Services' avowed mission was to "keep families together," no matter how dangerous the practice. "How can you stand it?" I asked her.

"I can't." As we settled ourselves on stools around the kitchen island, she poured me a cup of coffee and absentmindedly dumped in four teaspoons of sugar and enough milk to turn the liquid pale beige.

I sipped at it and tried to keep from gagging. "Nice."

"Liar." She made a similar face, having fixed the same concoction for herself and found it wanting. "Oh, hell. I hardly know what I'm doing today." Grabbing both cups, she dumped the coffee-sugar-milk concoction down the sink. "How about a Diet Coke?"

"That'll work for me."

After she'd fetched two cold cans from the refrigerator, we sat quietly for a while, listening to the electronic hums of an empty house until she finally broke the silence. "I did get some good news yesterday. The judge in Kyle's case vacated his earlier non-communication order and is allowing us to visit, so Glen and I are going over there this afternoon."

Next to finding out I'd get another copy of the Cameron case files, this was the best news I'd had all morning. "That's great, Fiona. I'm sure it will be of immense help to him. Psychologically speaking, that is. But, ah, I came over to ask you a few questions, so if you'll, ah, well…" Given her grief over losing the twins, I felt hesitant.

She waved away my doubt. "What do you want to know?"

"My sources tell me you didn't approve of Kyle's relationship with Ali."

"Who told you that?"

"I never divulge my sources." Especially when they're fourteen-year-old Gothettes.

Fiona shook her head. "Well, it's not quite true. Glen and I, we both liked Ali, and we were happy Kyle found someone he cared about and who seemed to care about him, but we didn't want him to get hurt. Foster care kids…" It was her turn to stop and consider her words carefully. "Well, this is something you would know all about, isn't it?" At my nod, she continued. "Foster kids tend to go one of two ways—either emotionally remote or overly attached. With Kyle it was the second. He attached himself to people immediately, which can lead to a lot of rejection. Since Glen and I got just as attached to him, it worked out well—on that front, at least—but with the Ali situation, apparently not so much." She studied her Diet Coke. The bubbles had almost disappeared. "Considering everything that's happened, you'll find this hard to believe, but as far as Ali was concerned, we never saw any problems with her. It was Ali's father we didn't much like."

This, coming hard on the heels of the mini-Goth's comment that Dr. Cameron was "creepy," made me sit up straight. "Why?"

She made a waving motion with her right hand, as if to brush something away. But there were no flies in the spotless kitchen, no motes of dust. Maybe she was just waving away the doubt in her own voice.

"We ran into him a couple of times, once at Trader Joe's, the other time at a PTA meeting, and, what can I say? There just seemed to be something…something lacking with him. Nothing I can exactly put my finger on, but, well, something. He acted friendly enough, but…" Her face changed. "That's it! He *acted* friendly, but really wasn't. Remembering back, I don't think he would have noticed if I'd fallen over and died right in front of him, which is odd, him being a doctor and all."

"Would you describe him as remote?"

"'Remote' is a good word, but it was even more than that. He looked at me as if I didn't exist, same way he looked at Glen. Maybe he was more normal at home, but the few times we tried to talk to him, no matter what we said, all he did was look right through us while yammering on and on about cars, even when it was obvious we were getting bored. It came across as rude." She stopped and gave me a baffled look. "Don't you think that's rude, not to care if you're boring someone?"

Not really. Asperger's people were frequently misunderstood, because unlike most of us, they existed in a logic-oriented otherworld, not an emotional one. Dr. Cameron wouldn't have been able to read the signals revealing his audience's discomfort. The high IQ and creativity that often go along with Asperger's folks usually allowed them to "act" an emotional involvement they didn't always feel in social situations outside their own family and small friendship circles. Some were good actors, and some weren't. The more I heard, the more it sounded like Dr. Cameron might have been among the bright but unlucky few who couldn't act his way out of a paper bag. At least he'd tried.

Then again, mini-Goth said that her friends' laughter stopped whenever Dr. Cameron entered a room. That didn't sound like Asperger's at all. It sounded—to use her word—creepy. The teens might have picked up on something adults couldn't. I told Fiona her description had helped, and left it at that. Dr. Cameron was dead, and whether or not he was creepy or simply had Asperger's was now a moot point. In the end, what really mattered was the fact that he had worked hard to create a safe, comfortable life for his wife and children.

At least until murder came to call.

The conversation had taken Fiona's mind off her own misery about losing the twins, enough so that I was ready to broach the topic that had brought me here.

"I need to ask a favor," I said.

"Which is?" she replied, cautiously.

"Since I'm working for Ali's attorney, I can't visit Kyle. I was hoping you would ask him one question for me."

She gave me a glare. "If you think I'm going to ask Kyle if he killed that family, you can get out of my house right now!" To punctuate her words, she stood up, prepared to show me to the door.

I didn't budge. "That's not my question."

"Then what is it?" She didn't sit back down, and she didn't stop glaring.

"Ask Kyle why he tried to kill the dog."

Chapter Twelve

Artists aren't early risers, but chances were good that Madeline would be up by ten, so as soon as I found a shady spot to park, I called and cancelled our dinner appointment.

"Don't bother driving in from Florence," I said. "Something's come up." I didn't mention the fire at Desert Investigations.

"Work related?"

"What else? You know I have no personal life."

"Lena, are you ever going to do something about that?"

Good foster mothers are like all good mothers: nosy. "Hey, how's that new painting class coming along?"

"Nice feint, since you'd rather not answer my question. Have it your way, then. My painting class, not that you're really interested, is doing well. A couple of my students even have talent."

"A couple? How big is the class?"

"Seven. Four of them are painting landscapes, another is reinventing Mondrian."

"The squares, right?"

"I taught you well, Grasshopper."

That gave me my first genuine smile in, what, twenty-four hours? "Look, I really am sorry about tonight, and I promise to call you and reschedule as soon as…" I caught myself before saying *as soon as I get word from the fire marshal.* "Uh, as soon as I clear away some work."

"See that you do, Hon. You know I worry about you."

Another thing all good mothers have in common: They never stop worrying about their children, even when their children are grown and carry firearms.

"I can take care of myself," I said.

"Said the cat to the crocodile. But fine, I won't nag."

"Said the nagger to the naggee."

She was still laughing when I killed the call.

Mission accomplished, I pulled away from the cool shelter of an overhanging Aleppo pine and back into the hot sun. Such early morning heat meant Hell's own temps for the afternoon, so getting interviews out of the way now made sense. The Jeep wasn't retrofitted with air-conditioning, and sweat was already rolling down my face when I parked in front of the Cameron house.

When the murders occurred, the Camerons' neighbors had been out of town, but from the signs of recent activity—a news-paper lying in the driveway at the territorial-style house, someone closing the south-facing blinds at the pseudo-Mediterranean—they were back. Not expecting much, I tried the house on the left, where I'd seen the vague shape of a man before the blinds snapped shut. The door opened before I had a chance to ring the bell.

"Well, hello, pretty lady," growled a massive, middle-aged man wearing too-tight jeans and tee-shirt. His accent hinted at New Jersey. "What you selling? Yourself, I hope."

Great. It was going to be one of those interviews. To fore-stall more wolfish behavior, I produced my P.I. card, a surefire flirtation killer. "Not selling anything today, sir, just looking for information."

His jowl-heavy face morphed from leer to caution. "This about the Camerons?"

"Yes, sir. It is. I know you were in Wyoming at the time of…"

"No, I was in Venice, the one in Italy, not California. The Newberrys were in Wyoming. They're into horses and cows, must own half the state up there. But you might as well come in. I never say no to blondes."

Big Guy motioned me into an elegantly furnished home which the air-conditioning had turned into a suburb of Nome,

Alaska. The mostly-white leather furniture echoed the Arctic chill, but here and there, colorful toss pillows matched the vivid reds, yellows, and blues of a painting that took up an entire wall. Unless I was wrong, it was a de Kooning.

Big Guy caught me gaping at it. "Left to me by an old pal when he passed. And the Giacometti?" He gestured toward a spindly sculpture in the corner of a skeletal woman standing on one leg. "Ditto my Aunt Grace, so I guess you could say I've profited from death in my time. Not that I'd do anything to bring it about, unlike some of my old buddies back in Bayonne, so you can cross me off your suspect list. Name's Ralph, by the way. But you can call me Ralph." A wink.

I was getting all kinds of mixed vibes from Ralph. A thin layer of Jersey geniality covered a much deeper layer of menace experience had taught me not to explore, so I decided to make the interview brief. Settling myself in a chair across from the long sofa, I asked, "How well did you know the Camerons?"

When he sat down, the sofa looked smaller by comparison. "Just to say hello to."

"No social contact with any of them?"

"None to speak of." He reached into his pocket and withdrew a pack of Marlboros, which explained the musty odor I'd noticed in the pristine room. "Smoke?"

"No, thanks."

"Suit yourself." He shook out a cigarette, tapped the end of it against his palm, then lit up. After a deep inhale, he blew a spiral of smoke into the air. "Two years now I been sayin' I'm gonna quit, but hasn't happened yet. Guy's gotta have some vices, right?"

"Right. Look, what can you tell me about the Camerons?"

He took another puff, then stubbed the cigarette out in a marble ashtray. "You know, the cops asked me the same question. Why I should go over it all again with you?"

The de Kooning wasn't the only picture in the room. On a table next to the sofa sat a beachside photograph of Ralph with a young girl who looked just like him, poor thing, but the camera had caught him smiling at her as if she was the most beautiful kid in the world. Figuring she was his daughter, I decided to take a chance.

"Because I think it's possible Ali had nothing to do with her family's murder."

He thought about that for a moment, then said, "Beauty and brains."

"Ali?"

"Nah. You."

I waited.

He shook out another cigarette. This time he didn't light it, just placed it between his fleshy lips and sucked. "I've got to stop this crap," he finally announced, then lit the thing. "You smoke?"

I shook my head.

"Like I said, beauty and brains. Okay. Here's what I know about the kid. Typical teen, half nasty, half nice, but she always waved and smiled when she saw me. Loved her mother, tolerated her brother, and more than a little edgy around her father, but don't bother asking me why, because I don't know, not being on what you'd call 'intimate terms' with the family. Which I consider a real shame as far as the lady of the house went. Jesus, what a woman. All natural, too, none of that cosmetic surgery crap you see so much of today. Totally wasted on that cold dick she was married to. She'da been mine, I'd of…" He took another draw at this cigarette. "I'd have shown her a better time."

"Do you think it's possible Dr. Cameron mistreated Ali?"

A shrug. "Hard to tell. He was always too controlled to be up front about whatever was going on with him, and there must have been something, because he was like this big blank page walking around. I'll tell you this, though, if I'da seen as much as one mark on that woman—or the girl or even the little boy—I'da done something about it. And by 'done something' I don't mean calling the cops."

I believed him. Call Me Ralph oozed all kinds of menace.

"What kinds of friends did the Camerons have?"

"You mean, like people who wouldn't think twice about wasting someone? Prissy-assed professional types, that's all I ever saw go in over there. Not many of those, either. Other than the little girl's friends, and the book club broads, they weren't much on entertaining."

"How do you know they were, ah, book club broads?"

"'Cause they'd arrive with AJ's pastry boxes in one hand, a book in the other. Last I saw, they was reading something by Philip Roth, another cold dick." At my expression, he smirked. "Roth lived next door to my Aunt Grace, who was all the time reading his books. I never could figure out why women read his crap, 'cause the prick sure as hell hates women and doesn't exactly make a secret of it, either. And before you go getting all shocked again, yeah, I got curious over some of the stories Aunt Grace told me about him, so I tried one of his books. Couldn't get past the dick's mommy issues."

"Fascinating. You say the Camerons didn't have many visitors?"

"Yeah, what I said."

"Did Mrs. Cameron ever, ah, entertain male guests while the husband and kids were elsewhere?"

A smirk. "Like me, for instance? I should be so lucky. But, nah, never saw any guys go in over there without some woman tagging along. At least not that I ever saw. If Alexandra'd been playing around and Cameron found out, he probably would've killed her long before this mess happened. He sure as hell was capable of it."

I tried to keep the shock out of my face. "That's a pretty strong thing to say about Dr. Cameron since he has no record of violence."

His laugh sounded like gravel on asphalt. "That cold dick could cut somebody down and not think twice about it. Believe what you want, gorgeous, but I got a sixth sense about these things."

"I'm sure you do," I murmured under my breath. "How about Kyle Gibbs? You ever see him over there?"

"Kyle Gibbs? Is that the boy people are saying was the girl's partner in crime? Yeah, I saw 'im a few times. Seemed nice enough to me, but I read what they said about him in the newspaper, about his slut mom and even more worthless dad. The kid's probably fucked up seven ways from Sunday. Jesus, some folks got no business havin' babies." There was no irony in his voice as he passed this judgment.

"Anything else you can tell me about the family?"

"You got it all. Say, you wanna go out sometime?"

I gave him my standard thanks-but-no-thanks smile-and-excuse. "I'm involved," I lied.

In return, he gave me a conspiratorial smile. "Doesn't have to be a problem, honey. Next time you feel like stepping out on the lucky bastard, gimme a call."

I felt like I needed a bath—some people have that effect on you—so as soon as I made it out the door, I decided to drive back to Desert Investigations and take a cold shower before I transcribed the interview. As soon as I climbed into my Jeep, I changed my plans. Due to the fire, there would be no cold shower in my upstairs apartment, and no transcribing of case notes on my office computer. Because of Monster Woman, I was temporarily homeless and office-less.

"Aw, hell," I muttered, not knowing where to go.

The motel? I had charged a week in advance on my Visa, which meant I could go there, but to do what? Sleep? Pace the floor? Although the motel offered a business center, I didn't relish typing out case notes where someone might read them over my shoulder. To turn my motel room into an even minimally-effective office, I would have to buy a new laptop and printer, but it could take a couple of days to load in the software. Then I'd have to figure out how to merge the new laptop with Jimmy's.

Deciding to get one more interview out of the way before attempting to solve the office problem, I stepped back out of my Jeep and headed across the street to the Camerons' other neighbor. According to the files Ali's attorney had given me, the two-story territorial was owned by Elmont and Margaret New-berry. After only one knock, the door was opened by a sunburnt man, who in naturally faded jeans and ancient cowboy boots, looked more like a ranch hand than most ranch hands do. But his long-nosed, patrician face partially ruined the effect. I showed him my ID and explained why I was in the neighborhood.

With a courtly gesture, he invited me in. "Sorry about the mess," he said, in an accent more Massachusetts than Arizona.

At first glance, the "mess" appeared to be two porcelain cups on the coffee table, one with lipstick on the rim. Once I sat settled myself onto a rough-out leather sofa, I did see a mouse-sized dust bunny hunkered down in the corner. The room also smelled faintly of horse and dog.

"Margie can probably tell you more than I can about the Camerons, since she was pretty close to Alexandra. Right now, though, she's at her law office taking an emergency deposition. But seeing as how you're already here, can I ask if you've heard anything yet about the funeral? We want to attend, of course."

I explained that the funeral should happen shortly since the bodies had finally been released, and told him how to reach Dr. Teague for details. "But when you do leave town, Mr. Newberry, you might want to do something about that newspaper in your driveway. A collection of them is a dead giveaway someone's on vacation."

He frowned. "Again? When I called the circulation office yesterday to complain, the guy I talked to guaranteed he'd take care of it. Used to be..." He cleared his throat, then added, "Alexandra used to check on things like that for everyone. Such a lovely, sweet woman. When she knew someone was away, she would pick up newspapers and take flyers off their doors. That was before, well, you know."

"Before the murders."

"Yes. Before the murders. And please call me Monty."

Like Ralph Parelli's house across the street, this one was filled with art, but of a vastly different genre. Oils of Indians hunting buffalo hung on textured walls. A sculpture collection that featured the rugged faces of even more Indians stood scattered around the room. My favorite was the life-sized sculpture of a war-painted Comanche who brandished a lethal-looking spear. The furnishings matched the art—rough-out tan leather sofas studded with brass trim and Navajo rugs thrown randomly across a saltillo tile floor. Elmont Newberry might have originated on the Eastern seaboard, but his heart was true West.

"You sound like you were on good terms with the Camerons," I said, avoiding the Comanche's glower.

"We never had much to do with Arthur, but my wife was friends with Alexandra."

I could picture Monty's wife now. Aristocratic, tall, lean, perhaps as beautiful as Alexandra. "Were they good friends?"

"I'd say so. But Margie is pretty much into her law practice and Alexandra is—or was, sorry—your basic soccer mom, always shuttling the children back and forth to this or that game or dance or piano lesson. Every now and then, she would fly out somewhere on behalf of that charity she was involved with, I forget the name, something about kids. But she and my wife got together all the time, chatting over coffee, things like that. You know, like women do. Ah, some women, anyway."

I hid my smile; despite his ranch garb, he'd been well house-trained. "Do you know if those chats included the sharing of personal information?"

"If you mean like the fact that Alexandra wasn't happy in her marriage, I guess you could say they did."

Well, well. Out of the mouths of Boston-bred cowboys. "I've heard about that," I lied. "Did Alexandra go into detail?"

"Not to me, but Margie might be able to give you the specifics."

At my request, he walked over to an ancient rolltop desk, hunted around though a drawer, then came back with a business card that said MARGARET NEWBERRY, ATTORNEY AT LAW. A Scottsdale address and phone number.

"When you talk to her, be gentle. Margie's...Well, she's a bit touchy these days. She and Alexandra were close."

"No problem." I tucked the card into my pocket. "You said you didn't have much to do with Dr. Cameron. May I ask why?"

He looked down at his jeans. Flicked away something. Didn't look up. "I didn't care for the man, and I doubt he cared for me. Hardly ever said so much as 'Nice day, isn't it?'"

I waited. Sometimes, if you wait long enough, the other person will say more to fill in the silence. That's what he did.

Pale gray eyes finally met mine. "Look, Arthur could be personable enough, but he was, oh, I don't know, he never felt like he was with you when he was with you, if you know what I mean. Removed, you could say. You usually don't experience that kind of thing around here." He paused for a moment, a thoughtful look on his fine-boned face. "Margie didn't care for him, either. If Arthur came home while she was over there chatting with Alexandra, she'd say she had to get back and start dinner, which was a blatant lie." A hint of a smile. "My wife can't even boil water. If it wasn't for Chinese takeaway and AJ's ready-to-eat meals, we'd both starve to death."

Fleetingly, I wondered what they were eating up on their Wyoming ranch. Raw elk? "How about Ali? What do you know about her?"

The half-smile broadened. "A lovely girl, simply lovely. Had her mother's heart. I'd see her around every now and then, skateboarding up and down the cul-de-sac—without a helmet, I regret to say—sometimes walking home from school with friends. That the police could believe that crazy confession of hers, well, it beggars belief."

"Why?"

He shook his head. "Ali is not the type to ever hurt anyone."

"And what 'type' is that?"

"You know. Troubled. Violent. Not Alison." Then an element of doubt entered his voice. "She appeared to be a typical teenager, but then again, Margie and I were never lucky enough to have children, so what do I know?"

"Ever hear any fights between her and her father? Or anyone else?"

Another head shake. "These houses are pretty much sound-proof. They could set off nuclear tests over there and we wouldn't hear a thing."

"Do you think…?"

My next question was cut short by someone coming through the door. I turned around and saw a tiny brown woman with the face of an enraged shark. "The bitch didn't show!"

When she noticed me, she looked even more furious. "Lady, if you're selling insurance, you sure as hell picked the wrong house on the wrong day."

To punctuate her comment, she lobbed her handbag across the room like a grenade. It bounced off the opposite wall, spewing shrapnel of keys, tissues, and pens across the tile floor.

Elmont "Monty" Newberry didn't flinch. Maybe this sort of thing happened all the time in the Newberry house. "Hi, Hon. This is Lena Jones, she's a private investigator. She's working for Ali's attorney, and would like to know about Alexandra's and Arthur's marriage."

"Don't want to know much, do you?" his wife muttered, plopping herself down on the sofa next to him. She ignored the wounded handbag and its spilled innards. "Whatever was going on between those two is none of your business."

Angry people not only say things they don't mean, but they also say things they do mean but were normally too cautious to verbalize, so I braved the firestorm and said, "I've heard from several people that Alexandra Cameron was unhappy. Did she ever mention divorce?"

Dark brown eyes glittered at me. Was it my imagination or did she resemble the photograph I'd seen of Geronimo at the fry bread restaurant? Margie Newberry definitely had Indian blood, and judging from the cragginess of her face, possibly Apache.

"Hate to disappoint you, Miss Jones," she said, "but regardless of what my husband might have told you, I wasn't Alexandra's Mother Confessor." She glared at her husband, then, surprisingly, gave him a peck on the cheek. "Monty here has a vivid imagination, should have been a writer, not a banker. That marriage was fine. Not perfect, no marriage is, but acceptable."

"Acceptable?" I allowed my skepticism to show.

Nonplussed, her husband smiled at her, a man besotted with his wife. "Just tell the woman, Margie. It might help Ali."

"Hmm." She left the sofa, walked over to her handbag, and began gathering up the spilled items. It seemed to take longer than necessary, but when she returned to the sofa, she had a determined expression on her face. "Poor Alexandra. All that beauty and look what it got her. Amazing, isn't it, how one mistake can ruin your life?"

"And that mistake was?" I asked.

"Marrying Arthur, of course. Talk about a cold fish. She did talk about leaving him. So there. Make of it what you will."

"He was cold, you say? That doesn't sound reason enough for a divorce."

"Depends on what a person wants from life. You Catholic or something, Miss Jones? Think marriage is sacred and all that?"

The question didn't call for an answer so I gave her none. Just waited.

She sighed. "Oh, all right. Alexandra is dead, along with poor little Alec, as well as that idiot she was married to, so nothing I say can hurt her now. However, before I begin, I want you to turn off any recording device you have in your bag or on your person and set it on the coffee table."

I reached into my carryall, pulled out my digital recorder, switched it off, and laid it down.

Mr. Newberry's mouth formed a perfect "O." "You didn't get my permission for that!"

"She didn't have to, Hon," his wife explained. "Under Arizona law, only one person has to know about a recording device, which almost always means the person who's making the recording."

"That hardly seems fair," he muttered.

"Since when does the law have to be fair?" To me, she said, "I don't want you taking notes, either."

I raised empty hands. "No problem."

She took a deep breath, then proceeded to reveal that she was, after all, Alexandra Cameron's Mother Confessor. "Once, Alexandra asked me if I could recommend a good divorce attorney."

"Did she say why?"

"Didn't have to. I already knew how unhappy she was."

Tolstoy's comment about marriage came to mind. *All happy families are alike; every unhappy family is unhappy in its own way.* "Can you explain?"

"Among other things, she suspected he might be having an affair."

Which was no more than I'd suspected myself, since secret bank accounts fairly reeked of extramarital activities on at least one person's part. Still, I pretended to be surprised. "Really! Do you know if she confronted her husband with her suspicions?"

"No."

"Yet she wanted a divorce attorney?"

"Yep. I think she just…" Margie's eyes unfocused for a moment, then snapped back to attention. "Besides her suspicions, I think she was just tired. That can happen in a marriage. One day you wake up and you're ready to pack it in. All you're looking for is an excuse. That's what happened to Alexandra, I guess."

Spotting the alarm that swept across her husband's face, she gave him a swift smile and a pat on the cheek. "You silly man."

The besotted expression returned. Tolstoy notwithstanding, even happy marriages are unique in their own way.

"Back to Alexandra," I said, to forestall any cuddling between the two unlikely lovebirds. "If she suspected her husband was having an affair, did she have a particular woman in mind?"

Husband duly reassured, she went on, "What difference does it make?"

"Surely she had grounds for her suspicion."

She glanced across the room at the Comanche sculpture, as if looking for advice on how much she should say. The Comanche remained silent.

"Her suspicions started several years ago, after he switched his hours from days—which he'd worked for years—to nights. He told her he liked fixing the gunshot wounds, the stabbings, especially on weekends, when they really started rolling into the ER. Arthur was freaky that way, when he talked shop, it sounded like he wasn't talking about human beings at all, just organs. You know, like 'Yesterday I worked on the most interesting kidney' or 'That aorta was exciting, never saw anything like that since med school.'

"Anyway, he switched his schedule to nights, working from around six in the evening to around two or three in the morning, but now and then he never came home at all. Not that that's anything unusual for an ER doc. Then one night little Alec got sick. Shivering, vomiting, cramps, the whole nine yards. Alexandra tried calling him at the hospital, but kept getting his voice mail. Again, not unusual for an ER doc. But she was all shook up, called me, said she didn't know what to do, but neither did I, so she kept calling and around midnight she finally reached a nurse over there she knew personally. The nurse told her Arthur had the night off."

Yes, that would have set alarm bells off in most marriages. "What happened then?"

"She took Alec to Scottsdale Health Care Emergency, where the pediatrician on duty diagnosed the flu and wrote out a prescription for the latest wonder drug. So that was that."

"No, I meant when Dr. Cameron came home, did Alexandra ask him what was going on?"

"Wouldn't you? Arthur got home around four in the morning, which was pretty much his normal time, and by then the kid had stopped barfing. Alexandra didn't exactly give him the third degree, she wasn't like that, but from what I understood, when she asked him where he'd been, he told her that where he went and what he did was none of her concern."

"He didn't even bother lying about it?"

She shrugged. "You had to know Arthur to understand. If he wanted to do something, he did it, and if you didn't like it, too bad. That might make you think he was a forthright person, but he wasn't. In his own way, he could be very secretive, like he knew something no one else knew and enjoyed knowing it."

Such as the existence of a secret bank account. "Sounds like Dr. Cameron was a complicated man."

A sharp laugh. "That's one way of putting it."

"Your neighbor, Ralph Parelli, told me Alison was 'edgy' around her father."

She looked at her husband. "Did you ever see anything like that?"

He shook his head.

"I didn't either," she continued. "Arthur irritated her sometimes, just like he irritated everybody, but edgy? Never. If anything, she seemed to understand him better than anyone else."

Monty nodded. "Ali wasn't afraid of anyone or anything. Especially not her father, maybe because Arthur was too remote to actually get mad at anyone, especially her, so…"

"You're wrong, Monty." Margie's fierce brown eyes narrowed. "Arthur did have a nasty temper. He had a run-in with me once."

I waited and watched her own anger build.

"It was over that damned Corvette of his, oh, yes, I remember now. A couple of years ago, right after he bought the stupid thing, on his days off he would park it in front of his house and start washing it, waxing it, fussing and pawing over it like it was a show horse. You never saw such a display of obsession in your life. Once I sent Monty over there to remind him the neighborhood R&Rs forbid that sort of thing, but next thing you know, Monty was right there with him, drooling over the damned car, too." She shot her husband a dirty look.

"Hon, it was a 1957 convertible," he said mildly. "Well worth the drool."

"Men are so useless." But she smiled fondly at him. "Anyway, Arthur kept doing it, washing and waxing that thing in front of the house, day after day, polluting the environment with God knows what chemicals. It became so irritating that I filed a complaint with the homeowners' board, and they sent him a cease-and-desist notice, and that was the end of that. Not too long afterwards, I was out front picking up the newspaper at the same time Arthur happened to be fetching his. When he caught sight of me, he walked over and told me to stop coming over to his house and pestering his wife. The nerve! Well, trying to bully Geronimo's great-great-granddaughter is always a mistake, so I told him I'd visit whomever I wanted whenever I wanted, and that according to the communal property laws of the great state of Arizona, the house was as much Alexandra's as it was his, so if she invited me over for coffee, as she often did, well, screw him and the horse he rode in on."

"What'd he say to that?"

"He called me an Indian bitch, then stomped back to his house."

A glower replaced the placid expression on her husband's face. "Bitch? *Indian bitch?* You never told me he called you that! If you had…"

"Yeah, yeah, you'd have gone over there and punched his lights out, then he'd bring assault charges against you, and there we'd go again. As if I don't have anything better to do with my time than play Courtroom when I'm not being paid to do it. Remember that time you…" She caught herself. "Anyway, that's why I didn't tell you."

Remember that time you… I made a mental note to have Jimmy run a background check on both Newberrys. Maybe good ol' Monty wasn't as mild-mannered as he appeared.

The story about the Corvette reminded me of something I'd meant to ask earlier, but it took a moment to figure out how best to phrase the question. "From what you've just described, Dr. Cameron had a dark side. It's my guess he kept a tight rein on his family. Would that be accurate?"

"Not really," Margie answered, the anger leaving her face. "At least not from what I observed. You have to remember, Arthur worked very long hours. Emergency room physicians don't exactly have nine-to-five jobs, or six-to-two, whichever. They stay 'til the bleeding stops. If anything, I'd say Arthur was more, ah, emotionally removed from his family than anything else. Alexandra ran that household, not him. She did everything, from researching universities for the children, to calling out the plumber. He couldn't have cared less. The only thing he cared about was his damned cars, and whatever ghastly, chewed-up mess came into the ER."

She'd just given me the perfect intro to bring up finances. And maybe secret bank accounts. "Sounds like Alexandra must've done all the bookkeeping."

Margie nodded. "As if she didn't already have too much to do. Sometimes when I went over there I'd find her half-buried in bills and financial reports, investment portfolios, the whole nine yards. Not that she ever complained. Number-crunching was her thing. Before she married Arthur, she was a CPA for Saxe, Hartnell, and Schaeffer, that big Phoenix accounting firm. She only quit because he wanted her to."

"Did she ever mention anything about missing money?"

"What do you mean, 'missing money'? Alexandra knew where every dime came from and where it went."

"Just wondering." It explained why Dr. Cameron had opened a secret savings account. His wife acted as chief financial officer at their house, and whatever secret thing was going on with him, he wanted to keep his extra income a secret. "You know, Margie, so far everyone I've talked to has described Alexandra as a near-saint, but in my business, and probably yours, we know that very few saints walk the face of this Earth."

A wry smile. "I know what you mean, but if Alexandra had a fault, I never saw it. She was beautiful, but even more than that, Alexandra was *good*." She didn't look at me when she said it, though.

"No hint of an affair?" At her narrowed eyes, I added hastily, "A beautiful woman whose husband worked long hours and sometimes vanished for an entire night, it wouldn't surprise me if she got lonely from time to time."

Margie pursed her lips so tight they almost disappeared. Recognizing that further questions about Alexandra's faithfulness wouldn't be welcomed, I changed the subject.

"How well did you know Alison?"

The fierceness disappeared. "Ali? Like her mother. Bright. Independent. Certainly no killer, regardless of what the papers are hinting, although for legal reasons they aren't outright saying."

"She did confess to planning the murders."

"Show me a teenager who isn't above telling a fib every now and then."

"A murder confession can hardly be categorized as a fib."

She snorted. "Semantics."

Further questioning gleaned no more useful information, other than the fact that Alexandra Cameron was as saintly as she was beautiful; Alison wouldn't hurt a fly; ten-year-old Alec was a budding Einstein; and despite his profession, Dr. Arthur Cameron had the cold soul of a snake.

As the lovebirds, holding hands, escorted me to the door, I asked one final question. "What you do you know about Ralph Parelli, the guy across the street?"

Margie laughed. "An interior decorator with a great art collection. And inherited money."

"Interior decorator?" There went that stereotype.

"Casinos," Mr. Newberry explained. "And nightclubs, the kind movie stars go to. Mobbed up, would be my guess."

Margie gave her husband a warning look. "Better not let Ralph hear you say that. We'll find a dead fish on our doorstep."

He gave her a pat on her skinny rump. "Don't worry, Hon. I'm not as dumb as you think I am."

When the door closed behind me, Geronimo's great-great-granddaughter was giggling like a schoolgirl.

Outside, the day had heated up even further, and the Jeep's upholstery felt like it would ignite any minute. I dug my phone out of my carryall and called Jimmy. He answered right away and he didn't sound happy.

"Why do you keep turning off your phone? I've been trying to reach you all morning. There's news…"

Before he could finish, I said, "Last time I drove around with my phone on I killed the battery. Anyway, I'd like you to run checks on an interior decorator named Ralph Parelli, and Elmont and Margaret Newberry. She's an attorney; I don't know for sure what he does, maybe something in banking, but I'm sure you can…"

"We need to talk, Lena. That's why I've been calling."

"We're talking, but it's hot as hell out here, so make it quick."

An exasperated sigh. "I've found the source of Dr. Cameron's secret bank account, but it's nothing I want to discuss over the phone."

"Great. I'm on my way back to the office…" Oh. There was no office. "For obvious reasons, scratch my last remark. Do you want to meet for coffee somewhere?"

"This isn't the kind of information you'll want bandied around a public place. Where exactly are you right now?"

"Indian Bend area, just west of Scottsdale Road."

"Then hop on Loop 101 and come down to my place. I'll put the coffee on. Or, considering the heat, would you rather have iced tea?"

My partner's tea—a mixture of tea leaves he'd cobbled together himself—was as good as his coffee could be when he wasn't getting fancy, so I pulled out of the cul-de-sac and headed for the freeway. Fifteen minutes later, after muscling my way through a herd of Volvos and Audis, and stopping-and-going around a jackknifed Ikea tractor-trailer, I took the McDowell Road exit east onto the Salt River Pima-Maricopa Reservation.

Although a frequent visitor to Jimmy's place, I'd never checked out his new home office. Last winter he had bought another single-wide and attached it to the back of his house trailer. On the outside, he continued the painted frieze of Pima designs so that from the road the two units blended together perfectly. But inside, the office extension resembled a NASA command center more than a tribute to his tribe's mythology and history. No friendly kachinas danced across those walls, no tribal rugs covered the dull gray linoleum floor. Instead, eight computers in various stages of construction sat atop a long workbench, while on a large U-shaped desk, two more hummed happily away. Another workbench hosted a scanner, two printers, and several machines I couldn't identify.

"Cozy," I said.

"It gets the job done."

When envisioning the life of a private detective, most people summon up the clichéd image of a fedora-hatted, trench coat-wearing man stalking the mean streets of some dark, rainy city. While that may once have been true, it isn't anymore. These days, seventy-five percent of all investigative work is carried out in these brightly lit computer rooms.

Jimmy sat down in an ergonomic chair and patted the seat of its mate. "Sit down. This will take a while."

I wasn't looking forward to that. While the temperature in his living area was cool and comfortable, the office felt like an igloo. How Jimmy had managed to attain meat-locker temps using only window air-conditioning units was a mystery, but goose bumps popped up on my arms the second I stepped inside. Grumbling, I sat down, prepared to make the best of it.

"See if you can hurry this up," I said. "I'm freezing in here, and while the tea is good, it's adding to my misery." I rattled the ice cubes in my tall glass for emphasis, then set it down beside an old Bakelite telephone that looked weirdly out of place in its high-tech environment.

Jimmy tsk-tsked. "Such a delicate flower. But all right, I'll make this fast as I can. Remember my telling you I'd check around to find out why Dr. Cameron received eighteen thousand dollars cash at irregular intervals?"

"Sure. It's one of the stranger elements of this case."

"So is the answer. To start off, I put together a program with a two-year window that compared the dates Cameron received those payments with events that happened around central Arizona at the same time, giving or taking a week. No more, though, because Cameron probably wouldn't allow that kind of money to kick around the house for long."

"Nobody in his right mind would." Especially when he was keeping it secret from his wife.

"Too true. Once I got the program running, it came up with too many possibles. Fatal car crashes. Marriages. Divorces. Births. Rotary dinners. Zoning meetings. School violence incidents.

The list of match-ups was extraordinary, so I narrowed the time gap to two days before and after the deposit. I wasn't optimistic, but lawdy lawdy Miss Clawdy, it worked. Here's the timetable. The hits started back three years ago, when Dr. Cameron made the first eighteen thousand dollar deposit into his account on, ah, October six. In the last couple of years, he made five more deposits, then there was another gap. Skip to this year and he made two deposits, one on the second of January, another on the twelfth. Then one on March twenty-three, another on May two. The date on the deposit slip you found was July eight, the very day of the murders. It all looked, well, weird, so I double-checked, and checked again. Wait'll you see this."

With an intent look, he hit a command on the other computer. A man's face popped up on the screen. I recognized him immediately. Sydney Hoyt: convicted in 1993 of burning his wife and three children alive to collect on the insurance money, executed by lethal injection recently at the Arizona State Prison. He appeared no more vicious than your run-of-the-mill bank clerk.

Jimmy tapped the key again and another man's face came up. I recognized his bland face, too. Kenny Dean Hopper, convicted in 1995 of the execution-style killings of four competing meth dealers and one sixty-seven-year-old grandmother, executed by lethal injection a few days days after Hoyt bit the big one.

Nine more taps, nine more murderers, nine more executions. Only a few of the men actually looked dangerous, which just goes to show.

"Did you notice the execution dates?" Jimmy asked.

"Not after the first two. I was too busy watching the beauty contest. The only state that executes more people than Arizona is Texas, so none of this comes as a big surprise. But why is this related to the Cameron case?" The chill in the room was making me cranky.

Jimmy swiveled his desk chair around to face the other computer, hit a command, and two columns of dates appeared on the screen. Neither column meant anything to me, and I said so.

"Patience," he murmured, then pointed at the screen. "The column on the left gives the dates of the last eleven executions in Arizona, all performed by lethal injection. Those two big gaps? Easily explained by the two times all state executions were put on hold while awaiting a ruling by the Supreme Court. Now look to the right. That column shows the dates Dr. Cameron made an eighteen thousand dollar cash deposit to his mysterious savings account. Look carefully and you'll notice that each deposit was made exactly one day after an execution at the state prison in Florence."

I felt a chill that had nothing to do with the room's hyped-up air-conditioning. "Jimmy, what are you saying?"

He pushed himself away from the computer and faced me. "Lena, unless there's a flaw in my program, and I'm confident there isn't, the good doctor was moonlighting as our official Arizona State Executioner."

Chapter Thirteen

Knowing what I had already heard about Dr. Arthur Cameron, it wasn't difficult to imagine him in pursuit of his state-sponsored duties.

In the execution chamber the condemned man lies strapped to a gurney, his arms outstretched. He is connected to a cardiac monitor which in turn is connected to a printer located in the curtained-off anteroom where the good doctor is waiting. The warden, standing next to the condemned man, asks him if he has any last words.

The condemned man shakes his head.

Outside, in the witnesses' gallery, the condemned man's mother begins to sob.

The warden begins reading the execution order aloud.

Dr. Cameron is listening. He smiles.

As soon as the warden finishes reading the execution order, he leaves the death chamber and joins Dr. Cameron in the anteroom.

He nods to Dr. Cameron. Aware that he is now being watched, the doctor has stopped smiling.

The doctor pushes a plunger, sending a lethal dose of the newest Supreme Court-approved drugs flowing into the condemned man's veins.

The condemned man yawns; he feels sleepy.

His mother's sobs increase.

Dr. Cameron can't hear her, not that it would make any difference. His focus is absolute.

Ten minutes later, the good doctor checks the readout on the printer.

Flat line.

It is finished.

"Seems Cameron didn't take the Hippocratic Oath all that seriously," Jimmy said.

I swallowed. "Guess not."

As I scanned the lists in Jimmy's home office, the computers hummed their electronic symphony while their master explained the results of his online investigations. "Ten executions at eighteen thousand per comes up to one hundred and eighty thousand dollars, the exact amount he had in his savings account. If Dr. Cameron had lived to make that last deposit, it would have been ninety eight."

"Talk about your Angel of Death," I muttered, watching the numbers scroll by.

"Not sure I'd agree with the 'angel' part." Jimmy had never been a proponent of the death penalty. Me, I'm on the fence. Some people are too evil to be allowed to walk this Earth, but… Well, mistakes can be made, and once someone's dead, apologies don't bring the dead back to life.

When I reached the bottom of the lists, I swiveled my chair around. "You realize this could be a game-changer for Ali and Kyle." As an ex-cop, I knew revenge was the third most common reason for murder, following closely behind greed and lust.

"That's what I thought, too. If word somehow leaked about Cameron's role in those executions, there's no telling what one of his victims' family members might have done."

"Victim?"

Jimmy looked thunderous. "I consider 'victim' to be the proper word here, yes."

I didn't feel like arguing. "Okay, okay. What it boils down to is that if Cameron's role in the executions was leaked—although

I can't imagine how, just look at the trouble you had coming up with this—then a number of people had good reason to want him dead." Torturing the doctor's family to death in front of him must have made the killer's revenge even sweeter.

Who made the most likely killer? The anguished relative of an executed man, or a love-besotted teenager? If nothing else, Alison's attorney could play up this information nicely in the defense strategy. And when I informed the Honorable Juliana Thorsson, she'd dance a jig.

"Ali's attorney needs to know about this right away." I said, picking up my cell. And to hell with ethics, Kyle's attorney deserved to know, too.

Jimmy's hand stilled mine. "Don't call the lawyers yet." With that, he slid a fat stack of papers toward me. "Once I double- and triple-checked everything, I did some research on each of the executed men's cases. One of them…Let's just say I came across something very, very interesting. Keep reading. You'll know it when you see it."

"No hints?" I stared down at the papers. The top page featured mug shots of each executed murderer. Grouped together like this, they looked more menacing.

"You won't need hints. Want me to fix us more tea while you read?"

Now that the first shock of Jimmy's discovery had worn off, I realized how cold I was. "Yeah, but let's get out of this refrigerator first."

We left the computers singing their electronic songs and went back to the living area of the trailer, where the temperature felt at least fifteen degrees warmer. While Jimmy busied himself at the kitchen counter, I started reading the account of Kenny Dean Hopper's storied criminal career. The first of his family to go to college, the blond, blue-eyed, preppy-looking Kenny dropped out in his sophomore year to pursue a more lucrative field than the teaching career he'd originally planned. Within months, he was the northwest Phoenix go-to guy for your crystal meth needs.

Three years and two missing partners later, his distribution area had inched up to Cave Creek, where even the bikers feared him.

The party ended in 1995, when a dust-up over Black Canyon City distribution left four men dead and a wounded Kenny Dean bleeding heavily. He hijacked a car at a rest stop off I-17, and after killing the driver—one Rosealee McMannus, an elderly volunteer at St. Mary's Food Bank—eventually crashed Mrs. McMannus' stolen Ford Contour into the guardrail near the exit ramp of Glendale Boulevard. Fortunately, the eight-lane shoot-out that ensued as soon as DPS officers arrived on the scene, hurt no one except Kenny Dean himself. He took another bullet, this one to the knee, which left him with a permanent limp.

Not that it mattered.

After more than twenty years of appeals, Kenny Dean was given a new pair of denims and a blue work shirt. He had already received visits from family members, the prison chaplain, and the warden. According to prison tradition, he ordered his last meal. Fried chicken, white meat only, corn on the cob slathered in real butter, green beans cooked with fatback, sliced tomatoes drizzled in Wishbone Italian dressing, lime Jell-O, and a liter of Mountain Dew.

A man of huge appetites, he finished everything. Then waited.

When the time came, the warden, the chaplain, and a gaggle of guards escorted him down the hall to the execution chamber. The guards strapped him onto the execution table.

He didn't put up a fight.

Kenny Dean's last words on Earth were, "Fuck you all."

"Nice guy," I said to Jimmy, as he set a fresh glass of iced herbal tea in front of me. "But I don't see the 'very, very interesting thing' you were talking about. Just the standard sleazebag bio."

"Take a look at next of kin."

I turned the page over. Kenny Dean left a mother, two sisters, and a fiancée.

"Someone wanted to marry this loser?"

"Love is blind. Keep reading."

"Nag, nag, nag."

Halfway down the last page, I found it.

"Oh."

"'Oh,' is right."

The name of Kenny Dean Hopper's fiancée was Terry Jardine. Otherwise known as Monster Woman.

Although not the most emotional person in the world, Ali's attorney sounded pleased with the information I relayed over the phone while sipping yet another glass of Jimmy's custom-blended tea.

"My, my," Stephen Zellar rasped. "Looks like you're well worth your exorbitant fee, Ms. Jones."

"Takes one to know one, Mr. Zellar."

"Hmm." A pause. Then, "Who would have thought that a respectable physician like Dr. Cameron would have been living such an odd secret life? Killing people for money, tsk tsk. In certain circles, he'd be called a hit man. Oh, well. Judge not, and all that. He probably had expenses. A mistress, perhaps. A gambling problem."

"Don't think so. From what I've been able to ascertain, he was obsessed with classic cars."

"Those can be more expensive than women. Or poker." Zellar sounded like he knew what he was talking about.

"You realize why this opens up our investigation."

A dry chuckle. "The revenge motive, of course. You've told me Dr. Cameron executed eleven men. Eleven! Which means there are eleven grieving families out there, five of them just this year! Any one of those men might have a son, brother, whatever, who believes in an eye for an eye. This will certainly make for an intriguing defense."

"If it gets that far. By the way, I might even have a name for you shortly, but I want to do a little more digging first." Not that I was looking forward to interviewing Monster Woman, aka Terry Jardine, since there was a good chance she'd rip my head off. "How are things on your end? Have you managed to get Ali's confession thrown out yet?"

"I'm afraid the wheels of justice grind more slowly than that, Ms. Jones. Yes, I'm working on it, have already had the papers served to the county attorney, but the whole process will take time. Even if I succeed in getting the confession thrown out, that won't guarantee her release from custody. Don't forget, besides the canine blood, her clothing showed a smear of the victims' blood, too. Her shoes were soaked in it. Yes, the clothing alone is a bit flimsy, and yes, I might be able to get that evidence thrown out, too, but again, it will take time."

Lawyers. With them, it was always one problem after another. "Whatever. I'm going to talk her into retracting that stupid confession."

"Unfortunately, due to a sense of misplaced loyalty to the boy, so far she's been unwilling to do that."

I stifled a groan. Ali's wasn't the only confession needing retraction. There was still a chance—however remote, it now appeared—that Kyle had, in fact, carried out the carnage at the Cameron house. I would know as soon as I got the answer to the question I'd told Fiona Etheridge to ask him.

"Speaking of the Cameron case, Babette's finished putting another hard copy of the case file in a box, and if you check your email, you'll see it duplicated in an attachment. We close at four, being Saturday, so I suggest you pick up the box before then."

"That'll be my next stop," I told him. I was about to end the call when Zellar added, "Ms. Jones, have you given any thought to what will happen if Alison is released? With no surviving relatives nearby, she has no place to go other than a group home, which could be risky for both her and the other children."

"Her uncle…"

He headed me off at the pass. "Dr. Bradley Teague is a resident of Pasadena, California, when he's actually in the U.S., and it's doubtful any judge would allow him to take her to California while she remains under indictment."

"He could move here. Temporarily, of course."

"You've met the man, Ms. Jones. Can you see Dr. Teague doing anything like that?"

I could almost see Zellar's dry smile. "No, I can't," I confessed. Which is where we left it.

Immediately upon ending the call to Zellar, I punched in the number of Kyle's foster mother. Fiona didn't answer, perhaps because she was already at Juvenile Hall visiting Kyle.

"Call me as soon as you get home," I told her voice mail. "It's important."

As I stuffed my cell back into my carryall, Jimmy said, "We have an appointment to meet with an arson investigator from Scottsdale PD and a representative from Scottsdale Restore at three. The insurance guy's going to be there, too. And, oh joy, the owner of the building. Have you had lunch yet?"

"I'm not really hungry."

He frowned. "Thou shalt not fib."

"Who says I'm fibbing?"

"Your growling stomach. Why don't you let me fix us something? Or we can head over to Denny's. It's on the way."

"You cook?"

"*Iron Chef* is one of my favorite TV shows. You'd be amazed at what I've picked up."

Soon we were lunching on chicken salad crunched up with slivered almonds, served on a mixture of Bibb lettuce, heirloom tomatoes, and alfalfa sprouts. The Parmesan whole wheat muffins he'd baked himself were pretty good, too.

"You keep surprising me," I said, licking herbed butter off my fingers.

"Maybe you should pay closer attention." He glanced at his watch. "We'd better get a move on. Want to ride over in my nice air-conditioned truck?"

I briefly considered it. Yes, I needed to talk to Kyle's foster mother, which I could easily accomplish by cell, but an in-person visit to Ali was definitely in the cards, and as soon as possible. If the interview with Ali proved as successful as I hoped, I would need to talk to the Honorable Juliana Thorsson, too.

"Separate cars," I answered.

Thirty minutes later we were touring what was left of Desert Investigations. Percy Simms, the building's owner, looked near-suicidal until a consultation with the insurance agent lifted his spirits. After that, he drove off without saying a word to me.

The conversation with Detective Howard Lopez was brief, too. "Other than this Terry Jardine person, do you have any other known enemies?" he asked.

This made Jimmy grin. "Would you like the list in alphabetical order or by date of threat?"

"Terry Jardine's vehicle matches an eye-witness' account," I said, heading off the long recital of people Desert Investigations had helped jail. "We had Ms. Jardine's vehicle towed for continually parking in our private space, which I doubt she was happy about. Besides that, there are indications she might have drug issues. As well as, ah, other personal problems."

Such as a history of being romantically attracted to homicidal maniacs like Kenny Dean Hopper.

After jotting down the names of other grudge-holders Jimmy so merrily supplied, Detective Lopez left, and Gavin Biddle, our insurance agent, took over.

"It could be worse," he said, ever the optimist. "The office will have to be rebuilt, although the contents of your fireproof cabinets may be salvageable. Still, the computers and furniture were totaled, as were the carpets and paneling. The good news is that the flames didn't reach your upstairs apartment. The bad news? Some water damage, plus the smoke odor permeates everything: walls, carpet, furniture, mattress, linens, clothing, et cetera. But Scottsdale Restoration will take care of that for you, no problem."

"How soon before I can move back in?"

"The apartment or the office?"

"Apartment."

"Two weeks, maybe. The office, well, that's going to take longer, because essentially, you'll be building a new one. What with the construction boom we're having now…" He shrugged. "Who knows?"

Oh, great. Not only was I homeless, but I would continue officeless for ages, stuck in that damned motel, driving back and forth from Jimmy's frigid computer room.

Unless…

I thought of chicken salad with almonds. Home-baked Parmesan muffins.

Then I thought of Desert Investigations' case files accessible at a mere keystroke. As long as Jimmy kept coffee or iced tea coming, I could put up with the temperature.

"Does your offer still hold?" I asked Jimmy after Biddle and Detective Lopez drove away.

"What offer?" He wiped some soot off his hands with a clean white handkerchief.

"To let me crash at your place."

He looked up. "Of course it still holds."

"You're not worried your relatives will talk?"

"No problem. Pimas aren't big on gossip."

"Then how about your girlfriend, what's-her-name. How will she feel about me staying at your trailer?"

When he raised his eyebrows, the tribal tattoo on his temple moved upwards a quarter of an inch. "You mean Cynthia? Also no problem. She's back in jail for violating parole. Been there three months, as a matter of fact."

"Oh."

Jimmy's love life was even more dysfunctional than mine. Whereas I tend to choose partners who are emotionally unavailable, Jimmy is a born fixer-upper. In the same way he fixes abandoned trailers, he tries to fix crazy women. The trailers work out. The women don't.

"I really am sorry, Jimmy. I thought you two…"

"You think too much." He put the handkerchief back into his pocket. "How about coq au vin?"

"Huh?"

"For dinner."

"Sounds delicious."

He flashed white teeth. "Take care of what you have to, then, and I'll see you when I see you. Dinner will be simmering on the stove." With that, he got back into his pickup and drove off.

As his truck turned the corner, my cell rang. It was Kyle's foster mother. To get out of the merciless sun, I moved down the street a few feet and into the shadowed entrance to Hugo White Feather's Indian Jewelry, where the temperature was a few degrees cooler.

"Glen and I just returned from seeing Kyle," Fiona Etheridge said, her voiced teary. "He's not doing well at all, just keeps saying he's sorry about everything and wants to come home. But when I asked him if he'd recant his confession, he refused. He's still protecting Ali. I know I shouldn't hate that poor girl but I think I'm starting to."

"Did you ask the question I told you to ask?"

"The one about why he tried to kill the dog?"

"Yes. That one."

Behind me, the door opened, and a whoosh of air-conditioning rushed out, followed by the store's owner.

"Lena, either come in here or go stand in someone else's doorway," Hugo White Feather pleaded. "You're scaring away my customers."

"Hold on," I said to Fiona. Turning to Hugo, I asked, "What customers? There's not a soul on the street. Too hot."

"Shows how much you're aware of your surroundings these days," Hugo answered. "A man and a woman almost came in a minute ago, then they took one look at the expression on your face and crossed the street. Just get in here and out of the doorway, okay? For old time's sake? Oh, and I'm sorry about your office. If you need any help cleaning up, let me know. I've got a big mop and an industrial-size vacuum cleaner."

Grateful for a respite from the heat, I followed Hugo into the store and stood by the counter. Indian chants were playing over the sound system—Pawnee, I think—but not loudly enough to interfere with my conversation.

"The question, Fiona. Did you ask it?"

She didn't answer right away because she had to blow her nose first. "Yes, yes, I asked."

"Did he answer? I need to know."

"In…in a way, I guess he did, but…but it didn't make sense, considering what I've heard about what…what happened at that house."

I took a deep breath to calm my frustration. "Just tell me what Kyle said. I don't care how nonsensical it sounds."

"Well, when I asked, he got even more upset and said that we should know him better than to believe he'd ever hurt an animal. After that, he refused to talk anymore. At least the guards let us hug him. That's when I started crying, which I swore I wouldn't do."

I let out my breath.

To my right, Hugo was rearranging a black velvet tray filled with turquoise and silver rings. One of them had two large, rough-cut ovals of turquoise embraced by fat squash leaves. It wasn't dainty, but it was beautiful.

"There may be good news for you soon," I told Fiona. "Just give me a couple of days. In the meantime, keep visiting and hugging."

A sniff. "As if Glen and I would do anything else."

When we said our good-byes, I stashed the cell into my carryall and walked over to the turquoise ring display. I pointed a ring-less finger.

"Hugo, can I try on that two-stone job?"

Time to celebrate.

Two hundred and thirty dollars and seventy-six cents poorer, but a whole lot more optimistic, I stopped by Zellar's office and picked up the new case file. Not taking any chances, I drove it straight to Jimmy's trailer—he was already working away—and stowed it in the guest bedroom. Then I took off for the juvenile detention center.

Since it wasn't normal visiting hours there was no wait, and within minutes a middle-aged corrections officer who seriously needed to diet showed me to an antiseptic-smelling interview room furnished with only chairs and a metal table. Almost as soon as I sat down, another corrections officer, this one a woman wearing magazine-cover makeup, ushered in a fierce-looking Alison Cameron and directed her to sit. She did, but she didn't look happy about it. Her arms crossed in defiance and the frown on her face appeared deeper than when we last met. A tic at the corner of her right eye was the only clue to her true condition. It ticced so hard that as she scowled across the table at me, she appeared to be winking.

"You again." She sounded hoarse. Did she cry at night, when no one was around?

"Yep, it's me again, your friendly pay-per-diem private investigator."

"Anyone ever tell you you're a smart ass?"

"Plenty of people, plenty of times. But I come bearing good news *if*—and it's a big if, Ali—you answer my questions truthfully. For a change."

Now she looked wary, as if concerned I was about to play a trick on her, which I was. "I'm not telling you anything, bitch."

"Doesn't take long in juvie to toughen a girl up, does it?"

The scowl deepened.

"Anyway, you might change your mind about things when you hear what I have to say."

"As if."

"Right. So let's get to it. As I'm certain your attorney has told you, we've received copies of your unwise statements to the arresting officers, and Mr. Zellar is at present trying to get your 'confession' thrown out. Should be a slam dunk, he says, since you're under age and the arresting officers didn't properly Mirandize you. And when…"

"Doesn't matter," she sulked. "I still did it."

"Don't interrupt. As I was about to say, when you were arrested, you and Kyle were together and you were covered in blood. Kyle, not so much. But know what? The lab tests are back and as it turns out, most of that blood on you was dog blood, probably Misty's. But just one small smear of human blood, and that was from your mother. Considering the violence of the crimes and the state of the house, that's an interesting detail. But here's the really fascinating part, Ali. Kyle claims he never hurt Misty, that he never laid a finger or a baseball bat on her. If he didn't, who did?"

"But…He said…he said…" She stammered to a halt, looking confused.

When I slammed my hand down on the metal table, my new silver-and-turquoise ring clanged like a hammer on an anvil. *"Kyle said what?!"*

Eyes wide in alarm, she responded, "He asked…he asked if I wanted him to put her out of her misery. But I told him no, that we should take her to the vet."

"When he asked you that, did he have the bat in his hands?" She nodded.

"Which is how his fingerprints wound up on the murder weapon. Not because he'd killed anyone with it. Or clubbed Misty."

"Of course not! Didn't I tell you he didn't kill anyone? I told you! Again and again! I told them all! But nobody listens to me!"

She yelled so loud the corrections officer stationed outside looked in, concerned. I told her everything was fine and waved her back out.

"Calm down. Ever think that no one believed you because of that cockamamie story about hiring a hit man with your allowance money? Here's another thing. I searched Kyle's room, and guess what I found? A big pack of love letters from you. In one of them, you wrote that you wished your parents were dead and suggested he kill them."

Her face resumed its former hostility, but her fingers dug so deeply into her crossed arms they'd undoubtedly leave bruises. "I changed my mind and hired a hit man."

One of the best tactics when interviewing a hostile witness is to switch subjects for a while, then circle back. That's what I did. "Who were you closest to, your mother or your father?"

She blinked several times. "Why's it matter?"

"Because now that your Uncle Bradley's in town to claim the bodies, the funeral can start. Want to attend? If you do, there's a chance your attorney can work out the arrangements."

More blinking. "I...I..."

"I've heard you were scared of your father, so maybe not."

A lone tear escaped all that blinking. Her tough façade was crumbling.

Once your subject's true self emerges, a certain amount of emotional cruelty is another effective interview tactic. Although I hated what I was about to do, Ali needed one more shock to complete the deconstruction process. Of course, I'd be taking a physical risk if I was wrong about her, but such was the reality of my job.

Watching her body language carefully, I sat back in my chair, increasing the distance between us, preparing myself for what I hoped would be the last necessary stab in the heart. Steeling myself, I vented a long, theatrical sigh.

"Oh, I get it. You were scared of them both, weren't you? Your father and your mother. No surprise there. Hell, the neighbors tell me both your parents beat you and your brother every day. What a nasty, dysfunctional family you had, your poor little thing. But how's this? Go ahead and attend, but keep your eyes and ears closed until they start talking about your brother. Then when burying time comes, it'll go by faster, his grave being half the size of your parents'."

She turned so white I feared she might come across the table at me. But I'd been right: the brave, loyal little fool didn't have a violent bone in her body. She just sat there wounded, lower lip trembling, a curtain of tears joining that first slippage.

Time to circle back around.

I softened my voice and said my first true words. "You really loved your parents, didn't you, Ali?"

Her breath came in short, sharp hitches. "They...they're lying."

"Who's lying?" Would I ever get over hating myself for this?

"The neighbors who...who said that...that ugly stuff about my parents."

"Your parents didn't beat you?"

"Never. They never ever hit me. Or Alec."

"You're saying they were good parents? The both of them?"

She looked at the ceiling. Gulped.

I sat there silently, giving her more time to recover from my unforgivable cruelty.

Finally she was ready. Staring red-eyed across the table at me, she wept, "They...they were the best mom and dad ever. I would never ever hurt them. And Alec? I loved that little kid so much!"

I handed her a fat wad of tissues, let her wipe her face and blow her nose. Then I allowed the compassion I actually felt to slip into my voice. "I know they were good parents, Ali. And I know something else, too. Kyle did not kill your family. He only said he did to protect you. Just like you've been shouldering the blame to protect *him*."

She glanced across warily, not yet ready to trust me. Smart of her, really.

"What makes you think that, Miss Know-It-All?" The old Ali spirit was back.

I crossed my heart in the global I'm-telling-the-truth gesture. "Because I think I know who killed them, but the police won't follow up as long as you keep saying you did it. The minute you stop copping to the murders, Kyle will stop playing hit man. Tell the truth and save him, as well as your own silly ass."

The scowl returned. "You bitch."

What spirit! For a fleeting moment I regretted not having a daughter.

With a smile, I said, "An astute observation, but this bitch is going to get you and your boyfriend out of juvie. Now, are you willing to meet with your attorney and formally retract your confession?"

She gave me a surly nod.

"Excellent. Then my work here is done."

I stood and headed for the door. The sooner I got out of this depressing place, the better.

"Wait!"

I turned. "Yes, Ali?"

In the seconds it had taken me to reach the door, she had deflated from woman to child. Her voice was so small I could hardly hear here when she mumbled, "You better catch who did it before I do."

Chapter Fourteen

Ali

I hate that Lena person, saying those awful things about Mom and Dad, even if she did say it just to make me talk. That my parents would, like, beat me? As if! Dad never hurt anybody, he saved their lives, and Mom, God, what didn't she do for people, especially kids?

Mom was the only adult any of them could talk to if something was wrong, and they did. They told Mom everything, even if it would cause trouble. When Elena told her what was going on at home, Mom called Child Protective Services on that awful guy who was messing with her and got him arrested, even though they had to let him out again when Elena took it all back and then told him who she told—Mom. Boy, was he mad! He came over and told her he'd get even with her no matter what. I wonder if he, like, did it. Just because he moved his family to Alaska doesn't mean he didn't, like, get on a plane and fly back.

Maybe I'll tell Lena about that. Even better, I can pretend I saw something, just to make sure the cops fly up to Alaska and arrest him again. All us kids know he was really messing with Elena, we talked about it all the time, but she was scared to admit it to anyone but Mom, so it wouldn't be bad for me to, like, lie if it gets him caught, would it?

I'm so mad at myself for thinking Kyle would do anything to hurt Mom and Dad and Alec and Misty, but he was so good to me I could really kinda see him doing something majorly extreme if he thought I was being hurt like Elena was being hurt, but I never actually told him to do anything like that, did I? I was just mad because Mom said me and Kyle should, like, cool it.

Me and Kyle, we've found true love! Why'd she want us to stop loving each other just so years and years could go by and I'd wind up in a marriage like hers and Dad's? I love them both, but Mom would've been happier with somebody else, maybe even with that weird old Ralph guy next door, he's so crazy about her he'd do anything for her, and everybody knows it. But he sure doesn't know I know it.

And Dad, he'd be happy with whoever, just as long as they stayed out of his way and let him buy a million cars. Why shouldn't Dad buy what he wanted? He worked hard, didn't he, so why shouldn't he buy up every car lot in Scottsdale?

Me, I'm gonna buy whatever I want, too. Once the cops let me out of this shitty place and Kyle and I make it big in Hollywood, we're gonna take our money and buy a whole library and, like, turn it into a house and we'll rescue all the abused and lonely animals, and we'll invite Mom and Dad and Alec over for dinner and we'll…

Oh.

Chapter Fifteen

Lena

It took a while to recover from my interview with Ali. Fortunately, I'd found a parking space on the shady side of the building, so I was able to sit in the Jeep until I stopped shaking. Cruelty never came easy to me, especially toward a child, but it goes with the territory. There are times we investigators must harden our hearts in order to get the truth. Those times always come with an emotional blow-back.

Five minutes and a couple of tissues later, I cleared my throat and speed dialed Stephen Zellar. I'd like to say Ali's attorney was all joy at the news she was ready to retract her confession, but I'd be lying. In an only mildly pleased voice, he said, "Nice work, Ms. Jones. I'll get down there before she has a chance to change her mind."

"She won't."

"You never know what kids will do."

I let that pass. "But now that she's retracting it, that'll help get the case against her dismissed, right?"

"It's a step in the right direction. What would really help is if you could get some proof to back up her new story."

He was right, of course. "So once she formally recants, what then?'

"We'll have to wait and see. But first, I have to arrange an emergency meeting with the judge and Aaron Hyatt, the county attorney. The weekend's coming up, and if I remember correctly, Judge Benson's taking his family up to Sedona. Six kids, the wife, two brothers-in-law, the mother-in-law, the whole clan." A laugh, then a very un-Zellarish comment. "Sucks to be him."

Judge Benson's family problems were none of my concern. "Can you manage it today?"

"Rest assured I'll have Babette clear my calendar as soon as we hang up. She'll also place calls to Benson and Hyatt. They are both reasonable men, which is a plus. One reminder, though. In the event that I am able to get Alison released, which isn't certain, mind you, since she is an orphaned minor and there is yet no designated guardian. If, and I stress *if,* she's released from juvenile detention, as a minor she will still be under the auspices of Child Protective Services. Their oversight will continue unless Dr. Teague is granted guardianship, or at the very least, temporary guardianship. Perhaps even then."

Given my own experiences with CPS, the fact that the girl would remain under their jurisdiction alarmed me. Most group homes and foster parents were fine, but the ones that weren't fine were horrific. "Will you call Dr. Teague or shall I?"

"I'm going to be very, very busy for the next few hours, so I will leave the honors to you. Then I'll finalize everything. If he accepts. Now, I have to go…"

"One more thing," I interrupted.

"There always is with you, Ms. Jones."

"Ali wants to attend the funeral."

After a moment's silence, he said, "Excellent. If I can arrange it, no guarantee there, either, it will look good, very good. Our Miss Alison has turned out to be a wise young woman, hasn't she? Do me a favor and convey her wishes to her uncle, and I'll take care of whatever red tape is necessary on that front. And then we'll see."

Agreeing to keep in touch, we ended the call, but not before the tenor of Zellar's final comments registered: he believed Ali was only playing to the court of public opinion by her request to attend her family's funeral. Did that mean he wasn't convinced of her innocence? If her own attorney wasn't sure she hadn't killed her family, how would her story fare with the public, which had already been incited to a near-lynch mentality by the non-stop news coverage? Only yesterday the *Phoenix Morning Herald*, a yellow rag seldom lauded for excellence in journalism, had published an alarming two-page spread on the upsurge of what they termed "killer kids," detailing the bloody deeds committed by children across the country during the past decade. It read like a horror novel.

Nothing like influencing potential jurors while two as-yet-presumed-innocent kids sat in jail.

Aware that I was entering verboten legal territory yet again, I called Curtis Racine, Kyle Gibbs' attorney and gave him a highly unethical summation of my meeting with Ali. His reaction was more emotional than Zellar's.

"Looks like someone finally talked that girl into showing some sense," he said, after venting a cheer. "Couldn't be you, could it, Ms. Jones? Unfortunately, there could be a downside to this. If the girl really does withdraw her confession, it could put my own client in a precarious position. But remember, we're not having this conversation. I would never talk to an opposing counsel's investigator. Never."

"Of course you wouldn't. And I'm not talking to you, either. Be that as it may, Kyle will only be harmed if he continues to cling to his own crazy story, which is why I called you, even though we're not, as you say, having this conversation. When you talk to Kyle, and I hope you manage it today, stress that Ali only confessed to planning the murders because she thought he was the killer. Once he realizes Ali had nothing to do with the murders, he'll tell the truth, too."

"I hope you're right."

"In matters like these, I usually am." My voice conveyed more confidence than I felt. There was always the chance Kyle would suspect he was being played by the authorities, and Ali hadn't changed her story at all.

After ending the call, the sweat rolling down my face alerted me that I had been sitting in the heat of the day for far too long. The outside thermometer on a billboard across the way registered a hundred and ten, and shade or no shade, I was beginning to feel light-headed. Time to hydrate.

A few minutes later I was ensconced at Echo Coffee, drinking a giant-sized latte and several glasses of water. Although it was too late for the lunch crowd and too early for the Early Bird dinner crowd, the place buzzed with customers yakking away on their cell phones. From the snatches of conversation I heard, most were job-hunting, although it sounded like the haggard-looking man in the booth closest to me was on a conference call, hashing through a financial settlement with his soon-to-be ex-wife.

Finally rehydrated, I joined the chattering masses by placing a call to Dr. Teague. It didn't take long for Ali's uncle to understand the rapidly changing game plan.

"Guess that means I'll have to accept responsibility for her." He didn't sound enthusiastic.

Poor Ali. Even if she escaped becoming a ward of the state, it didn't take a fortune-teller to foresee her future: a boarding school far away from her uncle, followed by a university equally distant. Unlike his murdered brother, Dr. Bradley Teague exhibited no desire to be a father. He was too busy saving the world.

"Tell me, Dr. Teague, did you know your brother worked as the state executioner?"

A pause, as if he was gathering his thoughts, then, "We had words about it, yes. And it created a rift between us, even more so than that IVF business. To tell the truth, I haven't spoken to my brother or his family since I found out. That was, what, three years ago. Doctors should save lives, not take them. We are pledged to…"

Fearing another self-righteous sermon, I cut him off at the pass. "You didn't feel it was necessary to tell me what you knew?"

"It's not like Arthur's extracurricular activities had anything to do with his death. I thought Ali did it."

Ali. *Your niece. The one you haven't seen in three years, you cold-hearted son of a bitch.* I took a deep breath and forced myself to calm down. "If you'd told me what you knew, it would have saved a lot of work."

"Why?"

Oh, for God's sake. "Because it means plenty of other people had a motive to kill your brother!"

The clattering and chattering in Echo ceased. Baristas and job-seekers alike turned their heads to stare, mouths agape. The man who had been arguing with his soon-to-be ex-wife stopped snarling at her and joined the gawking crowd. With difficulty, I lowered my voice.

"Don't you even care, Dr. Teague?"

Another pause. "When's the soonest my niece might get released?"

The man was hopeless. "There's no guarantee on that, and even if it happens, it'll depend on how fast Stephen Zellar can work his magic. In the meantime, we need to talk about the funeral. Have you arranged it yet? Ali wants to attend."

"She does?" He sounded downright disapproving.

"Yes, Dr. Teague. She does."

A sigh. "All right. As it stands now, the memorial service will take place at ten a.m. Tuesday, the interment following immediately afterwards. Side-by-side plots, of course. I've, uh, I've prepared a eulogy for Alexandra." His voice wobbled as he pronounced Alexandra's name, revealing feelings that ran deeper than toward his brother or nephew. Or his niece, for that matter.

But I let it go. "Call Zellar and tell him to draw up the guardianship papers. Or leave a message re that, if he's not in. As for the funeral, if the judge allows Ali to attend, remember that she will be under guard. What church and cemetery are we talking about?"

Teague named a church he probably wouldn't have chosen if he had known more about its liberal bent—a couple of its priests were always getting arrested for protesting various human rights abuses—but his choice of cemeteries was refreshingly old-fashioned. Instead of the new easy-to-care-for modern burial grounds that banned anything other than ground-level plaques, the cemetery hewed to the old custom of marble crypts and weeping angel statuary.

"See you at the memorial service, then," I said.

"Oh, you don't need bother to attend."

"Yes, I do." After today's conversation with Ali, the kid might hate me, but at the very least she deserved to be around someone with feelings.

After ringing off, I called Margie Newberry, told her the funeral plans, and asked her to get the word out. I didn't want the Camerons' last day on Earth to be accompanied only by Dr. Teague and a priest who didn't even know them. Margie, bless her crusty heart, agreed.

Next, I called the Honorable Juliana Thorsson. As soon as I started to explain Ali's new situation, she demanded I drive over for a confab. She actually used that word.

Twenty minutes later I was sitting across from Thorsson in her overly air-conditioned living room, but this time I welcomed the frigidity.

"You've done fine work, Ms. Jones," she said, after hearing the latest developments on the case. Despite her words, her blue eyes remained as chilly as her air-conditioned condo. I could feel goose bumps popping up on my bare arms.

"Thank you. Since I've managed to get Ali to recant her confession, as well as finding a host of new suspects, you may not need my services anymore. If you wish, I can mail my final invoice to you Monday." Not that I planned to stop working on the case. Just the opposite. I had every intention of finding out who had killed the Cameron family, but I could do that on my own dime.

Oblivious to my thinking, Thorsson gave me a wintry smile. "Final invoice? Oh, I think not."

"Well, then, you can wait until the charges are dropped against Ali, which they probably will be. Eventually, that is."

Those frigid eyes didn't flicker. "Our arrangement still holds."

"Which was to pave the way for getting charges dropped against your…" I'd been about to say "daughter," but was Ali really Thorsson's daughter in any accepted sense of the word? The politician was merely an egg donor. She hadn't raised Ali, held birthday parties for Ali, shuttled Ali to soccer games, bandaged Ali's bloody knees, soothed Ali's tears, or done any of the things real mothers do. Strictly speaking, Thorsson was a biological lend-lease apparatus, nothing more. "…uh, Ali." I rephrased. "Granted, even with the recanted confession, it can take a while."

She shook her head. "If there's one thing a politician is expert on, Ms. Jones, it's image control. Regardless of that 'person of interest' phrase the media so loves to use these days, most people will view Ali as a killer until the actual killer is caught and successfully prosecuted, and we're still a long way from that. Do you want suspicion to follow that girl for the rest of her life?"

I put aside my shock that Thorsson and I actually agreed on something. "Of course I don't. But you understand that many murders remain unsolved, right? I can't guarantee anything."

"Which is understandable. But these days our fine law enforcement officers labor under too many handicaps. That foolish Miranda business, for instance, informing criminals about their so-called rights, I find that disgraceful. And then there's the forbidding of enhanced questioning, all the new chain-of-evidence rulings, and now this DNA foolishness. It's a wonder the authorities ever bring any criminal investigation to a successful conclusion. But as a private citizen, you can ignore those encumbrances, can't you?"

Without waiting for an answer, she continued, "As you know, before I retained you, I checked you out thoroughly and discovered that on these sorts of cases, your solve rate is higher than Scottsdale PD's. So what if you skip over some of the legal niceties? You accomplish what's necessary, and that's the only thing that counts. In fact, if what you've just told me about Ali's father is true, I'll wager you already have some ideas."

"Yes, I do, and I plan on passing those ideas to the proper authorities for follow-up."

A faint expression of disapproval crossed her face. "Unfortunate. Nevertheless, I want you to continue your investigation into the case and identify the killer. Or killers, plural, as the case may be. I never saw how one person, let alone a fourteen-year-old boy, could have killed three people—including one physically-able adult male—without help."

"Well, there was a gun involved, but according to the case files, the boy's hand showed no gunshot residue. And the gun, a 9mm Beretta, was never found."

She grunted. "Nice firearm. Well. I have no problem, Ms. Jones, with you turning your findings over to the police department and letting them make the arrest." She pointed a stern, manicured finger at me. "But no overt vigilantism. Nothing that would jeopardize the case."

"You mean I can't waterboard anyone? Damn!" I gave her a cold smile of my own.

She matched it. "*Au contraire*, Ms. Jones. I would gladly pay to see that. However, given the abysmal state of the criminal justice system these days, I do want to make certain that the person or persons who ruined Ali's life will have no legitimate grounds for appeal once he has been found guilty in a court of law."

Ruined Ali's life. Those were Thorsson's beliefs, not mine. She hadn't met Ali, never experienced the girl's grit.

"Don't worry, I'll be careful not to screw up any subsequent trial," I assured her. "But before I start chasing down other suspects, I'm curious about something."

Blond eyebrows raised. "What 'something' is that?"

"What are your feelings about the fact that your biological daughter's father served as Arizona's state executioner?"

She shrugged those elegant shoulders. "Someone has to do it."

Regardless of the Honorable Juliana Thorsson's confidence in my investigative skills, Desert Investigations faced a daunting task. Finding the Camerons' killer—or killers, plural—could prove impossible. In the past three years alone, the doctor had executed ten men and one woman, each of whom had a family. One of those family members might have craved a certain rough justice of his own. True, Jimmy could come up with their names, but tracking them down would be time-consuming.

While I suffered through the afternoon rush hour traffic on Scottsdale Road, I let my mind roam, trying to ignore the acrid stink of hot asphalt, the complaints of the Jeep's over-warm engine. By the time I turned into the Best Western's parking lot on Indian School Road, I had landed on two questions I should have asked myself earlier, but didn't.

Question Number One: How had the killer found out Dr. Cameron's identity? For decades, the names of Arizona's state executioners had been a closely guarded secret. To keep them from being traced, the executioners were always paid in cash so that their names would not appear on a correctional department payroll check. And although the media always ran in-depth "Death Watch" stories every time an execution approached, no enterprising investigative journalist had yet been able to come up with an executioner's name. Jimmy had been able to do it, yes, but his level of skill was rare even in hacking circles.

Which led to Question Number Two: Let's say the near-impossible was true. If one of the condemned men's families contained a computer whiz kid who possessed the same talent, would Jimmy be able to locate him? Most of the websites Jimmy used to snuffle out Dr. Cameron's part-time job were public postings, merely dates and events. Anyone who cared had access to the same information. Backtracking visitors to those same sites would be a Herculean task, perhaps impossible, but given the execution dates…

Maybe. Just maybe.

Although Cameron had been performing his service to the state of Arizona for several years, I decided to confine my focus to executions taking place this year. Earlier than that, the passion for revenge would probably have cooled. As I climbed out of my Jeep, I ran the more recent execution dates through my mind.

Maleese Young—January 1
Sidney Hoyt—January 11
Beulah Phelps—March 22
Blaine DuCharme—May 1
Kenny Dean Hopper—July 7

That last date caught my attention. It was the day before the Cameron murders.

Parched from the long, hot drive, I made a beeline for the vending machine in the Best Western's snack alcove. Not a lot of selections, mainly water, presweetened teas, and artificially flavored fruit drinks. No Tab, my preferred drink, just several other species of Coke. I chose the least exotic: Diet Coke. When the cold can rattled down the chute, I picked it up and pressed it against my forehead. Ahhh.

As I climbed the stairs to my second-floor room, something else occurred to me. There was no guarantee that the killer was linked to Dr. Cameron's grim freelance job, and I might be jumping the gun here. I'd already discovered that his own brother didn't approve of him and his neighbors didn't much like him. Who else harbored negative feelings about him? People in the medical profession are notoriously closed-mouthed, but a visit to Good Samaritan Hospital was probably necessary. Maybe Cameron had saved the life of a gang member, to the disgust of a rival gang. Or maybe he'd failed to save a life, and a grief-addled relative decided to make him pay. Then again, maybe one of Good Sam's other doctors, or even a nurse, held a grudge against him. Granted, it would have to be a pretty big grudge to result in such a horrific crime, but at this point, anything was possible.

Something else bothered me. So far, everyone I'd talked to, especially the murdered man's brother, had described Alexandra Cameron as a near-saint. I didn't believe in saints. Everyone has secrets, especially beautiful women who sound too good to be true.

Then there was Terry Jardine. Monster Woman.

Interviewing her presented a problem in more ways than one. Since she was the leading suspect in the firebombing of Desert Investigations, I had to be careful not to muck up the arson inquiry. Still, murder trumped arson, and considering her relationship to the executed Kenny Dean Hopper, there was no denying that Jardine was a strong suspect. She was certainly strong enough to inflict the damage I'd seen in the crime scene photographs, and crazy enough to do it.

The clincher? Kenny Dean Hopper, Monster Woman's erstwhile fiancé, had been executed the day before the Cameron murders.

When I opened the door to my room, a gust of cool air rushed out to meet me. I scurried into its frigid embrace and kicked the door shut. After setting my carryall down on the bed I grabbed the TV remote and clicked on CNN, hoping Thorsson had somehow not graced that cable channel with an interview. I lucked out, in more ways than one. Her patrician face, backed by the avid, slightly crazed, faces of her supporters, never showed. Instead, while I'd been working, the world had become more peaceful than usual. Only one suicide bombing in a Baghdad market, only one little girl's face attacked with acid in Kandahar, only two drowning victims in a Bangladeshi typhoon, only one workplace shooting at a St. Louis factory, and only four teens murdered in Chicago.

Satan must have been napping.

Caught up on the day's carnage, I popped open the Diet Coke can and chugged it, reveling in its frosty run down my esophagus. Since I was already wired, I didn't need the caffeine, but what you gonna do? I made a mental note to stop by a Circle K on the way to Jimmy's and pick up a six-pack of some of the caffeine-free species, otherwise I'd be awake all night. Thirst slaked, I stripped off my sweaty clothes and treated myself to a cold shower. After I'd lowered my body temperature to a more comfortable level, I wrapped myself in a thick towel and checked my phone messages.

Six calls were from Desert Investigations' clients. They had read about the firebombing and wanted to know how it would affect their cases. Most were from companies wanting background checks of potential employees, but one was from Jennifer Longley, a too-doting mother who'd hired me to investigate her son's fiancée. I returned the calls and reassured the clients that work on their cases continued unabated. In the Longley case, nothing negative had yet been discovered about the fiancée in question. Mama Longley didn't sound pleased at this news; she'd hated the girl at first sight.

Telephone work finished, I dressed and went downstairs to the motel office, where the amiable manager told me that yes, he would cancel the rest of my reservation, but there would be a penalty. "Scottsdale in July isn't exactly the summer destination of choice, so I'm sure you understand," he said.

We commiserated with each other over the ungodly heat for a couple of minutes before I went back to my room and packed up what few things I'd brought with me.

Then I left for Jimmy's trailer.

A man of his word, my partner had dinner simmering on the stove. Coq au vin, served with slow-roasted potatoes, crusty French bread, and apple cobbler for desert. It was all delicious.

"I'll get fat staying with you," I said, staring at my empty plate.

Jimmy looked smug. "Enjoy it while you can. Besides, you could use a little more weight."

"What, I'm too thin?"

"How many meals do you average a day?"

"Two, usually. Breakfast and dinner. You know my schedule. Half the time I'm too busy for lunch."

"See what I mean? Another five or even ten pounds wouldn't hurt you."

I smiled. "In that case, I'll have some more cobbler."

After finishing the second helping, it was all I could do to keep from licking the bowl.

"I'll wash, you dry," Jimmy said, as he cleared the table.

When he handed me a dishtowel that had ARIZONA—THE GRAND CANYON STATE printed on it, he caught sight of my new ring. "That's a big hunk of turquoise and silver you've got there."

"Too big?"

"Not for you. In an emergency, you can substitute it for brass knuckles."

"There's an idea."

Companionably, we started on the dishes.

For a brief moment I missed my little apartment again, where after a meal all I had to do was throw away a paper plate. Then again, my usual dinner of ramen noodles didn't taste like coq au vin or apple cobbler.

"Did you check out the Camerons' neighbors?" I asked, as I dried a big serving platter. It had a picture of a smiling turkey painting on it.

"As soon as you called. That Parelli guy? No record, no wants, no warrants, but a lot of his friends look fishy, and two of his brothers got popped for mob-related activities. Extortion, mid-level dealing, et cetera. You know what they say about birds of a feather. Still, I saw some publicity photos of the hot spots he worked on and as far as talent goes, he's the real deal. Did you know that, besides other trendy night spots he's responsible for, he decorated the Python Lounge?"

The Python Lounge was one of Scottsdale's flashiest clubs, catering only to the very rich and very famous. Its regulars included the starting lineup of the Phoenix Suns, as well as a never-ending stream of visiting music, film, and TV stars.

"Fancy," I said.

He gave me a plate. "Not so fancy is the Camerons' other neighbor, Elmont "Monty" Newberry. He's been arrested twice for battery, although both times the charges were dropped. Never served a day, even though one of the guys he hit suffered two broken ribs and a fractured eye socket."

I remembered Monty's thin, aristocratic face, his obvious affection for his fierce wife. "Was a woman involved either time?"

"Only in the legal negotiations. The original complainants came into large sums of money shortly thereafter, and Margaret Newberry, Monty's wife, was the attorney of record. You going to hold that plate for the rest of the year?"

Pondering the old saw about not judging a book by its cover, I set the plate in the cabinet and took the new one he held out. "And he seemed like such a nice man. Oh, well. Sounds like you've been busy."

"Aren't I always? How about you? What's on tap for tomorrow?"

I told him I planned to drive over to Good Sam and see if I could get someone to talk about Dr. Arthur Cameron. Because of HIPAA regulations, I wasn't hopeful.

"No problemo," he said. "I'll hook you up with Valerie."

"Valerie?"

"Valerie Redhorse, R.N. Another one of my cousins, married a Paiute. Works in the ER over there. Probably knows Dr. Cameron all too well."

"And you didn't tell me this before because…?"

"Because she's been up on Second Mesa for the last week, helping vaccinate Hopi kids. I was going to tell you as soon as she got back, which will be late Sunday night. Here's another plate, belonged to my grandmother, so be careful. By the way, I put fresh linens on your bed and left you a clean towel and washrag."

"You're a fine host, Almost Brother. As well as a never-ceasing flow of information."

"Nice to be appreciated for a change." He grunted. "Hey, I've already gone to the gym, how about you?"

"Taking the day off."

Another grunt. "Usually after dinner I watch a little TV. Tonight *Animal Planet* is airing a special on endangered Southwest species. Want to watch it with me or are you going to work?"

I thought about the interviews that needed transcription, the additional case notes I had to finish. "Work."

"Why am I not surprised? Well, you know where the computers are and what the Desert Investigations password is. Me,

I'm going to relax and find out how close Arizona's mountain lions are to extinction. Or is that a non sequitur?"

"What's so non sequitur about that?" My partner's thought patterns often escaped me.

"The word 'relax' probably shouldn't be used in the same sentence as 'extinction.'"

"Oh."

"Have fun working. There's another non sequitur for you. No, on second thought, that's actually an oxymoron."

Once the last dish had been put away, we separated companionably; he to *Animal Planet*, me to the glacial computer room, where I worked nonstop for another three hours. When I finally emerged, Jimmy had already turned in for the night. Good. Maybe he was a sound sleeper and wouldn't discover the reason for my initial hesitation in accepting his hospitality.

As promised, the sheets on my bed were fresh and the mattress firm, but it made no difference. Sleep never came easily to me, this night was no exception. For hours I lay there staring at the ceiling, trying to still my overactive mind by listening to coyotes yip in the distance. It didn't work. The last time I looked at the bedside clock, it was half past one.

Chapter Sixteen

I was standing by the entrance to the mine shaft. At the bottom lay the dead children, their cries silenced by the same round of gunfire that killed my father. Next to me, my mother stood frozen, her grip on my hand so tight it hurt.

The Golden Boy, much bigger than I, stood on the other side of the mine shaft, his blue eyes dancing with joy. Now he was the only son. The One.

Because Abraham had sacrificed his first-born brother instead.

I had no older brother, no one to die for me. Did that mean I would be next?

As if reading my mind, Golden Boy said, "He won't touch you."

My mother tightened her grip on my hand even further. She leaned down, whispered, "Don't say anything."

But I, being only four years old, ignored her. Refusing to show fear, I asked, "How do you know he won't?"

"Because he promised you to me."

I began to scream.

"Lena! Wake up!"

Strong arms pulled me away from the mine shaft.

Not my mother's arms. Someone else's. I flailed out at them, then opened my eyes and saw Jimmy. He was bare-chested, wearing only boxer shorts. They were covered with cartoons of Roadrunner and Wile E. Coyote.

In one of them, a thought balloon over Coyote's head showed Roadrunner roasting over a slow fire.

Chapter Seventeen

By noon I was standing on Felix Phelps' front porch in an old Peoria subdivision imaginatively named Happy Acres, wondering if the man would ever answer the door. In case the doorbell was broken—everything else around the house seemed to be in disrepair—I knocked. Still no answer. The disintegrating Toyota Corolla in the driveway bore testament that he was home, but maybe he was out walking the dog. If he had a dog.

Thirty-four-year-old Felix was the son of Beulah Phelps. A few months earlier, Dr. Arthur Cameron had ushered Beulah out of this vale of tears for poisoning four elderly men, burying them in her backyard, and collecting their Social Security checks. Due to strange odors emanating from the yard, her neighbors eventually became suspicious and called the police. The appeals process had taken two decades, but in March, Felix had been granted the privilege of attending his mother's execution. According to the *Arizona Republic* story Jimmy pulled up for me this morning, the second Beulah had gasped her last, her son fainted, thus ensuring that neither mother nor son left the execution wing of the Arizona State Prison under their own volition.

The next month he moved back into the house he once shared with his mother, a renter this time. Why?

"Felix's home, he just don't answer the door," called a woman's voice. Somewhere in her sixties, she stood on her front porch, looking as wrecked as her house. Frowsy gray-and-white hair that eerily matched the peeling paint, an ill-fitting brown dress the exact color of the dead grass on her lawn.

"I need to talk to him," I called back.

"Then you might as well go on in. Asshole never locks his door. Probably gonna get his head bashed in by some hop-head burglar someday, not that Felix's got anything worth stealing." With that, she went back inside her own crumbling house, and a second later, I heard the sound of three locks sliding into place.

Peoria is a northwestern suburb of Phoenix, and its neighborhoods range from new, upscale planned communities settled alongside artificial lakes, to down-at-the-heels neighborhoods like this one. Although built with great optimism after WWII, over the years the area's lack of a strong economic base and the erosion of time laid bare the houses' hurry-up construction. Their shambling appearance wasn't helped by the tiny lots they sat on. Huddled as close together as they were, their unkempt yards and crumbling sidewalks announced the neighborhood's illness as terminal. One day the bulldozers would come along and that would be the end of Happy Acres.

The thought of bulldozers made me wonder if the backyard still retained the open maws of four graves. Or had the city filled them in?

I gave the door a final knock, then, taking the old woman's advice, opened it to the stench of cigarette smoke, mildew, and urine. "Hey, Mr. Phelps, you in there?"

A mumble from a far corner of the room. "What?"

The curtains, nothing more than none-too-clean sheets, had been drawn, so the living room was dark after the morning's white-hot glare. But I could hear him trying to breathe, emphasis on the *trying* part.

"My name is Lena Jones, and I'm a private investigator. I'd like to talk to you about your mother."

"She's...dead." His halting voice was a high tenor, similar to that of a child asthmatic's.

As I stepped into the room, I reached my hand into my

carryall and switched on my digital recorder. "I know, Mr. Phelps. That's what I want to talk to you about."

"The bastards…killed her."

"I know that, too."

"They…shouldn't a…done that."

"She was convicted of murdering four innocent men."

"She was just trying…to take care of me after…Daddy left. What'd they…expect her to do when she couldn't…get a job? Beg on the…street?" He was parroting the same defense his mother had used at her trial.

My eyes were becoming accustomed to the gloom and I focused in on him. Felix Phelps was morbidly obese, little more than a blue-lipped, glutinous mass. His rolls of fat spilled over a patched-together recliner surrounded by empty beer bottles, cigarette packs, fly-specked TV dinner containers, and empty Hershey wrappers. Urine stained the front of his giant-sized sweatpants. Diabetic, probably, but I saw no syringe, and no oxygen apparatus to ease his labored breathing.

There being no way this man could have committed the three torture-killings described in the Cameron case file, I removed him from my mental list of suspects. In his condition, swinging a baseball bat even once was beyond him. He needed medical attention as soon as possible.

"You look unwell, Mr. Phelps. Want me to call someone, get you some help?"

"Call who? Never…had no one…but my…mama, now don't even got her. She was just…an old lady. Who was she…gonna hurt anymore, huh?"

I looked around for something to sit on, saw nothing. The recliner and a cooler next to the recliner appeared to be the only pieces of furniture in the room. I didn't even see a television set. So I kept standing.

My vision finally back to normal, I finally spotted a rickety table placed catty-corner from him so he could look directly at it. The table held a yellowing photograph of Felix as a handsome young teenager, embraced by a smiling serial killer.

"You don't have any aunts, uncles, or cousins to help you? No friends?"

"Mama was all…I had."

Felix had been just shy of fourteen when his mother had been arrested. With no kin, he was turned over to Child Protective Services, where—like Kyle—he made the rounds of foster care and at least two group homes. Like other children in his situation, at the age of eighteen he'd been released from CPS protection to fend for himself. These damaged kids, first damaged by their parents, then by the state, were expected to get by with whatever skills and/or education they had already acquired, which wasn't much. If they had health problems, whether physical or mental, that was also too bad. Once they aged out of the system they were no longer insured, and their well-being was no longer the state's concern. The good news was that the kids' health problems seldom lasted all that long, the bad news was the reason why: there was a high suicide rate among eighteen-year-old foster care graduates.

I remembered some of the children I had met during my own long, orphaned slog through the CPS system. Johnny Frasier, dead of an overdose at eighteen. Harmony McMillan, seventeen, who overdosed with Johnny. After a year of hooking on Van Buren Avenue, D'Anne Otumbo, nineteen, drove a stolen car into a freeway abutment, leaving no sign she'd attempted to brake. Those were just a few of my fellow fosters who were no longer in this life.

Now Felix.

Maybe a visit from Adult Protective Services could help him. Then again, maybe not. The fates of so many of my friends had taught me that no matter how incapacitated, when a person wants to die, he can always find a way to accomplish that sad task. Felix had found his.

Under the circumstances this interview would be pointless, but I began anyway. Once he answered two questions, I would leave this house of past and present horror.

"Felix, what were you doing between noon and 2:45 p.m. on July 8?"

"Huh?"

"July 8. It was a Monday."

"Then I was…here. Prob'ly. Don't get…out much."

"Did you hire someone to kill Dr. Arthur Cameron?"

He squinted up at me through eyes that were little more than slits in an almost basketball-sized head. "Who's that?"

"He's an ER doc at Good Sam. Or to put it more correctly, he was."

Felix's fleshy mouth twisted in puzzlement as he struggled to speak. "Last doctor…I seen was Washrowski or…Kryzoski or something like that…over at Peoria General, couple years ago…but Good Sam's too far to drive…last time I drove more than…a mile, the engine light…came on. So sorry…never met any…Doctor Cammy." He drank the rest of his beer, tossed the empty bottle on the floor, and in the same smooth motion, retrieved a new beer from the ice chest. "Want one?"

I declined. "His name was Cameron, not Cammy."

"What I…said, isn't it? So this doctor…he got himself killed?"

"Yep. Plus his wife and his son."

"Geez…A kid?"

"Ten years old."

"Just as well…then."

It was my turn to be puzzled. "What do you mean, Felix?"

"No point in hangin' out after…your mama's gone…since she's the only one…ever loved you."

As soon as I returned to my Jeep I called Adult Protective Services and explained Felix' condition. The woman on the other end of the line sounded efficient enough, but promised little. Maricopa County was heavily populated, she said, and there were hundreds, possibly thousands, of adults in worse shape than Felix, adults who for one reason or another, were being victimized by their caregivers. Those cases were given priority status by Adult Protective Service. Compared to grannies being beaten by daughters and grandsons, a person killing himself slowly with food, cigarettes, and alcohol didn't even rate an in-home visit.

She didn't come right out and say that last part, of course, but by the time I ended the call, the between-the-lines hung in the air.

No point in hangin' out after your mama's gone since she's the only one loves you.

I placed another call, this one to Curtis Racine, Kyle Gibbs' attorney. He wasn't pleased because I'd apparently interrupted him in the middle of something.

"This better be important," he grumbled, sounding out of breath. In the background I could hear a woman's voice, soft, yet irritated. I could also hear clothes rustling. Or was it sheets?

"As per our earlier agreement, you're not talking on the phone to me, anyway, so this intrusion into your personal life never happened," I said. "Here's what I suggest you do. Visit Kyle, tell him Ali's about to retract her confession and that she's going to deny planning her family's murder. She's also going to say that the only reason she made up the story about hiring a hit man was because she thought she was protecting Kyle. Since then, she has come to believe that he doesn't need protecting because he had nothing to do with the murders."

No comment for a moment, just a hurried shush to the muttering woman before Curtis came back on the line. "Aren't you forgetting something? A certain person's fingerprints on a certain piece of sports equipment?"

"I'm sure he has an explanation for that. Especially since the crime techs found only one set of fingerprints on the bat. If Kyle killed those people, his fingerprints should have been all over it, not merely confined to the grip area. His prints should also have shown up in the master bedroom and Alec's bedroom, at the very least. But they didn't."

"I planned to use that in a certain person's defense. Dammit, stop!" This last wasn't addressed to me, but to the woman, who from the tone of her voice, was pleading for something. Having been around that block a few times myself, I could guess what.

"Curtis, just get the kid to tell the truth, okay?"

"The truth. Now there's a concept."

"Another thing, and you didn't hear it from me, remember. Desert Investigations has discovered that for the past three years, right up to his death, Dr. Arthur Cameron was moonlighting as the Arizona state executioner, during which time he put ten men and one woman to death. He was paid, in cash, a total of eighteen thousand dollars per head. So to speak."

An unlawyerly squawk.

I ignored it. "Which means there were a lot of other people who might have wanted Dr. Cameron dead, grieving family members and such."

"Holy. Shit."

"You can say that again. Well, it's been nice talking to…"

He interrupted, his voice lowered to a whisper. "You haven't been talking to me, and I've certainly heard none of this information from anyone, let alone you. But just out of curiosity, I have to ask, why are you doing this?"

Because I don't want Kyle turning into Felix Phelps, I could have answered. Instead, I just said, "If you can convince that dumb, deluded boy that Ali had nothing to do with the murders—and at this point I can assure you she didn't—he'll probably retract his confession, too."

With that, I let him get back to whatever important task he'd been performing for womankind and called Fiona Etheridge, the dumb, deluded boy's soon-to-be-adoptive mother and imparted much the same information. The only thing I left out was Dr. Cameron's lucrative sideline, which she didn't need to know.

After giving Fiona time to make happy noises, I added, "Get down to juvie today and start working on him. He needs to retract that bullshit confession."

"But what if he thinks he's still helping Ali?"

"It's your job to convince him otherwise."

I ended the call, then pressed speed dial for Jimmy.

The conversation was tense, but after first refusing, he gave me the local addresses where the families of four recently executed men lived. If nothing substantive turned up in my interviews with them, I'd range further afield.

"You okay?" Jimmy asked, before I could hang up.

"Considering what happened last night, I should probably be asking you that question. How is it, anyway?"

"How is what?"

"Your nose."

"Sore."

"You should have just let me scream it out. That's what I usually do."

"My partner starts screaming in the middle of the night and I'm supposed to ignore it?"

"You know how I am." A partial lie, because I'd never told him about my nightmares, and certainly not about Golden Boy.

"I knew you had issues, but I thought you were getting help."

"I did. My therapist was so good that yours was the first bloody nose I've caused in, oh, several months." *Keep it light, keep it light.*

When he took a deep breath, I knew a lecture was coming. He didn't disappoint. "This is serious, Lena. You should…"

"Hmm. Let me see. The address for the Hoppers was 4891 West Corinth, right? In Maryvale? You recited those numbers so fast I wanted to make sure."

"Yeah. 4891 West Corinth."

"Thanks."

I killed the call before he added anything else.

On Sundays the Black Canyon Freeway flows relatively smoothly, so as the Jeep cruised south toward the Maryvale area of west Phoenix, I erased last night's embarrassment by worrying about someone with worse problems than mine. Felix Phelps would be dead by the end of the year, but there was nothing more I could do. If God existed and if He was as merciful as some people believe, Felix would pass away peacefully in his duct-taped recliner, staring at his mother's photograph. Despite her horrific crimes, she had somehow managed to make her son feel loved.

Felix and I had one thing in common. My mother had almost killed me, yet despite the bullet scar on my forehead, I remembered her with longing. Were we damaged children programmed to love our mothers, regardless? And despite CPS' case files of horrific maternal abuse, those very mothers invariably swore they loved the children they nearly killed, too. Somehow, despite all evidence to the contrary, love continued to flow both ways through the polluted maternal stream.

Genetic mysteries being beyond my capacity to solve, I shuttered my mind by shoving a Big Joe Williams CD into the Jeep's newly installed under-dash player. As the blues singer growled his way through a song about a cheating woman, I exited the freeway at Bethany Home Road and headed west toward Maryvale, the childhood home of Kenny Dean Hopper. His parents, described in the news stories as staunch blue-collar types with no criminal history, still lived in the same house. They sounded like good people, but you never know. On the surface, almost everyone looks good.

Unlike Felix' ramshackle place, the Hopper residence was a perfectly maintained John F. Long one-story only slightly bigger than Felix' heap. But the tiny lot was adorned with pristine desert landscaping, and as I parked in front, the lifted arm of a saguaro appeared to welcome me. Splashing sounds and children's laughter floating over a high backyard fence completed the happy suburban picture, and by the time I made it to the front door, I smelled barbeque. Kenny Dean had been executed little more than three weeks ago, but they were having a pool party.

Life, regardless of the wounds it inflicts, goes on.

I leaned on the doorbell for what seemed forever, but eventually the sound of hurrying feet proved my strategy effective, so I switched my recorder on.

"Coming! Coming!" a man yelled. "Hold your horses!"

The door opened, revealing a fit, sandy-haired man somewhere between fifty and sixty. Over cutoff jeans and a wife-beater shirt that revealed well-toned biceps, he wore an apron that said MY GRANDKIDS ARE CUTER THAN YOUR GRAND-KIDS. Standing by his side was a mean-looking shepherd mix. The way it stared at my ankle made me nervous.

"Mr. Emery Hopper?"

His friendly smile conflicted with the worry lines around his mouth and the purple bags under his eyes. "What can I do for you?" he said. "Better make it quick, because I've got seven grandkids in the pool and my wife and one loopy teen are the only ones watching them."

When I gave my name and flashed my ID, the genial manner disappeared. "You here to talk about my son?"

"Yes, I have some questions about Kenny, and I…"

He slammed the door in my face.

I didn't hear him retreat, so I leaned on the doorbell again.

The door opened. Like its owner, the shepherd was growling. "What's the matter with you? Ring my doorbell like that again and I'm calling the cops. My family's been put through enough without having to put up with this P.I. shit."

Investigators don't mind confronting hostility; angry people tend to let things slip. "Mr. Hopper, do you know an Arthur Cameron, M.D.?"

The anger softened and a line of puzzlement formed on his forehead. "No, I'm pretty sure I don't. But the name sounds familiar."

"How about Terry Jardine?" *Otherwise known as Monster Woman, who had been foolish enough to get engaged to your homicidal, wacko son.*

A sneer. "Just another delusional Death Row groupie. My son had dozens. And if you think she was engaged to him like she claimed in the newspapers, ask to see the ring. There was none, because he was stringing her along, like he did with all the others, having his sick fun."

"I see. Back to Dr. Cameron. He was murdered a couple of weeks ago, along with his wife and ten-year-old son. His fourteen-year-old daughter is accused of murdering them."

"Yeah, I remember reading about that, but what's it got to do with Kenny?"

"Trust me, there's a connection. I'm just not free to reveal it right now. May I ask you where you were on Monday, July 8, between noon and 2:45 p.m.?"

"You're kidding, right? You're aware that Kenny died the night before, right? But I still had to go to work, God bless America. In fact, I work two jobs, seven days a week, and if you're interested, which I doubt, I'll be working seven days a week for the rest of my life in order to pay Kenny's legal bills."

"You're not working today."

"Laid off from one of the jobs yesterday. Looking for a new one tomorrow."

"I'm sorry to hear that."

"I just bet you are."

"Anyway, that girl—my client—needs your help."

A flicker of concern in his gray eyes, but it was only temporary. "What makes you think I can help some kid I don't even know? And why should I, anyway? She didn't just murder her parents, she murdered her little brother, too. After torturing him for hours, the papers said. Nice girl. Real queen of the prom."

"The girl has been accused of the crime, yes."

"Confessed, is what I read."

"There's confessions and there's confessions. Invite me in and we can talk more comfortably." Sweat was running down my neck, and there was no breeze to use it as a coolant.

"You're not taking one step inside this house. My wife's probably going to walk in any minute to see why I'm not back, and I won't have you upsetting her. This is the first day she's smiled since…" He didn't finish. He didn't have to. *This is the first day she's smiled since our son was executed.*

I tried again. The more he talked, the more I'd learn about him, regardless of how loud he yelled or what lies he told. "It's a hundred and five degrees out here, Mr. Hopper."

"Poor you." He crossed his arms, and that's when I realized that throughout this conversation he had been holding a barbeque fork with tines long enough to eviscerate me. The shepherd mix was drooling now, still focused on my ankle. Maybe having a long chat wasn't a good idea.

I tried once more. "C'mon, Mr. Hopper, you're a father, and

a grandfather, but you're making it sound like you don't care what happens to that little girl."

My question had ignited his earlier anger into something far more dangerous, and his eyes narrowed into slits. "Did you care what happened to our son?"

Having read Kenny rap sheet, no, I didn't. But I said, "I'm sorry for your loss, but I'm trying to help a child."

He gave a dry laugh. "Oh, really? Let me tell you what happened to *my* child. They say death by injection is painless, but my wife and I were both there. We saw him convulse. We heard him gasp for breath."

In the face of such grief and rage, further questioning was hopeless. "Thank you for your time, Mr. Hopper."

I walked away quickly, before he and his dog came through the screen door at me.

There were three more names and addresses on Jimmy's list, but my stomach reminded me I was starving. This morning I'd been too embarrassed about my late night scream-a-thon to hang around Jimmy's trailer for breakfast. Plus, there's something nerve-wracking about seeing your business partner leaning over you in bed, wearing nothing but his undershorts. Looking back, I realized I should have followed my instincts and stayed at the motel, but there was nothing I could do about that now, except make certain it wouldn't happen again.

Maryvale being a heavily Hispanic area, I headed out to the main drag in search of enchiladas. Four blocks from the Hoppers' house, a crowded parking lot next to Mi Casa Supremo made me ease up on the Jeep's accelerator. The scent of garlic and chilies wafting through the air held great promise, so I swung a sharp right and pulled into the lot. After a fifteen-minute wait, the hostess ushered me to a tiny table near the kitchen, which might have been able to seat two very thin people if they were in a close relationship, but it was more suited to one normal-sized detective. The fiery enchiladas were worth the wait, and having the table to myself enabled me to check my phone messages. There were six of them, five from clients.

The sixth was the most interesting: Detective Pete Halliwell, from Scottsdale PD, informing me that a Ms. Terry Jardine had been arrested early that morning as a suspect in the Desert Investigations arson. I returned the call immediately, only to reach Halliwell's voice mail. Disappointment led to disappointment as I responded to the client calls, only to wind up in their voice mail systems, too. Irritated, I turned my attention to my enchiladas and forgot everything else.

Thirty minutes later I was on the Black Canyon Freeway, headed toward the I-10 interchange. Several more minutes later, I glommed onto Loop 202 east until it dumped me out in Queen Creek, almost fifty miles away. Good thing I like to drive, even though the Jeep was becoming increasingly testy. Not as testy as some of the drivers I encountered on the way, though. In summer, road rage is the price you pay for living in Arizona.

The family of Sidney Hoyt, who had burned his wife and three children alive to collect on their insurance, lived in a once-quiet farming community that had now been gobbled up by suburbs. My seventh foster home, or was it my eighth, had been in Queen Creek, and it had been one of CPS' better placements. The Stearson family owned a dairy farm, and I had helped them out by attaching automatic milking machines to placid cows' udders. As a reward, I'd been allowed to ride Sparkle, the family's just-as-placid old quarter horse mare, and by the time I'd been yanked away from the Stearsons—I forget why—I'd become a passable rider.

The minute I hopped off the 202 at the San Tan Village Parkway exit ramp, I realized that the Stearsons' farm was only a memory. The drive down Greenfield Road toward Queen Creek showcased housing development after housing development, broken up every now and then by bustling shopping centers. The fact that the smell of cow manure no longer hung in the air came as no comfort. Then, after turning east at the new, stop-lighted intersection of Greenfield and Herford roads, I got a fresh surprise. While the Stearsons' dairy acreage had vanished, the farmhouse—the one I'd once lived in—remained. But something terrible had happened to it.

The clapboard siding the Stearsons had kept a pure white was now almost stripped of paint, all shutters but one were hanging askew, and the roof appeared beyond repair. Next to a cyclone-fenced lot with a sign FOR SALE, was a slapped-together chicken coop that boasted no chickens. In the front yard, two eucalyptus trees were in the process of dying from lack of care, and in the back, the dairy barns were gone. Bewildered, I double-checked the address Jimmy had given me. 37567 E. Keltie Lane. This was the place where the baby-burner's family lived, all right, only when I lived there with the Stearsons, the address had been Rural Route 37. No wonder I hadn't recognized it.

I parked my Jeep on the rutted drive behind two pickup trucks that looked like they'd been abandoned sometime during the Reagan administration, and picked my way up the path to the house. The snarls of several huge dogs chained to metal stakes near the front steps accompanied me on my trek. By the time I arrived at the stairs, burrs clung to my black jeans. Jimmy must have made one of his rare mistakes; surely no one lived here. They only dropped by every now and then to throw trespassers to the hounds.

Before I could mount the stairs, the front door flew open and an elderly woman hobbled out. She wore a printed housedress as faded as she was.

"What you want?" she yelled, in a voice harsh enough to finish stripping the paint off the house.

I flashed my ID but she didn't even look at it. Maybe she couldn't read.

"I said, what you want?"

Just what I needed, another hostile interview.

"Ma'am, I'm here to…"

Suddenly two men, both at least six-three, loomed up behind her. Middle-aged, red-faced, and dentally challenged, they looked enough alike to be twins, but only one brandished a baseball bat.

Bat Boy yelled, "Fucking reporters, think you can come 'round here botherin' us! Well, we got us some advice for you! Get the hell off our property!"

"But I'm not a…"

Bat Boy shoved past the old woman and started across the porch, accompanied by frantic snarls and barks from the hounds.

I like to think of myself as brave, but I'm also smart.

So I got the hell out of there.

Regardless of the distance between them, I had meant to visit all five families on Jimmy's list today, since on Sundays most people are home, but after my unsettling morning I decided to return to the office instead. Well, Jimmy's office, the situation at Desert Investigations being what it was. While fighting the freeways back to Scottsdale, I mulled over what I had already learned.

Unless Felix Phelps had enough money to hire a hit man, which I doubted, he hadn't killed the Camerons, and he was physically incapable of carrying out the crime himself. But the family of Kenny Dean Hopper harbored at least one individual who—half-mad with grief—appeared to possess the will and ability to kill for revenge. Ditto for the Neanderthal-ish Hoyts.

Grief does odd things to people. Whether a dull pain or a sharp knife, grief is a wound that never heals, no matter how or by whom it is inflicted. With these people it wasn't as if their loved ones had died of natural causes—they'd been purposely put to death by the state of Arizona. It might seem odd that innocent families grieved over the execution of a conscienceless killer, but in reality, such sorrow was the most natural thing in the world. After all, the survivors bore wounds, too. Kin was kin, regardless of what crimes had been committed. Some survivors were able to pretend they felt nothing, but the majority of the wounded limped along, dealing with what had to be dealt with as well as they could, day after sad day.

Thinking about the various ways of handling grief made me wonder how Ali was doing. Since I couldn't call her from my Jeep, I did the next best thing: called her attorney.

"It is Sunday," Stephen Zellar grumped, after picking up before the second ring had finished. "You think I don't deserve time off?"

I could barely hear him over the road noise, which even this far away from Phoenix proper, was considerable as a caravan of RVs, moving vans, and even a boat on a flatbed roared by. "I called your office number," I yelled over the din, "so apparently you don't think you deserve time off, either."

"That is not my point."

"How's Ali? Has she been released into her uncle's custody yet?"

A sigh. "There appears to be a problem."

"What?" Damned traffic.

"I said, there appears to be a problem."

Despite the new hands-free apparatus in my Jeep, Zellar's statement alarmed me enough that I nearly swerved out of my lane and into the '72 Cadillac convertible next to me. My inattention was rewarded by frantic honking.

"Don't tell me Ali decided not to withdraw her confession!" I said, steering the Jeep back into its own lane. As the Cadillac sped away, its driver, a silver-haired granny, flipped me the bird.

"Ali did exactly what she promised she would do and signed the appropriate papers to that effect. But we are faced with one more obstacle."

"Which is?"

"She will not disclose what she was doing the day of the, ah, incident."

Incident. An interesting word to describe charnel-house slaughter. "Why not?"

"I certainly wish I knew, Ms. Jones. As it stands now, our client has little chance of being released on bond. Or at least, not until we can prove she was elsewhere during the, ah, incident, and thus can satisfy the judge that she poses no threat to society. We need to remember that three people are dead, one of them a child, and Ali's retracted confession alone does not allay the seriousness of those charges."

No mention of Kyle there, not that I should have expected it, coming from the by-the-book Zellar, but still. Didn't he care about the boy? Not that I didn't already know the answer. I did, though, remind him of one thing. "The funeral is Tuesday. Were you able to get the go-ahead for her to attend?"

"With some difficulty I did, yes. Ali will be allowed to attend the memorial and the funeral both, albeit heavily guarded. And she'll be in shackles, which I find quite abhorrent."

"What?" A semi had taken up position on my left, and hung there belching fumes and noise.

Zellar raised his voice to a shout. "I said, she'll be there! In shackles! Guarded!"

The image of Ali in chains, standing over her family's graves, was so distressing that I would have wrung my hands, but I wasn't certain that the driver of the rig next to me even saw my Jeep. Attention was required.

Then Zellar surprised me. Still shouting, he said, "Perhaps you, being a woman and all, can talk some sense into the child's head. I've begun to suspect the reason she will not tell me where she was during the, ah, incident, is because she might have been involved in something that had an, ah, sexual component. With her so-called partner in crime."

Could this case get any messier? But it was the twenty-first century, and girls will be girls. I checked my rearview mirror. No tailgaters, and the ramp leading to Loop 202 lay less than a quarter mile ahead. I put on my retrofitted turn signal.

"I'm headed for juvie now!" I screamed to Zellar. "As soon as I find out what's going on, I'll let you know. "

He screamed back. "Be sure and do that, Ms. Jones. If I don't hear from you by then, I'll see you at the funeral. Wear black. Not that you ever wear anything else."

He ended the call as the Jeep cruised up the exit ramp.

"On Monday, July 8, where were you between noon and three p.m., when you showed up at the vet's office with Misty?" I asked Ali.

We were in a new interview room, this one, for some indecipherable reason, painted such a bright chartreuse I was tempted to put on my sunglasses.

Ali scowled, as usual. "None of your business."

"Didn't your attorney explain that merely retracting your confession isn't enough, that you need to provide an alibi, too?"

"I don't have to talk to you." Arms crossed, chin thrust forward.

"What'd you have for lunch today? Bile?"

"Bitch."

God, I loved this kid. "Back at ya."

My chipper tone must have disconcerted her, because her lower lip began to wobble. "You…you…"

"Me, what?"

"You promised you'd get us out of here, me and Kyle!"

"I said that if you retracted your confession, your attorney could start the necessary work to get you out. But when I talked to him a little while ago, he said you wouldn't tell him where you and Kyle were when—sorry, but I have to be blunt here—when your family was murdered, so there's nothing he can do unless you change your mind and open up. You need an alibi, Ali. Kyle's miserable, by the way. He doesn't have a high-powered attorney like yours, or a well-off uncle, either. All he has is you, so since you don't want to do what it takes to help him…" Guilt card duly played, I let my sentence trail off.

She looked down at the floor. Nothing there but a drain and our shadows, cast by yellowish overhead lighting. "I can't."

"Any day now, you realize, some banger or other punk might decide to make an example of Kyle. He's not locked up with a bunch of primped and powdered Valley girls."

"Neither am I," she muttered.

"Oh, kiddo, it's not the same."

I began counting through the ensuing silence, deciding that when I reached one hundred, I would get up and leave.

On the eighty-four count, she gave in. "Kyle and I, we weren't supposed to be there."

"Where?"

"At the party house."

"What house is that?"

Still addressing the floor drain, she said, "You know, the house where we, you know, were. We, we were kinda breaking the law, which is why I didn't want to say. We were, like, trespassing, and that could get us in big trouble."

Trust a fourteen-year-old to think that trespassing was worse than a triple murder charge. But the teenage years are the time of magical thinking, aren't they? Such as: I'm going to marry Justin Bieber; all I have to do is meet him. Or: If I admit we trespassed, me and my boyfriend will be locked up forever and ever, so I'd better keep my mouth shut.

I leaned forward. "Was anyone else there, Ali? Anyone who could testify they saw you both during the time of the murder?"

She still wouldn't look at me, just shook her head. "We were there all day, well, I'd left my house real, real early, like nine or something to meet him, but there was nobody else around, just me and Kyle." She finally raised her head, and stared me straight in the eye. "I swear."

Ordinarily I don't trust people who swear to something while looking you straight in the eye, but for Ali I made an exception. "Where is this house?"

"Maybe about a mile from mine, something like that, anyway. Takes around thirty minutes to walk there. There's signs on the door saying the bank owns it, and the windows are, like, boarded up. All the kids use it. There's a couple of sleeping bags, a camp stove, lots of neat stuff."

Graffiti on the walls, too, I bet. "Give me the address."

I finally got to see her eyes again. "I don't know it. Thing's just some old, boarded-up place. The owners probably lost their jobs and couldn't keep it. Lots of that going around."

"Old, you say?"

"Yeah."

In Scottsdale, the term "old" is relative. The house could have been anywhere from ten to forty years old, but since it was located near Ali's, I could estimate its age. The original Arabian horse farms had disappeared twenty years earlier, when subdivisions gobbled up the north end of the Valley. This meant the house could be no more than twenty years old, a spring chicken by most estimates in the U.S.

"You say the house is boarded up?"

"Yeah. Front and back."

"Is it east or west of your own place?"

She raised her hand to her mouth and chewed on a knuckle. It was all I could do not to move her hand away. "Toward the rez."

East, then. "Color?"

Some teenage eye-rolling. "Kind of a beigey-pink."

I made a mental note to find the house and give the address to Zellar. "What were you and Kyle doing in that house?"

A flush, followed by a silence that proved Zellar's dirty mind was right on.

"Okay, Ali, let's see if I can guess. You and Kyle were having sex."

The flush deepened. "Not totally. He, uh, when he got the condom on, I'd only brought one, and it split and it was like, so we, well, you know."

"So you did something else."

"Yeah." She was looking at the drain again, her long hair parted to uncover one stoplight-red ear.

"Ali, where'd you get the condom? Did you shoplift it?"

"I don't shoplift!" The genuine outrage in her voice convinced me she was telling the truth.

"Then where'd it come from? You told me you were the one who brought it to your little love tryst, not Kyle."

Ali's earlier embarrassment returned, this time tinged with sadness. "You won't tell on me?"

"I promise from the heart."

A long sigh. "I swiped it from my mother's chest of drawers, where she keeps her sweaters. She has lots of them, all cashmere, really beautiful. Anyway, I knew she wouldn't miss just one. Condom, I mean, not sweater. She'd miss a cashmere sweater big-time."

A warning flag went up, but I let it go. For now, anyway. "One more thing. Give me the name of your mother's closest friend, someone she might confide in." It was probably Margie Newberry, but I wanted to make sure before I accused Geronimo's great-great-granddaughter of holding out on me.

"Close? You mean like Kyle and me?"

"Exactly. Like you and Kyle."

She thought for a moment, then smiled for the first time during the interview. "Margie."

"Your next-door neighbor."

"Yeah. She and Mom were, like, besties."

"Good. I'll be talking to her later today. Um, in the meantime, Ali, when exactly did you get to the party house and how long did you stay there?"

Relieved that I wasn't going to cross-examine her about the ways and means of safe sex, she answered without thinking. "Like I said, I left my house around nine that morning. I told my mom I'd be back for lunch, but what with Kyle and everything, uh, you know, I forgot."

And a good thing, too, otherwise there would have been four bodies in the Camerons' living room. I didn't mention that, though. She had enough to deal with.

"So you were at this party house from around nine-thirty to around two or two-thirty? That's a long time to play around."

"We ate some Fritos. And drank some Mountain Dew. And I slept for a while."

Uh oh. "How long did you sleep?"

Ali shrugged, unaware of what she'd let slip. "An hour. Maybe two. Dunno."

"What was Kyle doing while you were sleeping? Did he go somewhere?"

Her head snapped up. "He was right there! With me! He didn't go anywhere! Not anywhere!"

Methought the lady doth protest too much. "Stop lying, Ali."

"I…I…" She swallowed. "You won't understand."

"Try me."

When her shoulders slumped I knew I was about to get the truth. She didn't disappoint.

"We'd planned the whole day so we could be, like, together, and Kyle got to the house real early, even before, like, me, and we were, um, kinda fooling around for a…uh, for a long while, like, at least a couple of hours, maybe more, and then later we heard this dog whining, and we shouldn't have, been able to hear a dog, I mean, because nobody around there had one, so Kyle went out to look."

She paused and took a breath. "He was gone for a couple minutes, then he came back to the window and he was holding this little scruffy thing. He'd found it eating garbage in the backyard, and said he recognized it from all the flyers tacked up around the neighborhood saying that it got scared and ran away because of the Fourth of July fireworks. Now it was all ragged and limping bad, and like, scared-looking." She paused for another breath. "Do you know how many dogs run off because of fireworks? It's terrible, people should keep them, like, inside. Anyway, Kyle said he was going to return the dog to its owner because she sounded real nice on the flyer, and if it turned out not to be hers after all, he'd, like, take it to his house, 'cause Fiona, she's his foster mom, she lets him do stuff like that."

"What did Kyle do then?"

She flushed again. "I couldn't talk him out of leaving, so he did. He stayed gone for a while."

"What time did he get back?"

"Twelve-thirty? One? One-thirty?" She shrugged. "I know it was way after the time I usually had lunch, because I remember my stomach was growling and we'd run out of Fritos, so I was getting kinda starved, but I don't know for sure because I wasn't exactly checking my watch, you know?"

I mentally reviewed the case notes. According to the autopsy, the Camerons had been interrupted while eating a lunch of Chinese takeout, then tied up and tortured for at least an hour, possibly two. If someone other than Ali had seen Kyle during that time, it could provide an alibi. "When Kyle he got back, did he say he'd successfully returned the dog?"

She nodded. "Oh, yeah! He wouldn't quit 'til he did. It had on tags, and one of them had the woman's phone number on it, so he, like, called the woman on his cell, and it turned out that she lived about a mile away, so because it was all limping and stuff, he had to carry it there. He said the owner was crying and kept trying to give him money, but he wouldn't take it." Another pause for breath. "Kyle never takes money for rescues."

"Did he mention the owner's name?"

"Alice something, I think. She was old, he said."

Remembering Ali's usual interpretation of the word "old," I asked, "Old like me? Or old like Minerva McGonagall, in the Harry Potter movies?'

A look of surprise. "You saw the movies?"

"The first one." I didn't tell her I'd hated it. "Answer, please. Old like…?"

"Old like Minerva McGonagall. Like, ancient."

"Kyle didn't happen to tell you Ancient Alice's address, did he?"

"I didn't ask."

No, of course you didn't. You had other things on your mind, such as having another go-round with the love of your so-far life. "Maybe Kyle remembers."

Hope flashed in her eyes. "Yes! He's good with numbers."

Street names, too, I hoped back. If the dog owner could provide Kyle with an alibi, there was a chance his attorney could get him bonded out. I was about to end the interview and rush off to make the necessary calls when I thought of something else. "So let's get this straight. After Kyle returned the dog, he came back to the party house sometime around one o'clock and you were together for the rest of the day until you showed up at the scene of…ah, at your house, right?"

The floor drain got interesting again.

"Uh, mostly." She didn't look up.

I sighed. "Define 'mostly.'"

"Well, he, uh, after a while he left again."

When she didn't explain further, I asked, "What time was this?"

"A little after we, um, we had a fight."

"A fight. About what?"

Her face went red again. "Can't remember."

"Don't hand me that 'can't remember' bullshit, Ali. What was the fight about? Did you hit each other?"

"No! Kyle never hit anyone! And I didn't either. We just, we just yelled a lot."

"And what did you two yell at each other about?

"Dunno."

If I hadn't liked her so much, I would have smacked her upside her lying little head. "If you want to get Kyle out of trouble, you'll start telling all of the truth, not just part of it. Do it. Now!"

She shrank back at the sound of my raised voice, the mysteries of the floor drain forgotten as the words spilled out of her between gulps. "It was all my fault 'cause I yelled that I was starving, I mean...I mean all I'd had to eat since breakfast was the Fritos and Mountain Dew and...and why had he been all that worried about a dog when I was there starving to death, so why didn't he stop at the Circle K on the way back and... and get me something, like, some more Fritos and Slim Jims or Twinkies or something. And he yelled back that I was selfish and never thought about anything but myself and I...I...I told him I was going to leave him there in that nasty old house all by myself and go home and get something to eat so he said all right he'd go get me something and...and then he left."

She hung her head, a perfect portrait of misery.

"This Circle K, where is it?"

"Corner of Scottsdale Road and Indian Bend. It's kind of halfway between the party house and mine."

"And?"

"And, what?"

"How long was Kyle gone this time?"

Silence.

"Ali?"

"He, uh, he didn't come back."

Not good news, that. "So what did you do then?"

"I felt really bad for the things I said to him and…and when he didn't come back in a long while I was afraid he was so mad at me we'd break up so…so I went looking for him to tell him tell him I was sorry and that I promised not to ever be selfish again."

"Did you find him?"

Eyes back to the drain. "Yeah."

"Where did you find him, Ali?" As if I hadn't figured it out already.

A tiny voice. "At my house."

There was little more to say after that, so I stood up. "Thank you, Ali. And don't worry, you've been a big help. If everything works out like I think it will, there's a good chance you won't have to spend much more time in here. If I don't see you again before then, I'll see you at the funeral."

She blanched. "Funeral?"

Oh, hell. She didn't know. I sat back down and softened my voice. "It's Tuesday, Ali. Your attorney is arranging for you to be there."

She looked at the drain, studied it for a while. I waited, let her take her time. Several shoulder heaves later, she faced me again. "Okay." That was all she could say.

I couldn't help myself. I reached over and stroked her hair. "I'll be there, in case you need me."

Maybe it was my imagination, but before I got up to leave I thought I saw a hint of relief on her face.

As the Jeep pulled out of the detention center's parking lot, I reflected on what I'd learned so far. Dr. Cameron was nobody's Dr. Feel Good. Ali probably hadn't killed her family. Kyle had the beginnings of an alibi, but hardly an iron-clad one. And Alexandra Cameron, the good and beautiful woman everyone so admired, a woman who had had so much difficulty getting pregnant that she needed the services of egg donors in order to have children? She kept a stash of condoms. The only reason an infertile woman needed condoms was to protect herself from

STDs, but Dr. Cameron's autopsy showed him to be free of sexually-transmitted disease. Being infected by her own husband wasn't what Alexandra worried about.

It sounded to me that the good and beautiful Alexandra Cameron wasn't so good, after all.

Chapter Eighteen

Kyle

I'm going to die in here. I know I am. I'll die without ever seeing Ali again, but that'll be okay as long as they let her go. I'm going to keep saying I did it did it did it as long as it takes because nothing matters anymore without Ali. As long as I know she's all right and they let her go I'll let anything happen to me that needs to happen. Maybe I'll even write a note saying again exactly how I did it and then kill myself. They'd have to let her go then, wouldn't they?

Ali is all the goodness in the world and no matter what she did to her folks, nothing's going to change my mind. For her, I'll keep saying I did it until the day I die and if I'm lucky that'll happen soon. Maybe one of the bangers in here will do it for me.

If I could only see Ali one more time. Just one. I'd die happy.

Life is a lonely place. I've always known it, even before I came here, but I didn't know it like I know it now. There's all this noise, all this pain, all this hate and fear, and so many people walking around all the time shouting mean things at everyone, just shouting and shouting and shouting. I didn't think anybody could be lonely in a loud place like this but it's true. The louder it gets the lonelier I feel.

I miss Ali.

I miss Mom Fi and Daddy Glen.

I miss Aunt Edith.

I wonder if Aunt Edith feels as lonely as I do? But if I let her visit it'll upset her and she's so old and sick she could die if she gets upset and then they'll take Pit Bull away and put him to sleep and I can't let that happen.

I can't let anyone else die because of me.

Chapter Nineteen

Lena

On the way to the Newberrys' house, I called Kyle's foster mom and told her to get from him the name and address of the woman who lost her dog during the July 4th fireworks. She promised to visit Kyle later that day and would call me immediately thereafter. Next, I called Ali's attorney and updated him on my progress so far, then did the same with Juliana Thorsson. Unlike Zellar, whose end of the conversation was hurried and brief, the congresswoman seemed inclined to keep me on the phone, even though from the clamor behind her, she was at another fund-raiser. Not that she was running for Senate, of course.

"My money's on one of those Hoyt creatures," Thorsson said, after I described the Queen Creek family's bat-wielding performance.

"Didn't know you were a gambler, Congresswoman."

I was temporarily diverted from her questioning when a red pickup truck belching oily exhaust swerved in front of me, almost clipping the Jeep's bumper. Only the fact that he immediately ducked onto an off-ramp kept me from giving him the finger.

"I never mind taking a flyer on a sure thing, Ms. Jones," Thorsson said, bringing my attention back. "By the way, pretend you don't know me at the funeral Tuesday."

"What!?" My turn to swerve, but at least I stayed in my own lane. More or less. "Surely you're not going!"

"Dr. Cameron and his wife were my constituents."

I doubted that she went to all her constituents' funerals. "Need I remind you that if the press happens to be there, you'll be spotted? Besides that, do you really think attending is a good idea, given your, ah, electoral situation and all?"

"If the press is there, I'll give them the same explanation I gave you, that I care for my constituents. As for whether it's a good idea or not, that's my business, not yours."

No one can talk politicians out of doing something they want to do, whether mismanaging campaign funds, hiring call girls, or sneaking peeks at biological daughters, so I didn't try. "Just don't try to talk to Ali."

"Give me credit for at least minimal brains, Ms. Jones."

With that, she hung up.

Twenty minutes later I pulled into the Camerons' cul-de-sac. Parked in front of their house were two vans, each bearing the legend, COYOTE CLEAN-UP: DISASTER TO DELIGHT. Regardless of their motto, I doubted things would ever be delightful again at the house.

I climbed out of my Jeep and walked over to the Newberrys'. Margie didn't appear happy to see me.

"Make it quick," she said, looking less lawyerly in a ripped tee-shirt and baggy jeans. "I'm in the middle of packing."

"Changed your mind about attending the funeral, then?"

"I'll be there, along with the rest of Alexandra's friends. But Monty and I are flying out right afterwards, and I expect I'll be upset, and so I…Ah, I'd like to point out to you that we're letting the air-conditioning out, so if you must talk to me right now, step inside."

I stepped. "Could you spare me a drink? Water, whatever, anything will do. I'm roasting."

She made an exasperated noise, but innate Arizonan courtesy made her head for the kitchen. I followed, entering a large kitchen/family room combination brightly lit by a wall full of sliding glass doors that led out a park-sized backyard. The Newberrys sure weren't hurting for money.

"Must be a hundred and ten out there," I said.

"July in Arizona, surprise, surprise." She opened the refrigerator and poured me a tall glass of trachea-freezing tea.

When I chugged half the glass, she poured some more. "Where's your husband?" I asked.

"Down at some camping gear store buying things we don't need."

No chugging this time, just a sip because I wanted to make the refill last. "As long as I'm here, there are a couple of questions I'd like to ask."

" 'As long as you're here,' " she mimicked. "Oh, please. I wasn't born yesterday. What new information have you garnered that brings you back to interrogate me on this balmy summer day?" She motioned toward the breakfast bar. "We might as well sit down so we can both be comfortable during the interrogation. And set your digital recorder on the bar so I can make sure its precious little red light is off."

I did as I was told and sat down on one of the tall bar stools grouped around the granite counter. Looking longingly at my now nonfunctioning recorder, I asked, "What makes you think I'm going to interrogate you?"

"The look on your face. Want a peach?" After sitting across from me, Margie gestured toward the filled fruit bowl on the granite bar. "I'll have to throw them out before we leave, anyway."

"Is it poisoned?"

"Try one and see."

"Don't mind if I do." I picked the largest and fuzziest and took a big bite. Juice ran down my chin. "Yum"

"In around twenty minutes, you'll die in agony."

I took another bite. "It's worth it. Why did Alexandra Cameron keep a box of condoms in her sweater drawer?"

She looked away. "For the usual reason, I expect."

"Not to prevent pregnancy. Alexandra couldn't get pregnant on her own, remember."

"There are other reasons to use condoms."

"The autopsy showed that neither she nor her husband had contracted STDs"

"Worked, didn't it?"

I took a final bite of the peach, then dropped the pit into a half-filled trash container by the counter. "Let's stop dancing around, Mrs. Newberry. Who was Alexandra's lover?"

She looked me straight in the eye. Unlike when Ali did it, I knew she was revving up for a lie. "I haven't the faintest idea," she said.

"That's interesting. Alison described you and Alexandra as, 'besties.' If I'm as up on teen-speak as I think, that means 'best friends.' And best friends tell each other everything. After all, you've already admitted that she and Dr. Cameron were having trouble."

"Yup. But I still don't know who her lover was, mainly because there was no 'lover' in the commonly accepted sense of the word."

"I don't understand."

"Have some more iced tea. And another poisoned peach."

There being no point in pushing my luck, I declined both. "What aren't you telling me, Mrs. Newberry?"

"Oh, what the hell. Poor Alexandra is dead, so it hardly matters now." She reached over, took a peach, and bit into it. After swallowing, she snapped, "And cut the 'Mrs. Newberry' crap. My name's Margie, as you well know. By now you and that sly hacker partner of yours have found out the brand of syrup I like on my pancakes and which color I prefer for my mani-pedis. What I'm telling you, Lena, dear, oh ye of the suspicious expression, is the God's honest truth. I have absolutely no idea who Alexandra was sleeping with. Alexandra didn't know, either, since she never learned their last names. But if the names 'Tony,' or 'George,' or 'Stu' or whatever will help in your investigation, have at it."

I tried to keep my eyes from boggling. "Multiples?"

"Gee, you can count."

"But…"

"But what?" She took another big chaw of the peach. Hers was even juicier than mine, and she had to dab away the juice running down her chin.

Outside, two emerald-colored hummingbirds were fighting over the rights to a feeder, while from a nearby olive tree's top limb, a red-tailed hawk watched intently. From its posture, I figured one or both hummers had seconds to live. A sudden, brown-flashing dive and a subsequent explosion of green proved me correct. Dinner secured, the hawk flew away with its prize, leaving the surviving hummer fleeing in the opposite direction.

"Was Alexandra moonlighting as an escort?" I asked Margie.

She brayed a laugh. "You've been watching too many art flicks. Or porn. No, my 'bestie,' as you so charmingly call her, was no escort." The harsh humor on her face disappeared, replaced by solemnity. "She was a normal woman trapped in a marriage with a man who either couldn't or wouldn't return her affection, so she took her pleasure where she could find it, mainly when she was travelling for BKDB."

I've always had trouble with acronyms. "What's BKDB? I never heard of it."

"Big Kids Dream Big, a charitable organization to which Monty and I are major contributors. BKDB does for healthy but financially-strapped children what Make-A-Wish does for sick ones, helps them achieve their dreams, which in some cases, means paying school fees, or in other cases, funding trips to summer camp. As you might imagine, keeping such a large organization going entails a lot of bookkeeping, among other things, and that's where Alexandra's background as a CPA came in handy. She pre-audited their books on a regular basis, while I watched Ali and Alec whenever she was out of town. Along with Eldora, of course."

"Their maid. Yes, I talked to her. But what's a pre-audit?"

"A check for discrepancies before things got out of hand. Or criminal. As I'm sure you know, fraud, or shall we say, 'irregular disbursements of funds,' can happen with any charity, especially one that size. A few times a year Alexandra would travel to

BKDB's various offices—they have branches in almost every state—to look over the books. She'd spend a couple of nights at a local hotel, and visit the bar. Every now and then, if things had been particularly bad at home, she'd take a new gentleman friend to her room. Being a wise woman, she never told any of her playmates anything about herself and she didn't bother learning anything about them, either. She wasn't looking for friends, just what the Bruce Springsteen song describes as 'a bit of that human touch.'"

Having walked a few miles in those moccasins myself, I could relate. Still, such behavior never comes without risk. "Did you ever warn her that what she was doing could be dangerous?"

"On a regular basis." A wry smile. "That's what 'besties' are for, aren't they? She claimed she took precautions, and not just of the condom type."

I stifled a groan. These days, all a bad guy needed to do to find out everything about you was to sneak a peek inside your purse. Or bribe the hotel night clerk to get your name and home address, not to mention shadow you as you went about your daily business. Alexandra Cameron might have been a smart woman, but she wasn't a wise one.

"Did she ever conduct any of these, ah, affairs, closer to home?"

"Depends on how close you mean."

"Tucson. Flagstaff."

"A couple of times."

"Each place?"

"Yeah."

"How about Phoenix?"

A flutter outside the glass doors made Margie turn around on her bar stool so she could see better. The lone survivor of the hawk attack had returned to lap sugared water from the feeder. "Aren't they pretty?" she said, ignoring my question.

I tried again. "Margie, did Mrs. Cameron have sex with a man other than her husband here in the Valley area?"

Still watching the hummingbird, she said, "One time, at the Wigwam Resort, way out on the west side. Nice place. They say Frank Sinatra stayed there once." A look of longing briefly appeared on her chiseled face; maybe she was remembering freer days of her own. Straightening her shoulders, she said, "Anyway, after that, she kept her adventures, as she called them, farther away."

"Why?"

"Because as she was leaving the hotel, she saw one of her husband's colleagues walking out of the bar. A Dr. Bosworth, I think she said."

I made a mental note of the name. "Did this Dr. Bosworth recognize her?"

"She wasn't sure, but the encounter spooked her enough that she never went there again." When Margie turned away from the hummingbird, her eyes were bleak. "Not that it made any difference in the end."

I let silence filled the air for a few seconds until I decided it was safe to bring up something else that had been bothering me, yet another inconsistency in a very inconsistent case. "The last time we talked, you told me that Alexandra was upset because she suspected her husband of having an affair. If she was being unfaithful to him, wasn't that rather hypocritical of her?"

With an expression of deep unhappiness, Margie shook her head. "All right. I admit it. I was covering up for her, not wanting to tell you what was really going on over there. And I wanted to place the blame for their trouble squarely on Arthur, not her. Yeah, I was covering up, but so what? Alexandra was my 'bestie,' remember. What she really told me was, since neither she nor Arthur could be faithful to each other, it was probably best to end the marriage before more damage was done. Then a few days later—Alexandra being Alexandra—she told me she'd changed her mind, that the children deserved an intact home. She decided to try harder to make Arthur happy enough that he wouldn't roam, and she in turn would stop having her 'adventures,' regardless of how lonely she felt."

"That's a pretty masochistic philosophy, don't you think?"

She actually laughed. "There's a single woman talking."

"What's that got to do with anything?"

"Marriage is marriage, and life is life. Neither is perfect. If a woman leaves her husband because there's something about him that drives her crazy, chances are good she'll pick another man who's even worse. And after one divorce, the second one comes easier. And the third. And the fourth. Before she knows it, she's racked up a small fortune in attorneys' fees, yet her life isn't one bit better. Ali has a friend whose mother is like that. Married three times already, she's still looking for Mr. Right, and what's it got her? A drinking problem, that's what, and trouble with the law for giving alcohol to minors. So, no, Alexandra's decision was not masochistic. For all her flaws—and she certainly had them—she chose the wiser path. And, considering the children, the more compassionate one."

Also, the more depressing. I thought back about my own love life. Dusty. Warren. The men before them. The good thing about being single was that when you decided to pack it in, you just left. No legal proceedings required. If you didn't want to go crazy, you had to believe that somewhere out there was someone right for you, someone you'd never get to know if you stayed in your current bad situation. If you wound up alone, so be it.

But Margie's revelations gave rise to another suspicion. "When Alexandra decided to stay with Dr. Cameron, did she clear the slate by telling him about her one-night stands?"

"I doubt it. Still, I can't be certain."

When Margie rose from her bar stool and looked toward the door, I knew the interview was over. "One more question before I go. Several people have described Dr. Cameron as either aloof or downright cold. When he wasn't obsessing over his cars, that is. His half-brother, who's also a physician, thinks he had a touch of Asperger's. Did you ever witness that kind of behavior?"

She blinked several times. "Asperger's? That would explain everything. Oh, good Lord, I can't believe I didn't think of it myself when Alexandra told me what he'd done, because it was so awful, so unforgivable…" Her face contorted into a mixture of shock and grief. "You…You have to understand, I'd never thought of Arthur as having a temper but never being downright cruel, so I was shocked when…" She shook her head, still aghast over some past incident. "That poor woman. And Jesus, that poor, poor kid."

"What did Dr. Cameron do?"

"It doesn't matter, what he did has nothing to do with what happened."

My interior alarm was shrieking. "Let me be the judge of that. What did Dr. Cameron do?"

She walked over to the sliding glass door. Looked out at a new hummingbird helicoptering near the feeder. When it saw her, it flew away in a glimmer of blue and green. She sighed. "I like watching them, the birds, and yet I always seem to scare them off."

"Margie, stop evading my question."

With nothing left to see, she returned to the counter. "Now I feel rotten for being so angry with Arthur. If what you say is true, the man didn't realize what he was doing. This was, oh, about a month ago, maybe a little more. First thing I need to tell you is that, well, as you've seen, Alexandra shared a lot with me. About everything, even the trouble she was having getting pregnant and what she and Arthur finally did about it."

"She told you about the IVF?"

"Of course. I even helped her with the shots." She looked at me defiantly, as if expecting some sort of negative reaction.

Instead, I said, "You were a good friend, Margie."

She looked at her hand, the one with the wedding ring. "I tried to be. Marriage…well, marriage can be complicated, and over the years, I became as open with her as she was with me."

Trouble in Newberry Land? But I didn't want to get sidetracked. "What did Dr. Cameron do that had Alexandra so upset?"

She heaved another sigh. "All right. I'll tell you. One morning Alexandra came over here in tears, distraught over something he'd said while they were eating breakfast. All of them were at the table, Arthur, Alexandra, Alec, and Ali. There'd been an article in the morning newspaper, something about in vitro fertilization, and Arthur became obsessed with the inaccuracies in the reporting. For obvious reasons Alexandra tried to distract him, but he just went on and on until he finally started comparing what was in the newspaper with what he knew and had had experience with. Unfortunately, he used Ali as his example. While she was sitting right there. Listening to him."

"You mean he let it slip that Ali was the result of IVF?"

"Not only 'let slip.' From what Alexandra told me, he pretty much battered the subject to death, then took its corpse out for a walk. He yammered about how many intramuscular shots she had to take, for how long a period, and how the whole thing had to be timed with the egg donor, who was taking the same shots. He went on and on, she said, and nothing she said or did would shut him up." She rubbed a trembling hand over her eyes. "God, that must have been ghastly for her."

And for Ali.

"Did Alexandra say how Ali reacted?"

A bitter laugh. "The poor girl locked herself in her room and didn't speak to anyone for two days." Margie closed her eyes. When she opened them, they were red. "You know what's really pathetic? Alexandra said that no matter how often or in how many different ways she tried to explain it to him afterwards, Arthur never could understand why Ali got so upset."

Deciding that I might as well lump all the misery into one day and get it over with, I re-checked Jimmy's list for the other two families who had lost loved ones via Dr. Arthur Cameron's deadly services, and headed for the closest.

Murderers cover the entire financial spectrum: rich, poor, middle class, and every financial state in between. True, the Death Row type of murderer was rarest among the rich, mainly because wealthy felons can afford better lawyers, but every now and then, one of them got himself—or herself—convicted. That happened to Blaine DuCharme III, executed May 1 for killing two police officers and a civilian in the aftermath of a bungled bank robbery initiated to feed his drug habit. There were so many witnesses to Blaine's crimes—among them, three surveillance cameras, and two squad car dash cams—that his conviction had been a slam dunk. So great was the outrage among Arizona's law-and-order populace, that despite his family's money, his execution had been fast-tracked to a mere twenty-one years after his conviction.

Unlike the families of Buelah Phelps, Kenny Dean Hopper, and Sidney Hoyt, the DuCharme family was rolling in the green stuff. DuCharme Chocolatiers, founded seventy-five years ago by Blaine DuCharme I, was Arizona's answer to Belgium's Godiva. The company started off as a small, mom-and-pop confectionary in Old Town Scottsdale, then over the decades, grew into an empire that enjoyed outlets in just about every high-end mall in America. But its very success guaranteed national coverage when Blaine Three—as the tabloids dubbed him—shot his way up Scottsdale Road. Somehow the DuCharme family survived the shame, and sales of their waist-expanding products continued to be brisk. Only one member of the DuCharme family, the younger brother, showed up to hear Blaine Three's final words: "Personally, I always liked the white chocolate hazelnut truffles best."

The family immediately pulled hazelnut truffles from their stores nationwide, and hasn't offered them since.

No love lost there, I figured, as I approached Casa DuCharme. Like many of the Valley's more expensive abodes, the house was located on several acres of scalped desert in far North Scottsdale, where blacktop driveways covered old Indian trails, and Cadillacs roamed where mountain lions once hunted. Kidney-shaped pools now replaced watering holes and gaudy gardens of bougainvillea drowned out the subtler tones of desert wildflowers. At least Casa DuCharme, a relic of the old Frank Lloyd Wright school of architecture, had the decency to mimic its surroundings. A spiky, copper-clad roof echoed distant mountains, and sweeping glass windows reflected the remains of the ancient Hohokam hill fort on a rise across the way.

I tried hard to appreciate the DuCharmes' desert-sensitive efforts as I climbed the stone steps to the front door, a cunning mockup of saguaro spines overlaid on what appeared to be a rusted mine entrance. Before I made it to the top, a uniformed maid opened the door. At her feet, a gray-snouted Chihuahua yipped at me out of a nearly toothless mouth.

"Mrs. DuCharme is seeing no one," the maid said, in a Hispanic accent. "Please go now."

"I just want…"

"I'll take care of it, Lucinda," a tall woman said, gently moving the maid and Chihuahua aside.

Mrs. Lorraine DuCharme, nee Hillier, of the Santa Barbara Hilliers, faced me. She had once been beautiful, but was much less so now, and not only because of age. Already bone thin, sorrow had bowed her back and despair haunted her dark eyes. Even her voice sounded laden with tears.

She wasn't too frail for *politesse*, though. "If you are a journalist, please understand that I do not speak to the press. Everything you need to know, I said in the press release my PR person handed out on the evening of my son's execution. Perhaps you did not receive a copy? If not, Lucinda can fetch you another, for I understand and sympathize with editorial deadlines."

"Ma'am, I'm not with the media."

She glanced toward my Jeep, which sat popping and pinging in the heat. "Are you having car trouble? If so, you may come in and wait until a tow arrives. This heat can be dangerous. Lucinda will serve you some iced tea."

Although tempted to lie, out of pity I didn't. "No, Ma'am, my Jeep's fine. The name's Lena Jones. I'm a private investigator and I'm here to talk to you about your son." Too late I remembered that there were two sons in the DuCharme family. The living one now ran the company business.

But Mrs. DuCharme knew which one I meant. Her face shut down and she stepped back. "Then you have wasted your trip." The door closed.

"But a young girl's life is at stake! And a boy's!" I yelled.

Nothing.

She was right. I had wasted my trip.

Twenty-three years earlier, Maleese Young, a black high-school dropout was convicted of killing his wife and her lover, a small-time South Phoenix drug dealer. This past New Year's Day he met his own end at the hands of the esteemed Dr. Arthur Cameron. Because diabetes and heart disease ran rampant in the Young family, the only two relatives left to mourn Maleese were Janeese, his thirty-six-year-old daughter, and Dorothea, his mother. The two lived together in a small condo near Arizona State University, where Janeese Young, PhD—she never married—headed up the Urban Planning Department.

When I showed up at their door, I was invited in, but only because they were initially under the impression that I had found proof of Maleese's innocence. The temperature in the room dropped considerably when I set them straight.

"If you're not here to help us clear my father's name, then why are you here?" Professor Young asked, hostility leaking out of every pore. Her mood was mirrored by two large black dogs that jumped off a chair and darted toward me, barking shrilly. They had all their teeth.

I shuffled my feet just inside the threshold, wishing I'd found another profession. "I just want to ask you a few questions, then I'll leave."

"Leave now!" she said, meaning it.

"Janeese, you were raised better than that," Her grandmother said, rolling her wheelchair forward. "And get her something to drink. Poor thing looks half dead." In her late sixties, she was missing a leg, and her skin, once a rich mahogany, showed patches of gray around her eyes. She wore an insulin pump at her waist.

"Sorry for my lack of manners," her granddaughter said, not sounding sorry at all, "but things have been rough around here since my father's been executed." She put stress on the last word. "But go ahead, take a seat, and I'll get us some sweet tea."

Sweet tea. The terminology reminded me that the family had moved to Arizona from Mississippi twenty years before Maleese married the woman whose sins eventually killed him. Unlike Alexandra Cameron's multiple lovers, Janet Young—Professor Young's mother—was reputed to have had only one: the late, unlamented Willie 'Pig Eye' Wyms.

"Tea would be lovely, thanks." I hate sweet tea but this was neither the time nor the place to stick to the truth.

She disappeared into the kitchen, leaving me to field the polite scrutiny of her grandmother. And the not-so-polite scrutiny of the dogs. They stared at me like I was dinner.

"Have a seat, Miss Jones. I don't bite, although Duke and Shasta might." She patted the seat cushion of a beige tweed sofa. "You'll be safer over here."

Although small, the living room comfortably combined two divergent tastes. A four-foot-high abstract sculpture of "found" materials stood guard in the corner, while a brightly colored African print scarf was thrown across the back of the muted-toned sofa. Dr. Young was probably responsible for the various awards and degrees on one wall, but I imagined that her grandmother had hung the many family portraits decorating every other wall. Most of the people in them, including the murdered Janet Young, were now dead. So was Maleese, whose smiles beamed down at us from five different photographs. Adorable as a child, he had grown into a handsome man.

Maleese's defense attorney had made much of his near movie-star looks, arguing that it was unlikely a woman would cheat on such a handsome man with the likes of the appropriately nicknamed "Pig Eye." His argument failed, the jury deciding that there was no accounting for taste.

Seeing me stare at the pictures, Mrs. Young said proudly, "My family."

"Very nice." I didn't know what else to say.

"My son didn't kill Janeese's mother. Or that Pig Eye fellow."

I was saved from replying by the return of Dr. Young, who bore three glasses of iced tea on a hammered bronze tray. She set the tray down on the glass-topped coffee table, then handed one glass to her grandmother.

"My father never hurt anyone," Dr. Young said. "Regardless of what those people testified to in court, my mother didn't involve herself with other men, especially not a lowlife like Willie Wyms."

Tea service complete, she lowered herself into a chair across from me, where she could keep those cold, hard eyes on my face. The dogs followed suit, but when she reached down to pat them, the animosity in their eyes disappeared and they looked at her with adoration.

"You know why I have two black dogs, Ms. Jones?"

"Uh, no."

"Because more black dogs are euthanized at the pound than any other color."

I knew what else she was about to say, and she didn't disappoint me.

"Just like the American penal system. More black men in prison than white, more black men executed than white."

There was no arguing with that. Racial profiling continues right into the Death Chamber. But this wasn't the time to get into a civil rights discussion, so I merely said, "The court records show there were eyewitnesses to the murders. Two men testified that they saw your father shoot your mother and Mr. Wyms." I took a sip of the tea; its sweetness was tweaked with lemon slices.

A bitter laugh. "Oh, sure, a couple of drug dealers, both of whom made deals with the prosecutor for lighter sentences. They lied."

Maybe, but more than twenty-three years of unsuccessful appeals said otherwise.

What must it be like, I wondered, to be descended from a killer? To recognize that everyone knew what your father had done? To find every eye leveled on you in judgment, or even worse, pity? What was it like to attend your father's execution, to sit there and watch while he breathed his last? Did it break your heart? Or did you bury your heartbreak under an avalanche of rage?

However the deaths of her mother—and years later her father—impacted her soul, Professor Janeese Young was no fool. When I asked her where she was between noon and three p.m. on Monday, July 8, she told me oh so politely it was none of my business. Then she added, "Put your tea down, Ms. Jones. The welcome mat has just been withdrawn."

Despite an admonition from her grandmother, Dr. Young escorted me to the door. Just before she opened it, she leaned toward me, the desire for vengeance sparking from her eyes. "Do you know what my father's last words were?"

Having already briefed myself, I did, but she wanted to tell me so I let her.

"My daddy said, 'I'm sorry for everything I done put my family through. Oh, sweet Jesus, here I come.'"

Chapter Twenty

The late afternoon sun blazed a fiery outline behind the cumulus clouds that had collected in the west during my interview with the Youngs. It held out hope that an evening rain shower might bring some relief to the heat, but I was so depressed, even that possibility failed to cheer me.

Although I was no fan of capital punishment, after some of the horrendous crimes I had helped solve I couldn't say I was one hundred percent against it, either. Yet most of the arguments for or against capital punishment focused on the death itself, not the years leading up to the execution. After a short trial in which most of the other evidence was circumstantial, Maleese Young spent twenty-three years on Death Row with the knowledge that each sunrise brought him one day closer to the padded gurney where he would reach his earthly end. Could such knowledge be considered cruel and unusual punishment? Or was Maleese's awareness little different than the same fear of death we all lived with, that each new day brought us closer to dying?

Still…

I had once interviewed a retired prison guard who pointed out that, given most of the condemned men's violent pasts, their decades spent on Death Row actually lengthened their lives. "Drugs, brawls, knives, shootings—hell, Ms. Jones, left to their own devices, most of these guys wouldn't have made it to their thirtieth birthdays. Say what you will about Death Row being a grim place and all, it's still safer for them than the streets. Here they live twice as long as they would have out there."

His words had creeped me out at the time. They still do.

When I exited the freeway at McDowell, I made a snap decision. Instead of turning east toward the Pima Rez and the dangerous comforts of Jimmy's trailer, I turned west toward Scottsdale and the Best Western. The arrangement might be inconvenient, but I'd be able to have my nightmares in peace. Besides, his trailer and computers were only fifteen minutes away.

As soon as I checked in, I called Jimmy and explained.

He wasn't happy. "Did you forget you left your things here? And that big box of Cameron material."

Yes, I'd forgotten, but wasn't about to admit it. "As to the clothes, I'll pick up more at Walmart. And I'll get the box tomorrow."

A grunt. "With all the business you do at Walmart, they've probably run out of black."

"Then it's on to Target. Maybe it's time I moved up the style ladder."

"This is about last night isn't it?"

"Don't be silly."

"Lena, you need to…"

"Oops! Landline's ringing. Gotta go!"

I ended the call before remembering there is no landline in a car.

Shopping at Walmart did not take long. It never does when you limit your clothing choices to black and don't care much what shampoo, deodorant, or toothpaste you buy as long as it's on sale. The only thing that merited careful consideration was a laptop, but since I'm not fussy there either, I bought a basic Samsung and let it go at that. All I needed was something to tie me into Desert Investigations' records so I could update the case file.

Two hours later an emergency technician at Data Doctors had loaded enough basic software into the Samsung to get me started, so once ensconced at the Best Western, in the same room as before, I was able to transcribe the day's interviews before they went cold on me. As soon as I finished typing, I merged all my transcriptions with the case file Babette had emailed me. Then I sat back and reread everything twice. When you get things down in black and white, inconsistencies can leap out at you, and today was no exception. I found several, which meant that follow-up interviews were in order.

I checked my watch. Seven-thirty. In July the days are long, giving me plenty of time to find Ali's party house, so I grabbed the usual equipment and headed out into the heat again.

Due to the economic downturn, finding the party house took longer than planned and the light had dimmed. More than one bank-owned home lined the streets of North Scottsdale, so by the time I snuck my way into its backyard, dusk had fallen. No matter. Like any good Girl Scout, I came armed with a flashlight. Although the house was well-hidden from the street by high, untrimmed oleander bushes, entrance to 17712 East Appaloosa Way presented no problem. The houses on both sides sported FOR SALE signs and appeared empty. No snoopy neighbors to worry about. By now, the plywood sheeting across the back window which gave party-minded teens their egress had slipped to the ground. The only thing to worry about was the prospect of cutting myself on the few pieces of glass that remained in the window. Wrapping a couple of towels around my latex-gloved hands helped on that front.

When I finally made it through, only to land in a puddle of water, the stench of mildew, old beer, and rotted junk food almost knocked me off my feet. Talk about your Teenage Babylon.

A quick walk-through proved that this formerly two-million-dollar property had hit the skids big time. Apparently so many properties been repossessed of late that the banks had given up policing them. A smashed crystal chandelier hung crookedly from the living room's twenty-foot ceiling, and graffiti, most of it of a sexual nature, defaced the Tuscan plaster walls. Someone had taken a sledgehammer to the travertine marble flooring, which was further insulted by layers of used condoms and junk food wrappers. The nasty sleeping bags tossed here and there were more Goodwill Reject than Montbel.

Ignoring the heat and smell, I searched through the rubble, hoping to find something that would back up Ali's story. I hit pay dirt in what appeared to have been the master suite, where a relatively clean duvet and a backpack were tucked into a walk-in closet. I leaned closer and with the aid of the flashlight, read KYLE GIBBS printed on the side of the backpack with a Sharpie. The pack had been scavenged and most of its treasures, such as graded term papers and shopping lists for his pets, were torn to pieces. But zipped into a side compartment, I found several sales receipts and a still-intact but grubby note in Ali's handwriting. It asked him to rendezvous with her at the house to "make mad, passionate love." It gave time and date for the assignation: the day of the murders.

Although any halfway decent prosecutor could shoot holes in my find—and in fact, the backpack's contents proved little, other than a plan to get together—this was something the police needed to see, so after taking several pictures with my smart-phone, I made my way back outside and called Scottsdale PD. Then, my hands still covered in the latex gloves, I took a closer look at the receipts.

And everything changed.

Eight thirty is a relatively slow time in Scottsdale, at least by police standards. The late-night bar fights hadn't yet begun, and the drunks were hours away from wrecking their Porsches. Within minutes of my call, I was being given the third degree in the overgrown backyard by my old buddies, detectives Bob Grossman and Sylvie Perrins, as a squadron of crime techs made their way into the house.

"We could arrest you for breaking-and-entering," Bob said, sounding sorrowful.

I gave him a smile to cheer him up. "You could, but you won't. At least not for the 'breaking' part. As anyone can plainly see, that plywood's been off the window for a while."

"Then how about we just kick your skinny ass all the way to Nogales?" Sylvie snarled. She had always been the more violent of the two.

"That's police brutality, Sylvie. Besides, you guys owe me."

"Yeah? For what?" She was so close I could tell she'd switched perfumes, from an oriental citrus blend to a musky floral. New boyfriend? I hoped so. A few rolls in the hay might take the edge off all that aggression.

"You owe me because of that money I found for you at the crime scene. And for this." I waved a receipt at her. "Proof that neither of those kids killed anyone."

"Nogales isn't all that far. Just a simple dropkick…"

"Point taken. I'm irritating. But what you don't know, Sylvie, is that while doing my work for Ai's attorney, I uncovered several other suspects, people who had stronger reasons to kill the Camerons than Ali and Kyle ever did."

Her glower deepened. "And you're going to surprise us with those mysterious suspects' names at the trial, right? That's withholding evidence, another reason to arrest you."

"Everything I've found out will be forwarded to the prosecutor at the appropriate time. In the meantime, consider this receipt a gift to old friends. Auld lang syne, and all that."

She wasn't ready to let it go. "How do we know you didn't plant that backpack? And the receipt?"

"The backpack will prove to have Kyle's fingerprints all over it, certainly not mine, since I'm wearing these stylish latex gloves, but until the techs bear out my story, you'll have to take my word. As for this particular receipt, it'll match the records at Circle K. The receipt shows that at 1:30 p.m. July 8, when the Camerons were being tortured and killed, Kyle was buying eight Slim Jims, four bags of Fritos, and two packs of Twinkies." I pointed at the receipt again. "And a *Cosmopolitan Magazine.* If I remember correctly, the July issue has an article titled '40 Sex Tips to Please Your Man.' Excellent article. I picked up a few hints, myself."

"Oh, the sex tips will go over big with the county prosecutor. I hear he's lonely. But that's all you got? Kyle Gibbs bought fucking Fritos?"

"Timeline, Sylvie, timeline. Get sex out of your head and listen. That receipt is time-stamped at 1:30, which proves that Kyle was elsewhere when the murders and house-trashing were taking place. According to the interview you guys did with the delivery boy at Zhou's Mandarin Wok, he dropped off an order of almond chicken, moo goo gai pan, and egg rolls just before noon. We know from the medical examiner's report that the family had just begun to eat when they were interrupted. The few bites of food found in their stomachs were only partially digested before they died, which narrows the time of death to between a few minutes after twelve and sometime before two thirty. Probably closer to the later, because of the time it took to torture them."

That finally got Sylvie's attention. "Go on," she said.

"Not to sound monotonous about this, but remember the Circle K time stamp? I'll say it again. One thirty. According to the autopsy, the Camerons were either dead or dying then, so let me ask you this. Do you really think that in, say, ten or fifteen minutes, a fourteen-year-old boy walked almost a mile from the Circle K at the corner of Indian Bend and Scottsdale Road to here, dumped his backpack, then went back out again, and walked another mile to the Camerons' house, got inside, tied them up, tortured them, trashed the house, smeared dog droppings all over the walls—then walked away with only a couple of drops of blood on him? He just didn't have enough time, Sylvie."

"He could have killed them earlier, say, around one, before he got to the Circle K. The autopsy doesn't rule that out."

I didn't want to bring up Kyle's dog rescue, which could provide a further alibi, until I'd found the dog's owner, so I just said, "Only if he could fly. Granted, the M.E. said the murder could have been committed a little earlier, but he also stressed that it was doubtful since the food in the victims' stomachs had already begun to digest. Also, if the kid killed the Camerons earlier, then went to the Circle K for his junk food fix, why didn't the Circle K clerk notice he was covered in blood? Or later, at the vet's? The vet certainly noticed blood on Ali when they dropped Misty off, but he never said anything about blood on Kyle."

"Maybe the kid changed clothes."

"That makes no sense, Sylvie. I'd also like to remind you the crime lab found two very small smears of human blood, and no spatter at all, on Kyle's clothes, not enough to account for the kind of slaughter that went down. Lots of canine blood on Ali's. Yes, when the kids were arrested, faint traces of human blood were under one of Kyle's fingernails, but that probably got transferred from the murder weapon when he picked it up. But let me remind you, Kyle didn't leave enough fingerprints on the bat to have clubbed the Cameron family to death. That's always been the weak point in the case against him. Yes, yes, I know, he and Ali both had the victims' blood on the bottom of their shoes, they'd tromped around in it, but that's it. You saw the crime scene. How could either one of them slaughter three people without getting drenched in gore?"

Sylvie might have been a Grade A bitch, but she was also honest and smart so I gave her time to digest this. After clicking her tongue against her teeth for a few moments, she finally gave in. "Shit. You're right. Thing is, we stopped looking at other possibilities when the kids confessed."

"And now they've retracted those confessions."

"Double shit."

"You can say that again." This from Bob.

Before I could add anything else, one of the crime scene techs exited the party house and walked up to us. She was a heavy, middle-aged woman who looked like she'd attended one too many parties herself. Addressing Sylvie, she said, "Detective Perrins, how thorough do you want us to be? There's a god-awful mess in there, everything from rat feces to smashed wine bottles. We've got a cookstove with Chef Boyardee ravioli slopped all over it, dozens of empty food cans ranging from Vienna sausages to canned peaches, and some pretty nasty sleeping bags."

"Do your damned job!" Sylvie snapped. "Scrape every inch of the place!"

The tech snapped a snarky salute and waddled back into the house.

"What a bitch," Sylvie muttered.

I could have said something about pots calling kettles black, but let it go. "Why don't we forget about the kids for a minute and talk about the murder scene and what it suggests. An awful amount of rage went into that attack. Tell me, have you looked into the doctor's background and thought about whoever else might have wanted to kill him? And his entire family? Don't forget, if Ali had been home, she would probably have been killed, too."

Trying hard to keep her temper in check, Sylvie said, "Why would we bother checking into Dr. Cameron when we thought we already had our perps? Two kids who'd kill to be together, simple as that. Fuck that now. What else do you know? The name of someone or someones who held a grudge against Cameron?" She stressed the plural.

"Because of my arrangement with Ali's attorney, I can't give you any names right now, but I can say this. If you look into the doctor's background more closely you might get a big fat surprise."

"Such as?"

I sighed. "Sylvie, I'm not going to do your work for you." *At least not until Ali's attorney tells me I can. Until then, all you'll get is hints.*

Before Sylvie could erupt again, Bob nudged her. "Ease up. Lena's on file as Stephen Zellar's investigator, which means she doesn't have to tell us anything she doesn't want to. Not now, anyway."

She transferred her glower to him. "It's still withholding evidence." Her eyes narrowed. "And there's that little problem with breaking-and-entering, and no, I don't buy her lame-ass story that the window was intact when she got here. We can haul her in for that."

Ignoring his partner's refreshed temper tantrum, Bob said to me, "Let's handle it this way, Lena. Next time you find something of interest, why not let us know before we all have to put on our good clothes to show up in court? Hmmm?" Turning to Sylvie, he said, "Lena might not have broken in. It rained last night, and if you'll remember, once we got inside, we had to wade through the collected water right below the window. Worse comes to worst, Lena can claim she was doing her civic duty by checking out the safety of the structure. Sure, we could get her for trespass, but under the circumstances, she wouldn't even get her wrist slapped. That's an awful lot of paperwork to go through for nothing."

I'd always admired Bob's ability to pour oil on Sylvie's troubled waters, so I added my two cents. "Especially since upon entering the house, I just happened to come across evidence I thought the fine ladies and gentlemen at Scottsdale PD should know about. Not to mention my concern over the safety issues you just brought up, Bob. Gee, what would happen if one of those kids accidentally burned the place down with that Stone Age cookstove in there and didn't make it out in time? This place is not just an attractive nuisance, it's a dangerous one."

I directed my next comment to Sylvie. "Another thing. Since the receipt has the exact time Kyle was in the Circle K, he should be on their surveillance video. Look, Sylvie, you may talk a mean game, but I know you're no more interested in railroading a couple of innocent kids than I am."

"Hmph." But her glower had vanished. After a few moments' silence, she said, "Get the hell out of here before I change my mind and cuff you."

"I'm already gone."

As I drove away, something occurred to me.

The Circle K probably wasn't the only structure around with a surveillance camera. This was a pretty expensive neighborhood, and that meant expensive security. Chances were good that somewhere between the party house and the murder scene, some of those houses probably had their own surveillance systems.

All I needed to do was find them.

Chapter Twenty-one

Another night, another nightmare, but this time I was able to scream it out without bringing a half-naked Indian to my bed.

After a hasty and overpriced breakfast at the restaurant next door, I headed up to North Scottsdale, where I traced the route from the party house to the murder scene. What I found made me wonder if another meeting with Ali was in the offing. The path from the two places was a straight shot, so how could she have missed seeing Kyle when she went to apologize for her temper tantrum?

But on my second drive-through, I discovered that the boy could have taken another route from the Circle K back to their little love nest. Instead of walking along Appaloosa Way, he could have used Pinto Lane, a small side street, to connect with Indian Bend, then over to Appaloosa. If Ali had gone the other way— Appaloosa to Scottsdale Road, then south to the Circle K—they would have missed each other by two blocks. Still, I would ask her to make sure. Just not tomorrow, when her father, mother, and brother would be buried.

I then set off in search of Ancient Alice, the woman whose dog Kyle said he rescued. Tracking her down didn't take long. A block from the Circle K, I found a faded LOST DOG flyer tacked to a telephone pole. The owner's telephone number was attached to pull-off tabs at the bottom, and yes, one was missing. I called, and five minutes later was sitting in a chair covered with dog hair, listening to Ancient Alice tell me about the wonderful boy who had kept a spectacularly ugly mutt named Precious from becoming a coyote's dinner.

"Kyle said when he found Precious she was headed straight for the Pima Reservation, and you know what would have happened to her there, what with all those coyotes running loose. Awful things are always prowling around this neighborhood, looking for strays. A good friend of mine, her Chihuahua got loose once, and she found it the next day, nothing left of the poor thing but a bit of fur and its collar." During all this, Precious, who looked half possum and half javelina, sat on her lap, drooling and farting. Ancient Alice didn't seem to mind.

Trying not to breathe too deeply, I said, "The flyer offered the finder a one hundred dollar reward. Did you give it to him?"

Ancient Alice, who was only around fifty and in tennis-player shape, answered, "I tried, but he refused to take it, told me to make a donation to Liberty Wildlife instead. So I did. Two hundred, as a matter of fact, and in his name. Kyle Gibbs. Too bad more young people these days aren't like him, instead of playing that awful rap and wearing their pants down around their knees. Why, it's terrible how…"

I broke in before she was well away into her diatribe. "Don't you watch the news? Read the newspapers?"

She gave me a look. "Of course I do. Why do you ask?"

"But…" I remembered that because of Ali's and Kyle's ages, neither their names nor their faces had appeared in the media, a practice set in place years ago to protect minors' identities. This time, the compassionate practice had worked against them.

I wasted no time in bringing Ancient Alice up-to-date on Kyle's situation.

"But he was here a little after noon. I'd just come back to take a lunch break from looking for Precious before I went out again. I was eating and watching *Arizona Live*, that news program, and they'd started to do their feature section, which is around halfway through, so that would be, um, about 12:15. I can assure you that boy had no blood on his shirt whatsoever. It was white with a small blue logo that said LIBERTY WILDLIFE, and the only thing on it, besides the logo, was a little bit of hair from Precious. She was limping so bad he had to carry the poor thing."

It was all I could do to keep her from rushing down to the police station to demand Kyle's release, and she settled down only when I told her that placing a call to Curtis Racine, Kyle's attorney, would be the wiser course. I gave her his number.

When I left, she was already reaching for the phone.

During my search for Ancient Alice, I had listed the addresses of every home between the crime scene and the party house that sported surveillance cameras. Now I doubled back, making certain I hadn't skipped any. Then I called Detective Sylvie Perrins.

"I have some addresses for you," I told her. "All the houses with security cameras along the routes Ali and Kyle took the day of the murders."

"About how many are there?"

"Twenty three."

"Oh, for Christ's sake, Lena. I'm not your secretary. Email the addresses to me."

Click.

Once back at the Best Western I typed up the list on my new laptop and sent it to Sylvie, as per her command. The woman might be a pain to get along with, but I knew she and Bob would waste no time viewing whatever action all those surveillance cameras caught. Unless I was wrong, Kyle and Ali would be released from custody in a matter of days. To make certain, I followed up with calls to their attorneys. Although I got Curtis Racine's voice mail, Zellar actually picked up the phone.

"Tell me you have something good for me," he said.

I told him what I'd found out about the party house and my hopes for the security cameras.

"Good news for the boy, but what about Ali?"

"I'm going to check for surveillance cameras on her, too. By the way, when Ali gets released, and I'm certain she will be, where will she go?"

"To her uncle's, I imagine. Remember, as per the deceased's wishes, Dr. Teague has filed for legal custody."

"Wish I felt better about that."

"Life doesn't always cooperate with our wishes, Ms. Jones."

"Tell me about it. Ah, about the funeral tomorrow. Were you able to talk the judge into letting Ali attend?"

"He's allowing her to attend, but she'll be in shackles." He didn't sound happy.

When we said our good-byes, I didn't sound happy, either. In fact, I felt less optimistic than I'd felt at the start of our conversation. Shackled at a funeral, Jesus. And the idea of loyal, sensitive Alison Cameron being raised by her uncle wasn't pleasant, either. But Zellar was right and there was nothing I could do about it. Deciding that a trip to the gym would take my mind off the situation, I changed into my Walmart workout clothes and headed back out into the heat. But since the drive took me within spitting distance of Desert Investigations, I stopped by to see how Scottsdale Restore was doing with my apartment.

Not well, it appeared. At least not as far as my moving back in was concerned.

"Bad news," said, Cal Kinsley, the project foreman, after taking off his face mask. A hands-on type of boss, he was as grungy as his workers. Soot stained his overalls and flecks of sawdust peppered his light brown hair. "You've got extensive smoke damage to the carpet, drywall, and ceiling, so they'll all have to be replaced. Yes, yes, I know you're anxious to move back in, but right now the place is a health hazard. Plus, the fire damaged the meter box, and the city inspector can't make it out to look at it until Thursday. That's at the earliest."

"But I could…" I was about to tell him I was willing to sleep wearing a painter's mask to keep out the fumes, but he saved me from myself.

"It really is a safety issue, Miss Jones. Count yourself lucky we didn't find asbestos." When he smiled, I realized that underneath all that grime was a handsome man, so I didn't mind when he looked me up and down. "Headed to the gym?"

I nodded.

"Good. It'll help work off all that anxiety."

"I didn't realize it was that obvious."

"Well, you are wearing workout clothes."

"I meant the anxiety."

He laughed. "Which gym you belong to?"

"L.A. Fitness. And Scottsdale Fight Pro."

"Hey, same here! Maybe I'll run into you at one of the smoothie bars."

After checking his left hand for a wedding ring and finding none, I smiled back. "Maybe at the smoothie bar."

"I'm into the Banana Strawberry with Power Boost. How about you?"

"Mango Delite. But I'm always willing to try anything new."

"Me, too." He waggled his eyebrows.

There's nothing like a flirtation with a good-looking man to cheer a woman up, so I was whistling a happy tune when I rolled into the Fight Pro parking lot, which for a change, still had a few spaces open. But I rolled back out when I saw Big Black Hummer parked near the entrance. Hell. She'd made bail already? On an arson charge? With her damned Hummer, yet? For a moment I sympathized with Congresswoman Thorsson about the laxity of our criminal justice system, but there was nothing I could do about it. While I wasn't averse to having a face-off with Monster Woman, legally speaking it wasn't a good idea so I turned the Jeep around and headed for the Best Western. Seeing the Hummer had reminded me of something, though, so I pulled to the curb and placed a call to Jimmy.

"Find out everything you can about Terry Jardine," I told him. "I'm thinking we might have dropped the ball there. If she's crazy enough to get engaged to a multiple murderer like Kenny Dean Hopper, and firebomb Desert Investigations just because I had her Hummer towed, she might be crazy enough to kill the Cameron family."

Jimmy made negative noises. "No woman would commit that kind of crime, Lena. Remember, a child was one of the victims."

"You saw the crime scene pictures, didn't you?"

"Unfortunately, yes."

"Man or woman, steroid abuse does strange things to the mind. And who says women can't be stone cold killers, or have you forgotten one of our recent cases?"

He grumbled some more, but in the end, agreed to do it. Then, before I could hang up, he said, "Lena, we really need to talk."

"About what?"

"About your nightmares. About you moving back to the motel."

"No we don't."

"Yes, we do. You keep avoiding the issue, and that's affecting our work relationship."

"It was just a dream, so what's the big deal? Don't you ever dream?"

"Not like that."

"Lucky you." Irritated beyond measure, I ended the call.

In summer, a cool shower always relaxes me, so I stripped off my sweaty clothes and went into the bathroom. Twenty minutes later I emerged, smelling like Best Western soap and Best Western shampoo. Best of all, something had occurred to me while the water rained down.

Mrs. Lorraine Hillier DuCharme, matriarch of DuCharme Chocolatiers, may have refused to talk to me, but there could be a way around that problem. A mecca for chocoholics everywhere, her Scottsdale-based chocolate company offered tours of the factory, each of which culminated in a visit to the factory's retail outlet in the same building. I had just enough time to make it over there to sign on for the one o'clock. Besides, they say chocolate's good for whatever ails ya, so a few truffles might be the medicine I needed to lift my spirits.

Although the DuCharme home store was located in Old Town Scottsdale where herds of tourists roamed, the factory itself sat a couple of miles southeast. Mere minutes later I was pulling into the parking lot. Once inside the building, I realized throwing questions at Carl DuCharme, who conducted the tours, wouldn't work. Still, I went along as a busload of tourists and senior citizens trailed after him through a factory that was so clean you could have eaten your chocolate truffles right off the floor.

Carl was the younger of the two DuCharme brothers. In his thirties, tall, and with a lean physique that hinted he didn't avail himself of the family product too often, he only vaguely resembled the old booking shot of his infamous older brother. Unlike Blaine DuCharme's manic stare, Carl's eyes gleamed with intelligence, not drugs, and his gentle manner with the older people on the tour hinted at a different personality altogether.

Due to the infirmaries and advanced ages of some of the tour-goers, he led us slowly alongside a contraption he jovially called the "*I Love Lucy* Assembly Line."

"Whenever we get a new hire," he said, flashing a good-natured smile, "we turn up the speed of the conveyer belt."

Obediently, we all laughed.

He directed his next remark to the senior members of our group. "Just kidding, of course. We wouldn't do that to our worst enemies. I'm sure some of you remember what happened to Lucy and her pal Ethel when the conveyer belt got too fast for them. They started eating the chocolate instead of processing it." He wagged a finger, and added, to more laughter, "We need to ration our sins, not overindulge them, even when chocolate is involved. But remember, one DuCharme truffle a day keeps the doctor away."

More laughter.

Since the sound level in the factory was so high—something I had not expected—he spoke through a hand-held mike. I'd expected to see huge vats with dark chocolate dripping down the sides. Instead, the chocolate—both white and dark—ran through the gleaming, stainless steel pipes hanging from the ceiling until their addictive cargo gushed into the appropriate containers. From there they were mixed with different flavorings, coated with something equally addictive, or pressed into bars. At no time during this sanitized procedure did I see a drop spill. The factory was so sanitized you couldn't even smell the chocolate.

"I'm actually not kidding about the health benefits of chocolate," DuCharme continued, as we baby-stepped along in deference to our elders. "Dark chocolate helps lower the risk of heart failure, reduces blood pressure, reduces stroke risk, and is loaded with flavonols which boost cognitive function. Plus, as we all know, chocolate gives us energy. Great energy! Why, eating one chocolate chip alone gives you enough energy to walk a hundred and fifty feet, and if you could manage to eat eighteen thousand bars of dark chocolate—although I don't advise it—you'd have the energy to walk around the world!"

Ooohs and ahhhs.

Picking out the oldest person on the tour, an eighties-something woman who hobbled behind a walker, he added, "Just think, Ma'am, chocolate's good for your heart, your blood pressure, and your mind—plus it gives you energy. Imagine what that can do for your love life!"

The elderly lady giggled. So did the elderly man hobbling along next to her.

On we went, past spotless, gleaming machines that covered pretzels in dark chocolate, machines that popped out white chocolate golf balls and every other shape imaginable, past mixing machines that blended various flavors of mousse, and so on. The addictive, albeit healthful, delights the DuCharmes manufactured seemingly continued into infinity. By the time the tour was over, I, along with the rest of the crowd, was eager for Carl DuCharme to lead us into the retail area where he himself stood ready to ring up our purchases.

And did we buy.

After availing myself of a small shopping basket, I filled it with three dozen singly-wrapped and boxed white golf balls for Desert Investigations' regular clients, a bag of white chocolate-dipped pretzels for Madeline, a six-inch high dark chocolate cowboy boot for Jimmy, and for myself, five dark chocolate bars and an assortment of truffles that included orange spice, vanilla mousse, crème de pistachio, caramel walnut, and a brand new variety labeled Original Sin. There was method to my madness. I hung back until DuCharme had rung up the last customer, approached him with my overstuffed basket.

"Methinks the lady doth have a taste for chocolate," he said, smiling.

"You thinks right. But not all of that's for me. The golf balls are for my clients."

His smile grew hesitant. "Um, may I ask your business?"

"Certainly. I'll tell you what it is as soon as you ring me up." I didn't want to get thrown out of DuCharme's until I had those chocolates.

Once the deal was done, and he'd placed my treasures into a chocolate-colored tote decorated with DuCHARME CHOCO-LATIERS printed in metallic gold, I handed him my business card and watched the remnants of his smile fade away. He took a quick look around. No one was near, but when he spoke his voice was so low I could hardly hear him over the noise of the chocolate-making machinery in the back.

"You're the investigator who upset my mother the other day."

"I'm sorry about that."

"Leave. Us. Alone."

"But…"

The visitors' door to the factory opened and several women walked in. Each had salon-treated hair, wore expensively casual clothing, and carried an empty DuCHARME CHOCOLAT-IERS tote. Back for a fill-up?

"Hi, Carl!" one of the women said, sashaying up to him. "We were talking about Original Sin at our last meeting, and we're just dying to try it. Since we all came in together, we thought you might give us a group discount. Pretty please?"

Carl's frown vanished into a big hail-fellow-well-met grin, but before he could answer her, I seized my chance. Leaning toward him, I whispered, just loud enough for him to hear, "I can ask my questions right here and now, or we could go someplace private. Your choice."

For a brief moment he looked like he wanted to throw me into one of the filler machines and squash me into a truffle. But after a hesitation, the smile came back, although I doubt it was for my benefit.

Turning around, he said to a Hispanic woman replenishing the truffle stock, "Herminia, would you please help these lovely ladies from the Scottsdale Racquet Club? And when you ring them up, be certain to give them our Loyal Customer discount." Then, to me, "C'mon, Ms. Jones, we're going to my office." After giving a brief apology to the racquet club ladies, he headed toward the back without asking me to follow him. I guess he knew it wasn't necessary.

Carl DuCharme's office was as clean as his factory. Maybe too clean. Offices should look worked-in, but the surfaces of his chrome-and-glass desk and the matching credenza behind it were bare of any papers, rubber bands, or paper clips—none of the usual refuse of the busy worker bee. The man didn't even have file cabinets. The only décor hung on the wall: several certificates for something or other; a photograph of his mother and deceased father, Blaine DuCharme II; one of his grandfather, Blaine DuCharme I, the founder of DuCharme Chocolatiers; and a photograph of himself and another man in a dog show ring setting, both holding large, purebred boxers on short leashes. Unlike his mother, he was no Chihuahua man. All photographs had glass-and-chrome frames that perfectly matched his chrome-and-glass desk, and like everything else in the room, gleamed as if they'd been polished for hours. Other than the compulsive sterility, one thing caught my eye. Or rather *didn't* catch my eye.

There were no pictures of Blaine DuCharme Three.

"Sit down if you want," he said, pointing to an overly modern chair that looked too spindly to hold up a gnat, "but I'd prefer you didn't. This conversation is going to be brief. There's another tour starting in a half-hour, and I really don't have time to discuss my brother. Not that I'd discuss him even if I had the time."

"Okay. Where were you between noon and three, Monday, July 8?"

"Huh?" His cross expression morphed into one of bewilderment.

"It's a simple question."

"Monday, July 8? How the hell do I know?"

"Maybe you were working."

He made a sound of disgust. "No shit, Sherlock."

I motioned to the iPhone his hand. "Could you check?"

"Oh, for Christ's sake." But he punched in the date on his phone. "Yep, I was here. All day, as a matter of fact."

"Did anyone see you?"

A sour look. "Only everyone in the factory, including my mother. We had a big shipment going out to Seattle and…Hey, what difference does it make where I was? You told Mother you wanted to talk about Blaine."

"The brother who was executed for killing two police officers and a civilian."

"Yes. And he paid the ultimate price for it, too."

"I'm wondering how you felt about that. Seeing him die like that."

"Felt? How do you think I felt?"

"The witness list said you were the only family member present."

"Correct. Mother refused to go, so I had to. It wasn't pleasant." He looked at his watch. "Next question. And it better be your last."

"Do you, or did you, know Dr. Arthur Cameron? Alexandra Cameron? Alec Cameron?"

A blank look. "Who?"

"You heard me."

He stopped in the middle of an annoyed head-shake. "Wait a minute. Those names…Isn't that the family…?" When he made the link, he didn't look happy. "Hey! Just what the hell is this?!" His rage growing, he stood up and stabbed a finger at me. "You! The nerve! Come into my plant and threaten to embarrass me in front of valued customers, then bring up that poor murdered family as if it had anything to do with me. Get out of my office right now, you hear? Get out of the whole damned building. And from now on, buy your chocolates elsewhere."

I got out before he snatched my DuCHARME CHOCO-LATIERS bag out of my hands.

But I wasn't fast enough. Before reaching the end of the hall, I spotted an elderly woman walking slowly toward Carl's office. At first I mistook her for one of the tour group who had become separated from the others, but as she drew closer I recognized her: Lorraine DuCharme. From her expression—which suddenly devolved from a mask of patrician politesse to fury—she recognized me, too.

"You!" she snapped.

"I just wanted to talk to your son about…"

She didn't wait for me to finish. Shouldering roughly past me, Mrs. DuCharme hurried into her son's office. She was still screaming at him as I reached the exit.

Chapter Twenty-two

Chocolate doesn't do well in the desert heat, so after leaving the DuCharme factory, I made a side trip to the Best Western and dropped off my belt-expanding—but healthful!—bag of goodies. Then I hit the road again in search of the delivery boy whose name was printed on the receipt found at the murder scene. Zhou's Mandarin Wok was located less than a mile east of the Cameron house, probably the reason the Camerons and their neighbors, the Newberrys, used their delivery service so often. The food must have been good, too, because as I drove up, a satisfied-looking group of office workers was leaving. Most carried takeout containers, the same kind found at the murder scene.

Inside, the scents of sesame oil and ginger reminded me I hadn't eaten lunch. Well, that could be remedied. After taking a quick look around—eight tables, six booths, deep red walls with a gold dragon emblazoned on the farthest one—I walked up to the counter, perused the menu, and ordered the special: General Tso's chicken with fried rice and egg roll, and a large Diet Coke.

"Tso spicy or not?" asked the middle-aged Chinese woman taking my order.

"Spicy."

"Extra spicy or regular spicy?"

"Extra."

"It gonna burn your mouth."

"I can deal with it."

"That what they all say. No refund if too hot!"

Convinced by her attitude I was talking to the owner of Mandarin Wok, I asked, "Are you Mrs. Zhou?"

"Who wanna know?" She gave me a glare that could have stir-fried shrimp. "You a cop?"

"Used to be. Now I do private investigative work." I handed her my card.

When she looked at it, her face softened. "Ah, you a P.I. then. Like Clint Eastwood in *Dirty Harry*."

A movie fan, thus her son's name: Clint Zhou. "Yes. Kind of like Clint Eastwood, except in that movie he played a San Francisco police detective, not a P.I."

"Not important. Boss always mad at him. Funny. Yeah, I Mrs. Zhou. You been P.I. long?"

Boy, we were getting along like a house afire. "It seems like forever, Mrs. Zhou."

A glimmer of a smile. "I like you stick to stuff, not like kid always goofing off like youngest son. So what you want, Miss Forever Detective?"

"I'd like to speak to your son, if I may?"

"Got six sons. Only one daughter, damn. Girls more careful drivers."

"The son named Clint."

"Ah! You lucky. He just back." She turned around and bawled something in Mandarin through the kitchen service window. Almost immediately, a jumpy teenager joined her behind the counter. From the iPhone clutched in his hand, I could see he'd been interrupted while texting.

"What'd I do now?" he asked, trying to hide the phone behind his back. He hadn't yet grown into his Adam's apple, and it bobbed up and down as he spoke.

Mrs. Zhou missed nothing. "You tell Miss Forever Detective what she need to know. You hear? And stop that text stuff." To me she said, "We make General Tso extra hot. You no say I not warn you." Looking thrilled at the chance to show me up, she shooed us to a booth by the window.

"This is about the Camerons, isn't it?" Clint Zhou said, slumping as far down in the booth as he could while still staying upright. "I've already talked to the police."

"But I'm a private detective."

"Same thing."

I let it slide. "You didn't tell me, so tell it again."

He did, reciting almost word for word the interview in the case file. According to the computerized receipt, at 11:30 a woman identifying herself as Alexandra Cameron called in an order for almond chicken, moo goo gai pan, and egg rolls. She specified she needed enough to feed four people.

I interrupted. "Four? Not three?" Ali had told me she was expected back for lunch.

"Yeah, four."

"What time did you leave the restaurant?"

"Around ten minutes later. Mom makes sure we get the orders right out."

"How long did it take you to drive to the Camerons' house?"

"Same, I guess. Ten minutes. I had another order, this one for the Lindells, but I hit the Camerons first because they were on the way." He flushed. "And Mrs. Cameron always tipped better than the Lindells."

"So that put you at their house at about noon?"

"Yeah. Around that. Maybe a few minutes earlier."

I thought for a minute. "When did you deliver the next order? The one for the Lindells."

His Adam's apple began bobbing, and his eyes slid away as if he'd spotted something interesting on the other side of the small restaurant. I looked. Nothing was there. Their last customer had straggled back to work.

"Clint? Answer my question. When did you deliver the next order?"

He looked down at the table. "Um, a little after 12:30. Maybe 12:40. Something like that."

"How far is it from the Camerons' house to the Lindells'?"

The phone in his pocked buzzed, signifying an arriving text. He fished it out of his pocket, read it, and typed a reply until his mother saw him and screamed something in Mandarin. Muttering under his breath, he put the phone back in his pocket. Then he sank back into his seat and sulked.

Teenagers.

Thanks to Ali, I was getting used to the species. "C'mon, Clint, how far is it from the Camerons' house to the Lindells'? And tell the truth."

"Pretty far," he told the table.

I whipped out my own iPhone and punched up a Scottsdale street map. "Give me the name of the street the Lindells are on."

He mumbled something I couldn't quite hear.

"What's that?" I asked.

"Pinto Lane."

According to the map, Clint's next delivery was less than a mile from the Camerons' house. Exasperated, I said, "Are you telling me that it took you thirty or forty minutes to drive from Yellow Horse Drive to Pinto Lane? A route that's all quiet neighborhood streets, except for that one intersection at Scottsdale Road?" I held the screen up so he could see for himself. "What's wrong with this picture, Clint?"

There had been no comments about this time discrepancy in the police file, no explanation of why it took so long for the Zhous' delivery van to get three-quarters of a mile from Point A to Point B. Then again, thanks to the confessions of two idiot teens, the cops believed they already had their killers.

Clint shot a look back at the counter, where his mother was screaming again at someone through the kitchen service window. Probably another son, God help him.

"Should I discuss this with your mother?"

From the expression on the kid's face, you'd think I'd just sentenced him to the Death of a Thousand Cuts. "Well, I wasn't driving all the time." he whined.

"Then what were you doing?"

His cell phone buzzed again. This time he ignored it. "I, uh, I kind of got in a wreck," he told the table.

"*Kind* of got in a wreck? Where?"

"When I was turning from Palomino Circle, uh, the big roundabout near the Camerons' place, back onto Indian Bend to make my next delivery."

That would have been the entrance to the Camerons' circle of cul-de-sacs. I leaned so far forward across the table that my forehead almost touched his. "Who, or what, did you get in a wreck with? Bicycle? Horse? Car? UFO?"

"Some van."

It was all I could do to keep breathing. "Tell me about the wreck, and don't you dare leave anything out or I'll tell your mother."

He opened his mouth to explain, but Mrs. Zhou picked that very moment to personally deliver my lunch. "You try now," she said, with a smirk of satisfaction.

I tasted. Although I could feel blisters blooming all over my mouth, I smiled up at her. "Best General Tso's chicken I ever tasted."

"Not too hot?"

"It's just the way I like it."

Crestfallen, she walked away.

"All right, you," I hissed at Clint, after chugging down my entire glass of Diet Coke. "On with it. I don't have all day." And I needed to go buy some Mylanta.

"Well, I was pulling out of Palomino and I, um, hit this van."

"Palomino Circle is a wide street with no parking on either side. How the heck could you hit anyone? Were you driving blindfolded or something?"

His Adam's apple began bobbing again. "I was, um, well, I was kind of texting my girlfriend."

"You were 'kind of texting' your girlfriend. While driving."

"If you tell my mother she'll kill me."

"Okay, I won't tell her, but don't expect to live to a ripe old age if you continue texting while driving. I'm sure they told you as much in Driver's Ed."

His face turned as red as the peppers in my General Tso's chicken, but he plunged on. "So I stopped. I mean, that's what you're supposed to do after a wreck, right? Stop and exchange information?"

"Oh, yeah. Especially when you're dumb enough to text while driving. That's if you live through the accidents you cause."

"You shouldn't call me dumb," he whined. "It's not nice."

I looked toward the counter, where Mama Zhou was screaming at someone on the phone. Another son, no doubt. I rose from my seat.

With a yelp, Clint grabbed my wrist. "Oh, Jesus, please don't go over there!"

I sat back down. "Then cut the crap and tell me what happened."

He gulped, and started again. "Like I started to say, I opened the glove compartment and took out the registration and insurance card, then I got out my driver's license and exited the van, just like you're supposed to do."

"Gold star for you. So what'd the guy, if it was a guy in the other van, do? And by the way, did you see more than one person in there?"

"Maybe a couple of people, maybe just one, the windows were tinted pretty dark. Anyway, the driver didn't stop, just, like, kept going, didn't slow down or anything."

"Kept on going? After you'd run into him?"

"I swear!"

I managed to keep a straight face when he flashed the Boy Scout salute. "What'd you do next?"

The words poured out. "Got back in the van and split. Then I, uh, went over to my girlfriend's house, she lives right around there and she, uh, she'd been out of town for two weeks and I hadn't seen her and I missed her so much, and she, uh, she texted me while I was handing the delivery to Mrs. Cameron, so as soon as I got back to the van I texted her back, but I wasn't driving then, I swear I wasn't, just sitting parked outside the Cameron house for maybe five minutes, until we were done, and I put the phone back in my pocket. But then she texted me again and I texted her again and, uh, I remembered I had to get over to the Lindells', so I drove off..."

"Still texting."

He took a deep breath and started in again. "Yeah, but you can't tell Mom, because then I had the wreck, and I knew she would kill me if she found out, so I drove over to Sandra's house..."

"Sandra?"

"My girlfriend. We, uh, after we said hi and some other stuff, we checked out the van's fender. There was a big dent, but heck, there were already so many dents on our van you couldn't really tell unless you looked hard that I'd just put in a new one, so I figured I didn't need to tell Mom."

Or the police. "She'd have found out once she got the insurance bill. You think of that?"

He looked horrified. 'Uh, no. I guess I was too upset. Oh, geez, oh my God, if she..."

"How long were you at Sandra's house?"

Pulling himself together, he said, "Fifteen minutes? Twenty? I was really worried about the van, so I, uh, I kind of popped the fender back out a little. I thought it'd be easy to do, but it wasn't. It took longer than I'd planned."

Which is why body work costs us all an arm and a leg. "What did the Lindells say when you finally showed up with cold takeout?"

"I didn't. My girlfriend, she zapped it in the microwave for me."

Ah, true love. "Describe the van you hit."

"White. Mostly."

"What do you mean, 'mostly'?"

"Well, it was really, really old, older even than our van, and besides the white, there were bits of different colors all over it, and even some sections of primer. It looked like it'd been painted a million times."

"Was there lettering on the side? A logo?"

He shook his head. "Nope."

"Make?"

He shrugged. "Ford, I think. Maybe a Chevy. I'm not all that good with cars, especially old ones, but I think it was something from the seventies. Or maybe early eighties."

"Panel van? Recreational van?"

"Plain old panel. No windows, except for the driver's."

"Where'd you hit him?"

"Left front fender."

"Did you see any damage to his vehicle?"

"You kidding me? That whole van was messed up. Dents all over, even worse than ours. Like I said, it was old. Really old."

"You didn't think it was odd that the driver didn't stop?"

"Well, yeah, looking back I guess it was kind of weird, but at the time I was more worried about what Mom would do if she found out I'd been…" He trailed off.

"Texting while driving."

He had the decency to look embarrassed. "Something like that."

"How old are you?" I asked, hoping he wasn't a minor.

"Eighteen. Mom wouldn't let me do deliveries if I wasn't. She's picky that way."

No, kid, she's smart that way. "Have you washed the van since then?"

"Not me, but maybe one of my brothers did." Then he second-thought himself. "No. Wait. They usually drive their own cars while making deliveries. I don't have a car yet, but Mom said if I'm real careful and don't get any tickets, she might buy me one for Christmas. I'm hoping for a Camaro, but a Mustang or a…"

Sensing a long teenage wish list coming on, I interrupted him again. "Just ask your brothers if they washed the damned van, okay?" I leaned across the table again. "Now listen carefully, Clint. As soon as I leave, I want you to call Detective Sylvie Perkins and tell her everything you just told me. Everything, you understand?" I wrote down Sylvie's number on a napkin and handed it to him. "If she's not in, ask for Detective Bob Grossman. And get me a doggie bag."

"Huh?"

"For the General Tso's chicken."

He fetched me a large Styrofoam container, to his mother's obvious delight. She probably suspected I was going to throw the fiery stuff out, and she was right. I just didn't want to give her the satisfaction of seeing me do it.

"One more thing," I said, after scraping my uneaten meal into the container. "You need to show me the van you used that day."

Eager to get rid of me, he gestured toward the door. "It's out back. Tan. Has ZHOU'S MANDARIN WOK painted in big red letters on the side. And it's all banged up." In a burst of independence, he added, "You can't miss it."

"Clint, Clint. You still don't get it, do you? It sounds like you might have had a run-in with the Camerons' killer, and I want to see the exact area where your van whapped the other van. Ever hear of paint transfer?"

His Adam's apple went into overdrive. "*Killer?!* You…you think that guy, the guy I hit, was, like, the Camerons' killer?"

"There's a good chance. C'mon. Time's a-wasting." Now my stomach was beginning to get blisters, too. Good thing there was a Walgreen's two blocks away.

The Zhous' delivery van looked like something left over from a demolition derby. There were dents along the sides, the front bumper hung down at an angle, and the rear one was attached to the body with baling wire. The red, two-feet-high lettering—ZHOU'S MANDARIN WOK—wasn't bad, though. You could read it from a mile away, which I guessed was the point.

"There," Clint said, pointing at on the front bumper and fender. "See those scuffs? That's where I hit him."

I leaned down to take a closer look. The left front fender was crumpled from his clumsy body work and the bumper had experienced numerous run-ins, so in addition to white, streaks of yellow, blue, and some dark color—it might have been brown—nearly obliterated the original chrome.

One of those streaks had come from the killer's van.

"Clint, forget what I said about calling Detective Perkins. I'll call her myself right now. And no matter what your mother tells you, don't take this van anywhere until Perkins gets here."

"What's she gonna do? Interview me again?" The worry-lines on his forehead deepened.

I was already punching in Sylvie's cell number. "Without a doubt." What I didn't tell him was that after I told her about the van's adventures with oncoming traffic, she'd probably get a warrant and have it towed to the impound lot.

After considering the emergency of the situation, I remained with the vehicle until Sylvie and Bob rolled in. They took one look at the fender and bumper, heard the kid out, and made some calls. While we waited in the sizzling heat, Sylvie caught me up on hers and Bob's side of the investigation. Finally, assured that a friendly judge had issued an emergency search warrant and a tow truck was on its way, I left Clint to the mercies of his tiger mother and took off.

But as I drove toward Walgreen's to pick up some Mylanta for my burning stomach, I couldn't help but think what would have happened if the kid had arrived at the Cameron house five minutes later.

Chapter Twenty-three

After spending part of the night hugging the commode, I arrived early the next morning at St. Simon's Catholic Church. I positioned myself in a back pew, the better to see who showed up, and in what order. The light that filtered through the church's multitude of stained glass windows washed the interior in jewel tones of color, easing the gloom. The flowers helped, too. So many decorated the three caskets that their scent competed with the omnipresent incense.

Detectives Bob Grossman and Sylvie Perrins came in together and like me, found a place in the back, but on the other side of the aisle. As was the custom in homicide cases, they hoped someone might dance down the aisle, singing, "I did it, I did it, I did it and got away with it!" The fact that this seldom happens makes no difference; hope never dies in a homicide detective's breast.

Stephen Zellar, Ali's attorney, arrived shortly after the detectives as a show of support for his client. He gave a nod as he passed by. Next came a tearful Eldora Morales, the Camerons' former maid, chauffeured by Armetta Zielsdorf, her new employer. They took a middle pew. Right behind them came Margie and Monty Newberry, then Ralph Parelli, the Camerons' other neighbor. Parelli appeared much more subdued than the vulgarian I'd first met; real grief was etched upon his face.

As the church slowly filled, it was obvious that Scottsdale had turned out in full force to support one of their own. I thought I spotted the members of Alexandra's book club: six well-dressed women sitting together, looking equally traumatized. Sitting not far from Bob and Sylvie were teachers, students, and staff at Four Palms Middle School, wearing orange and green ribbons, the school's colors. Near them, I saw what could have been little Alec's entire fifth grade class. It hurt to see so many young faces looking so solemn.

I tried not to look at the smallest casket in the front of the church—Alec's—but seemingly independent of my will, my eyes kept drifting back. Ten years old. Tortured for God knows how long, then murdered. I remembered his room, the sports posters, the photograph of Einstein, the advanced science books. What discoveries had the world lost when he died? Next to Alec's, Alexandra's coffin. So beautiful, so unhappy. Yes, her promiscuity was troubling, but if there was one thing I could understand, it was the desperation a lonely woman could feel. In that way, we were two of a kind.

The casket on the end was Dr. Cameron's. A saver of lives, a taker of lives. An aloof, sometimes cold man, the fibers found on the back of his shirt proved that in his last minutes of life, he'd held his wife and child behind him, attempting to shield them from harm. How could anyone understand a man like that? Had he understood himself?

One of the reasons I hate funerals so much is because they make you ask too many questions.

There was no way to know how many of Dr. Cameron's associates at Good Samaritan Hospital were in attendance. From his lack of popularity, I guessed not many. Then again, I could have been wrong, because the Valley medical community held his skills in high esteem. Judging from the size of the crowd in the church and the expensive cut of their clothes, a third of the mourners could have been other doctors showing up as a final gesture of respect.

One of the last people to enter the church was U.S. Representative Juliana Thorsson. There was an expression on her face I couldn't quite identify, and it made me uneasy. Once more I wondered about the wisdom of her attendance. If anyone noticed her resemblance to Ali, she could kiss that U.S. Senate seat good-bye. But try telling a politician anything.

Then the door opened again, and here came Ali, wearing an ill-fitting black dress instead of jailhouse orange. Arms and legs shackled, she hobbled out of the bright sunlight and into the dark church, flanked by two stern-looking women, each of whom could have wrestled on the WWF circuit. Her eyes were red, but dry. *That's my girl.*

"Hi, Lena," she whispered, as she her guards guided her into the pew in front of me.

"We warned you, Miss Cameron, no speaking!" the guard to her left snapped. She sounded like a drill sergeant.

My hand itched to brush an errant strand of blond-rooted black hair away from the child's face, but I controlled myself. No point in getting her in more trouble than she already was in, so I just nodded a hello and smiled.

Ali forced a smile back.

Finally, here came Dr. Bradley Teague. As soon as he saw Ali, he moved to the other side of the aisle as if she carried some infectious disease. He said nothing to her, no hellos, no words of condolence, nothing, just hurried away toward a pew near the front.

I wanted to slap the son of a bitch.

Maybe I would have, but just then Eldora Morales turned around in her seat and spotted Ali immediately. With a loud sob she left her seat, rushed up the aisle, and climbed over the knees of one of Ali's guards. Before the guard could react, she wrapped Ali in her arms.

"*Mi pobre pequeña!*" Eldora wailed.

She was still wailing as the guard grabbed her and hustled her away.

The service began.

Not being the religious type, I paid little attention, just kept my eyes and ears attuned to Ali, who never once cried.

Dr. Teague made up for it.

He wept so loudly throughout the service, much of it conducted in Latin by a priest old enough to rival Methuselah, you'd
have thought Alexandra had been his wife, not his half-brother's.
This made me wonder if his admitted love for her had ever been
consummated. If so, how had he felt when their love affair, either
a one-nighter or longer, ended? Heartbroken? Angry? But on the
day of the Cameron killings, Dr. Teague had been thousands of
miles away in the African bush, vaccinating children.

Or had he?

By the time the service was over and we drove in a long proces-
sion to the cemetery, Dr. Teague was pretty much all cried out.
After we wended our way through weeping angel statuary to a
canopied area where three empty graves waited to be filled, he
stopped his outright sobbing and ground down to a hiccup here
and there. As the graveside ceremony progressed, he was able to
make it through a Shakespearean sonnet extolling Alexandra's
virtues with only a few hitches. His control was complete while
delivering a short eulogy for his nephew. He said nothing about
his murdered brother.

Bastard.

At ten a.m. it wasn't too hot. Not yet, anyway. A soft breeze
blowing in from California took the edge off the heat. A mockingbird perched in an olive tree added musical accompaniment to
the sound of passing traffic, while the barking of a nearby dog
provided a staccato counterpoint. Since the sun almost always
shines in Arizona, all that light and all those flowers can often put
a funeral in danger of taking on an unintentional festive aspect,
but there was no danger of that happening today. Yes, the sun still
danced its merry dance over the Superstition Mountains, but a
pall of guilt and gloom hung over the three side-by-side graves.

Unlike her uncle, Ali remained dry-eyed at the graveside service, but she didn't fool me. From the condition of her swollen
eyes, she had cried all night with no one to comfort her, no one
to hug her or whisper that old, well-meaning lie—*There, there,
sweetheart, everything will be all right.*

Poor damn kid.

Juliana Thorsson stood unnoticed and alone in the shade of an Aleppo pine, her eyes riveted on her biological daughter. She still had that odd, unidentifiable look on her face. When she saw me watching her, she moved further into the shade.

Finally it was over. Without allowing Ali to speak to anyone, her guards hustled her into a van and drove her back to juvie.

Detectives Bob Grossman and Sylvie Perrins followed me out of the cemetery. "Notice the uncle?" Sylvie asked, after we had put enough distance between ourselves and the others. "Weird, huh? Bet he was getting it on with the wife."

Bob tsk-tsked. "Weird family, period. Kid didn't even cry. Hey, Lena, were my eyes deceiving me or was that Congresswoman Thorsson standing under that tree? What would some fancy-ass politician be doing here?"

"The family lived in her district, I believe," I answered, careful not to say too much. "At least that's what I hear."

"Damned decent of her to show up like that, then."

Sylvie snickered. "She's running on the Decency Platform, didn't you know? I'm surprised she didn't drag along some whore of a photographer to get a picture of her feeling someone else's pain."

After a hurried good-bye, I went back to my Jeep. But as the Jeep pulled away from the curb, I finally identified Juliana Thorsson's odd expression.

It was hunger.

Chapter Twenty-four

Emotionally exhausted, I headed back to the motel to shower off the cloying scents of incense and flowers. Sometimes I do my best thinking in the shower, and today was no different. While soaping myself under the cool water I realized something had been missing from the case file Babette had sent me. After drying myself off, I logged onto the file and double-checked.

I was right. Probably because by then Kyle and Ali had already confessed to the murders, the cops hadn't bothered to look at Dr. Bradley Teague's passport.

So I picked up my cell and called Sylvie Perrins.

For all Sylvie's sound and fury, I trusted her more than any other detective at Scottsdale PD. She didn't care what you thought about her, she just wanted to get to the truth, even if the truth would benefit someone she loathed. Me, for instance.

"I wish you'd stop being right for a change," she muttered, when I told her about my rising suspicions re Dr. Bradley Teague. "Oh, by the way, remember those surveillance cameras? Well, we already got the results, and they're gonna make a lot of people happy, not to mention you and that liberal schmuck Curtis Racine. He's the boy's attorney, right?"

"Right. Lay it on me. Don't make me beg."

"But wouldn't that be fun?" Not waiting for my answer, she reeled off information that, yes, did make me happy.

The security camera at the Circle K showed an unbloodied Kyle Gibbs buying Slim Jims at 1:30 p.m. the day of the murders, an hour and a half after Clint Zhou made his delivery. By that time, the Camerons were either already dead or in the process of dying. Furthermore, several homeowners along Kyle's route back to the party house had allowed access to their own security cameras, and those cameras captured the boy walking along innocently, no blood on his white tee-shirt.

But the clincher was the home security camera three doors down from Ancient Alice's house, which had picked up Kyle at 12:12 p.m., carrying a small ugly dog, and wearing the same clean tee-shirt that appeared more than an hour later on the other cameras.

Alibis don't get much better than that.

"Those kids'll be out of juvie by this time tomorrow, Thursday at the latest." Sylvie had said. "At least as far as the girl goes, since she's got that hotshot attorney you're working for."

I placed a call to Curtis Racine, Kyle's non-hotshot attorney. He received the information with glee.

"I'd stay on the line and flirt, you sexy thing, but I can't wait to call the prosecutor's office and give him a kick up his fat ass. If that doesn't cut Kyle loose, I'll contact the judge. In the meantime, have a glass of champagne on me."

Dial tone.

I wouldn't be taking his advice. Not knowing what genetic predisposition I was born with, I had always stayed away from liquor and drugs. For all I knew, my biological parents were drunkards, addicts, or a combination of the two. What other kind of parents would shoot their four-year-old daughter in the head and leave her in the street to die?

So no champagne for me. But I did have a big pile of chocolate waiting at the Best Western. After stopping off at the nearby Walgreen's for another bottle of Mylanta, I headed back to the motel.

A half-cup of Mylanta, two chocolate bars, and twelve white chocolate-covered pretzels later I lay back on the cool sheets of my Best Western room and thought about the case.

Ordinarily, my job would be over as soon as Ali Cameron was released from juvie, but with Congresswoman Juliana Thorsson as my client, that wasn't the case here. I also had to prove—or at the very least provide strong clues to—the real killer's identity. The problem here was the case's many dimensions.

For instance, who was the primary target of the killer's rage? From what I had discovered so far, it could have been either Dr. Arthur Cameron or his wife Alexandra. But that was where the case became even more messy. If Dr. Cameron's identity as the state's executioner had somehow been discovered, he possessed the longest list of people who wished him dead, although Alexandra was a strong second contender. Extramarital liaisons sometimes led to murder, but the torture murders of an entire family? Yes, that would be stretching it, but during my years with Scottsdale PD I'd once seen a single mom and her three children decapitated in a parking lot when she refused to give the killer—who'd been standing in line next to her at Costco—her phone number.

It was never a good idea to get fixated on one suspect, which is where Scottsdale PD had gone wrong. Just because Dr. Cameron had executed people so he could earn the cash for a fancy sports car didn't necessarily mean one of their grieving family members had killed him.

On the bright side, there was now new information to consider. While driving back to the motel something Clint Zhou said had niggled at the back of my mind: the killer drove a white van.

Where had I recently seen a white van in connection to this case?

I got up, ate another chocolate bar, then lay back on the bed and closed my eyes. With the noise of my conscious mind blissed into silence by the chocolate's sweet, buttery high, the answer floated up to me. At the cemetery. A white van from Good Samaritan Hospital had transported some of the hospital's staffers to pay their respects. Granted, that van had been fairly new and in excellent condition, but it was white, and hospitals had always been partial to white. Maybe Good Sam kept an older van around to run errands.

And hadn't Margie Newberry said something about Alexandra running into one of the Good Sam doctors when she'd indulged in a one-night-stand at the Wigwam Resort?

Yes, I remembered now. Margie said, *As she was leaving the hotel, she saw one of her husband's colleagues walking out of the bar. A Dr. Bosworth.*

Dr. Bosworth.

I'd meant to sniff around Dr. Cameron's workplace but knowing that getting information from medical types was like pulling teeth, I'd kept putting it off. But maybe I could get someone to help me.

I grabbed my cell and called Jimmy.

"Didn't you tell me you have a cousin who works at Good Sam?" I asked, as soon as he answered, hoping to ward off any more comments about last night.

"Yeah. Valerie. She's a nurse over there. Why?"

"Because I need a contact."

After I'd given him the highlights of Alexandra's sex life, he said, "Poor woman. She must have been so lonely."

That was Jimmy for you, always giving women the benefit of the doubt.

"From what I've been hearing about her husband, I'm sure she was. But back to Valerie. Do you know her schedule? I need to go down to Good Sam, talk to some people. She can give me an in."

"Last I heard she was working the night shift, but here's her cell number. Call and ask."

I wrote it down.

"Lena, before you hang up…How are you? I've been worried."

Sigh. "I'm fine, Jimmy. Fine. Could you please stop obsessing about my dream?"

"I'm not obsessing."

"Coulda fooled me. Just please, please, stop worrying about me some time before the next Ice Age rolls in, okay? I can take care of myself."

Silence.

Now I felt guilty. It wasn't a capital crime to worry about someone, so why the discomfort when Jimmy worried about me? Easy to answer. I hated the fact that the man could always see right through me.

"Look, I'm sorry I'm being so...so..." What was the word? "...*abrupt*, but I really have to push this investigation along, which right now means tying up loose ends. Talking to some doctor down at Good Sam is one of them. Got it?"

"Got it." He did not sound happy.

I let a rare note of softness enter my voice. "Bye, then, Jimmy. You're a good friend."

Then I stabbed the OFF button.

Next, I called Valerie. Her husband Andrew answered the phone. Kids were screaming in the background; it sounded like someone was being murdered. After I'd introduced myself, Andrew said, "Aha, the famous Lena. Jimmy talks about you all the time."

"Nothing bad, I hope."

"Worse than bad."

When I gasped, he laughed. "Ha ha. Just kidding."

Those Paiutes. Barrels of laughs.

When I explained the situation, Andrew said Valerie had switched her schedule to days and would be getting off at six. Why didn't I drop by this evening? They'd feed me.

Just thinking of those screaming kids terrified me, so I lied and said I'd already made other plans. Maybe I could catch Valerie as she left the hospital?

He suggested I meet her in the employee parking lot, and that he'd send a text message telling her to expect me. I didn't like the idea of waiting in the hot sun, but anything was better than those screaming kids, so I agreed.

"How will I recognize her?"

"Just a minute." He yelled for the kids to shut up. They didn't.

Once back on the line, he said, "Head for Employee Parking Lot B, the one on the east side. She likes the first row 'cause it's closest to the entrance, so she always arrives early to get it. Val's short, plump, a cute little bowling ball. Black hair in ponytail, maroon streak in bangs to match her car. Name tag says V.REDHORSE, R.N. Car's a maroon, yep, 2012 Buick Verano. 'Pima Pride' sticker in the rear window. License plate number VFINERN. Valerie's a fine R.N., get it?" He laughed. "Expect her to be cranky. Always a bearcat when she gets off work, probably 'cause she hates to come home, ha ha! Compared to this house, the ER's a snooze room."

There was nothing pressing to do until I left for Good Sam, so once I ended the call I started typing up the day's case notes on my laptop. I'd made it halfway through the interview with young Mr. Dumbass-Texting-While-Driving when my cell rang.

Congresswoman Juliana Thorsson.

"Do you have time to stop by my house for a minute?" she asked. "There's something I want to discuss with you."

I looked at my Timex: 3:09. There'd be plenty of time to confab with my client before heading into downtown Phoenix. Since I'd be driving against rush-hour traffic, it shouldn't take me more than a half-hour.

"Sure," I said. "I'll be right over."

On my way to the parking lot, I passed the dumpster where two days ago I'd thrown in Mama Zhou's fiery General Tso's. A noisy group of ravens had finally managed to peck their way through the Styrofoam container and were gobbling it down. Unlike my own poor craw, the heat didn't seem to bother theirs one bit.

When I arrived at Congresswoman Thorsson's condo, Ali's dog Misty met me at the door. Although still bandaged, spirit had returned to her eyes, giving her the temerity to nip at my ankles as I entered.

"Misty's feeling better," Juliana said, studying the dog fondly, the first indication of warmth I'd ever seen from her. With gentleness, she picked the animal up, cuddled it for a moment, then gestured me to a chair. On the side table was a glass of iced tea she had already prepared for me.

"This won't take long but you might as well be comfortable," she said.

Something seemed different about the condo, about her. The living room was still too cool and too sleek, as was its owner, who was dressed in an ice-colored linen sheath. And the campaign poster mock-ups had been added to by one that showed Thorsson in her Olympics uniform, skeet rifle at the ready. It proclaimed HIT THE TARGET WITH THORSSON.

But there was something else...something...

Then I spotted it. The photograph of Ali walking home from school with her friends. Although out of focus and poorly composed, Juliana had put it in a silver frame and placed it on the stand next to the sofa where she now sat with Misty on her lap. After easing the dog into a comfortable position, bandaged side up, she explained why she'd needed to see me.

"Ali's attorney called me a little while ago and said he was on his way to see the judge to arrange for her release. He says that barring any snags in the red tape, she'll be freed from the detention center sometime tomorrow afternoon."

I felt like dancing, but merely said, "Excellent news."

"In a way. But there's a problem. I haven't been totally honest with you."

What politician is? If politicians didn't outright lie, they stretched the truth and hid the in-between. I sat back, waiting for her to confess to some trivial sin. She surprised me.

After giving Misty a quick kiss on the snout, she said, "I knew Alexandra Cameron."

"*What?!*"

"Drink that tea before you go into shock. Now tell me, how much do you know about in vitro fertilization?"

I took a swig of the tea. "Just the part you told me about, that it entails a number of hormone shots."

She gave me a cold smile. "A simplification. The full process takes several weeks, sometimes months, and I can assure you it's not without pain. For instance, I had to inject myself with Lupron—intramuscularly, you understand—for fifteen days in order to synchronize my periods with Alexandra's. After her periods and mine were in sync, there were more injections, then more, until finally, three months later, my eggs were…" The smile disappeared. "The term the doctor used was 'harvested.' Under anesthesia, of course."

"What does all that have to do with you knowing Alexandra?"

"Plenty. Alexandra and I supported each other throughout the entire process."

I shook my head. "While I'm no expert on IVF, I know that's not usual.'

"It's not. But fifteen years ago, when I first met the Camerons, I was already pretty savvy about people and their motives, and one thing I'd learned was this—that evil often masquerades as compassion. Or need. Being in the business you're in, I'm sure you've noticed that, too. So I was cautious, and when I answered the ad in the *New Times*—the phone number was an attorney's—I insisted upon meeting both prospective parents. Yes, I'll admit that I did what I did mainly for the tuition money, but I needed to find out what kind of people would be raising the, ah, product, of my egg donation."

Product. What a word for a child. "So the story you told me about seeing her at Fancy Feet and noticing her heart-shaped birthmark, the one that matched yours, was a lie?"

She frowned. "It wasn't a lie. Before buying this townhouse a year ago, I was living in a leased condo near Shea and Ninetieth Street, several miles from here. I'd long ago put the IVF situation out of my mind…" She paused, then started again. "Oh, well, from time to time I'll admit I wondered about the girl—yes, I knew Alexandra had given birth to a girl, she wrote and told me—but such thoughts were fleeting. I was too busy living my life."

And entering politics, where her egg-selling past could be a career-destroying scandal.

Unaware of my thoughts, she continued. "It was only coincidence that I happened to be at Fancy Feet that day, Ms. Jones. I usually get my shoes at Nordstrom, but I was in a hurry and the store was just down the street, so…" She swallowed and paused for a moment, the first intimation this confession was difficult for her. "Anyway, when I walked in, I recognized Alexandra immediately. She'd hardly changed. True beauty is like that, you see, bred in the bone, not at the cosmetic counter. Then, when I took one look at Ali's face…Well, you've seen the resemblance. The birthmark on her foot, the one exactly like mine, merely confirmed what I already knew, but…" She swallowed again. "Anyway, I got out of the store before Alexandra saw me."

It had the ring of truth, but I was still suspicious. "Tell me more about Alexandra. At what point you two actually met, and what you talked about."

A dismissive wave. "The usual. Marriage. Children. I came away from that initial meeting convinced she'd be a wonderful mother for any child."

From everything I had heard so far in my investigation, her assessment of the woman had been correct. "What was your take on Dr. Cameron?"

"I didn't warm to him, and he didn't warm to me, either. From his manner, I doubt if he ever saw me as anything other than a means to an end, but that didn't matter, since my expectations of him were no more elevated. He was just semen in a petri dish. As far as I was concerned, all I cared about was his ability to provide a comfortable, safe home for…" She paused, as if struck by the irony of her statement.

Shaken, Thorsson looked beyond me, several miles beyond me, I guessed, to a cemetery where three graves lay covered with dying flowers. I, too, allowed a brief memory—that of my own father standing in a faraway forest, telling my mother to take me and run, while he provided the distraction that would save us.

And kill him.

In the end, Dr. Cameron tried to save his family, too.

And he had failed. Just as my own father failed.

Recovering herself, Thorsson said, "During the fertility process, when Alexandra and I were both undergoing the injections, we met several more times at different coffee shops around

Scottsdale, once in her home. She wanted me to see how well they lived. By the time the, ah, biological process was completed, I'd learned a lot about her. Her childhood, the career she was willing to walk away from, her marriage." Another brief, distant look, then her eyes focused on me again. "Did you know she was a very lonely woman?"

"I've heard something about that, yes."

She shook her head. "How could a woman be that beautiful, and still so lonely?"

"Life is strange. So are people."

"Anyway, ours was only a temporary friendship, one which ended as soon as she became pregnant. Yet then, as well as now, I was convinced that Alexandra Cameron was one of the finest women I ever met. She was elegant and kind and…" Her voice trailed off.

And you fell in love with her, didn't you, Congresswoman? Another secret you're keeping from your radical right constituents.

As if afraid she had already revealed too much, Juliana's manner became brisk. "Well. I'm certain you found all that fascinating, but I didn't invite you over here to dwell on the past. It's the future I'm concerned with."

Here it came. The real reason she'd summoned me.

"I want you to arrange a meeting between me and Ali's uncle."

"The purpose of that being?" As if I hadn't already begun to suspect.

Like all good politicians, Congresswoman Thorsson began to build her story point by point. "When I was watching the uncle at the service this morning, I noticed he never once touched that girl. No hugs. No kisses. He couldn't even bring himself to talk to her."

"I wouldn't call him demonstrative, no."

Her mouth twisted in contempt. "That's putting it mildly. Well, the girl simply can't stay with him. He'll just pack her off to some dismal boarding school so he can return to his real love—some damned Kenyan village."

"Inoculating children against disease isn't the worst crime anyone ever committed."

"Of course not. But charity begins at home, don't you think?"

"I live alone, Congresswoman, so I wouldn't know. So do you, by the way."

"Not for long."

"Oh?"

She frowned. "Don't play dumb, Miss Jones. You know exactly where I'm headed. I'm going ask Dr. Teague to relinquish guardianship of Ali to me."

Chapter Twenty-five

Ali

My uncle hates me. I mean, really, really hates me. At the funeral today he wouldn't even look at me. Wouldn't sit next to me.

Everybody hates me.

Especially the girls here in juvie. Yesterday, as soon as I got back from the funeral, three of them jumped me in the shower, and although I yelled, nobody came to help because they all hate me. I'm too rich. I'm too snobby. I'm too much everything that's bad.

I killed my family.

That's what they all think, anyway.

Since I had, like, three girls on me there was nothing else I could do except fight back. I got a hank of somebody's hair, and bit somebody's finger nearly off. But three against one isn't fair, is it, so they got me down and kicked me around until I almost cried.

Almost.

Instead, I pretended they'd knocked me out, and I just laid there in that nasty water and bled for a while until they walked away and finally one of the matrons, or whatever they call themselves, came in and found me.

Then I was taken to Medical, where they fixed me up some. Just some. When I wake up tomorrow, I know I'm going to have, like, a black eye. And a bunch of cuts.

They gave me ten demerits for fighting.
When I get out of here, I'm going to kill myself.

Chapter Twenty-six

Lena

Question: what is a mother?

Answer: in Congresswoman Juliana Thorsson's case, the answer had once been easy: a mother was the biological entity that produced an egg and allowed it to be fertilized.

Period.

What was the answer now?

Philosophy didn't come easy to me, so I did what I always did when my brain hurt.

I headed out for another interview.

Tuesday at six is a good time to show up at Good Samaritan Hospital. The victims of Friday night car wrecks, overdoses, and shootings had either died or been patched together, so I was able to park in the visitors' lot without too much trouble and make my way to the other side of the hospital to Employee Parking Lot B. The second car on the east end was the maroon Buick Verano, license number VFINERN. After a few minutes a cute brunette faintly resembling a bowling ball approached.

"Are you Lena? If not, get away from my car."

An astute man, her husband. She was cranky.

"Yep, I'm Lena. And you're Valerie Redhorse, right?"

Scowling, she said, "Ditto the yep. Let's make this fast, okay? I've had a bad day."

"Busy?"

"Yeah, not that I'm going to divulge the gory details. HIPAA rules. Anyway, I've already told the police everything I know about Dr. Cameron, which isn't much. Here's what I told the cops. He was an excellent doc. A great one, even. When he worked on a patient, bombs could have gone off around him and he wouldn't notice, the man was that focused. No drug habit to speak of and I never saw him drunk. Don't think he stepped out on his wife, either. With his focus, he had the opposite of a roving eye. But personally? He wasn't friendly and he wasn't chatty. Bit of a bastard, really, but most doctors are. Especially ER docs on a rough Saturday night, which we call 'Gunshot Saturdays,' God bless the NRA."

"No drug habit *to speak of,* you said?" Her phrasing sounded odd.

A fierce grin. "Show me an ER doc who doesn't need a little pick-me-up after being on duty four nights straight and I'll show you a dumb-ass kid straight out of med school." Seeing my expression, she cracked a weak smile. "Not to worry. NoDoz is the drug of choice around here. It's right up there with black coffee and pizza."

My alarm disappeared. "Did you ever hear anyone threaten Dr. Cameron?"

She shook her head. "Nope."

"No angry gang members?"

"Nope."

"No crazed, grieving kin after one of their loved ones died?"

"Nope. You gotta understand, we don't let relatives—or unshot or unstabbed gang members—into the working section of the ER They'd just clutter up the place, and what would be the point anyway? They'd either go into hysterics or faint, and then we'd have to attend to them, not the patient. That's why we have a separate waiting room off to the side. Comfy place with lots of Kleenex. We keep that door closed so they won't see the blood."

"If you keep the door closed, then you wouldn't have heard them if they made threats."

"Got a point there, don't you?" She actually laughed. Nurses. Hard as nails when they're not grieving over some battered child. "Now, if you're finished, I wanna get home. Dinner's waiting, and Andrew's a great cook."

"One more question."

She jangled her car keys. "Make it snappy."

"Do you know a Dr. Bosworth?"

"Dr. Edwin Bosworth? Tall, dark, and handsome Bosworth?"

"Sounds like the one."

"I work with him all the time. Another good doc, though not as good as Dr. Cameron. Nobody was as good as Cameron. What do you want to know about Bosworth?"

"Ever hear any rumors about him and Mrs. Cameron?"

Her earlier laughter was nothing in comparison to the belly laugh I heard now. When she finally calmed down, she said, through giggles, "Tell me another one. Bad day or not, I'm always up for a good joke."

"I don't understand."

A final giggle as she unlocked her Buick and slid into the seat. "Nope, no rumors about Mrs. Cameron and Dr. Bosworth. Mainly 'cause he's gay as a day in May."

Having gained nothing other than the elimination of one possible subject from my conversation with Jimmy's cousin, I headed back to Scottsdale, the setting sun at my back. No matter the heat, this was the Valley's most beautiful time of day. As I drove east along McDowell, the reflection of a rosy-orange sun bounced off the rear windows of the cars ahead of me, and once I'd made it to the red sandstone Papago Buttes, the glow was so intense the Buttes appeared to be on fire. Mounting the top of the hill, I saw Scottsdale spread out before me, washed in such a vibrant golden halo that it looked like the Promised Land.

But beauty can do only so much for you. It can't tone your muscles, and what with one thing and another, I needed a serious workout. I stopped by the motel for my gym bag, then drove over to L.A. Fitness. When I arrived, the machines were so crowded with nine-to-fivers wearing designer Spandex, I decided to take my chances at Fight Pro.

Because of Fight Pro's ongoing construction, parking opportunities were slim and it took several passes around what was left of the parking area before I found a spot at the far northwest corner, near a fenced-off empty lot. At least, during my cruise-around, I'd seen no sign of Big Black Hummer, which didn't come as a surprise. Monster Woman tended to haunt the gym during the day, and in the evenings usually stayed home, probably to spend her time watching reruns of *Pumping Iron* and penning love letters to psychopaths on Death Row.

Best laid plans of mice and men, and all that. I had been pounding the treadmill for fifteen minutes when Monster Woman stalked through the door. Because the treadmills were located near the back of the gym, she didn't see me. That left two choices open: continue working out or leave immediately. I chose the first, knowing she seldom used the treadmills. Besides, I wasn't about to let Monster Woman's craziness run my life.

But since I'm not crazy myself, as soon as I finished with the treadmill, I made a wide arc around the free-weights area where she had planted herself, and set my sights on the Nautilus machines. Making the best of the situation, I spent ten minutes on the abdominal, ten on the leg press, fifteen on the rowing torso, and finished with the back pull. Then I returned to the treadmills and ended my workout with a fifteen-minute sprint.

Tired, sore, and happy, I showered quickly—secure in the fact that I'd seen Monster Woman leave the gym twenty minutes earlier—dressed, and headed back to my Jeep.

Night had fallen during my workout, swallowing the golden glory of the Arizona sunset in its inky craw. Now a flickering, weak light from a sole tungsten lamp lengthened the cars' shadows as I crossed the lot. I stayed alert, because even though Scottsdale has a low crime rate, you never know.

I was just about to climb into my Jeep when a truck hit me from behind.

When the fog cleared, I was lying on hot asphalt, staring up at Monster Woman. She was holding a rock. The back of my head felt wet and I smelled blood.

"Get my Hummer towed, will you, bitch?"

She must have seen me all along, and been out here waiting for me. In most cases when faced with physical threat, I try to talk the would-be assailant down, but I'd already been hit and the look on Monster Woman's face proved she wasn't in a listening mood. She was too intent on inflicting further damage.

And here it came.

After swinging a massive leg backwards, she kicked me in the face.

Now, you don't actually see stars after taking a hard blow to the head. What you see are little pinpoints of light against a dark red background. It looked nothing like the night sky, which hung above me, oblivious to what was going down in the parking lot of Scottsdale Fight Pro.

Fortunately, Monster Woman was wearing workout shoes, not steel-toed boots, so the light show was brief. Since I'd seen the blow coming, I'd prepared for it by turning my head. Also by raising my arms. While the lights fancy-danced around my field of vision, I managed to grab onto her leg. Although burdened by my weight, she was still able to swing her leg back again, taking my whole body with her.

The woman's strength was amazing, but in a fight, more than strength and weight was involved. Skill and agility came into play, too, as well as the brand of dirty fighting taught in Krav Maga. So instead of struggling as she swung me back and forth, I just went with the flow and hugged her leg tighter.

And bit.

God bless strong genes and good dentists. Thanks to my own Dr. Sheffield's skill, I was able to gnaw all the way through her leathery skin to the tough gristle inside. Disregarding her howls, I kept gnawing until she bent down to pull me away.

Which is what I was waiting for. I let go of her leg and with one hand, grabbed her long blond hair, and drew her closer.

With my other hand, I poked her in the eye with a stiffened forefinger. The pain she'd felt before was nothing compared to what she felt now, and she staggered back, shrieking. I jumped to my feet.

Ignoring my wet forefinger—vitreous humor? God, I hoped not—I flattened my hand, turned it to the side, and gave her a chop to the neck.

She went down.

But it wasn't over yet. She reached up and snatched at me blindly, hoping to hook my leg and bring me down with her. If she got me between those massive thighs...

I wouldn't allow it. Instead, I drew my right fist back, leaned over, and smashed her in the nose. Only when her eyes rolled into her head and blood spurted all over me did I remember my heavy new turquoise ring.

The Navajo version of brass knuckles.

Ten minutes later I was filling out a police report as an ambulance carried Terry Jardine, aka Monster Woman, away. Before I got the chance to call the police myself, the commotion had alerted two sweaty accountants as they exited the gym, and they had performed that kind service for me.

After I refused treatment, against everyone's recommendation, the uniformed officers interviewed me.

"You say she attacked you first?" the tall one asked. He was thin as a snake but had a genial personality. His name tag identified him as Bruce Leavitt. I didn't know him, but I had once worked with his partner, a hard-ass little snip named Gwyneth Pronzini, whose ferocity made my old frenemy Detective Sylvie Perrins look like Tinker Bell.

"Yes, she hit me from behind with that rock..." I gestured toward the offending mineral lying near my Jeep, "...as I was about to climb in my vehicle. If you check your records, you'll find she's out on bail after being charged with firebombing my office."

Pronzini turned to Leavitt. "That'll be Desert Investigations. Over on Main Street. Arson guys have it." To me, "What'd you do to Ms. Jardine to make her act like that?"

"Had her car towed. She kept parking in our space."

"Definitely a major crime against humanity." Like most female cops, including Sylvie, Pronzini had to act twice as tough to be taken half as seriously as the male of the species.

I was about to say something cynical in return, but then something wet trickled down my back. When I raised my hand up to the wound, it came back red. Uh-oh.

"I'm bleeding again." I tried not to sound pathetic.

"Didn't we warn you not to refuse treatment?' Pronzini said, outraged. "You lied to the EMTs, didn't you, when you said you didn't lose consciousness?"

I shook my head before I remembered how much it hurt. "But I didn't. Not totally, anyway. Just saw a few stars."

Leavitt stared at my hand, then my head. "She really needs to go to the hospital."

"Sure looks like it." Pronzini turned her glare on me. "Lena, you smear any blood on our squad car, I'll kill you myself. We just had it washed."

With that, they drove me over to Scottsdale-Osborn Hospital, which luckily, was only eight blocks away from the gym so I didn't have to listen to Pronzini's caterwauls too long. Once there, she shut up. Copious amounts of blood are great attention-getters from ER folk, so I was immediately separated from the bloodless but groaning herd and ushered into a curtained examination area. As per protocol, Pronzini and Leavitt trailed along. Once a nurse helped me onto a gurney, the two cops turned to go.

But not before Pronzini got in a final zinger. "Oh, and you'd better get that blood around your mouth HIV-tested, too. Just in case."

An hour later, minus a little hair but the brand new owner of sixteen staples in my scalp, the ER released me with orders not to drive or operate heavy machinery for the next twenty-four hours. All hopped up on adrenalin, I ignored the doctor's warning and hoofed it back to the gym, where I picked up my Jeep and drove to my motel. The adrenaline wore off as I was climbing the stairs. It was only with difficulty that I summoned enough strength to get through the door to my room.

After latching the door behind me, I flopped across the bed in my bloody clothes, and fell into a deep, and thankfully, dreamless sleep.

Chapter Twenty-seven

Boom. Boom. Boom.

Cannon fire?

No. Someone pounding on my motel door. For a while I tried to ignore the racket, but that's hard to do when your head pounds along in time. *Boom. Boom. Boom.*

I opened my eyes to narrow slits and found the room full of light. Wha...? A check of the digital clock on the nightstand informed me that it was only 9:04 a.m. Damn noisy hotel maids.

"Go away!" I yelled, then wished I hadn't. My head felt like blood would spurt from my ears any second.

"Open this door, Lena, or I'll break it down!"

Jimmy.

I knew the man well enough to know that once he decided to do something, he did it, so with a groan I rose from the bed, staggered to the door, unlocked it, then staggered over to the nightstand. Leaning against it for balance, I dry-swallowed one of the pain pills the ER doc had given me and lay back down.

"It's unlocked!" I yelled. More pain. I remembered reading that anything ingested took twenty minutes to get into the bloodstream. Maybe I'd be dead by then. Buoyed by that hope, I lay there and waited for the coming storm.

It arrived in the guise of one furious Indian. "Why do I have to be alerted by the police that you've been hurt?"

"Police? That would be...?"

"Somebody named Gwyneth Pronzini, and she sounded pissed."

I didn't bother to lift my head off the pillow. "Gwyn's always pissed."

"Yeah, well, she called fifteen minutes ago and said you probably needed looking in on. Said she'd have called me earlier, but right after she and her partner dropped you off at the hospital, they were radioed about a missing three-year-old and looked for him all night. As soon as they found the kid sleeping in the backseat of a neighbor's car, she got on the phone to me."

Here's the thing about cops. They may hate each other, but in the end, they all stand together. Even when the cop is no longer a cop.

"So here you are. Well, as you can see, I'm alive. You can leave now." I put the pillow over my head, to either dull the sound of his voice or smother myself. Either way, it was a win-win.

He snatched the pillow away. "You're coming back to the trailer with me."

"No I'm not."

"Are too."

"No..."

Strong arms heaved me off the bed and dope-walked me to the door.

"I'll yell 'kidnap'."

"No you won't."

"Will too."

"Won't."

The problem with Jimmy is that he's so often right. Not really wanting to get him in trouble, I didn't yell, and he hustled me all the way down the stairs without anyone noticing. By the time he dragged me into his truck, I'd stopped struggling. I just wanted that pain pill to hurry up. It finally kicked in as we turned onto the gravel road that led to his trailer, and after that, I no longer cared about anything.

Around one o'clock, the smell of something wonderful woke me up.

"Lunch is served," Jimmy said, pushing a bowl under my nose.

"What's that?"

"Pima stew."

He turned on his heel and carried the bowl into the kitchen area. Led by the heavenly aroma, I followed, and found the table set for lunch for three.

I asked, "Who's joining us?"

"Madeline. She'll be here any minute. In fact, I think I hear her van coming down the road right now." He cocked his head. "Yep. I'd recognize that rattle anywhere."

"How…?"

"She called about twenty minutes ago, told me she'd been delivering some paintings to one of the Main Street galleries and decided to drop by our office. Then oops, she found nothing but a burnt-out shell where Desert Investigations used to be. Imagine that. Being the curious type, she went across the street to Cliffie's gallery, and he told her what happened, so when her call to you rolled over to voice mail, she got on the phone to me. Why in the world didn't you tell her about the firebomb?"

I rubbed my head. It still hurt, although not as badly as before. "Didn't want her to worry. You know how she is."

He frowned. "Well, now she's gets to see you all beat up, with staples in your head. Good luck with that."

Outside, a car door slammed. Steps crunched on gravel. A polite tap-tap at the door.

Jimmy liked Madeline, my former foster mother, so when he greeted her, his smile was genuine. "Welcome to my humble abode."

Her smile matched his as she took in the Pima designs painted across the cabinetry and said, "Not so humble. Love the art." When she turned to me, her smile faded.

"Why am I always the last to know, Lena?" Her long, dark hair, usually tied neatly behind in a low-slung ponytail, was in disarray, and the fine lines around her amber-colored eyes seemed more pronounced than ever.

After repeating the excuse I'd given Jimmy, I added, "Besides, you were all the way down in Florence. There was no point in making you drive up here."

"Less than an hour's drive, big deal. I've been going crazy ever since I saw what happened to your office. For a minute I thought…I thought…" She gulped. "Sweetie, how are you? You look like crap."

Question: what is a mother?

Answer: the woman who worries about you.

"It's not as bad as it looks," I lied.

Jimmy's welcoming smile turned sour. "She has sixteen staples in her scalp."

Madeline sat down and put her arm around me. "Oh, Lena."

"I'm fine, I'm fine."

"The crazy woman tried to kill her," Jimmy continued. "Back in jail now, bail revoked, cooling her heels at Tent City where it's a hundred and fifteen in the shade."

"Good!" Spleen vented, Madeline gave me a thoughtful look. "You've lost weight, too, Sweetie. Are you eating right?"

I thought of my usual diet of ramen noodles, topped off every now and then with a raspberry jelly doughnut from Bosa's. "Of course I am. In my business, you have to keep up your strength."

"Speaking of eating…" Jimmy said, stepping over to the trailer's tiny refrigerator. "I'd already made some Pima stew— mutton, you know—before you called, but I've put together a nice big salad for you."

"How thoughtful of you, Jimmy." Madeline had been a vegetarian for as long as I could remember.

We ate more or less in silence until Madeline brought up the issue I'd so desperately avoided thinking about. "Jimmy said the woman who attacked you used steroids."

"Sure looks like it."

"Intramuscular?"

"Probably."

She took a deep breath, then finally got around to it. "Lena, Jimmy told me that since you got her blood in your mouth, they'll have to test you for HIV."

For a moment I hated my partner for sharing so much. Didn't he know what a worrywart Madeline was? "Oh, sure, but it's just a matter of routine. While I was in the ER, they took a base blood sample from me, and just to be on the safe side, I'll get tested again after a month. Then again after another two months. If Monster Woman is HIV positive, which I doubt she is, I'll take one final test around the six-month mark. No big deal. This sort of thing happens all the time, and in ninety-nine percent of cases, everyone's in the clear." An exaggeration there, but what the hell.

"They tested her, too? This...this 'Monster Woman,' as you call her?"

I sighed. "Actual name, Terry Jardine. Since there was a lot of blood flying around, they probably gave her a viral load test, but those results won't be available right away. In the meantime..."

"In the meantime, we worry," Jimmy muttered.

"Not me," I lied again. "I'm too busy working the Cameron case to worry about anything else."

This started another discussion, an abbreviated one, since there was little I wanted to share with Madeline, including Juliana Thorsson's identity. After I'd finished my recital of the basic facts of the case, Madeline said, "That poor child. Well, at least she has someone who'll take care of her, love her."

I thought about Ali's uncle, about her egg donor.

"Maybe," was all I said.

An hour later, her concern about me somewhat abated, Madeline left for her studio in Florence, abandoning me with Jimmy. I wasn't happy and neither was he. I looked longingly at my laptop, which Jimmy had thoughtfully retrieved from my motel room. It was all I could do not to rush over and fire it up.

Jimmy caught me looking. "Lena, go back to bed and get some rest." He'd already refused to let me help with the dishes, leaving me alone at the table, watching him as he put away the last dried dish.

"I'm rested enough to be bored out of my mind," I complained. "Tell me what you've dug up on the Cameron suspects."

"Forget about work. You look awfully pale."

"I'm a natural blonde and wear lots of sunblock. Tell me about Kenny Dean Hopper's family. Any other murderers lurking around in their gene pool?"

"They're the salt of the Earth." Yet something in his expression told me there was more to the story.

"But? C'mon, Jimmy. I met Kenny's father. The man has a temper."

"The problem isn't the father."

I raised my eyebrows. "His mother?"

"Oh, all right. Let me go into the office, get the printouts…"

"I'll go with you." I rose from my seat.

He stepped in front of me and crossed his arms across his broad chest. "Absolutely not. It's too cold in there and I'm not taking any chances with you, so sit your ass back down."

I'd never heard Jimmy swear before; Pimas were known for their clean speech. Out of shock, I sat my ass back down.

A minute later I held a stack of printouts in my hand. I stared at the pages for a few moments, then confessed, "I can't read this."

"Vision still blurry, huh? Well, that's what you get with a concussion." He took the papers from me and set them on the table. "I'll sum up, then. When Estella Hopper, Kenny's mother, was sixteen—she was Estella Vargas then—she and her boyfriend, one Sean McKitteridge, got drunk at one of those desert parties and stole a cherry 1968 Jag XKE and wrapped it around a telephone pole on Camelback and Thirty-fifth Avenue. Sean died at the scene, Estella escaped with minor injuries. She wound up serving six months."

I digested that for a moment. "But she wasn't driving."

"They popped her for car theft and underage drinking."

"Still, a pretty stiff sentence for that, considering she was a minor and all."

"Not when there's a vehicular homicide involved."

"More like vehicular suicide," I muttered. "Anything else?"

"Not so much as a blip on the radar. Looks like she stopped going to desert parties, and a few years later, while working on her AA at Phoenix College, she met and married Emery Hopper, who became the father of the ill-fated Kenny Dean. But like I said, Emery's clean as a whistle, never so much as received a parking ticket."

If it wasn't for bad luck, Mrs. Hopper would have no luck at all. First her boyfriend gets himself killed drunk driving, then her son murders five people and she and her husband have to attend his execution. What a life.

"Next?"

A wry smile. "Ah, yes. That would be the Family Hoyt, they of the attack dogs and the baseball bat-swinging Bubba. How much do you want to know? Their list of transgressions is lengthy."

I put my hand to my staples. They still throbbed. "Read on, big man. I've got nothing else to do."

He cleared his throat. "It'll be easier if I take them one by one, according to the severity of the crimes. Sidney Hoyt you already know about. He burned his wife and babies alive to collect on the insurance, thus earning a visit from the esteemed Dr. Arthur Cameron in the Death House. Sidney's previous crimes included a nickel in Arizona State Prison for three Circle K robberies. In the last, he shot and wounded the female clerk, but the clerk—unlike Sidney's unfortunate wife and children—recovered. By the way, Sidney's brother Horace, who I'm betting is the one you refer to as Bat Boy, played backup in the robbery, and he, too, wound up doing five years. Horace has had several more scrapes with the law since then: three DUIs, two Assaults with Intent, one Resisting Arrest, and a half-dozen or so domestic violence calls before his wife—Edith is her name—sent him home to Mama Hoyt. I'll get to Mama later."

Oh, great. Even the mother had a sheet. "There were two more brothers, I believe."

"Yes indeedy. Gilman Hoyt, the baby of the family, blew himself up in a meth lab he was running in a Phoenix apartment. Once he was released from the hospital, he served seven years.

"And then there's Chester, the eldest. A failed liquor store robbery, for which he did two years. He is now suspected of running a dog-fighting ring, but they haven't found the venue yet. At one point, all four Hoyt brothers were residents of the state pen at the same time, which made it kind of homey in a way. Which brings me to Mama Hoyt."

"Wait a minute. Where's Papa? Something tells me the four brothers weren't virgin births."

"Mr. Something is right." A small smile. "Earl Hoyt was beaten to death in a barroom brawl one month before the birth of bouncing baby Gilman."

"A Hoyt as victim. What a refreshing change."

He shook his head. "Not really. Earl started the fight, which spread to such an extent that the detectives couldn't figure out who supplied the fatal blow. He'd cold-cocked a man who innocently brushed up against him on the way to the men's room, and a couple of the guy's buddies didn't take kindly to that. You ready for Mama now?"

"Lay it on me."

"Two shoplifting convictions, earning her a thirty-day stay for each in Tent City, and one three-year-long visit to Perryville for identity theft. She's on parole as we speak. Oh, and you'll like this, she's currently the Maricopa County president of M.W.A.—Mothers for a White America."

Jimmy was right. I liked it. I liked it so much it made the staples in my head hurt, and only with difficulty did I finally manage to stop laughing.

"The best and the brightest," I said, winding down to a snicker.

He snickered back. "Yea, verily." Then his voice turned solemn. "The Youngs, different story. Before Maleese Young was executed for capital murder, he'd received two parking tickets, one for double parking after he'd stopped to help a cat that'd been hit by a car. The cat survived. He took it home and gave it to his daughter Janeese. As for his wife, not even a parking ticket. Same with the daughter. Both of them clean right down the line, no ties to any fringe organization, unless you count the mother's membership in United Methodist Women as 'fringe.' And before you ask, it's the same story with the DuCharmes, the DuCharme chocolates family. Other than the cop-killing Blaine, who went nuts after he got hooked on crystal meth, no one in the family has ever had a police record. Their memberships are confined to Kiwanis and Rotary, and they're regular contributors to several charities, among them St. Jude's Children's Hospital, Meals On Wheels, and Adopt-A-Pet. Good people, it sounds like."

Good on paper, anyway. Ted Bundy had been good on paper, too.

Call me cynical.

"Where's Papa DuCharme?"

"Dead. But Mrs. DuCharme is the brains behind the company. Has been since it started."

I narrowed my eyes. "Anything irregular about Mr. DuCharme's death?"

"Slipped in the bathtub, cracked his skull open, drowned. Nobody home at the time. And before your suspicious mind goes into overdrive, I checked. Mrs. DuCharme and the kiddies were in the Bahamas waiting for Mr. DuCharme to join them as soon as he finished supervising the installation of some new factory equipment. When he didn't show at the airport or answer his phone, his wife called Scottsdale PD and asked for a welfare check. Cops found the body, and you know what they say."

"What do they say?"

"At least fifty percent of the time, and I'm quoting the most excellent Lena Jones here, the person who finds a dead body is the person responsible for helping it get dead in the first place."

"Gee, you sound just like a detective."

A big smile.

Time to get serious again. "How about Felix, Beulah Phelps' son?" Not that I believed the grossly overweight man could have had anything to do with the torture-killings of the Cameron family. He was too sick to do it himself, too poor to hire it done.

"As a juvenile, Mr. Phelps stayed off the radar until his mother went down for multiple homicides. While in foster care, he went on a shoplifting binge, did a six-months' stint in juvie, came out, was transferred to a group home, got some therapy, and stayed clean after that."

Clean but doomed.

"One other thing. While you were sleeping, I took a call from Valerie. She'd forgotten about this while she was talking to you over at Good Sam, but this morning she remembered that Dr. Cameron was instrumental in getting a nurse fired. You might want to call her, get the story yourself. But why don't you wait until you're feeling…"

His voice trailed away as I scrambled for my cell phone.

Valerie's story went like this: Approximately a year before the murders, Dr. Cameron complained that some prescribed Oxycodone hadn't made it to his patients. The following investigation revealed that Wanda Dorset, R.N., had hijacked their medications for her own use. After she refused rehab, Cameron pushed to have her terminated, and she was. Since word of drug addiction and pilferage sweeps like wildfire through the medical community, she couldn't find another nursing job.

"Lance, that's her husband, he was already out of work," Valerie said. "You know, one of those 'furlough' things with no end in sight. They were already on thin financial ice, so once Wanda's paycheck vanished, they lost their house. I hear he even came down to the hospital—I wasn't there that night, so I missed the drama—somehow made it into the ER and had it out with Dr. Cameron. Some shoving was involved. Security broke it up and tossed him out before it got too physical."

"Wanda's husband, he a big guy?"

"Better believe it. Because they were down to the one car, Lance always picked her up at the end of her shift, and we all met him at one time or other. That's how he got his nickname, The Hulk. Man looked like he never met a set of heavy weights he didn't like."

I winced. Just what the Cameron case needed: another suspect.

Although I'd planned to catch up on my case notes, the ER doc was right. I ran out of steam by two thirty and shuffled off to bed, leaving Jimmy to man the fort. My nap didn't last long. At three, blues riffs from my cell phone woke me and when I blearily looked at the display, saw Stephen Zellar's number. Hoping for good news, I took the call.

And was glad I did.

In a voice more animated than usual, Ali's attorney told me she had just been released into the custody of her uncle.

Chapter Twenty-eight

Ali

Ali didn't like the hotel room. It was furnished like something out of a sitcom she'd once watched with Alec on TV Land, but at least it was better than juvie. And Uncle Bradley, who she barely knew, was better than any guard, although most really weren't all that bad, to tell the truth. But Uncle Bradley didn't order her to do this, do that, and hurry up for Christ's sake. If he tried to order her around, he might have to touch her, and she knew he couldn't, like, stand the idea. It was why he didn't do anything about the marks on her face that stupid gansta girl put there. Some doctor, right?

But the food? Heaven.

"Want some more ice cream, Alison?" he asked, for what had to be the umpteenth millionth time.

"No, thanks, Uncle Bradley. I'm stuffed. Can we go shopping now? I need some clothes." She'd walked out of juvie wearing hand-me-downs, and from the way they smelled, they'd been wadded up in some Goodwill bag for a zillion years. With rat turds.

"Ah, about that. You see…"

Oh, great. Here it came. Another turndown.

She looked out the sliding glass door. They were eight stories up with a parking lot below, high enough that she'd probably die right away.

Tonight. She'd do it tonight.

"I don't know anything about young ladies' clothing and haven't been in a mall for over a year. I wouldn't even know where to take you, so…"

See? Anyway, what did it matter? If she couldn't get up enough nerve to kill herself she'd just walk around stinking for the rest of her life, and if people didn't like it, too bad. Once your mom and dad and brother had been murdered and you saw what they looked like lying there in their own blood, there was nothing anybody could do or say to make it…

No. Don't think about that. Don't think about them, not ever, or she'd start screaming and screaming and never stop, she'd…

"…so I've asked someone else to, ah, help with that," Uncle Bradley finished.

"Huh?"

"I meant to say, someone else will take you to the mall."

Handed off to a stranger. Well, what did she expect? The world sucked and just kept on sucking. She didn't care. She'd never care. Caring hurt too much.

"She'll be here any minute."

She? Well, at least that was something. But if whoever it was thought she was up for any cutesy pink girlie crap, she'd better think again. It was all black for Ali, black for remembrance.

A knock at the door, Uncle Bradley rushing to answer it, anything to keep from having to talk to her. He didn't know she knew that about him, but she did. He couldn't stand the sight of her and never would.

Not that it mattered. It didn't. Nothing mattered anymore.

Except for Kyle, but he was still in…

"Alison? I'd like you to meet Juliana Thorsson."

Chapter Twenty-nine

Lena

How can a person feel exhausted and restless at the same time? After awakening *un*-refreshed from my second nap of the day, I found myself incapable of following the ER doc's orders to take things easy. Instead, I wobbled over to my laptop and read through the Cameron case file. To my frustration, I found too many gaps, too many inconsistencies.

Around sundown, Jimmy interrupted me to inform me that we could count out the Oxycodone-pilfering Wanda Dorset, R.N., as a suspect.

"Three days after their house was repossessed, the Dorsets moved back to Malden, Missouri, their hometown," he said. "She was offered a job as a school nurse, and not being totally drug-addled, took it. He's working at some power plant. I seriously doubt they flew back here to slaughter the Camerons."

"So all's well that ends well for them, then?"

"Not really. They're living with her mother."

I gave him a bleak smile. "Maybe she's a sweetie."

He shrugged. "Anything's possible. I'm still following up on everyone connected to the case, including Bradley Teague, Dr. Cameron's brother. According to my sources, he really was in Kenya at the time of the murders."

"What sources would those be?"

"If I told you, I'd have to kill you."

"Funny man."

"I'm known for my one-liners."

He returned to his cold office, leaving me sitting there trying to figure out what to do next. I didn't have to think too long because minutes later my cell rang again. Fiona Etheridge, Kyle's foster mother.

"I wanted you to be the first to know, well, after my husband, of course, so I guess that makes you the second, I just have to thank you for everything you've done, because without you, everything…"

"Kyle's being released, right?" It was the only thing that could have reduced her to babble.

"Isn't that what I said?"

"Kinda."

She babbled on, telling me about the call she'd received from Curtis Racine, Kyle's attorney. After convincing the county attorney's office that surveillance videos proved the boy couldn't have killed the Camerons, Kyle had been granted a release, the only condition being that he, like Alison, could not leave the state.

"Mr. Racine assured us all charges will certainly be dropped," she finished. "It's just a matter of red tape now."

I felt almost as happy as Fiona, but for a different reason. "What time are you picking him up from the detention center?"

"At five. He'll be home in time for dinner, isn't that wonderful? I thought I'd never get over having to give up the twins but…"

"I want to talk to him."

"Huh?"

"The case is still open, Fiona, and he may be sitting on valuable information."

"Oh." A long silence, then, "I guess we owe you that much, don't we?"

You sure do. "How about after dinner?"

A small gasp. "That soon?"

"And do me a favor. Do not discuss the case with him before I get there. How about eight? No, make it seven. You folks will be done eating by then, right?"

"Uh, I guess so, but…"

"Good. See you then."

Before she could change her mind, I hung up.

I arrived at the Etheridge house at seven on the dot. When they opened the front door—letting out a strong aroma of pizza—both Etheridges were smiling, but their smiles faded when I stepped in and they saw my battered face.

"Something fell on me at the gym." No point in telling them that the object was a woman and she fell on me on purpose.

"You sure you're okay to drive?" Fiona asked, concern in her voice. "If you need to, Glen can drive you home. We can do this interview some other time. What matters is that Kyle is home where he belongs. And safe."

"No need to fuss, I'm perfectly fine." My head was killing me, but I didn't want to put off this interview. The longer the delay lasted, the more tainted Kyle's memory would become. Given the more than two weeks that had lapsed since the murder, it was tainted enough already. But regardless of the hitches in his memory, he was still the first person to arrive at the murder scene. Other than the killer.

Or killers, plural.

Fiona remained hesitant. "You just look so…so…tired."

Glen, towering behind her, spoke up. "Fi, let the poor woman sit down, okay?" Although he wasn't a handsome man—his nose was too broad and his chin too narrow—his face radiated kindliness. "Tell you ladies what. I'll go in the kitchen and pour us some coffee. Decaf all right, Miss Jones?"

I nodded, despite not being into decaf. While he was gone I could get the important questions out of the way. Fiona acted protective, but not as protective as I sensed he'd be.

Seeing my assent, he disappeared into the kitchen, leaving his wife to steer me to the family room. "I'd rather you not ask

Kyle any questions about the case until Glen gets back," she said, quashing my plan. "We've already seen what can happen when he's questioned without parental supervision. I'm sure you understand."

"Of course." I didn't let my disappointment show. The fact that both parents preferred to be present during the interview wasn't good, because children—especially young teens—were notoriously circumspect about what they reveal when their parents are listening.

When we reached the family room, I saw Kyle sitting on a vinyl-covered sofa with a fat brown puppy in his lap. Two kittens played with a Nerf ball at his feet. He appeared entranced by the view out the sliding glass doors that opened into the backyard. It wasn't particularly attractive or even well-tended, but he didn't seem to care. Neither would I, if I'd spent two weeks in the confines of the Mesa Detention Center. Studying him, I was surprised at how old he looked for his age, and how handsome. Clean movie-star features, glossy black hair, blue eyes so dark they were almost violet. The boy radiated good health, but there was no mistaking the burn scars up and down both of his arms, parting gifts from his biological mother.

Seeing me, he tucked the puppy under one muscular arm and stood up, careful not to step on the kittens.

'Thank you for all you've done for Ali," he said in a deep baritone. Almost as an afterthought, he added, "And for me." He stuck out his hand.

When I shook it, my hand came away covered in brown puppy hair.

"Sorry," Kyle said, wiping his own hairy paw on his jeans as he sat back down. "He's shedding."

"No problem. I've had worse on me." Monster Woman's blood, for instance.

Fiona fussed around with some pillows on a raggedy chair across from the sofa. "Sit down, sit down. This is nice and soft. Or do you need back support? How about an aspirin?"

"I'm fine." I plopped into the chair before she could fuss some more. "I'd really like to get this interview started."

"Not until…" She left off as Glen entered the room, carrying four unmatched coffee mugs on a tray.

"Here we are," he announced. "Sugar and milk, for those so inclined."

I grabbed a mug, took the digital recorder out of my tote, clicked it on, and set it on the coffee table.

Glen looked at it, then glanced at his wife, who'd joined Kyle on the sofa. "Is that really necessary?"

"I'm afraid so."

"Speech-activated, right?"

"Now that it's on, yes."

"Then understand that we reserve the right to stop this interview at any point." His voice, though gentle, was firm.

"Of course," I said.

"Good. Since we've got that settled, Miss Jones, have at it." Glen put his coffee mug down on an end table, then walked over to the sofa and stood there, arms crossed, fists clenched. Now Kyle was flanked by both foster parents. All gratitude forgotten, they'd circled the wagons.

I cleared my throat. "Kyle, after you returned to the abandoned house and found Ali gone, how long did you stay there? Did you leave right away, or wait for a while, thinking she might come back?" I already guessed the answer, but wanted him to tell me himself.

Kyle, after pouring enough milk into his coffee to turn it pale beige, answered. "As soon as I saw she'd left, I headed for her place. We'd been fighting and I figured she'd gone home."

"Weren't you worried about showing up at the Camerons'? Word I hear is that Ali's parents wanted to break you two up."

He shook his head. "Not really. Her mother didn't mind me seeing her, as long as it didn't get too…" He paused, searching for the word.

"Hot and heavy?" I suggested.

A pained smile. "Something like that."

"Did you see anything unusual on the way to Ali's house?"

He took a sip of his coffee. Made a face. Put it back down. "Like what?"

"Anything. A person on the street, maybe, who didn't look as if he belonged in the neighborhood. Or an unusual vehicle. Anything."

"Not that I can remember. It was awfully hot, and not many people were out."

"Not many? You saw some*one*, then. Who? Where?"

"Well, there was the mail carrier. Is that the kind of thing you mean?"

"That's exactly what I mean. Tell me about him."

"Her. She was driving one of those little trucks they have. You know, just delivering the mail."

"Where was this?"

"Couple blocks before I got to Alison's house. Colt Street, I think it was."

"Did you see the mail carrier get out of the truck and actually put mail into the mailboxes?"

He gave me a look that said, *Are you for real?* "Uh, yeah, I did. That's how I know she was a she. She left mail at a couple of houses. She was getting back into her truck as I rounded the corner."

The police report had logged in several unopened bills and junk mail from the Camerons' mailbox. Maybe the carrier had noticed something. Since the post office kept a log of who was on what route any given day, it should be easy enough for the police to check.

"Good, Kyle. Now we're getting somewhere. You see anyone else?"

"Well, there was this air-conditioning truck. Some guy getting stuff out of it."

A man. A truck. "Where was this?"

"Waaay before I saw the mail carrier. He was, like, closer to the party hou…uh, closer to the abandoned house than to the Camerons'." He looked over at Glen, who shrugged.

Fiona put her hand on Kyle's shoulder, the better to squeeze a warning if necessary.

I soldiered on. "How do you know he was the air-conditioning guy?"

Another *you must be some kind of stupid* look. "Because it said BINGHAM'S HEATING AND COOLING right there on the side. It's the same company Mom Fi uses."

"What color was the truck?"

A sigh. "Red, with white and black lettering, aluminum ladder on the top. Just like the truck that always shows up here."

"Same guy, by any chance?"

"Nah. Our guy's skinny. This other one was kinda fat. Or maybe muscular. Heck, I don't know. I wasn't exactly checking him out. Guys aren't my thing." He blinked, looking startled at what he'd just said. "Not that there's anything wrong with that."

Mom Fi patted him on the shoulder.

I thought about the air-conditioning guy. With the Camerons' neighbors out of state, their cul-de-sac was deserted, so there couldn't have been any complaints about overheating units on their street. "Is there anyone else you might have seen that you've forgotten about? Think hard, Kyle."

He looked up at the ceiling, where a fan was busy stirring the air around. His eyes tracked it for a few seconds, then he closed them for a moment, thinking. Mom Fi started to say something, but I raised my hand to silence her. Finally Kyle opened his eyes again. "Sorry. I can't remember seeing anyone else. Like I said, it was pretty hot out. Most people were indoors. Or at work. Or on vacation, you know?" He turned those startling blue eyes on me. "I mean, c'mon, wouldn't *you* be on vacation someplace cool if you didn't have to work?"

Relieved chuckles from Glen. A nod from Fiona.

Considering everything, the interview was progressing well. Kyle felt relaxed enough to act snarky.

I smiled, prolonging the feel-good moment. "You got that right, Kyle. They say Switzerland's nice this time of year, Iceland, too, so maybe I'll check them out sometime. But for now, yeah,

I have to work, which means asking you all these pesky questions. So far, you've been very, very helpful, and I really, really appreciate it."

He beamed. Not only handsome, nice, too.

But in my business you do what you have to do, even to nice kids. "Kyle, tell me exactly what you saw and heard when you approached the Cameron house."

Kyle flinched, and the puppy in his lap yelped. Stricken, the boy leaned his head down and nuzzled it. "So sorry, baby," he cooed. "I didn't mean to do that."

Fiona glared. "Lena, we've spent hours trying to make him forget what he saw that day!"

Exactly what I'd been afraid of. "In your place, I'd feel the same way, Fiona, but please understand, there's a vicious killer out there somewhere, possibly in this very neighborhood. Have you thought about that?"

The look on her face proved she hadn't, so I pressed my advantage. "The Cameron case isn't closed just because the authorities turned your son loose. The detectives will be going over old ground, trying to figure out what they missed last time." *Such as eighteen thousand dollars stuffed into a pillow sham.* "If they can't come up with any new leads, new suspects"—I stressed the word 'suspects'—"they might go back to where they started. With Kyle and Ali. We need to make certain that doesn't happen, and if it means dredging up a few bad memories, well…"

She didn't buy it. Neither did Glen.

To my surprise, Kyle did. Speaking directly to Fiona, he said, "She's right, Mom Fi. Just because they let us go for now doesn't mean they can't arrest us again." Then he blushed. "After all, we did…uh, I did sign that, um, statement."

"You mean your confession," I said, to make certain his foster parents understood the nature of the ongoing threat.

"Yeah, my confession. And I get it, it was a dumb thing to do. But we were scared, and I thought…Never mind what I thought. Ali didn't do anything bad, she didn't do anything at all. She just said what she did to protect me. She's telling the truth now, but if they start in on me again I'm afraid…"

"You're afraid she'll go back to telling the same old story."

"Yeah." He gulped, close to tears.

I reframed my question to give him a few moments to collect himself. "All right. Let's start again at the beginning. When you returned to the abandoned house from the Circle K, Ali wasn't there, so you left again, this time for the Camerons' place, thinking that after your argument she went home. Now pay attention. The minute you turned into their cul-de-sac, did you see anything or anyone in front of their house or leaving their street?"

He shook his head.

"Did you hear anything?"

Another head shake.

"Was the front door open or closed?"

"Open, but not by much."

"So you were able to walk right in?"

"I knocked first."

"And?"

"Nobody came. But when I knocked, it made the door open more, and when it did, I, uh, smelled something strange."

"Tell me about the smell."

He looked down at the puppy, which had fallen asleep on his lap. "Uh, like, uh…" He took a deep breath. "Like dog poop."

"Right. Is that when you went in?"

"Yeah. I was trying to figure out what was up, you know? 'Cause, Dr. Cameron, he was a doctor, I mean, like, a medical doctor and had this thing about dirt, so even with Misty, that place was always spotless, so I walked in, just a couple of steps at first, calling for Ali, and at first I didn't see anything, but then, but then, I saw, well, you know."

The puppy woke up, stared at him, then struggled to get down. That's when I realized how tense Kyle had become. His hands were clenched, and he was biting his lip so hard I thought it might bleed.

"Kyle?" Fiona's voice.

"It's all right, Mom," he said, easing the puppy down to the floor, where it joined the kittens tormenting the Nerf ball. Looking back at me, he said, "I saw Dr. Cameron first. He was sitting in that chair with tape over his mouth, covered in something red, but I didn't know what it was at first, I thought maybe he'd been painting, but I didn't smell paint, just the dog poop, and then I noticed his hands were all taped up, and then I saw Mrs. Cameron, she had tape over her mouth and her hair was sopped in the same red stuff as Dr. Cameron's and I knew then it wasn't paint because her hands were taped too, and I saw Misty all in red next to Ali's brother and he was all covered in red too and I...and I...I didn't still get it and I walked over there 'cause I was going to take the tape off and make them tell me what happened and maybe help them wash off all the red...but then...but then when I got close I saw that they weren't going to tell me, not ever going to tell anyone anything not ever again, and then I saw the bat and then...and then Ali came in and I thought...I thought..."

"You thought she'd done all that," I said, so softly I could hardly hear my own voice.

A gulp. "I must have been crazy."

"No, you were in shock."

Violet eyes ringed in red, he continued. "Ali...Ali saw Misty wasn't dead but I thought Misty was so awful-looking that I just knew she was dying and suffering and suffering, and I can't stand to see an animal suffer like that and all I could think was to put her out of her misery real fast so it wouldn't go on any longer and Ali was standing there saying all this crazy stuff and I was, like, remembering this note she wrote me about wanting them all dead so we could always be together and it was...it was...it was just...it was just awful."

"What happened then?" I couldn't seem to talk in a normal tone anymore, just whisper.

"Ali grabbed her mother's purse, the purse with the car keys in it and we took Misty to the vet."

"Then you headed for California."

His handsome face twisted. "Oh, God, we were so stupid!"

Glen, who hadn't said a word during all this, stepped forward. His hands were still clenched, as if ready to throw a punch. "Okay, Miss Jones. That's it. I want you to leave now."

"But:.."

Glen started toward me, fist raised.

Not wanting to get beat up again, I grabbed my recorder, threw it in my carryall, and hurried to the door.

As I turned the knob, I heard footsteps. I turned to see Kyle, standing at the entrance to the family room, Glen and Fiona clutching at him, trying to drag him away. He was too strong. "Wait, Miss Jones! I just remembered something else!"

Braving Glen's threatening fists, I asked, "What do you remember?"

"The van."

I frowned. "The air-conditioning van?"

"No. The other one."

"What other van, Kyle?"

"The panel van, the one that drove by me when I was still a few blocks from Ali's house, I think it was around Shetland Street and Appaloosa Way, you know, the intersection just before you go into the neighborhood where she lives. Anyway, this van, I think it was a Ford or a Chevy, a real old one, too, maybe even from the seventies, it was coming from that direction, the direction of the big circle, I mean, like it had been in there, and it was weird, you know? I didn't think too much about it before, but when I was talking to you in there, telling you about finding the Camerons all covered in bl…finding the Camerons like that, I remembered the van."

Fiona looked at Kyle nervously, tugged at his shirt.

He pushed her hand away. "Don't. I need to tell her."

"What color was it, this van?"

"Mostly white, but it was all beat up and you could see other colors on it, too. Looked like it had been painted over and over, a real bad paint job each time, like some dumb kid did it."

I already had the door open, but despite the heat rushing in from outside, the room's temperature must have dropped thirty degrees. "You say the van was weird, is that because it had a bad paint job?"

He shook his head. "No."

"Then what, Kyle? What was so weird about the van?"

"Because when it drove past me, it…it smelled like dog poop."

Hacking the Motor Vehicles site to find the registration for a 1970s to 1980s Ford or Chevy panel van would be impossible; even Jimmy couldn't work miracles. But Kyle's description correlated with Clint Zhou's, so there was little doubt both young men had seen the murder vehicle.

As I drove back to the Pima rez through the twilight, I ran the timeline through my aching head again.

Clint made his delivery to the still alive-and-well Camerons at 11:56 a.m., stayed parked in front of the house texting his girlfriend for a few minutes, then drove off and hit a white van while leaving the neighborhood. Later, Kyle, while on his way to the Camerons' house to find Ali, had passed the same van near the intersection of Shetland Street and Appaloosa Way, mere blocks from her house. Kyle didn't know the exact time he arrived at the Camerons', but according to the veterinarian who'd taken care of Misty, Kyle and Ali arrived in his office—a thirty-minute drive away—at 3:02. This meant the murderers entered the Cameron house no earlier than noon, and finished their bloody work around two thirty.

Time is relative. Two-and-a-half hours doesn't seem long, but it would have seemed an eternity for the Camerons.

Scottsdale PD had already checked with the Camerons' immediate neighbors to see if their houses had surveillance cameras and came up with a negative. But now that I had confirmation of the killers' vehicle, a concrete timeline, and a new intersection, there was a chance one of the houses near Shetland and Appaloosa caught the van's license plate on a better-angled camera. Too dark now to check the neighborhood for cameras myself, but Scottsdale PD needed to be aware of this right away.

I placed a call to Sylvie Perrins, only to have the call roll over to voice mail. I left a message, then tried Bob Grossman. Same thing. Frustrated, I thought about giving my information to Captain Ulrich, their boss, then thought better of it. All I'd get from Ulrich was a lecture about sticking my nose into police business.

When I arrived back at Jimmy's trailer, I found him sitting outside on his chaise, looking up at the stars.

"You do this every night?" I asked, getting out of the Jeep and into the warm night, where cricket songs and the rustlings of other small wildlife chased away the vast silence. For some reason, the coyotes weren't out yet, giving some rabbit a temporary stay of execution.

"When there's no dust storm." He waved toward the other chaise. "Have a seat. And by the way, how are you feeling? You look terrible."

"Thanks for the compliment." If I joined him, it would make twice in one week I'd wasted time sitting outside. Last time I did, Monster Woman burned down Desert Investigations. I sat down anyway. What could she do now, throw another firebomb all the way from Tent City? Still, I felt as bad as he said I looked, and the chaise offered comfort.

"A little thing like a dust storm scares you?" I teased. "I thought you Pimas were tough."

"We Pimas are peaceful farmers, cotton mostly, and farmers know better than to stay outside letting dust blow into their eyes when they could be sitting comfortably in their houses filling up on prickly pear ice cream."

I gave him a sideways glance. "Prickly pear ice cream? You're making that up."

"Go check in the freezer."

A minute later I returned to my chaise with a large bowl of bright pink ice cream.

"Bought a new ice cream maker yesterday," Jimmy continued, as if I'd never left. "On sale at Fry's. Gonna try to duplicate Ben & Jerry's Chunky Monkey tomorrow. Already have the bananas, chocolate, and walnuts. Maybe I'll throw in a little mint, just as an experiment. Or would that be gilding the lily?"

"Gilding." I dug into the prickly pear concoction and tasted Heaven. "You never stop surprising me, Almost Brother." As I swallowed the gooey stuff, my headache receded.

Jimmy didn't reply, just continued looking at the stars. I took the hint and looked at them, too, but it took no strain on my part. I'd always felt at home on the Pima rez; it had once taught me how tough I was.

Years earlier, Jimmy's father, a tribal policeman, saved my life. I was around six or seven, in my third or fourth foster home, and deeply unhappy. With all the magical thinking of a child who'd seen too many Disney cartoons, one hot day I set off across the desert to find my biological parents.

That morning I had awoken fresh from a dream of my red-headed father and blond mother standing in a lush forest, looking at a creek as it danced around lichen-covered rocks. I didn't remember much, but somehow I knew they lived "east," in the direction the sun rose. All I had to do was get back there, where they'd be waiting with kisses and candy. So I snuck down to my foster parents' kitchen, stowed two cans of Tab in my school bag, and left the Scottsdale house before they woke up. It was July, and the temperature already in triple digits. But by the time the sun was high overhead, I had already made it to the Pima reservation just in time for a dust storm.

As the curtain of red-brown dust rose before me, I tried to shield my face with my school bag, but it provided little protection. Sand bit into my face, my arms, my legs. When the storm was finished, so was I. Panting with fear and exhaustion, I lay in the sand, covered with dirt and debris. When I finally regained enough strength to look up, I saw vultures hovering above, big black birds I'd once seen in a John Wayne movie. I knew they ate the dead.

But they wouldn't eat me.

Fear turned to anger, and when they dove, I was ready. When the first one landed and started to hobbeldy-hop toward me, its knife-like beak dripping with menace, I shouted, "Go away, bird!"

I glanced at the long-empty Tab I'd pulled from my school bag. Not desert-wise, I'd planned on finding a cool stream where I could fill it again.

"Bird! I'll hit you!"

The vulture continued its progress.

I threw the can. It bounced off those glossy feathers, but at least halted the bird's advance.

I reached out and snatched the can from where it had rolled almost back to me, then filled it with rocks and dirt. "I'll hurt you bad this time!" I warned.

The vulture paid no attention, just hopped forward again as several of its friends swooped down to join the impending feast.

"I mean it, Bird! I'll hurt you! I'll hurt you all!" I didn't really want to hurt any of them, but in that John Wayne movie birds like them did terrible things to people, sometimes before the people were totally dead. I didn't want the same things done to me, so I had to make them go away.

The Tab can felt heavier now, more like a weapon. "I'll break your wing!" I screamed to the lead bird. "Then your friends will eat you!"

The bird kept coming.

I threw the can and struck the bird in the head. With a squawk, it flew away. A small victory only, because the others remained.

The fight had taken a lot out of me, and I slumped against a rock. Sensing weakness, the rest of the vultures closed in. I had no weapon now, just my hands.

I clenched my fists. I'd fight them until they ate away my fingers, then I'd hit them with my stumps.

One bird reared up and…

A gunshot.

In a great flurry of black, the birds flew away.

Through the roaring in my ears, I heard a man's deep voice. "Well, now, Little Miss. What're you doing way out here on our rez? Why don't I take you home?"

*I gazed up into a mahogany-colored face, gentle brown eyes, and
saw a policeman holstering his gun. His name tag read...*
SGT. JAMES EDWARD SISIWAN.

"I remember your father, you know," I said to Jimmy, as we
studied the Milky Way.

"So you've told me."

"He was my hero."

"Wish I could remember him, too, but I was only a baby
when he died. Then my mother died, and, well, I wound up in
Utah. But unlike you, I lucked out."

"I know." I turned on the chaise and faced him. They say
Indians don't show emotion, but that's bullshit. "How about I
remember him for the both of us?"

It took him a moment, but when he spoke again, he had
worked through his feelings. "Deal. For now, though, let's forget
the past. Too depressing. Tell me about Kyle. Bet his family was
happy to have him back."

I licked the last bit of ice cream off my spoon. "Oh, they were."

Once I finished recapping the interview, Jimmy said, "Maybe
that van will show up on some surveillance camera, but that
would be almost too easy, don't you think?"

"What do you mean?"

"It was probably stolen."

I groaned, for two reasons. Jimmy was right: the possibility
that the van had been stolen had occurred to me, too. And now,
notwithstanding the ice cream therapy, my headache was back.

"If the van was stolen," I said, trying not to think about the
pain in my head, "the killer probably dumped it long before now.
Still, I'll keep bugging Scottsdale PD until they track the thing
down. Maybe you could check with your buddies in the tribal
police since the rez is such a popular dumping ground. Bodies,
stolen cars, the usual. Even the most careful killer can screw up
and leave something behind, especially in a vehicle. A scrape of
DNA on a door latch, a hair on the floor...Speaking of DNA,
it works with dogs, too. The dog feces on the Camerons' walls?

Evidence. Let's not forget the case in Tennessee, where a man was convicted of murder based on a lone cat hair transferred from the victim to him."

"That conviction's being appealed, so don't get your hopes up."

"I'm an ex-cop, remember, which means I live on hope. Oh, look." I pointed to the sky, where one of the bright dots appeared to be moving, albeit very, very slowly. "Is that a comet? And if you wish on a comet, does your wish come true?"

"It's probably just another communications satellite. But go ahead and wish. Can't hurt."

So I did.

And it worked.

Chapter Thirty

I had just finished the Spanish omelet Jimmy had whipped up and was savoring my second cup of coffee when my cell rang. Up until then, he'd been cross-examining me on the state of my health, especially the part that concerned my sore head.

On the phone, Detective Sylvie Perrins sounded excited. "Couple of weeks ago, Phoenix cops found an '78 Ford Econoline van abandoned in the lot at Papago Park and had it towed to the impound lot. I just called over there and the manager said that, yeah, it's white. Techs are on their way as we speak. Thanks for the phone tip."

Before I could cheer, she added, "I already ran the VIN and it's registered to one Reuben Alvarez, of Buckeye. Reported stolen from the Pebble Creek Club House parking lot, where he was doing some yard work. Guy's a gardener."

"That's clear on the other side of Phoenix. He have any connection to the Camerons?"

"We're checking it out. Him being a yard man, there's no telling where-all he works. Or admits to working. These guys, they do a lot of under-the-table jobs. Maybe the whole car theft story's one big lie and he once did some work for the Camerons, got stiffed, and took his sweet revenge."

Anything was possible, but it didn't feel right, so I asked, "He have a sheet?"

"Couple of traffic tickets. Otherwise, no wants, no warrants. No history of domestics, either."

A man's propensity to violence often announces itself in a string of domestic violence calls, yet that didn't seem the case here. Then again, women don't always report the abuse. Alvarez could have been beating his wife, if he had a wife, black and blue for years and there could still be no record.

Sylvie knew that, too, so there was no point in mentioning it. "What happens now?"

"Since the van might be connected to a high-profile case, the techs' prelim report could reach us tomorrow. Or maybe early next week. Then we sit around and wait to see if there's a DNA match to anything from the Cameron house. Hey, even dog shit DNA! Wouldn't that be fun?"

"A laugh riot. What's the lab's back-up these days?"

"Oh, around fifty, sixty other cases, the usual. But, and don't tell anyone I said this, you know how it works, some cases have higher priority than others. We got us bunch of dead transients with no ID. Heatstroke, of course. Got around twenty, twenty-five illegals down by the border, thirst, more heatstroke, then we got that serial rapist working south Phoenix—he's still doing his thing—a couple of drive-by fatals in Maryvale, and a decomposed female some hiker's dog dug up in the Superstitions last week. The lab's overwhelmed."

These days, with violent crime on the increase and lab workers being laid off willy-nilly because of county budget cuts, DNA tests often took months to complete. In many states, the back-up ran into years. But as Sylvie pointed out, some cases had higher priority than others. DNA connected to the torture/murders of one physician's family rated higher than a host of dead illegals and transients. Death, as in life, had its own caste system.

Sylvie was being so helpful I almost hated to ask the next question. "What about the possibility of surveillance cameras near Shetland and Appaloosa? You do anything about that yet?"

She vented a string of expletives for a while, then calmed down enough to snap, "What?! You think Scottsdale PD's got nothing better to do than do your footwork for you? Send me a list of addresses and I'll get to them when I can!"

She hung up.

Jimmy stared at me. "Sounds like a rough call. By the way, you look worse than yesterday. If you ask me, you'd better take it easy."

"I didn't ask you."

He shrugged. "Just making an observation. That was Sylvie, I take it. I could tell by the squabbling. She get anything on the DNA yet?"

"Nope." Ignoring my headache—worse than yesterday's—I grabbed my carryall and headed for the door. "I'd help with the dishes, but I need to look at some houses."

He gave me a wry smile. "Not to purchase, right?"

"Oh, sure. I'm going to buy me a tract home in Scottsdale, join the local women's club, and live happily ever after."

As I left, I heard him mutter, "Stranger things have happened, although in your case, probably not."

At the intersection of Shetland and Indian Bend, I found two houses with security cameras. The good news was that they were situated kitty-corner from each other, thus able to videotape the murder van from different angles. The bad news? One camera looked old enough to have been used on Noah's ark. I phoned in the addresses to Sylvie, who accepted them with nary a thank you. Police work sure played hell with a person's manners.

Deciding I could use another cup of coffee to chase away my growing fatigue—so early in the day?—I headed for the Starbucks I'd passed on the way over. The crowd was thin enough that I was able to get an iced Frappuccino in what seemed like seconds, and after a couple of quick glances at my black eye, I was ignored. Frapp in hand, I made my way to an isolated seat in the corner, the better in which to think.

I felt certain that when the DNA results came in, the van in the impound yard would be turn out to be the murder van, and the surveillance cameras—if working that day—would give a jury something to look at. But the real question was this: did the killer leave any DNA of his own in the van? And if so, would that DNA match up with any already on file? Unless it did, the

DNA wouldn't be that much help in finding the killer, only in convicting him when he arrived in court.

It occurred to me that I might do some DNA collecting of my own, at least as far as doggie-do was concerned. With the exception of Felix Phelps, each of the people I'd interviewed owned at least one dog. From the sound of its barks, Monster Woman had something big, the Hoppers owned a German shepherd mix, the white trash Hoyts' property was overrun by a whole pack of ravenous mutts, the Youngs owned those two black something-or-others, and Carl DuCharme had a prize-winning boxer. I doubted if Mr. Hopper or his grieving wife would let me anywhere near their shepherd mix, and if I dropped by the Hoyts asking to borrow a cup of dog feces, I'd be lucky to get off their property alive. If I asked the Youngs for a sample of their dogs' doggie-do, Janeese would call the nut squad on me. And Carl DuCharme? He'd probably dropkick me into a vat of molten chocolate.

However, now that Dr. Bradley Teague had been proven to be in Africa at the time of the killings, and the nurse Dr. Cameron had fired was pretty much ruled out, too, I considered the prime suspects to be the Hoyts, with Monster Woman a close runner-up. The entire Hoyt family was vicious, and one of them liked to swing a baseball bat. As for Monster Woman, aka Terry Jardine, she was crazy-mean enough to do anything. At least the judge had raised her bail to five hundred thousand, so I might be able to gather her dog's feces in peace.

Frustrated by the incongruity of collecting dog poop, I decided to do something more pleasant: see how Ali was getting along. A call to her uncle elicited the fact that the girl had spent yesterday afternoon clothes shopping with Juliana.

"You're kidding, right?" I asked.

"Why would you think I'm kidding, Miss Jones? The girl couldn't keep wearing the clothes they gave her at her release, and she certainly doesn't want to go back into that house…" He paused for a moment, then continued. "…back in her house for her other things. Later, maybe, but not now."

"I meant that you had to be kidding, letting her leave with Juliana."

"What's wrong with that?"

He probably didn't know Juliana was Ali's biological mother, which might explain his obtuseness. But I remembered the way Juliana had stared at Ali during her family's funeral, the hunger in her eyes. Would the ice queen be sensitive to the girl's needs? I doubted it. Ali needed someone warm, not a senatorial candidate.

"There's nothing actually *wrong*, Dr. Teague, just that, considering everything, getting those two together could wind up being problematical in several ways. Leaving that aside, tell me how they got along?"

"Fine, I guess, because they're shopping again today. Miss Thorsson's already picked her up for another trip to Scottsdale Fashion Square."

I let that sink in for a moment. "Um, I'm curious, Dr. Teague. How much do you actually know about Ms. Thorsson?"

"Enough to know she's probably going to make a run for the U.S. Senate. We had a nice discussion about politics and there's a lot of agreement there. I found her quite refreshing."

"Oh, for…" In these cynical days, when politicians smoked crack and texted pictures of their penises, Juliana's being a politician might make a more cautious person think twice about handing an impressionable young teen over to her care for a carefree day at the mall. But not Ali's uncle, who had the sensitivity of a doorknob. "You mean, based on the fact that she's a senatorial candidate, you turned your niece over to a woman you've just met?"

"Well, that and the fact that she's Ali's biological mother."

"Thorsson told you?!" I yelled so loudly, that everyone in Starbucks, baristas included, turned to look at me. After mouthing "Sorry" at them, I lowered my voice. "She actually said that?"

Dr. Teague sounded surprised by my surprise. "Why wouldn't she? And she didn't just tell me, she showed me her copy of the contract she'd signed with my brother and Alexandra."

So Juliana had kept it all these years. Interesting. I forced myself to calm down. "Has she told Ali yet?"

I could almost hear his shrug. "I didn't ask."

The man was emotionally tone-deaf, so I ended the call as civilly as possible. Compared to Teague, Juliana Thorsson was a heaving mass of unrestrained emotion, but I wanted to make certain she treated Ali with more sensitivity than he did. Given the death of the girl's family, followed by a three-week stint in the corrections system, she had been traumatized enough. The last person she needed to be around was someone who knew diddly-squat about kids. It was one thing to experience a brief yearning for your biological child, another thing entirely to care for her. During my twelve-year stint in Child Protective Services, I'd lived in two foster homes where the people had loved the idea of children, but wound up hating the reality. As a result, they took their disappointment out on their foster kids. In some cases, the kids fought back.

Remembering the gun cabinets in Juliana's condo, I hit Thorsson's number on speed dial. She picked up right away, sounding hurried. From the bits of bad canned music I heard on the other end, they were already in the mall. "What do you want, Lena? I'm busy right now."

"Yeah, shopping with Ali."

A sniff. "You talked to Dr. Teague, I take it."

"Yep."

"Then that's one conversation we don't need to have."

With a feeling of dread I realized how much the woman took for granted. We could turn back time, and as some high-toned medieval philosopher once exulted, all would be well, and all would be well, and all would always be well. Except when it wasn't. Careful not to let my frustration show, I said, "Although technically you are my client, I'm as concerned about Ali's welfare as I am yours, so I'm just checking in to see how she's doing."

"She's doing fine." A hint of amusement.

"You haven't already told Ali about your, ah, relationship, have you?"

The frost returned. "Give me credit for some common sense."

Common sense? When she was out in public with a young teen who looked just like her? When I mentioned that, she laughed.

"It's common knowledge I have a sister and niece, but so far, no one's said anything about the resemblance. If and when they do, I'll deal with it. In the meantime, say hi to Ali. She's been asking about you."

Rustling sounds, then a new voice. Lighter. Warmer. "Lena! Guess what? I'm out of juvie!" For the first time since I'd met her, she actually sounded like a fourteen-year-old.

"That's great, kiddo. I hear you're at the mall."

"Yep. I got new jeans, new tops, new skirts, a couple necklaces, and a bracelet. Oh. And shoes and underwear."

I remembered she was going through a Goth stage. "All black?"

Her tone sobered. "I'll never wear colors again." The way she said it, I knew it wasn't a reference to style. "Anyway, Julie showed me this new color, Arctic Black. It looks black, but in certain lights, it's bluish-gray."

Julie? "Sounds pretty. I'll have to look that up for myself. Now pass the phone back to, ah, Julie."

"Told you so," Juliana said, as soon as she was on the line.

"Well, don't rush things."

The note of amusement returned. "Says the expert on teenage girls. Oh, well, since you're so concerned, why don't you drop by my place around five? We should be finished shopping by then, and you can check out Ali's emotional health in person. I'll make us some more iced tea."

I'd thought more along the line of going back to Jimmy's trailer for a nap after my next two stops, but I didn't want to pass up this chance. "Sounds good. Uh, just as a warning, I got into a bit of a scrape the other day…" *when a lunatic tried to kill me* "…so I'm sporting a shiner and a few other cuts and bruises. Better prepare her for that."

"She's seen worse."

I remembered the photographs of the Cameron crime scene. "Yes, she has."

It was only after the dial tone that I wondered how long Ali's visit with Juliana would last. Surely Dr. Teague wouldn't let her spend the night with a woman he'd just met. Then again, given the man's utter cluelessness, he might.

The crowd in Starbucks had thinned out by the time I stashed my cell back into my carryall, so I walked up to the counter and ordered a venti to go. No fancy flavors or froths, just twenty ounces of high-test straight stuff. Thus fortified for my next appointment, I went back to my Jeep.

Monster Woman's roommate was happy to see me. Due to a misunderstanding I hadn't bothered to correct when we spoke on the phone, she thought Terry Jardine and I were friends. Like Terry, Phoebe MacIntosh was a bodybuilder, although I'd never seen her around Scottsdale Fight Pro. But unlike Jardine, Phoebe wasn't insane. Her pink Spandex workout clothes revealed her body; she'd stopped at the apex of terrific.

With a welcoming smile, she brushed frosted brown hair out of her eyes and invited me in. "Don't pay any attention to Brunhilda," she said, gesturing toward the slavering Rottweiler at her side. "She's really a sweetie."

Brunhilda didn't look like a sweetie to me, but I walked in anyway and sank onto the softest sofa I'd ever encountered. The living room was a riot of pastels. Pink walls. Rose and cream-colored sofa and chairs, pale gray Berber carpet accented by a pink, cream, and mint-green throw rug. A menagerie of delicate glass animals capered across several antique-white occasional tables. The only evidence of a bodybuilding lifestyle was a series of framed photos on the wall showing Phoebe, bronzed and beaming, holding large trophies. No photographs of Terry. Women who overdevelop themselves to the point of psychosis don't win trophies.

"How's Terry?" I asked Phoebe, after explaining my face away as the result of a dropped barbell, thus continuing her belief that Monster Woman and I were workout buddies from the gym.

"Not so good. You know about the 'roids?"

"They're kind of obvious."

"If I've warned that girl a million times…Well, now she's detoxing from them and she's miserable. Not that she wasn't miserable before, what with the eye injury that vicious bitch who jumped her in the gym parking lot gave her."

"Hmm. Say, could I have some water? It's really hot out there. And I need to pop an Excedrin."

She gave me a look of concern. "Geez, where are my manners! I've also got iced tea?"

Of course she had iced tea. Everyone in Arizona makes iced tea in the summer. "I'd love some, but don't put yourself out for me."

"Don't be silly, it's already made." With that, she jumped up and headed for the kitchen, followed by Brunhilda and me, carryall in hand. The kitchen was pink, too. Pink walls, pink and green-striped curtains, marbled pink dinette set. At least the refrigerator was white. When Phoebe opened the refrigerator door and began rattling things around, I snuck a look out the window. Small concrete patio with two chairs and a glass-topped table, desert-landscaped yard area, kidney-shaped pool. Was that dark lump in the far corner a rock or a turd?

Phoebe carried a big pitcher of tea over to the sink and poured us both full glasses. "Want sugar? I don't use it, myself."

"Naw, this'll be fine." I washed down an Excedrin. It got caught halfway down, so I took another big drink. After it had cleared, I said, "You were telling me about Terry's eye injury. Is it serious?" I settled myself in a pink chair and sipped at my tea, showing no eagerness to return to the living room.

Phoebe took the hint and sat down, too, Brunhilda at her feet. "Oh, Terry's eye. She can see out of it again, thank God, but it's still blurry. The doctor told me they won't transfer her to jail until it's back to normal, and like I said, 'cause she's detoxing off the 'roids, she's got stomach cramps, muscle aches, she's hurling all over the place, and she's lost a ton of weight. She hates that more than anything 'cause she's so proud of her body."

Despite everything, I felt a pang of pity for the demented Terry Jardine. "They let you visit her in the hospital?"

"Oh, yeah. After her brother OD'ed, she listed me as her emergency contact, so I was the first person they called. It was awful, I'm telling you, seeing her handcuffed to the bed like that."

I acted surprised. "Handcuffed!"

Brunhilda growled. She was a sweetie, all right. Her and Cujo.

I was still trying to figure out how I could get a sample of the Rottweiler's feces when Phoebe added in a near-whisper, "Cops said she broke parole when she hit the woman back, but I'm not buying it. Terry wouldn't hurt a fly."

Not flies, maybe. Human beings and innocent office buildings, different story. But Phoebe had given me the perfect opening. "I'm sure you're right. Terry's judgment isn't always the greatest, though. The steroids, that pen pal of hers, the guy in prison, what-his-name."

Phoebe mashed her Cupid's-bow mouth into a grim line. "Kenny Dean Hopper. Talk about slime! Why she bothered with that creep..." She shook her head. "Only way I can figure it, he looked something like her brother. You ever meet Ashton?"

I shook my head.

"Terry showed me Ashton's picture once. Same build as Kenny Dean, same wild look in his eyes. From what she told me, he was a sicko, too."

I wasn't sure I wanted to go there, so I moved the subject back to the late Kenny Dean.

"She was pretty shook up after Kenny Dean was, uh..."

"After he rode the needle," she finished, a gleam of satisfaction in her eyes. "I comforted her as best I could, but to tell the truth, I'm glad the whole thing's over. He wasn't exactly the world's greatest influence, if you know what I mean. That 'roid business and that stupid Hummer of hers, it only started after she began writing him. He told her all kinds of stuff, such as liking tough-looking women who could handle themselves like men. Why do they let those creeps write naïve women like her and spread the crazy around like they do?"

Because even creeps have civil rights, I wanted to tell her. But I kept the conversation on track. "Did Terry ever say anything about getting even?"

Phoebe gave me a puzzled look. "Even with who? About what?"

I shrugged. "Oh, I dunno. The warden. Maybe even the executioner. Anybody who had a hand in killing Kenny."

A laugh of disbelief. "That sounds too crazy even for Terry."

"You're probably right." I was trying to figure out how I could reasonably ask for a tour of the backyard when Brunhilda, bless her vicious heart, trotted over to the door, sat down, and whined. "Looks like she wants out."

Phoebe stood up. "Yep. Wanna wait here?"

"Sure."

"Won't be but a minute."

"Take your time."

As soon as she and the dog were out the door, I reached inside my carryall and took out a baggie. Hiding it behind me, I went to the door and opened it.

"On second thought," I called, stepping outside, "maybe a little fresh air would be nice."

"It's awful hot."

"I like it." I didn't, actually. It must have been a hundred and ten by now, and my head hurt again.

But there was Brunhilda, hunched over in the corner, near the other dark mound. Regardless of breed, dogs are creatures of habit; they like to crap in the same spot. Once Brunhilda had done her business, she scratched some gravel over it, and began to caper around, snapping at flies and chasing her non-existent tail.

"She's so cute!" I exclaimed. "Why don't we have our tea here and watch her? I'll go in and get our glasses."

"You'll do no such thing," Phoebe said, all politeness. She tsk-tsked me and went back inside, declaring she'd get the glasses herself. The minute she closed the kitchen door behind her, I ran over to the fresh turd and, to the Rottweiler's amazement, scooped up a sample. By the time Phoebe returned with the tea, the turd was in my carryall and I was back in my seat.

For the next few minutes we discussed various workout routines and Terry Jardine's problems—they extended far beyond murderous boyfriends, although that was definitely the most spectacular—until I could leave without appearing rude. Feeling guilty about my dishonesty toward Phoebe, a pleasant enough woman, I climbed into my Jeep and headed straight for Arizona Pet Lab.

I had once used the lab's services to settle a homeowners association's squabble over whose mutt was responsible for depositing fecal matter all over the condominium community's lavishly landscaped green area. The guilty party turned out to be the shar-pei in 4710-D, and the owner was given a hefty fine. To ease the pain, the HOA gave the shar-pei's owner a month's supply of doggie-do bags. Arizona Pet Lab, although expensive, offered a much faster DNA turnaround than the overburdened county lab. I dropped off the baggie, then left to see how the work was coming along on my apartment. The sooner I got out from under Jimmy's eagle eye, the better.

After making sympathetic noises over my beat-up appearance, Cal Kinsley, the good-looking foreman from Scottsdale Restore, said he was pleased with his company's progress. As far as I was concerned, my apartment remained a disaster. The ceiling was finished, but the new drywall hadn't yet been installed so the walls, with their two-by-fours showing, looked skeletonized. The floor wasn't much better. Having decided that neither the carpet nor the pad could be saved, Tinsley's men had ripped up both, exposing an expanse of algae-green linoleum.

"We'll get rid of that, if you want," he said.

Envisioning another week added to the original estimate, I shook my head. "Carpet over it. Same color, same style."

He made a check on his clipboard. "I suggest new drapes."

"Can't the old ones be saved?"

"They got ripped at some point. We can stitch them back together, but due to the moisture they were subjected to and the subsequent stretching, there's no certainty they'll ever hang right again."

I sighed. "Replace them. Same color, same style."

"Wish all our clients were as amenable as you." He made another check on his clipboard. "Next item. That Navajo rug and Navajo-print pillows on your sofa? They'll be fine, but they're still being treated at our plant."

"How about my 'Welcome to the Philippines' pillow?" It was no work of art, but it had memories.

He gave me a curious look, as if wondering why I sounded so concerned about such an obviously cheap souvenir. "Same story there. It's at the plant."

"Good." Then I asked him the question I hated to ask. "My vinyl record albums. How are they?" Especially the album on which my long-dead father played back-up guitar for John Lee Hooker, I wanted to say. But since that would open a subject I was too tired to deal with, I didn't.

Unaware of the album's value to me, he answered, "Most will be okay, but a few, well, let's just say you'll have to replace them. Nice blues collection, though. And they say vinyl's coming back."

My heart hurt, so I returned to a safer subject. "My Navajo things. How long before I get them back?"

"Another week. But they're worth it, right? At least the Two Gray Hills rug is. Gorgeous."

"No kidding." I knew the weaver. Anna Begay, from Shiprock. Young, but she belonged to the new wave of Navajo traditionalists whose work was currently displayed at the Heard Museum.

Decisions made about the living room, we moved onto the bedroom, which looked even worse. No new drywall here yet, either, and the closet door had been ripped from its hinges, exposing a row of empty clothes hangers. The bed was stripped down to the frame.

"We couldn't save the mattress," Cal said.

As Gertrude Stein once said, a mattress is a mattress is a mattress. "Replace it."

He smiled. "Same color, same style, right?"

"Right."

"I like your style, Lena. No muss, no fuss."

I started to smile back, then remembered. "Oh. My Lone Ranger bedspread, is that okay or…"

"It's fine. Cute. You into fifties collectables?"

"Something like that."

The rest of the tour went quickly. Kitchen, fine. Bedroom, fine. New drywall up in both. The only casualties from the kitchen were the packets of ramen that had to be junked, no big deal because you can find ramen anywhere at any time. As for the bathroom, it needed a new shower curtain, toothbrush, bottle of Excedrin Extra-Strength gel tabs, a loofah, and some Yardley's lemon verbena soap. Oh, and shampoo, whatever was on sale. As the man said, I wasn't fussy, except when it came to bath soap.

"How long before I can move back in?" I asked.

Cal looked at his clipboard. "According to my calculations, the place will be good to go by, say, next week. Maybe even Monday or Tuesday. That's if we can get the carpet guys out by then, but I don't foresee a problem there. For obvious reasons, there's not a lot of redecorating going on in July. But just in case, are you willing to approve overtime? That's what weekend work costs."

Desperate to get back into my apartment, I nodded.

"Then sign on the dotted line."

When he passed me the clipboard, I saw that Scottsdale Restore charged double for overtime. Still worth it. I signed.

"That's it, then!" Big smile. "Say, I didn't see you at Fight Pro yesterday. Still recuperating from your dust-up with Terry?"

"You heard about that?"

He gave me an *Are-You-Serious* look.

I wished people would drop their obsession with my health. "Doc says I need to take it easy for a while." For another week, actually, but I refused to wait that long.

"Word's going around Terry's membership's been cancelled."

Gyms are like small towns; everyone knows everything. "A wise move."

"Absolutely. Say, how about I take you to dinner tonight? If you're up to it, that is."

I almost said yes, but for now I had too much on my plate. "Ask me again next week. After I've moved back in here." And out of Jimmy's trailer.

Downstairs, reconstruction continued. Out with the old and burned and water-damaged, in with the new. Like the Phoenix bird, Desert Investigations was rising from the ashes. After a brief conversation with the foreman, my après-beating fatigue caught up with me, and I headed back to Jimmy's trailer. I needed more Excedrin and a nap.

I slept until four and awoke feeling nauseated. When I staggered into the kitchen area of the trailer, Jimmy had a big frown on his face. "You need to see the doctor."

"It's just a headache. Nothing to worry about." I didn't mention my nausea.

"How many Excedrins did you just take?"

"Only four." I'd stopped counting at six.

"Are you seeing double?"

"No, Doctor, I'm not. Just one nosy Pima. Give it up, already. I'm fine, just fine."

"Don't lie. I heard you barfing in the bathroom."

"An auditory hallucination on your part."

"Hmm. While you were out roaming around this morning, did you stop anywhere for lunch?"

Finally. A question I didn't have to lie my way through. "Nope. Too busy."

"Then you must be hungry. How's some more Pima stew sound? It's easy on the stomach. Takes only seconds to heat up."

"Bring it on, Chef."

A few minutes later I was eating stew and warm Parmesan bread rolls, thinking that they would help settle my stomach if

I could just get enough down. I waved a roll at him. "Did you make these?"

"Trader Joe made them." He sat at the table, watching me with an intensity that made me nervous. Or maybe it was all the Excedrin I'd taken. The stuff was loaded with caffeine.

"Why are you looking at me like that?" I asked.

"Checking your reflexes." Without warning, he slapped the Parmesan roll out of my hand. It flew across the room and bounced off a cabinet.

I stared at him. "Why the hell did you do that?"

"To see how quickly you'd react. And you didn't react at all."

"Don't be ridiculous. I have the best reflexes of anyone I know, including you." He began to blur around the edges, and I was having trouble seeing where he left off and the cabinet began. How could that be possible?

As I fought for balance, he leaned over me. "One of your pupils is dilated, the other isn't. I'm calling Valerie."

"Your cousin the nurse?"

"I only have one cousin named Valerie, and yes, she's a nurse."

"Well, then, she works summers…" Did I just say 'summers' when I meant days? "Uh, days, and she sure as hell isn't going to leave work cactus, uh, leave work early just because you're playing the piano, uh, I mean overreacting." I blinked rapidly, trying to bring him into focus again. My tongue wouldn't behave, either.

"Today's Friday, her day off." Before I could stop him, he was on his cell phone, telling Valerie she'd better get over here right away, that he didn't like the way I was acting.

"Pay no attention to rattles, uh, to Jimmy, Valerie," I yelled, hoping she'd hear me. "I'm Chinese! I mean, I'm fine! Fine!"

When Jimmy ignored me and kept talking, I stood up and tried to snatch the phone away. He blurred some more, and because I couldn't see where the phone was in relation to his hand, I missed.

Then the floor hit me in the face.

Chapter Thirty-one

"He means it, Helen. We need to get out of here while we still can."

I was half-asleep in the back of our tent, but not so much that I didn't understand that my father and mother were having another argument. They whispered, but I could hear. Four-year-olds have good ears.

"It was just talk," she said. "Abraham's always quoting the Bible."

"Not like this. Listen, we'll be in Flagstaff in another couple of hours, and he'll have to stop for gas. That's our chance to get away. I still have some money left, enough for bus tickets back home and enough for food until we get there. Then all I need is to play a few gigs at that tonk down the road, and Nashville, here we come. Just like we originally planned."

"But I don't want to get away. These people are our friends. And she's happy here. It would break her heart if we left. She'd especially miss Abraham's son. She adores him."

No I don't, I thought. I just pretended to like Golden Boy so he won't know how much he scared me. "You should never let anyone know they scare you, because that would give them the advantage." Whatever 'advantage' meant. Who'd said that? Grandma? But she said that a long, long time ago, before Mom and Dad met the man with the big white bus. Abraham. I was scared of him, too. Even more scared of him than I was of Golden Boy.

"Helen, I'm telling you we have to get away before something bad happens."

"Oh, you silly. Nothing bad is going to happen. It's just that wild imagination of yours, which is what I get for taking up with you." *When she laughed, it sounded like Christmas bells, but it wasn't Christmas now. "You bluesmen, you always look on the dark side, but that's why you're so good, isn't it? All those songs about doom and gloom. Even John Lee said you were right up there with the best."*

Listen to Daddy, I wanted to scream. Wherever Flagstaff was, I wanted to run away there, get away from Abraham and his Golden Boy. I didn't want to do what they want me to do and I'd told my mother but she wouldn't believe me and it was coming closer every day and Daddy was right and we had to get out before…

"I see you're finally awake."

The room was so bright I had to squint to see a dark blob against the glaring white. "How are you feeling?" A woman. Her voice sounded familiar but I couldn't place her.

I closed my eyes against the glare. "Headache. Light doesn't help."

"You have a subdural hematoma. They had to drill a burr hole in your skull to relieve the pressure."

I opened my eyes again. "Hole in my head?"

The dark blob leaned closer, came into focus. Black hair, amber eyes, faint scent of turpentine. Madeline.

"Just a small one, Lena. Don't worry, your prognosis is good. Excellent, even, if you behave yourself. It's a good thing you were at Jimmy's. He scraped you off the floor and drove you straight to the ER, then called me."

"Don't remember."

"Well, you were unconscious at the time."

"Where is he?"

"In the cafeteria getting breakfast. He slept here last night. Night before, too, same as me. You had us scared for a while." She sat in one of two plastic chairs next to my bedside. The painting smock she wore looked crumpled.

"I've been here two days?"

"Three. It's Monday."

"I was supposed to be someplace, I think."

I tried to sit up, but the IVs attached to my arms made it too complicated, so I lay back down. At least my eyes worked better. What I had first experienced as a surrounding whiteness turned out to be pale peach walls lit by a high-wattage overhead light. A framed print hung on the wall next to the bathroom. Almost Disneyesque, it portrayed three deer standing in a yellow-tinted forest glade. Papa deer, Mama deer, Baby deer. They shimmered and glowed so much they looked drenched in butter. Thomas Kincade. There was no escape from him.

Madeline noticed me staring at it. "Piece of crap, huh?"

Thomas Kincade. Why did he remind me of someone? I thought hard. Dolphins, for some reason. And a mermaid. Then I remembered Ali's uncle walking past the art galleries on Main Street.

Ali.

"I need to see someone." Despite the IVs, I struggled to a sitting position.

Madeline pushed me back down.

"Lie still, Sweetie. You'll have to put up with this for a couple more days to make sure you don't develop an infection. Then you're going home with me. At least you'll be surrounded by better art."

I looked around the room, noticed the bathroom, the lack of a neighboring bed. "I can't afford a private room for five days."

"You didn't start off in one, but all the screaming kept waking your roommate up."

"I was screaming?"

"Something about a gold boy and a white bus. Anyway, don't worry about the cost. Turns out you've got great hospitalization insurance."

"That must have been Jimmy. He takes care of the business side of things."

"He's…Speak of the devil, here he comes." But she was smiling as Jimmy came through the door and took the seat next to her.

"Look who's awake," he said.

"I need to see Ali. And Juliana. I made an appointment."

"You're three days late. When you didn't show at Juliana's house Wednesday, she called and left a message on the office phone. I got back to her and told her what happened. Ali wants to see you, but I don't think that's a good idea right now. Oh, and here's some advice. Don't look in the mirror."

"Here's some advice for you, buddy. Don't tell me what not to do." There had to be a mirror in the bathroom, so I struggled up again. This time it was Jimmy who pushed me back down. "Vanity, thy name is Lena. If you really have to know, your face is the size and color of a pumpkin and just as scary. You've got an even bigger bald spot on the back of your head than before, not that it matters. You're supposed to be resting, not fussing about your looks."

He didn't understand. "I need to get back on my feet and take care of business."

"Oh, for God's sake," Madeline interjected. "Jimmy, explain to her what a subdural hematoma is. Maybe she'll listen to you."

"Lena doesn't listen to anyone," he growled, then proceeded to tell me that Monster Woman's blow to my head caused bleeding in my brain, blah, blah, blah, and the consequences could have been life-threatening, blah, blah, blah, especially since I'd ignored my first doctor's orders and continued running around town, blah, blah, blah, and all that movement resulted in complications, blah, blah, blah, and I was old enough to know better, and blah, blah, blah...

"Cut the lecture," I snapped. "It's making my head hurt."

"Blame it on me, why don't you?"

"Would you two stop bickering?" This, from Madeline. "You sound like some old married couple."

That shut us up.

With a smile of triumph, she continued. "Here's what we're going to do, Lena. The minute your doctors discharge you, you're coming home with me, and you'll stay in bed until I say you can get up. We don't need any more emergency trips back to the hospital, now, do we?"

Annoyed by her hospital-ese use of the royal "we," I pointed out the flaw in her plan. "No, *we* don't. But if something happens, *we* don't need to be way out there in the Boonies, do *we*? *We'll* be better off if *we* stay right here in Scottsdale where *we'll* be right down the street from a hospital."

"There's a perfectly good hospital right down the road from my studio. Florence General. Excellent ratings. Jimmy checked it out."

Jimmy added his own unwelcome opinion to the mix. "Furthermore, if you're out there in the Boonies, as you so delicately call the Florence area, you won't be so quick to hop in your Jeep and go back to work. And just to make sure, I'm keeping your Jeep at my place. You won't get the keys back until the doctor clears you to drive."

"That's car theft. Now just you listen to me, I'm going to..."

The nurse picked that moment to come in, carrying a hypodermic on a tray.

I didn't like the looks of it. "What's that?"

"It's our sleepy-bye shot," she said, and jabbed me.

Before I could protest, we went sleepy-bye.

Chapter Thirty-two

The clouds were pretty, the desert was pretty, but other than sitting around admiring all the prettiness, there was nothing to do at Madeline's. I had been cooped up in her two-story studio for almost a week, bored out of my mind. My Jeep was at Jimmy's, along with my cell phone and laptop, yet Madeline—overprotective to a fault—wouldn't let me cook, clean, or even read, declaring that given my fragile condition, reading might give me a headache. As for entertainment, forget it. Madeline didn't own a television, and as for music, she was into New Age Ambient, better known as "mood music." She played it over the studio's sound system until I threatened to one day hunt Yanni down and set fire to his piano. Phoning anyone was out, too, because Madeline had no landline and kept her cell phone in her handbag. The only thing left to do was stare out the window and watch the wind move dust around.

Once, in a seemingly lenient mood, she allowed me to sit in on one of the art classes she conducted in her downstairs studio, but as it turned out, she correctly guessed it would bore me so much I'd go back upstairs and stare out the window some more. Now that the pain from my sore head had diminished, I was restless but had no outlet for it.

Madeline's converted barn/home/studio sat on an unpopulated area off SR-79. Her nearest neighbors to the east consisted of several thousand white-faced cattle; to the west, thousands of acres of assorted cacti; to the north, the Superstition Mountains. The only hint of human habitation I could see from the upstairs window was the dome-shaped top of a water tower at the Arizona State Prison complex two miles south.

Not much action there, either.

Every now and then a jackrabbit would hop by, sometimes a coyote. Then there were the buzzards. I don't have anything against buzzards—they keep the desert clean—but they made for depressing viewing. They only swooped down when something was dead or about to be dead, which brought back memories of the times they'd dropped in on me. Once, when I was a runaway child; the other, when a murderer tried to add me to his list of victims.

I was safe now.

And bored out of my sore skull.

Knowing that painting always put Madeline in a good mood, I clumped down the stairs and threw myself on my imprisoner's mercy. "If I don't get some exercise I'm going to go nuts. You want that on your conscience?"

She stood at her easel, adding finishing touches to whatever-it-was, a brown blob sporting a purple halo. It looked like something Mark Rothko might have painted if he'd been half-blind and shooting heroin.

I loved it.

She gave me a paint-smeared smile. "Tell you what, Sweetie. You can take a walk today. A short one."

"Define 'short.'"

"Fifteen minutes tops. I'll time you." She shook her watch at me.

As I headed toward the door, she called out, "Make sure you don't get dirty! The doctor warned me infection's still a possibility!"

"I promise not to play in the mud." Not that there was any. Too dry.

I've always been happy living in Scottsdale, but there's something about being out in undeveloped desert that lifts my spirits.

Out here you don't smell car exhaust, you smell sage. There were no shopping malls, just cacti: tall saguaro, with their arms lifted to an unpolluted sky; teddy bear cholla nestling in family groups; fat barrel cacti, their wet pulp often serving as lifesavers for lost desert wanderers; the purple prickly pears, with their rose-to-lavender pads glimmering in sweet contrast to the surrounding miles of gold, gray, and pale green. At the tail-end of July, it was still hotter than hell, but because the ground beneath me was earth instead of asphalt or concrete, the temperature was at least ten degrees lower than in the city.

I inhaled the sweet fruits of the desert, and in the spirit of full disclosure, yes, I also got a faint hint of manure from the neighboring cattle. At least they grazed downwind.

I walked.

Madeline's property sat on a raised, triangular-shaped wedge of land bordered by two deep ravines that met in a tangle of boulders at the apex. The triangle's base was the wiggly two-lane blacktop that ran from U.S. 60 to Florence, a small desert city, then on toward Tucson. Exulting in my new freedom, I race-walked the property's perimeter again and again, once narrowly avoiding stepping on a rattler seeking shade beneath a mesquite. As I walked, I thought about the Camerons, especially about Ali. In a way, we were sisters, united by grief, kept company by the ghosts of murdered parents.

Was Ali back with her cold uncle, living in a hotel? Or was she still at Juliana's? If so, how had Juliana explained such an unusual arrangement, not only to Ali, but to her campaign manager? Kids have always been my weak spot, so I thought about Kyle, too, and his horrific life. Although I had only met the boy once, I'd been impressed by his courage and his devotion to Ali.

Maybe someday someone would love me as much as he loved her.

Then I caught myself. Fairy tale endings? I've never believed in them. In this modern world, the best we can hope for is an absence of pain.

"Time's up!" Madeline's voice silenced the sweet call of a cactus wren.

"Yeah, yeah," I muttered, turning back toward the big red barn. My own private prison.

Given my constant state of boredom, the sound of Madeline's students arriving downstairs a couple of hours later came as a relief. Her Sunday afternoon class proved her most advanced, several of them having slipped loose the surly bonds of photographic realism to explore the more demanding realm of post-modernism and whatever the hell else they called contemporary art these days. Boredom aside, there was another reason I was glad for their arrival.

I had a plan.

It's always easy to pick out the rebel in a group. This one's name was June-Mae Ronstadt, a grim-looking woman of about fifty. When Madeline instructed the class to mix their pigments with sand, June-Mae mixed them with bird droppings and weeds. If Madeline told them to stretch their canvases into rhomboids, June-Mae created a perfect disc. Oppositional temperament aside, she remained Madeline's favorite student because her work was flat-out brilliant, if distressing. Finding her inspiration in Florence's state prison complex, she turned out canvas after canvas filled with shadowy shapes hunched at the base of forbidding gray walls. But her most useful trait, at least to me, came from the fact that June-Mae was the only person in Madeline's class who smoked.

Five minutes before the class took its regular break, I asked Madeline if I could go outside again and get some fresh air, explaining that the turpentine fumes drifting upstairs were making me sick. Ever alert to my health needs, she agreed.

"Just don't wander off the property," she said.

"Oh, I won't."

Smiling sweetly, I headed straight for the big boulder where June-Mae regularly befouled her lungs, and waited.

A few minutes later the studio door opened and the students streamed out, breathing in the clear desert air. June-Mae split off from the others and headed for her usual spot. At first she looked disconcerted to see me, but her tobacco craving trumped her irritation.

"Nice day," I said, as she lit up.

Nothing. Just a big inhale, then a phlegmy exhale of poisonous fumes.

"That your '92 Nissan over there?" I asked, pointing to a decrepit sedan parked under the mesquite.

A grunt.

"Windshield's cracked."

"Tell me something I don't know."

"It could get you a ticket. A very expensive one."

Another grunt.

"Bet you could use some extra money. Maybe enough to fix that windshield."

"You're cute, but I don't swing that way."

I chuckled. "Neither do I, but I need a ride into Florence tomorrow, and I don't have a car."

"Use Madeline's panel van."

"See, there's the problem. She's delivering a couple of paintings to a Scottsdale gallery tomorrow, which will leave me high and dry at the very hour I need to be in Florence. Didn't I once hear you tell one of the other students you have Mondays off?"

She flicked her eyes toward the front of the studio, where Madeline stood chatting with the other students, then gave me a slit-eyed stare. Mimicking me, she said, "Didn't I once hear Madeline say you're recovering from a head injury?" In her own voice she added, "What kind of numbskull do you take me for?"

"A broke one. Tell you what, June-Mae. If you pick me up tomorrow at nine, that's when Madeline's leaving for Scottsdale, drive me over to the public library so I can take care of some business, and get me back here before she returns, I'll buy you a tank of gas as well as a new windshield. Oh, and I'll need to borrow your cell phone for the duration, which means I'll throw in another hundred to pay for the calls."

She flashed nicotine-stained teeth. "Deal."

The next morning she picked me up at nine-fifteen, five minutes after Madeline disappeared down the road with a load of paintings. When I hopped into June-Mae's Nissan sedan, I found the backseat occupied by three toddlers whose identical faces and identical pink clothes suggested they were triplets. They took one look at me and started to scream. The car's decibel level rose high enough to make your ears bleed, but its driver's expression was stoic.

"Who're they?" I asked.

"*They* are my granddaughters. They live with me. Along with my bat-shit crazy daughter-in-law. Don't ask why."

"Wouldn't dream of it." Oh, people and their traps. No wonder her paintings looked so depressing.

The triplets screamed all the way into town, where June-Mae shoved an old flip-top cell phone into my hand along with two estimates for windshield replacement, and dropped me off in front of the Florence Public Library. As soon as she drove away, I sat down on a bench near the entrance and placed my first call.

"How's Ali?" I asked Juliana.

She answered my question with a question. "How are you?"

"I'm perfectly fine. Tell me about Ali."

"She, too, is perfectly fine, and is staying with me for the interim. Right now, she's over at Kyle's house. Fiona said they're all going to the movies."

When I expressed surprise, she said, "Trying to keep those two separated would be more trouble than it's worth. You know teenagers."

I was starting to. "You said she's staying with you 'for the interim.' Define 'interim.'"

"Dr. Teague and I are waiting for an emergency hearing on the custody issue. It'll be just a formality, because he and I are in perfect agreement as to the girl's best interest. Meanwhile, Ali and I are using the time to get better acquainted." Before I could ask, she added, "At this point she knows only that I'm an old friend of her mother's, but that will eventually change. Speaking of Alexandra, the police haven't been exactly forthcoming about the case, so I applied a little pressure in certain quarters. I don't know yet if it worked, but we'll see. Now, as for you, I know you've been injured because I had a long chat with your partner." Her voice took on a new seriousness. "The charges against Ali may have been dropped, but the public's perception of her remains one of guilt, and that must be remedied. It's been a month since the Cameron murders and there's still no arrest."

Sometimes there never is. Sometimes a case just drags on and on until it's filed away in a back room. I didn't share that possibility with Juliana, just assured her that despite my injury I was still working the case and promised to inform her of any new developments.

"See that you do," she said, and hung up.

My second call was to Arizona Pet Lab, which for a hefty surcharge, had promised a faster than usual turnaround. The technician I talked to told me the DNA results on Monster Woman's Rottweiler had been completed, and what did I want done with them.

"Hang onto them until the police pick them up," I answered.

My third call was to Sylvie Perrins, who, wonder of wonders, was at her desk, probably filling out the reams of paperwork that are a cop's lot. After a too-long discussion of my physical health, I told her about my visit to Arizona Pet Lab.

She laughed. "You don't miss a trick, do you, Lena? Okay, Bob and I'll get over there as soon as we finish up here. By the way, you'll be interested to know that our own lab completed the tests from the murder scene, so we'll know right away if there's a match-up."

I was surprised. "That was fast."

"No shit, Sherlock. Apparently your big deal client became impatient and placed a call to a higher authority, namely the governor. Next thing we know—ta da!—we had the DNA results from the murder scene in our hot little hands. Bob was so thrilled he did the Dougie dance all over the office, talk about one butt-ugly sight. This brings me to the bad news. That impounded van, the one belonging to the Pebble Creek gardener? Turns out he was telling the truth. He didn't use it to kill the Camerons. The stench came from common fertilizer, not doggie do."

"How about those two surveillance cameras from the neighborhood? Did the real murder van show up on either of them?"

"Fat lotta good that was. Both cameras caught a white '83 Ford Econoline tooling down the street at the time the boy was headed to the Cameron house, but the plate was rigged out with one of those anti-radar film overlays, as well as some good 'ol Arizona dust. Our tech did what he could, but it was a no go. Got nada. We sent out a statewide BOLO on that model, though, and ran it through the Motor Vehicles base, but there's a couple thousand '83 Econolines still on the road, and with the manpower problem being what it is, well, you know. Say, did I tell you what Bob did the other day? He…"

I tried not to let disappointment leak into my voice. At least the DNA results from the murder house were in, and that was something. But we needed something to match them to.

Sylvie was still talking. "…and that was that. You should have seen Bob's face. Hey, what's this number you're calling me from? It's not your phone."

Rather than narc off June-Mae, I muttered a quick good-bye and rang off.

Maybe the DNA results at Arizona Pet Lab would match the DNA from the murder scene, maybe not. Terry Jardine, aka Monster Woman, was out-of-control enough to kill someone—she'd sure as hell tried to kill me—but where the Camerons were concerned, it didn't feel right. Too much planning there for an off-the-walls 'roid rage situation.

Calls completed, I got off the bench and went inside the library.

Florence may be small, but that doesn't mean it hasn't joined the twenty-first century. Same for its library, which offered a bank of new Internet-connected computers on the second floor. Once a helpful librarian showed me how to sign on, I was off and running.

I'm no Jimmy Sisiwan, but using my Desert Investigations password allowed me access to the Cameron case files. Although I'd been careful not to let anyone know, that blow to my head had fuzzed my memory to the point where it could no longer be trusted, so a refresher course on the facts seemed wise. I'm a quick study, and within minutes, had brought myself up-to-date on the investigation. Jimmy's own recently added notes weren't as helpful as hoped, but at least I found out how much we still didn't know. Sighing, I closed out the file and stared at the red and blue FLORENCE PUBLIC LIBRARY welcome screen until my head started hurting again and I had to look away. As I did, something nagged at me, something about those case notes…

Whatever it was, I couldn't track it. A glance at my watch revealed I'd been at the library a little more than an hour. From her studio, it would have taken Madeline around forty minutes to drive to Scottsdale, a few minutes to fill out some papers and chat with the gallery owner, then another forty for the drive back, let's say two hours total. Enough time to give my poor, under-exercised legs a good tune-up.

I shut down the computer, waved good-bye to the librarian, and went outside. After calling June-Mae at home and telling her where and when to meet me, I hitched into a race-walk and tooled along Florence's mesquite-shaded streets for a while, finally slowing down to study the authentic Western storefronts once used in the Sally Fields-James Garner film, *Murphy's Romance*. Like much of the town, they took me back to a simpler time, a time when you were on speaking terms with your neighbors and knew which ones to be wary of. Finally tiring, I ambled over to the bank and made a large withdrawal from Desert Investigations' account—windshield replacement is expensive these days—then headed for one of my favorite places: the Pinal County Historical Society & Museum, where I'd told June-Mae to pick me up.

The museum was an oddity in a town filled with oddities. Like everything else in Florence, the prison complex dominated its exhibits. Not unusual, when you realize that of the town's population of twenty-five thousand, only eight thousand were civilians; the other seventeen thousand were inmates. Besides the Indian and pioneer artifacts, which included furniture built from saguaro cactus spines, the inspiration for my own apartment's décor, one full room of the museum was dedicated to prison memorabilia. My favorites were the actual nooses used to hang condemned prisoners. Placed in the center of each noose was a small card giving the prisoner's name and his death date.

A few women's nooses numbered in the exhibit, too, including that of infamous Eva Dugan, a former cabaret singer who, after being found guilty of murdering a local rancher, was sentenced to death by hanging. In 1933 Eva became the last guest of honor at a state-sponsored necktie party. It didn't go well. Due to a miscalculation by the state executioner, when Eva dropped through the scaffold floor she was instantaneously decapitated. The resulting mess (several witnesses fainted when her head rolled toward them) spelled the end of official hangings in the great state of Arizona. Today we no longer pop off a condemned person's head. We just put them to sleep via the needle, in the same way we would a sick dog.

Until recently, Dr. Arthur Cameron had been Arizona's dog-killer-in-chief.

June-Mae was prompt. Her raggedy Nissan clattered to a stop in front of the museum at the appointed time. I saw no sign of the triplets.

"Where are your beautiful granddaughters?" I was trying to be polite, because from what I had been able to view under all that red-faced, snot-nosed screaming, they didn't even rate as cute.

"At home with my husband. Thank God his shift's over."

I hadn't thought about her being married, and a quick look at her left hand revealed how inattentive I'd been. "He work at MacDonald's, too?"

"No, Miss Nosy. He works at the prison complex. Most people in Florence do, except for the lucky few, such as myself."

Still trying to be polite, I asked, "He like it? Working at the prison, I mean."

"Don't make me laugh. Where's my money?"

I forked over the fat envelope the bank teller had given me. Before we pulled away from the curb, she counted it right down to the last penny.

I was staring out the upstairs window when Madeline returned home. A coyote was dragging something furry into the arroyo.

"How you doing up there?" Madeline called out.

"Just watching good old Mother Nature, red in tooth and claw," I called back, clomping down the stairs. "I'm hungry. You going to make lunch, or should I?"

My offer came too late. She was already in the kitchen, concocting something that involved rice, beans, and carrots. While I had to admit her vegetarian lifestyle was healthier than mine, I was jonesing for a Big Mac. Put it down to June-Mae's unhealthy influence.

"Uuumm, that looks good," I said.

She gave me a maternal smile. "I sure wish you wouldn't lie so much, Sweetie."

"Caught me."

"Vegetables are good for you."

"I know," I said, glumly. "Here, I'll help you chop."

Lunch was ready in an hour, and by then I was hungry enough to eat anything. To Madeline's satisfaction, I cleaned my plate.

"Looks like you got your appetite back, Sweetie."

I opened my mouth to answer that it was probably due to my morning's exercise, but caught myself in time. "I'm feeling better. So much better I think it's time for me to get out more, say into Florence, maybe pick up some library books." Something about the Cameron case file still niggled at the back of my mind. If I could just log on again, maybe I could figure it out. There was something…

"You're still too sick to read," Madeline answered, stopping my train of thought.

"No I'm not."

"Yes you are."

"But Madeline, I'm bored!"

That maternal smile again. "See? You've got your spirit back. It proves rest is doing you good. No, don't bother arguing. We're staying with the plan. The doctors said it would be a mistake to let you overdo it, that it would set you back."

"I wouldn't call a trip to the library 'overdoing it.'" True, that. My morning out and about made me feel almost like my old self. My brain was working better, too.

"With you it wouldn't stop at the library, Lena."

The woman knew me well. "Okay, if you won't drive me to the library, how about letting me take another walk? Just around the property, like yesterday."

"Now you're talking sense."

It was early afternoon and hot outside, but the heat didn't bother me. Thrilled to be on the move again, I race-walked the triangle several times, then sat down on the large boulder to rest.

And to try to figure out what was bothering me about the Cameron case file.

Chapter Thirty-three

"Lena! Get back in here!"

Madeline, hands on hips and looking fierce, stood at the door of her studio.

I rose, stunned. Why hadn't I thought of it before? Why hadn't Jimmy?

But I knew why. Sometimes you get so mired in small details that you forget about the Big Obvious. And in the Cameron case, the Big Obvious was the fact it had taken Jimmy days to discover Dr. Arthur Cameron was the official executioner of the state of Arizona. Even given the clue of Cameron's secret bank account and those mysterious eighteen thousand dollar deposits on certain days, finding the doctor's freelance job stretched Jimmy's hacking skills to the limit.

Unless I was wrong, none of my suspects knew the exact amount of money Dr. Cameron charged for his services. Certainly not the obese, doomed Felix Meyers, the white trash Hoyts, Kenny Dean Hopper's father, neither of the Youngs, nor anyone in the DuCharme family. As for Terry Jardine, who definitely had the makings of a murderer, her steroid-pickled brain wouldn't have been able to focus long enough for the kind of deep Internet crawl required. Sure, most of them, with the Hoyts as the lone exceptions, probably had the needed brainpower to slither through the dark side of the Net, but Jimmy knew the identities of Arizona's other web outlaws, and none of our suspects' names triggered an alarm.

Then how did the killer discover Dr. Cameron's big secret? *The Big Obvious was that he must have had a connection to the prison.*

I was trembling with excitement when someone grabbed my arm.

"Are you having a seizure?" Madeline asked, her voice filled with concern. "Should I take you to the hospital?"

"I'm…I'm fine," I forced myself to calm down. "I was just thinking, that's all. Come on, let's get out of this heat."

As we walked back to the studio, my mind raced.

The prison complex was a tightly guarded place, the Death House even more so. Access to the Death House was confined to the execution team, made up of guards, the prison medical staff, the clergy, and the warden. Of those, only the warden and the medical staff— nurses present to place the IV catheters into the condemned man's arms— could know the executioner's identity. The warden certainly wouldn't reveal anything, neither would the clergy. That left the medical staff and a small number of guards as the only possible sources of the leak.

Madeline's air-conditioned studio came as a welcome relief after the heat outside, and I gratefully accepted the tall glass of iced tea she poured for me after I'd settled myself into a rocking chair by the window.

"Sure you're feeling okay?" she asked.

"I'm feeling better than I have in weeks."

"It's all the rest."

"Must be. Say, aren't you going to paint today? I know you're probably beat after that drive into Scottsdale, but…" I needed more time to think, and chatting with Madeline, while pleasant, was getting in the way.

She glanced toward the big easel at the end of the great room. "Maybe in a few minutes. Right now I'm a bit distracted because while you were out there, I got a call from my accountant. Seems I'm being audited. Damned IRS."

"My condolences." Having once been audited myself, I didn't have to fake sympathy, but I did want her to return to her easel. When it came to painting, Madeline's "a few minutes" could be hours. "Painting will take your mind off it. Don't worry, I'll be fine right here, rocking in my chair, looking out the window at the pretty desert."

"Just as long as you're all right."

"Oh, I am, I am."

She frowned. "Lena, you almost sound like you're trying to get rid of me."

"Why would I do that?" I tried to look innocent.

After studying me through narrowed eyes for a moment, she headed toward her easel.

Now, where was I when Madeline had so lovingly interrupted me? Oh, yes. I was thinking about the prison and the possibility that someone working there must have leaked Dr. Cameron's identity to the killer.

Right.

By necessity, everyone working the Death House was hand-picked, the cream of the prison crop. Their very numbers, though, made me wonder. Bill Wycliff, the journalist covering Kenny Dean Hopper's execution, reported three medical techs in attendance, with the doctor himself hidden behind a partition. The journalist spotted eight guards, but I doubted they ever entered the alcove where the executioner stood ready. Still, at this point, the number of people who might, just might, have caught a glimpse of Dr. Cameron totaled twelve.

But what about the guards manning the gate?

A decade earlier, Arizona executions took place at one minute past midnight, but for the past few years they've taken place in the afternoon. So in his article, Wycliff reported that on a sweltering Arizona day, Butte Avenue, the street in front of the prison, rang with the chants of death penalty protestors. Trying hard to ignore the crowds were the members of Kenny Dean's family, who had to enter the complex through the main gate. That gate was heavily fortified and guarded, not only to keep prisoners in, but protestors out.

Wycliff described the security procedures in effect that afternoon, including the methods used to protect the identity of those involved. For instance, the executioner never used the Butte Avenue gate. To avoid the crowds, the doctor—in Arizona the executioner had to be a doctor—drove his car around to the back of the prison and into the industrial yard. Once parked inside the secure perimeter fencing, he walked through the less fortified, but still well-guarded pedestrian gate, where he was met and escorted to the Death House by a member of the execution team.

The question I now had was this: by the time Dr. Cameron pushed the plunger that sped a fatal dose of drugs into the condemned man's body, how many of the prison staff, in total, had seen his face? Twenty? Thirty? Because the doctor wore no standard-issue name tag, nothing connected his face to his name. His car, with its easily recognizable medical license plate, would seem his only identifier.

"Maybe you should take a nap," Madeline called, looking around the edge of her latest canvas.

I forced myself to smile. "I will later." Unless I was too excited to sleep. "Don't worry about me."

She muttered something I couldn't quite make out, and returned her attention to her canvas. Before she'd returned from Scottsdale, I'd stolen a look at it. Long ago, when I was her foster child, her work had been vibrant, colorful. This new work wasn't. Today she was putting the finishing touches to a gray-and-black coffin-shaped canvas. Like June-Mae, my new BFF, living so close to a prison had an effect on Madeline's work.

"Mind if I borrow some drawing materials?" I called.

"Knock yourself out."

Snagging one of Madeline's sketch pads and a Wolff's carbon pencil, I made a rough drawing of the prison yard as I remembered it from the time I'd visited an inmate during a recent Desert Investigations case. I'm no artist, but by the time I was through, it was plain Dr. Cameron would have passed through two separate guarded areas: the vehicle entrance to the industrial yard, then on foot through the pedestrian gate.

I knew that preparations for the execution began hours before the actual deed was done. The doctor would have arrived at the prison well before lunch, his silver Escalade standing out like a sore thumb from the inexpensive compacts, motorcycles, pickup trucks, and other vehicles in the lot. Only once his ID was checked and his license plate run, would he be waved through.

In my mind, I pictured him parking, the Escalade shining like an angel in the bright sun. I saw him exit his car, lock the door, then proceed alone across the wide expanse of the lot. Waiting for him was a second set of guards.

At that point, I realized, the second set of guards could also connect that solitary, walking man with his vehicle, a vehicle with an easily traceable M.D. license plate.

I stared at my drawing and thought for a while.

Finally, not bothering to check in with my conscience, I swiped Madeline's cell phone out of her handbag, and tiptoed upstairs to make a call.

"No," June-Mae said, after picking up. I heard the triplets bawling in the background. "My husband works in CB-2, nowhere near the industrial yard. Anyway, why do you need to know?"

Politicians have this kind of conversation down flat: if you don't want to answer a question, ignore it. So I countered her question with one of my own. "Does he know anyone who worked the industrial yard any time from the beginning of January to the first week in July?"

"That's when the Supreme Court ruled to allow executions again! Tell me why ours are any of your business."

"Just curious."

"Don't try to play me, Jones. I don't live in a prison town for nothing. Look, if you want to hire me to chauffeur you around again, have at it, but you're not going to get any names from me, so save your breath. Those men deserve their privacy. That aside, how about another ride into beautiful downtown Florence? I could use the money."

I know a hint when I hear one. Taking the bait, I said, "Five hundred for the list of names. I promise not to bother them." *Liar, liar, pants on fire.*

A long pause, then a smoker's cough. "Eight."

"Seven."

"Done. When do you need the list?"

"When's the soonest you can get it to me?"

"Later today, but you have to promise me to never tell anyone who gave it to you."

This time my promise was no lie. "I understand. Your husband needs his job."

"And I need mine, crap though it is."

After a brief discussion on method of payment—cash on the barrelhead, again—I added, "Uh, one other thing. I'm calling you from Madeline's phone, and you can't call me back on it. How will you get the list to me?"

"I'll just drop it by later this afternoon." Before I could protest, she said, "I'll tell her I left my Winsor Newton red sable No. 3 after class, and while we're hunting for it, I'll slip the list to you."

I'd been around artists long enough to know that a Winsor & Newton red sable was a top-of-the-line brush, more expensive than you would expect the driver of a broken-down Nissan to own, let alone carelessly leave behind after an art class. "Maybe you left it by the easel you were using. I'll take a look."

A phlegmy cough. "Don't bother. You're not the only liar around."

We rang off in mutual admiration, and I went downstairs and returned the cell phone to Madeline's handbag. Less than an hour later, June-Mae's old Nissan came chugging up the gravel road to the studio. Her timing was perfect. Madeline was in the middle of applying a glaze, so I told her I'd see what June-May wanted.

"When you gonna pay me?" she whispered when I answered the door.

I whispered back, "Next time I make it into Florence. Scout's honor."

Without further ado, she slipped a piece of paper into my hand.

I saw seven names, one with a star beside it. I pointed to that name, and said in a whisper, "Why the star?"

She put a finger to her lips. "When I leave, walk me to the car and I'll tell you." Then, she shouted, "Hey, Madeline, I think I left my Winsor Newton No. 3 here yesterday!"

Madeline craned her neck around the canvas painting. There was a patch of Payne's gray on her cheek; it looked like a bruise. "Don't worry. If it's here, we'll find it." She went back to her glaze.

After a brief search by June-Mae and myself resulted in no Winsor Newton—gee, what a surprise—June-Mae suddenly remembered that, silly her, she might have dropped the brush into the trunk of her Nissan. "And in this heat, I'll bet it's ruined!" she wailed. Not an Academy Award-winning performance, but good enough. Madeline murmured a few words of condolence and returned her attention to her canvas.

I told Madeline I'd walk June-Mae out and help look through the car trunk.

As soon as the Nissan's trunk went up, we both leaned forward and pretended to search.

"Okay, tell me about the name with the star."

"First you're going to have to explain why you needed this list," she said, her voice echoing around the surprisingly neat trunk. All traces of deceit were gone from her face, replaced by a combination of anger and fear. "I know you're a private investigator, but for the life of me, I don't understand why you're so interested in the prison staff. Do you think something's about to happen, like a riot, or an escape? Because if you know anything that might jeopardize any of those people, you better tell me right now. My husband and most of our friends work there. If their lives are in danger, I need to know."

Where had all this concern been when I'd first asked her for the guards' names? Something must have happened within the last two hours.

As it turned out, I was wrong. The "something" had happened the day before the Cameron killings. The only reason June-Mae was alarmed now was because a dead man's name, the name with the star, was on the list. It being put-up-or-shut-up-time, I filled her in on the Cameron case. Once she recovered from her shock—she'd read about the murders in the newspaper—she pointed to the name with the star.

"Sam Provencio," she said. "He was killed by a hit-and-run driver the day before that family was murdered."

Provencio had been killed on July 7, the same day Kenny Dean Hopper had been executed.

But I said nothing, while she went on to tell me that Provencio, who worked the outer industrial yard gate at the prison, left home to go jogging on the morning of July 7, before the heat became too intense. Three hours later, when he hadn't returned, his concerned wife put the kids in the car and went out looking for him along his usual route. She found his crumpled body lying by the side of a gravel road several miles south of Florence. A subsequent investigation showed that Provencio had not only been knocked down by a vehicle traveling at a high rate of speed, but that the vehicle had backed up and run over him two more times. So far, the search for the driver had been unsuccessful.

It was too much of a coincidence to be a coincidence. "I take it there were no witnesses."

June-Mae shook her head. "Just about the only people who use that road are joggers and a couple of ranchers, because after a couple of miles it dead-ends at a feeder lot. Besides, he was always out there well before sunup."

I thought about that for a moment. "What shift did he work?"

"Day shift."

Which meant that Provencio would have normally been at the industrial yard gate on execution days. "He jogged before went to work?"

She gave me a you've-got-to-be-kidding look. "With these temperatures, when else could he jog? Besides, he was training for the Iron Man."

The Iron Man was a rugged triathlon consisting of a two-mile swim, a one hundred and twelve-mile bicycle race, followed by a twenty six point two marathon. All in one day. Only the most fit and most obsessed athletes could survive the brutal challenge. I knew one such man. He trained for hours before work. After work, he trained some more. But my friend was a young guy, not quite thirty, and most prison guards I'd encountered were middle-aged or older.

"How old was Provencio?"

"Thirty-six," she answered. "Two kids. Pregnant wife. She's due next month. I went to the baby shower."

Jesus. "I need to talk to her." Unless I was wrong, the vehicle that had struck down Provencio would be a white '83 Ford Econoline van.

"Okay, but if you do, I want to…"

"What's going on out here?" Madeline, standing just outside the door to the house. Apparently she hadn't been too engrossed in her work not to notice that I'd been out of the house a suspiciously long time. Either that or she'd finished the troublesome glaze. She walked toward us, frowning. "Lena should come back inside. She needs her rest."

June-Mae saved the day. "Oh, sorry. We were just talking art. She's thinking about trying her hand at some oils."

Madeline's frown disappeared, mainly because she had been trying to get me to an easel for years. "Well, that's a great idea, but I suggest she work with acrylic first. It's faster, so she'll learn more quickly."

"You're probably right," June-Mae slammed down the car trunk. "Leave it to me to give bad painting advice. Well, see you folks next Sunday!"

"Hope you find your brush," I said loudly, for Madeline's benefit.

"Me, too." With a wave, June-Mae drove off.

An hour later I had learned more about acrylics vis-à-vis oils than I ever want to know, and finally begged off Madeline's Art 101 lecture, claiming exhaustion. Leaving her to her canvas, I climbed the stairs to the loft, where I lay down on the futon and despite my excitement, promptly fell asleep.

Three hours later I awoke to the smell of dinner.

When I made it downstairs, I found the table already set, the food piled onto the plates. Mine was a mini-Mt. Everest, with a three-decker mushroom, cheddar, avocado, and sprouts open-face sandwich towering over a field of sweet potato fries. Enough to feed a linebacker.

Intimidated, I said, "You expect me to eat all that?"

Madeline sat down across from me. Her sandwich was half the size of mine. "You need to keep your strength up."

For what, I wanted to ask. *More sitting around?* But of course I didn't. The food was delicious, if healthful, and she had even baked her own bread, a multi-grainer shot through with rosemary and nuts.

"Delicious," I said.

"If you want the recipe…"

Cooking-averse, I hastily changed the subject. "How long do you think this heat spell will last? I hear it got up to one-eighteen yesterday in Scottsdale."

She cocked her head, a quizzical look on her face. "Where'd you hear that?"

Oops. When I had signed onto the library's computer, one of the sites I visited listed the day's temperatures across Arizona. I scrambled to cover myself. "June-Mae mentioned it when we were looking for her brush."

"Mmm. Speaking of Scottsdale, I'm going to have to leave you alone for a while tomorrow. While you were napping, my accountant called again and said we needed a long sit-down. Apparently there's a problem with some of my deductions because the IRS prefers not to believe I spend so much money on paint, brushes, and canvas. So there goes my morning. Again." She sighed. "At least I've finished that glaze. By the way, is there anything you'd like me to pick up for you while I'm in town?"

Plenty of things, I thought. Several New York strip steaks. A bucket of Colonel Sanders original recipe. Slim Jims, extra spicy. Two cases of Tab, if you can find it, Diet Coke if you can't. But I shook my head. "Can't think of anything. About how long will you be gone?"

"Several hours, I'm afraid. You know how accountants are. You'll be okay, won't you? I was really nervous about leaving you alone yesterday, and now, to do it again a second day…" She trailed off, guilt written all over her face.

For once, her concern about my health worked for me. "I'll be fine."

She gave me a relieved smile.

As soon as she began showering off the day's accumulation of turps and linseed oil, I snuck her iPhone out of her purse and called June-Mae. By the time Madeline had emerged from the shower singing the final chorus of "Age of Aquarius," I had set up an appointment to meet with Sam Provencio's widow at ten the next morning.

Maybe she knew something, maybe she didn't. Whatever the case, I was sure as hell going to find out.

Chapter Thirty-four

Bella Provencio lived in a small tract home on the south end of Florence, where the town ended and the desert took over. A riot of children's toys littered the front yard, but the house looked in prime condition. The stucco was the same color as the desert stretching behind it, the trim and door painted a bright turquoise. Wind chimes and dream catchers hung from the beams of a shallow porch, adding a whimsical touch to a home that otherwise stood out little from its neighbors.

Two vehicles stood parked in the driveway, a tan Honda Civic, and a silver Dodge Ram pickup. Neither was new, but unlike June-Mae's heap, both appeared in perfect condition.

"Remember, Bella's husband's been dead only a month," June-Mae said, as we climbed the steps. "I want to find out who killed Sam as much as you do, but we're talking my best friend here, and don't you dare say or do anything that will cause her any more grief."

June-Mae needn't have worried. One of a cop's saddest duties is delivering the news of a loved one's death. After doing that a few dozen times, we get good at it. Or as good as you can get when telling someone something that will half-kill them. My face was already set in an expression of condolence, so imagine my surprise when a hugely pregnant, brightly smiling woman answered the door and chirped, "Oh, how nice of you to stop by! And you must be Lena!"

A closer look at Bella's bloodshot eyes revealed how she really felt, and once we entered the house, I saw the reason for her bubbly act. Two little girls, one a toddler, the other just short of kindergarten age, were playing some sort of Dora the Explorer game. Neither looked unduly distressed, which I took as a testament to their mother's grit.

The living room's décor reminded me of that I'd seen in the homes of so many young families. Brown carpet designed not to show dirt. Colonial-style sofa and matching chair covered in a red, green, and brown floral print. A comfy-looking recliner in a blue that just managed not to clash with the rest of the furniture, probably Sam's favorite de-stressing spot. It looked terribly empty. The only thing unusual about the room—other than three obese cats snoozing on a large pet bed in the corner—was the collection of blue ribbons hanging above the sofa.

A scarred credenza stood against one wall, and on top, Bella had created a memorial to her deceased husband. Sam's photograph, taken in his uniform, was surrounded by candles, U.S. Army medals, condolence cards, and a large memory book. As I studied Sam's photograph, he looked vaguely familiar, but maybe that was because of the Kirk Douglas dimple in his chin. His gentle smile made him appear kind, a man drawn to prison work out of financial necessity, not because he sought power over others.

"Say, I made us some cookies! And some coffee!" Bella chirped. "I hope you like chocolate chip!"

"I love chocolate chip," June-Mae echoed immediately.

"Great! Have a seat on the sofa! I'll be right back!" Still bubbly, still smiling, Bella, accompanied by June-Mae, moved past the children and toward the kitchen, the entrance to which had been blocked off by one of those expanding gates used by protective parents.

But when Bella opened the gate, the true reason for the gate rushed out: a huge, tan boxer, its coat gleaming as if brushed within an inch of its life. The dog headed straight for the children, sniffed them quickly as if to reassure himself they were all right, then with hackles raised, advanced on me. Unless I was mistaken, he wanted to eat my leg.

"Jingo! No!" Bella shouted, hurrying toward us. She grabbed the boxer's collar and dragged him back to the kitchen. "Sorry about that," she said, shutting the gate again. "He's very protective of the children. He knows June-Mae, but you're a stranger, so…" She shrugged, her tone no longer chipper. "I should really have been more careful, but I'm a little distracted these days."

"No problem." Anticipating the attack, I'd tucked my legs under my butt, and now I lowered them to the floor again. "I like dogs. And that one's especially beautiful." If you were into big teeth and drooly dewlaps.

"Oh, he is that!" Back to the chirps.

I didn't know which was the worst for her, round-the-clock sobbing or forced cheerfulness. The strain of keeping up a good front probably took its toll at night, when the children were asleep, but at least her babies were spared her grief. In the long run, that was the only thing that mattered.

Bella and June-Mae returned shortly with a platter of cookies and some coffee, along with containers of cream and sugar. Jingo tried to escape through the gate and run back into the living room, but this time June-Mae was ready for him and pushed him aside. He let his feelings be known by staring at me through the gate and venting a series of snaps and snarls that would intimidate a grizzly. After settling herself on an overstuffed chair, Bella shushed him. It worked for a couple of seconds, then he started up again.

The cookie was heavenly. She had made it from scratch, anything to keep the mind off that new grave on the outskirts of town.

"Lovely," I said, over the sound of Jingo's snarls. "I must have the recipe." I would give it to Madeline.

As I had hoped, she flushed in pleasure. Anything to give her one bright moment before I started my questioning.

"It was my great-grandmother's," she said, "passed down to me. I'll give it to Christy and Rose when they get married. But, sure, I'll write it out for you."

"I appreciate it." Now was the time. Gesturing toward the children, I said, "Um, perhaps they could play in another room for a few minutes?"

"Of course." She rose, and with a few murmured words, swept the children and Dora the Explorer out of the living room.

June-Mae whispered, "She's taking this harder than it looks. If you upset her any more than is necessary, you'll be walking back to Madeline's."

I was sure she meant it.

Once Bella returned and settled herself, I started slowly, asking her about the show ribbons above the sofa.

"Those are Jingo's," she said. "He's doing really well on the AKC circuit. But there probably won't be anymore shows, at least not for us. They were Sam's thing, I'm not that into it. I just like to have a dog around to pet. And for protection. He scared you, didn't he?" She smiled.

"He sure did. Speaking of Sam, he must have been a really busy guy. His work at the prison, the dog shows, and June-Mae told me he was quite the runner, too. It's amazing he could fit all that into his schedule."

"Oh, Sam had energy to burn. And he dearly loved to run. I don't think there was a marathon here in the state that he hadn't completed, plus a few out of state, San Diego, San Francisco, even Boston."

"You must have been proud of him."

Her face changed slightly. "It wasn't always easy. He'd get hurt from time to time, and that bothered me. At least we have good insurance through the state."

On an off-chance, I said, "You say he ran every marathon here in Arizona. Would that include the Phoenix Marathon?"

She nodded. "He ran the Phoenix four times, but only finished three. He got hurt there a couple of years ago when another runner tripped him up during a turn. It was an accident, of course, but he wound up in the emergency room with a torn tendon. Good thing I was there to bring him home. It was his right foot, so he couldn't even drive."

When she said "emergency room," I tensed. I controlled my voice carefully, when I asked, "Which hospital was that?"

She shrugged. "Can't remember."

I reeled off some names. "Phoenix Baptist, St. Joseph's, Phoenix General, St. Luke's, Good Samaritan…"

"Good Sam! That's it! Near downtown. On McDowell, I think. Yeah. McDowell."

I didn't think there was a hope in hell of her answering my next question, but I asked it anyway. "You went with him to the emergency room, right? Do you remember his doctor's name?"

"Sorry, I just…He was good, I remember that. Not much of a bedside manner, kind of cold, but really efficient. Maybe I can't remember his name, but after…but a few days after Sam's funeral I was throwing out all the newspapers that'd accumulated during…well, you know, when I wasn't paying attention to much else other than missing Sam…and as I was stacking them I saw an article about those awful murders in Scottsdale, and wondered if by any chance it could be the same doctor who'd treated Sam, and when I saw the picture I realized yes, it was. Sam's ER doc was the very same doctor who got killed along with his family. Oh, it was just the most terrible thing, and if I remember right, everyone thought the doctor's daughter and her boyfriend did it…Wait a minute, wait a minute. Maybe I do remember his name. Dr. Cummings? No, but it was Cam something. Cam, Cam, Cam…Cameron, that's it! Dr. Cameron. He and his family were murdered the day after Sam was killed. Isn't that a horrible coincidence?"

Horrible, yes. Coincidence, no.

We were getting close to it now, so I asked her if Sam ever talked about his work at the prison.

She shook her head. "He never brought his work home with him. None of the guards do. Too depressing."

"Smart, that. And considerate. How about some of the people he encountered? Especially the prisoners."

"Like I said, Sam was close-mouthed about that sort of thing, but lately he didn't really have that much to do with the prisoners, mostly just construction crews coming in and out of the gate. People like that. Regulars."

Except for one lone man on execution days, a man whose face he would have recognized.

She continued, "Anyway, I was glad he never talked about it, because he said the stories he'd heard from the other guards would upset me, especially in the condition I'm in now. Sam was very protective that way."

"I'm sure he made the right choice."

After asking her a few more softball questions, all answered in the negative, I finally arrived at the hard part. "I'm aware that Sam worked the day shift on the industrial yard, so I'm wondering if on, ah, execution days, when sometimes..." I had to be careful not to put any ideas in her head. "Where sometimes, ah, a *special* person needed to be admitted." Oh, the hell with it. "I'm talking about the executioner. Did Sam ever mention recognizing him?"

"Never!" She seemed to change her mind in mid head-shake. "Wait. Wait. There was this one time..." Then she finished shaking her head. "See, Sam was new on the gate. Normally he worked CB4, but back in January they transferred him. I knew he didn't like working there, not only because he was just standing around in that shack for hours at a time, but because he doesn't, uh, *didn't* believe in capital punishment, and he really, really didn't like working those days when they, uh, had to, um, when it happened. But he never complained. Sam wasn't a complainer, he just did his job. The only thing he ever said about those occasions was that at least it happened by IV, not the noose or the chair, that compared to them, the IV was merciful, just like putting a sick animal to sleep. But there was this one day he came home pretty upset, and I think it was in March or April or May, back before it got really hot. He wouldn't talk about it, though, so I can't help you."

Not necessarily. "Can you remember which execution this might have been? The prisoner's name?"

"I'm like Sam on that. I don't want to know so I make sure I don't know. But I remember I was pregnant and having trouble sleeping. I'm not sure. It was fairly cool during the day and still chilly at night, that's all I can tell you. My memory isn't that great. Especially now. A lot of stuff that happened this year is all mushed together in my mind because of…" Her lower lip began to tremble.

To my relief, June-Mae took over. "You know what, Bella? I'll bet Lena would love to see your memory book. There are some lovely photographs of Sam in it." Turning to me, she said, "Bella is quite the amateur photographer, and I'm not the only one who thinks so. Last year she won first prize in the formal portrait category at the Pinal County Fair, and that's for someone who never took a photography class in her life. When Madeline saw it, she said she'd help Bella put together a show of her work."

Getting of the subject of the prison for a while was a good idea, so I said I'd love to see the memory book. Bella appeared so eager to show me that I realized going through the book brought her comfort.

The memory book was more than pictures; it was the story of a marriage. I saw the first note Sam had passed to Bella when they were in the second grade. He'd misspelled the word "love" but his drawing of two hearts pierced with one arrow was moving. On another page, I saw a photograph of them dancing together at their senior prom; it had been taken by Sam's mother, one of the prom chaperones. Pressed between two pages were dried flowers from a bouquet he'd once given her. Bella's photographs started halfway through. A delighted Sam holding a baby. A delighted Sam holding a different baby. A sweating Sam running through several marathons. A half-naked Sam getting out of bed, his dark hair a wild mess. A grinning Sam looking at the puppy that had grown into the blood-thirsty Jingo. In each case, Bella used available light to evoke mood, giving the photographs a subtlety I found surprising in an untrained photographer. No wonder Madeline had been impressed with her work.

"You really *are* good," I said, meaning it. "Let Madeline help you get a show. It'll take your mind off…" I stopped before I said "your grief." Nothing would do that.

Bella blushed, as if such talent was nothing, but June-Mae was determined to sing her friend's praises. "She once sent a picture to the *Arizona Republic* and they printed it. They even sent her a check, and the editor called and said someone had even requested a copy. Sam looked so handsome in his new suit, didn't he, Bella? C'mon, show Lena. I forget what page that one's on."

Bella took the heavy book and flipped through several pages. "Here," she said, handing it back. "I taped the article about the dog show across from it, but in the caption under the photo you can see Sam's name. Sam Provencio, big as life! And doesn't he look handsome?"

Smiling, I looked at the photograph, then the article. Read the caption.

And understood.

Chapter Thirty-five

Several minutes later, I was driving Sam Provencio's truck toward south Scottsdale. It was a stick shift, but since my Jeep was, too, I had no problem. When I had explained what I wanted to do, Bella had insisted I take it, saying that using her husband's truck to catch his killer was poetic justice. The money-hungry June-Mae had even turned her phone over to me, for free this time.

Chances were nil that I would make it back to the studio before Madeline returned home, but under the circumstances, listening to one of her lectures was a small price to pay for identifying a killer.

Sam had kept his truck in tip-top shape, and it quickly ate up the miles. These days, once you have a name, you can usually Google a person's address, and today was no exception. Less than an hour after leaving Florence, I was parked under the shade of a mesquite a block down the street from 6883 Avonlea. An earlier phone call had already given me the information that the owner was at work, but I still needed to be quick. Already the temperature was much higher here than in Florence, and as a result, the street was deserted. Not even dog walkers were out.

Just what I'd bargained on.

The size and appearance of the killer's property didn't surprise me. Situated on a corner lot, it was three times larger than its neighbors, a holdover from before the days of elbow-to-elbow zoning. The front yard's tall border of pink oleanders was groomed within an inch of its life. So, too, was the desert landscaping visible through a break in the oleanders; not a leaf or twig appeared out of place. To make certain the earth-toned gravel didn't go where it wasn't supposed to go, a series of rocks the size of soccer balls lined the drive leading around the house toward the detached garage in back. The house, a long, one-story ranch, mirrored the owner's compulsive sense of order. Not a flake of stucco chipped away, not a roof tile missing. The windows sparkled as if they'd been washed just that morning.

In an odd coincidence, I saw that the house's color palate was the same as Bella's—beige stucco highlighted by immaculate turquoise wooden trim. This house, however, probably cost five times as much as the Provencios'. South Scottsdale might not be as toney as the northern end, but it's still Scottsdale.

In my earlier drive-by, I had noticed an alleyway running the length of the block, so I grabbed the items I brought with me, exited the truck, and set off on foot. Even from the alley it was easy to find the right house; all I did was follow the sound of barking dogs. Once I reached the back of 6883 Avonlea, I checked out the dumpster, hoping it would yield a fresh crop of dog feces. Unfortunately, it looked like garbage pick-up had already happened that morning because the dumpster was empty. To get what I needed, I would have to go over the property's masonry back wall.

As a general rule, boxers are a friendly breed, but as evidenced by Bella's Jingo, they can be territorial. When the three show dogs spotted me scaling the wall, they went nuts. The din they raised could have woken the dead, yet no angry neighbor opened his window to scream out the standard curses. They were either used to the noise or they were at work.

Like the rest of the killer's property, the kennel area was immaculate, unless you counted a small pile of dog feces in the corner nearest the garage. At the southern end of the chain-linked dog run sat three doghouses painted the same color combination as the human house. They were even roofed in the same shingles. Each doghouse had a boxer's name painted in Old English letters above the doorway. Tiberius Maximus of Avonlea, Octavius Maximus of Avonlea—and the prize-winning boxer Bella had captured in her photograph—Augustus Maximus of Avonlea.

Altogether, the kennel area measured approximately twenty by fifty feet, plenty of room for the dogs to get exercise when their owner was gone. An automatic waterer dribbled fresh water into a sparkling clean trough. To further insure the dogs' comfort, half the kennel was covered by a giant tarpaulin, casting all three doghouses and most of the run into shade. The killer was kind to his animals.

I noticed one more thing. The gate to the run was only latched, not locked. Good. No more climbing.

"Such good doggies," I murmured, as I approached the kennel where the boxers awaited me with slavering mouths. "So good. So pretty." Standing well away from sharp canine teeth, I reached into the grocery sack and pulled out the five-pound tube of extra-lean ground beef Bella had given me. "Are the good, pretty doggies hungry?"

Upon smelling the meat, the din immediately subsided. Ears perked up. Stumpy tails wagged. Instead of trying to climb over the chain-link fence to rip out my throat, they sat expectantly, smiling as only happy dogs can smile.

"Oh, such good, hungry doggies!"

I continued cooing as I separated the ground beef into six equal portions, then stepped up to the fence. Aiming carefully, I tossed half the beef into the run's far corner, away from the neat pile of feces. The second the boxers bounded after their treats, I unlatched the gate and hurried in. I had only seconds, so I worked quickly, scooping up three different turds—each from a different dog, I hoped—into three of the baggies I'd brought. I hadn't finished tying off the baggies before the dogs bounded back.

"Here's more goodies for the good, good doggies." I tossed the rest of the meat.

Off they bounded again. While they were busy gobbling up the rest of the beef, I slipped through the gate and latched it behind me with a sigh of relief. No nosy neighbors had shown up to ask me what the hell I was doing, and my throat remained unripped. I dropped the baggies into the grocery bag, and headed for the garage.

Like most detached garages, the structure had a front door, but this time my luck didn't hold. The door was locked. When I tried the window, I found that locked, too.

I didn't have my lock picks with me—along with most of my equipment, they'd been victims of the fire at Desert Investigations—but so far the day had been a lucky one, and maybe my luck would hold. Taking a credit card out of my wallet, I slipped it between the doorknob and the jamb, and the lock popped right open. Note to self: always use deadbolts.

I opened the door to a strong smell of bleach. After the blinding light outdoors, the interior of the garage was dark, but rather than flip on the light, I waited until my eyes adjusted. When I could see again, I found the garage further testament to the owner's obsessive cleanliness. The concrete floor was swept, a work table's surface was spotless, and a large collection of tools hung in orderly rows on a wall-long wooden pegboard. You could have performed open heart surgery in that garage.

A late model Chevrolet Explorer conversion van, probably used to chauffeur the boxers to dog shows, gleamed under the light filtering through the window, but the item that most interested me sat parked next to it, covered by a tarpaulin.

Ignoring the garage's furnace-like heat, I crossed the cement floor over to the dark shape and stood there for a second, strangely hesitant to raise the tarp's flap. What if I was wrong? What if the dog show connection had been a figment of my ever-hopeful, still damaged brain? What if Sam Provencio's death had nothing to do with the Cameron murders?

Like hell it didn't.

I lifted the corner of the tarp...

And found a mostly white 1983 Ford Econoline van with a crumpled front fender.

The van no longer smelled like dog feces because Carl DuChar-me, president of DuCharme Chocolatiers, had thoroughly washed and bleached it.

I had no time to celebrate before I heard the sound of tires on gravel, approaching the garage. The boxers raised their voices in yaps of welcome. DuCharme—despite his secretary's assurance when I'd called his office earlier—had returned home.

And here I was, trapped in his garage.

Maybe he'd just come home to check on the dogs. I stood stock-still, hesitant to move, in case I made a noise.

A car door slammed.

Then another.

Voices. A man's and a woman's.

"Well, if you have a better idea, why don't you share it?" Carl DuCharme sounded cross.

"Shush!" the woman hissed. "The neighbors."

"They're all at work," Carl said.

The woman's voice sounded familiar, but...

"It's your funeral, then, but as usual, you never think anything through. If you'd listened to me, that ridiculous vehicle of yours would be long gone. I still feel soiled after my ride in it." Lorraine DuCharme, his mother. Also the mother of Blaine DuCharme III, executed three months earlier for killing two police officers and a civilian in a botched bank robbery.

"You're lucky I hung onto it, because it certainly came in handy."

"You never could let anything go, could you?"

"It was Dad's first delivery van, or don't you care? I kept it just the way it was when he...he died."

"The Daddy Museum," his mother sneered. "You're as fool-ish as he was."

"I wish you wouldn't talk about Dad that way."

"I'll talk about him any way I want. If it hadn't been for my direction, we'd still be selling chocolate out of a cheap storefront."

Footsteps on gravel, coming closer. They were headed for the garage, not the house.

I tiptoed back to the Chevy and looked inside, hoping to see the automatic garage-door opener so I could flee out the back. None on the seat. Maybe in the console? The glove compartment? But there was no time to hunt around for it.

Silently cursing Jimmy for taking possession of my .38, I looked around for something to use as a weapon. There. On the peg board, second row from the top. A monkey wrench longer than my forearm. Making as little noise as possible, I hurried to the board and grabbed the wrench. It was so heavy I almost dropped it, but its very heft made me feel more secure. Ever aware of the way sound carries on concrete, I then made my way over to the Chevy conversion van, praying it wasn't locked.

Once again, I lucked out. Not only wasn't the Chevy locked, but due to its owner's compulsive nature, its back door opened with nary a squeak. Clutching the wrench, I crawled into the cargo area, which had been refitted to transport the dogs back and forth. I moved aside two large dog carriers, then hunched down behind them on a pile of leashes. If the worst happened and I was discovered, at least I had a weapon. Of a sort.

Then I waited.

Keys jangling. A click. The door to the garage opened.

"If I've told you once, I've told you a thousand times," said Lorraine DuCharme, the brains behind the family business, "take the nasty thing to one of those chop shops we're always hearing about."

"Oh, really?" Carl snarled. "You have an address for me? A phone number?" When she didn't answer, he said, "Just what I thought. You like telling people what to do, but can't give any decent advice on how to do it."

The sound of a slap. "Don't talk to your mother that way!"

Hard breathing from Carl.

"Why do I have to solve everything for you, Carl? Drive the thing out to the desert and set fire to it."

When her son answered, his voice trembled with rage. "The van's registered to me. You think they can't read a vehicle identification number, even after a fire?"

"Then get rid of the VIN before you set fire to it."

More heavy breathing. "I already tried that. Took a hammer and chisel and chipped the VIN off the back of the engine block, as well as I could, anyway, then took a blowtorch to the imprint on the doorjamb. But sometimes VINs're hidden in places you can't get to, like on the frame itself. What then? If they ever ID'ed the thing, I'm sunk. Shit, since this whole revenge crap was your idea, we'd both be sunk."

Another slap. "Watch your language!"

Ah, the incongruity. Torture and kill three people, one of them a child, yet be offended by a curse word.

Mrs. DuCharme's cold voice could have frozen the Amazon. "As for it being my idea, well, of course it was, since you're just like your father, never had a creative idea in your life. If it weren't for me and my vision, the company would have collapsed due to your mismanagement. Why, I even had to design the Camerons' punishment myself, you incompetent! That vile doctor murdered your brother! No one kills a DuCharme and gets away with it."

"I do have ideas!" He sounded like a whiny child. "The dog shi…feces was my idea, wasn't it?"

She grunted a weak agreement. Yes, of course the dog shit had been his idea. Torture and murder aside, the almost-pathologically neat Carl DuCharme saw trashing a house and smearing everything with dog feces as the most horrible thing possible.

As if having to agree with her son irritated her, Mrs. DuCharme rekindled her abusive tirade. "Left on your own you'd have done nothing. Nothing. You'd allow that man to kill your brother and would just turn away to resume your foolish little life with your nasty dogs as if nothing ever happened. You have no family loyalty and never did."

The whining child whined louder. "I proved my loyalty three times! Four if you count clubbing that little dog, which believe me, I wasn't happy about. But I did it for you, so why can't you ever show any loyalty toward me? Never mind, don't answer that. Blaine was always your favorite. For twenty-five years I've worked my a…my butt off for you and never got one word of thanks. I've stopped expecting it, but it's still a disappointment. You never felt one bit of…Wait."

"What?"

"There's something…something wrong."

I looked at the wrench in my hand, thought about the now-empty spot on the pegboard. If Carl DuCharme had noticed the wrench missing, I was in trouble. He was a big man, a couple of inches over six feet, and despite his sedentary job, well-muscled. Whatever happened, I couldn't let him get his hands on me. Especially not my head. One more trauma there and I'd be sitting in a nursing home drooling into my lap for the rest of my life.

That's if he didn't kill me outright.

When Carl murmured something low to his mother, I was certain he'd spotted the missing wrench. I heard feet move away from me, then a scrape and a click, a metallic object rubbing against wood. It told me I didn't have much time.

I had to get in the first blow or I was doomed.

Then I'd deal with his murderous mother.

After wiggling my toes to get the blood moving again, I leaned forward on the balls of my feet.

If Carl opened the passenger's or driver's door, I would be hidden behind the dog carriers. But he didn't. Like me, he opened the back door to the van. The minute he saw me crouched there, he slammed the big hammer toward me. Given no other defense, I blocked the blow with my left forearm and heard a crack. The pain almost blinded me, but now Carl was off-balance. Taking my only chance, I sprang through the open door, and swung the wrench at him with all my remaining strength.

The wrench connected with his head.

The cliché is true. The bigger they are, the harder they fall.

When Carl landed facedown at his mother's feet, the hammer skidded out of his hand and under the front bumper of the

Econoline van. She bent down and grabbed it, leaving me with a decision.

Could I hit an elderly woman? No. I couldn't, no matter what she had done. I wasn't that kind of person, I wasn't Lorraine DuCharme. Not only was I more compassionate, I was stronger, younger, more flexible. I'd tackle her barehanded—one-handed, even, given my broken left arm. But then I remembered ten-year-old Alec, his tortured little limbs bent into impossible shapes.

As soon as the doyenne of DuCharme Chocolatier straightened up with the hammer, I broke the bitch's nose.

Chapter Thirty-six

As the two murderers lay unconscious I one-handedly hog-tied them with dog leashes, then called Sylvie. After an explosion of curses that would have enraged Mrs. DuCharme's delicate sensibilities, Sylvie deployed a fleet of uniformed officers and crime techs to the garage, followed by Bob and her own sweet self.

"If the tests on that Econoline come back negative, you're up for kidnapping and assault," she snapped. "What the hell were you thinking? And why does your arm look like that?"

"I didn't exactly plan this whole scenario and I think my arm's broke, thank you for asking," I grumbled, as the uniforms replaced the DuCharmes' dog leashes with handcuffs.

I was handcuffed, too, although loosely enough that I could have slipped out of the cuffs if I'd wished. Throughout the odd procedure, Sylvie had been surprisingly gentle. "Just a formality," she said, grinning. She was enjoying this.

At this point, the only reason the DuCharmes were being taken into custody—although after being read her rights, Lorraine was rushed straight to the hospital—was because the Econoline van matched the vehicle seen on the CCTV cameras near the scene of the Cameron killings. Well aware that my own legal situation—trespassing, assault, kidnapping, etc.—was shaky, I'd had the good sense to rip the tarp off the van before the cops arrived, leaving the vehicle in plain sight. This gave the Scottsdale PD detectives enough ammunition to obtain a search warrant.

Animal Control took custody of Tiberius, Octavius, and Augustus, all of whom trotted peacefully to the rescue truck. They probably thought they were on their way to another dog show.

Several days later, when the tests came back on the Econoline van—the speed due to Congresswoman Juliana Thorsson's influence, again—Sylvie informed me that a strand of Sam Provencio's hair was found lodged under the rim of the right headlight, paint from the delivery van belonging to Zhou's Mandarin Wok was present on the left fender, and a speck of Alec Cameron's blood had been scraped off the carpeting under the passenger's front seat. Furthermore, the feces the techs collected from Tiberius, Octavius, and Augustus, matched the feces found on the walls of the Cameron house.

When a search of the house found a 9mm Beretta Millennium, and the ballistics test matched the bullet found in Dr. Cameron's brain, it sealed the deal.

Confronted with this avalanche of evidence, Carl DuCharme, still aggrieved that Mommy didn't love him as much as she loved Blaine Three, started talking. Seemingly proud of his actions, he bragged about using his lunch time to scope out the Cameron house. Over a couple of weeks' reconnaissance, he discovered that their neighbors were out of town, and that none of the houses on the cul-del-sac had surveillance cameras. The Camerons were sitting ducks, he'd told his mother.

Lorraine DuCharme didn't hold back, either. When questioned about her motive for the Cameron killings—yes, she'd been present for every vicious minute—she said, "Of course we killed them. Arthur Cameron killed my baby, so it was only fair that he suffer the same pain I did."

Question: what is a mother?

Answer: an animal that avenges its young.

Since my left arm was out of commission and Sam Provencio's truck was a stick, as soon as the doctor cleared me, Jimmy drove the truck back to Florence with me riding shotgun. My new cast had been signed by just about everyone in Scottsdale PD, including Sylvie and Bob. Sylvie had even drawn a big heart on it; the heart had a smiley face—with fangs.

Once we arrived in Florence, Bella met us at her front door, her newborn son in her arms. He had his father's chin dimple.

June-Mae was there, too. She had been helping out since Bella went into labor. After introducing Jimmy, I handed June-Mae the phone I'd borrowed, explaining, "I only used it to look up Carl DuCharme's address. Oh, and to call the cops."

She smiled for the first time since I'd met her. "After you'd bashed him and that bitch mother of his?"

"Yep."

"Good on you. And thanks for the check. It was more than I expected."

Her smile faded when she saw Bella heading for the kitchen. "Bella!" she yelled. "Sit down! You're not ready to do all this running around. Didn't I tell you I'd get the iced tea?"

Bella sat.

Knowing how it felt for a grown woman to be baby-sat against her will, I gave Bella a sympathetic look. When June-Mae hustled off to the kitchen, she said, simply, "Thank you."

I shook my head. "No, thank *you*. If you hadn't taken that picture and sent it to the newspaper, it would have taken me a lot longer to figure everything out. If ever."

"You'd have gotten there eventually, Lena," Jimmy said, his voice hoarse. "You always do." Since he'd lectured me about my foolhardiness all the way from Scottsdale to Florence, I was surprised he could talk at all.

I crossed the room to the credenza memorial, picked up Bella's memory book with one hand, and pointed out the photo and caption to Jimmy. "Jingo, that's her boxer's name, won his class at the Saguaro State Kennel Club show. Bella was there and took the picture. That's Sam on the left, the guy with the dimple in his chin. Look who else is in the frame."

Included in the shot was Augustus Maximus of Avonlea, who had taken Best of Show. Standing behind Augustus and beaming proudly was Carl DuCharme.

"Were Sam and DuCharme friends? Or just acquaintances?" Jimmy asked Bella.

"More like acquaintances. The dog show world, it's kinda small. They'd run into each other at shows from time to time, and they'd talk, maybe have a beer together, stuff like that, talk about dogs, sports, that kind of thing. Once I even heard Sam and that DuCharme guy talking about their exercise routines. DuCharme was into weight lifting, and Sam..." Bella's face clouded over. "Sam told him he was more into running, that he was training for the Iron Man. He even talked about his favorite running route out by the Jefferson ranch, said he ran there every morning before going to work."

We would probably never know the entire truth for certain. Carl DuCharme kept changing his story to put himself in the best light and his mother in the worst, but it was easy enough to imagine what had happened. Sam had seen Dr. Cameron enter through the industrial gate and immediately recognized him as the same ER doc who had once treated his torn tendon during the running of the Phoenix Marathon. Because of the press coverage in the days leading up to Blaine DuCharme's execution, he would have known the condemned Blaine was his dog show-buddy's brother. As the day for Blaine Three's execution approached, Sam must have decided to ease his buddy's pain as much as possible.

At least these days it's done by IV now, not the noose or the chair. Compared to that, the IV is merciful, I guess, just like putting a dog to sleep, he'd told Bella.

And so he told Carl that the fatal drug would be administered by the skilled, efficient Dr. Arthur Cameron, hoping to alleviate any fears the man had about his brother dying by a botched and painful execution.

Because it would be just like putting a dog to sleep.

With that act of compassion, Sam had sealed the fate of not only the Cameron family, but his own as well, because Carl, although vicious, wasn't stupid. He'd known that once news of Dr. Cameron's death reached Florence, Sam would put two and two together.

Therefore Sam had to be removed.

After some tea and cookies, I called Madeline and told her we were ready for her to pick us up and drive us back to Scottsdale. By now, Jingo knew we weren't going to eat the children so Bella let him out of the kitchen to see us. He slobbered on my new black Reeboks, then walked over to Jimmy and jumped into his lap.

"That's exactly what he used to do with Sam!" Bella said, clapping her hands.

As Jingo turned in a circle, making himself comfortable on Jimmy's lap, I laughed at my partner's discomfort. He always said he wasn't a dog person, but dogs knew better.

"The boxers," Bella suddenly exclaimed. "What's going to happen to Carl DuCharme's dogs?"

"Don't worry," I told her. "They're with Arizona Boxer Rescue and there's already a long list of people wanting to adopt them."

A happy ending for Tiberius, Octavius, and Augustus. Not so much for Carl and Lorraine DuCharme, since capital punishment was still popular in Arizona. Lorraine wouldn't live long enough to be executed, though; she was suffering from esophageal cancer. Her last wish on this Earth had been to avenge her precious Blaine. She carried that out the moment when, after two hours of torture—as she bragged to Sylvie during a videotaped interview—she shot Dr. Cameron in the face.

As for Carl, twenty years down the line he would die in the same small room in which his brother died.

It would be just like putting a dog to sleep.

Chapter Thirty-seven

A week later Desert Investigations was back in business. So was my apartment and my blues collection, even the album featuring my father playing back-up guitar for John Lee Hooker. As I surveyed Desert Investigations' new walls, new carpet, and new furniture, I breathed a sigh of relief. No more working out of Jimmy's trailer, no more fears that my screaming nightmares would bring Jimmy to my bed. Some people don't mind sharing their fears. I'm not one of them.

"Didn't you tell me Juliana Thorsson is dropping by this morning?" Jimmy asked. He had already personalized his new office computer and was doing the same for mine as I stood over our new coffeemaker, waiting for the brew to trickle into my cup.

"Yep. Says she wants to pay her bill in person."

"Should be a whopper, what with all those bribes."

"Bribes?"

"You bribed June-Mae to ferry you around behind Madeline's back."

"That wasn't a bribe, it was payment for services rendered."

"Whatever."

It was even nice to be bickering again. Especially knowing that at the end of the day, Jimmy would drive home to his trailer, and I would walk upstairs to my apartment.

Life was beautiful, even though my left arm was still in a cast.

I raised my cup to my lips. No-frills black. Just the way I liked it.

"Here she is," Jimmy announced.

I turned to see Juliana enter, dressed in politician chic. Ali, blooming like a rose in Arctic Black, was with her. My morning was now perfect.

Since Jimmy was busy with my new computer, I took Juliana into the conference room, while Ali hung back to watch Jimmy work. The kid was into that sort of thing.

To my surprise, Juliana closed the conference room door behind us. She needed privacy to pay a bill?

"Nice," Juliana said, looking around.

The old color scheme was gone, and the conference room was now a hymn to the desert. Sand-colored carpet, sandalwood walls, a reclaimed-pine conference table, chairs upholstered in hand-worked Pima designs. One of Jimmy's cousins had furnished the art, a series of petroglyph-style paintings, featuring Earth Doctor, Spider Woman, and Night Singing Bird. It no longer looked like some Yuppie's refurbbed basement; it looked like us.

Like Desert Investigations.

"Out with the old, in with the new," I said. "You're here to pay your bill, right?"

"And to dispute a portion of it."

It figured. No politician could rest easy unless he—or she, as in this instance—had screwed you over one way or another.

Ten minutes later, we arrived at a settlement which was only eighteen dollars less than the entire bill. All in all, it had been a pointless exercise in miser-dom, but if it made her happy, what the hell. "Nice doing business with you," I said, as she wrote out the check from her private account. No campaign fund hanky-panky for her.

She gave me a genuine smile, not her usual camera-ready one. Motherhood apparently became her. "Same here, Ms. Jones. We'll do business again sometime. Meanwhile, I'll be sure to recommend you to my friends."

Ms. Jones. So we were back to formality. Fine with me. It's always wisest to hold a politician at arm's length.

"Desert Investigations can use the business," I replied. "Especially now. Turns out our insurance policy has a larger deductible than I realized."

"Insurance companies. You can't trust them, can you?"

"Among other professions I could mention. But so much for that. How's Ali doing?" But I didn't need to ask the question, because the girl would be fine. Her laughter drifted through the closed conference room door as she chatted with Jimmy. She had learned to enjoy any moment of pleasure that came her way.

"The judge signed off on the custody agreement," Juliana continued, "which makes it easier, now that Dr. Teague has returned to Africa. For the life of me I can't understand abandoning a blood relative for children you've never met."

Neither could I. "I hear you're going to be a mom full time, now. Wonder what your electorate will think when they hear about the IVF, and they certainly will."

She laughed. "Fuck the electorate."

Yep, motherhood most definitely became her. I just might wind up liking the Honorable Juliana Thorsson. I already liked her kid.

"I hear you're moving," I said.

"That's putting the cart before the horse, but yes, we're looking at houses."

We. Meaning, *Ali and I. The both of us.*

"Does she know yet?" I asked. "About her real relationship to you?"

She shook her head. "I'm leading up to it. Once I've told Ali who I really am, there'll be a formal adoption, which is why we're looking for a family home, something permanent. Maybe a house closer to Kyle's. He's a good kid and their bond seems unshakable, but time will tell."

Our business finished, and a big fat check in my hand, I started to rise. I didn't have another appointment for a while, and I wanted to spend some time chatting with Ali. I'd missed the brat.

Juliana motioned me back down. "Sit, sit. I have something else to discuss."

What now? Another case?

"It's about Ali. She's one of the reasons I wanted to meet you here in person, rather than simply mailing a check. That girl admires you, and she wants to know if you'll serve as her honorary godmother. In case something ever happens to me, the political scene being what it is these days."

I looked down at the reclaimed pine table, the new carpet, then over at the sandalwood walls, eventually settling on one the Pima paintings. Spider Woman, who'd woven a giant blanket to protect the Earth. It gave me time to get my breath back.

"Yeah, okay." My reply sounded more like a croak, so I nodded my head, to make sure she understood me.

"Excellent. I'll tell her you said yes. In case you're confused about the duties of a godmother, I'm sure Jimmy will look it up for you on the Internet." For once, there was no edge to her voice; it was almost tender. "Another thing. Some advice."

"Yeah?"

"The man who raped you when you were a child. He's getting out of prison next week."

I narrowed my eyes. "I am well aware of that." In fact, I was planning a little welcome home party for the bastard, having already chosen the knife.

"Here's the advice."

She could give me all the advice she wanted to, but that didn't mean I had to take it.

"Don't let yourself turn into Lorraine DuCharme, Lena."

What little breath I'd recovered left me again. I felt like I'd been hit in the stomach. "Well, thanks for the advice, but you don't understand."

"Actually, I do. You're an excellent detective, Ms. Jones, but like every other human being, you have your blind spots."

Considering the near-impossible case I had solved for her, I felt offended. But only slightly. The check in my hand would more than cover any insult to my ego. And after next week, I would be relieved of a grudge I'd been carrying around since I was nine.

The knife was lovely. Part of the Interceptor series, it was appropriately called The Vindicator. Over ten inches long, with a double-edged tip for extreme penetrating capability, it had a serrated top edge for cutting and hacking. I couldn't wait to use it, to finish the job my nine-year-old self had failed at.

Unaware of the way my mind was working, my congress-woman continued. "You're good at putting two-and-two together and coming up with the right answer, and God knows you're not short on grit. But I suspect you don't yet fully understand the human heart, at least not its softer side. Probably because of all those foster homes you were raised in—abused in, rather—you learned to be more attuned to threat than to love."

No argument there, so I just shrugged. The ability to guess where the next blow was coming from had kept me alive.

So had my dreams of vengeance.

Juliana looked down at her long, slender fingers. Although her husband had been dead for more than twenty years, she still wore her wedding ring. For her public? Or because she still loved him? I was beginning to suspect the latter.

"Back to the idea of vengeance," she said.

I blinked to hear her use the very word I'd so lovingly used over and over in my dark imaginings.

"When I came to you, Lena, I used the word 'justice,' remember? That's what I wanted, justice, not vengeance. And that's what you gave me. You arranged for Ali to be freed from custody, and you found the people who killed her family. They're headed for prison, if Mrs. DuCharme lives long enough to ever see the inside of a cell. But for all your questioning, for all your sleuthing, you never once asked me an important question."

"Which was?" I was getting tired of this. I've never handled lectures well. I was impatient to visit with Ali. And to return to my bloody daydreams.

"Are you…?" As if what she wanted to say was more difficult than she'd planned, like me she stared at the painting of Spider Woman, at the giant blanket sheltering the Earth. Then she focused on me again. "Are you aware that you never asked what happened to those extra eggs the fertility doctor harvested from me?"

"Why ask when I already know the answer? Unused eggs get dumped. Everyone knows that." *Although not everyone was happy about it.*

The highlights in Juliana's hair, usually a cold white-blond, were softened into warmth by the colors in the room. "Yes, sometimes they're dumped. But eggs can also be stored for future use. As in my case. Several years after Ali's birth, Alexandra decided she didn't want the girl to be an only child, so she underwent the procedure one more time. The result was Alec."

"Are you saying…?"

"Yes, Lena. The DuCharmes murdered my son."

Chapter Thirty-eight

Question: what is a mother?
Answer: the woman who cries out for justice.

Epilogue

Ali

Ali frowned at the closed door. Juliana was great, but all this secrecy was getting irritating. Whisper, whisper, whisper. What did Juliana think she was protecting her from?

As if she needed protection, like, if she hadn't already lived through all the hell a person could live through, finding her family dead like that, then spending all that time in juvie with the gangster girls threatening to kill her every day.

Yet whisper, whisper, whisper.

So random.

Ali had, like, a whole list of questions she wanted to ask Lena, mostly things like how you become a private investigator, do you have to be a cop first, or can you just go out and do it? Ha! Just do it, like the Nike commercials. Just do it!

Not a bad way to live. That's what she wanted. To be a private investigator.

Just like Lena.

Ali smiled, and sure enough, that Indian guy, Jimmy Sisiwan, thought she was smiling at him because he smiled back, all white teeth and brown skin. That was okay. He was a good-looking dude, a hunk, even, with that big curvy tattoo on his forehead. Tribal, that's what it was. Not tribal like some of the lame-ass phony tats the kids at school wore, but real-deal tribal, like old Indian tribal. Pima, that was his tribe. Cool dudes, those Pimas.

She looked down at her new watch. If Juliana didn't hurry up in there, she wouldn't have time to have a nice long talk with Lena about becoming a private detective like her someday, and helping people like she did, because helping was important, maybe the most important thing in the world.

But if they didn't stop yakking…Well, then Ali and Juliana would have to rush straight out to see that real estate lady and it would be rush rush rush and Ali hated to rush. This house might be THE ONE, Juliana had said, all on a single floor, four bedrooms, three baths, new kitchen, big pool, a block from Kyle's house and all that crap. Juliana was so fussy, she was all "our house has to have this and our house has to have that," but all Ali needed was a yard for Misty and to be close to Kyle and most of all a house that didn't look anything like her old house, the house where…

No, better not think about that.

Never ever think about that. Never again.

It hurt too much.

Do what Juliana said to do, think about the good times, about the way things were before…

Just before.

Like, think about the time her and Alec and Mom and Dad all went to Disneyland and Dad couldn't stop obsessing about that stupid Small World ride, and he made them go through it four times and would have made them go through it ten-dozen more times, but then Mom put her foot down and said enough was enough, it was driving her crazy, but Alec said, no, let's do it, I wanna do it, so to shut him up Ali said c'mon, Mom, just once more, crazy never hurt anybody, that Alec was just as obsessive as Dad, and what was wrong with that, Dad's kind of crazy got him through medical school and helped save people's lives, didn't it, and then Mom started laughing, and then they were all laughing like crazy people, even Dad who never really laughed all that much, he just laughed and laughed and so they went through the stupid Small World ride again and came out singing that stupid song and even Mom was singing it too…

Yeah, that was the kind of thing to think about.

Juliana knew all kinds of things, about what to do when you got knots in your stomach and that tight feeling in your chest and what to do when your eyes started burning…Yeah, Juliana knew, all right, because a couple of times Ali had walked in on her and saw Juliana crying like she was about to die, but then she would always hide it, saying some bullshit about allergies.

As if.

Ali knew why Juliana cried, oh yes, she did.

That was something else she'd learned, that Juliana wasn't half as smart as she thought she was, and Ali—after everything that had happened—wasn't half as dumb as she used to be.

Because Ali knew. The only thing was, she had to figure out how to say it so it wouldn't upset Juliana too much, because Juliana wasn't half as tough as she pretended to be, either. In a kind of way, she was just like Ali, all big and tough on the outside while on the inside was all this hurt.

But Ali would figure out a way to tell her because she wanted everything out, no more secrets, even if it meant admitting she'd snuck around Juliana's condo and looked through a bunch of stuff she wasn't supposed to look through, and for sure wasn't supposed to find what she found.

So now she wanted to tell Juliana, tell her what she knew. She didn't know yet exactly how she'd tell it but maybe she'd start as soon as they got to the car. Ali would just blurt it right out, no matter how stupid it sounded.

And once Juliana got through being mad about her sneaking around, Ali would finally be able to say the word she wanted so much to say again.

She'd say, "*Mother.*"

To receive a free catalog of Poisoned Pen Press titles, please contact us in one of the following ways:

Phone: 1-800-421-3976
Facsimile: 1-480-949-1707
Email: info@poisonedpenpress.com
Website: www.poisonedpenpress.com

Poisoned Pen Press
6962 E. First Ave. Ste 103
Scottsdale, AZ 85251